"I'm telling you, tests don't make you an architect."

She tried to take a breath but got a lungful of man again, the smell of someone who did not take no for an answer.

"Life gives you enough tests," he said.

Like...how long could she sit here, inches from the sexiest man she could remember meeting in her life and not kiss him? That, right there, was a real test.

"True success comes from meeting and beating every one of the challenges you're thrown." He got a little bit closer with every word.

"Here's all you have to know about me, Lacey." He brushed her knuckles with his fingertips, ostensibly to underscore the point he was about to make, but the touch sent chills over her skin and made her curl her toes around the barstool. "I don't believe in obstacles, barriers, road-blocks, or anything else that says I can't. I get what I want and I don't quit until I have it. Now, can I have the job to design and build your resort?"

Someone who didn't quit? Didn't find excuses? Wasn't that exactly what she needed?

He put one finger under her chin and tilted her face toward his. "Just say yes."

Barefoot in the Sand

roxanne st. claire

FOREVER

NEW YORK   BOSTON

Copyright © 2012 by Roxanne St. Claire
Excerpt from *Barefoot in the Rain* copyright © 2012 by Roxanne St. Claire

Forever
Hachette Book Group
237 Park Avenue
New York, NY 10017
www.HachetteBookGroup.com

Printed in the United States of America

First Edition: May 2012

10 9 8 7 6 5 4 3 2 1

Forever is an imprint of Grand Central Publishing.
The Forever name and logo are trademarks of Hachette Book Group, Inc.

The Hachette Speakers Bureau provides a wide range of authors for speaking events. To find out more, go to www.hachettespeakersbureau.com or call (866) 376-6591.

The publisher is not responsible for websites (or their content) that are not owned by the publisher.

ATTENTION CORPORATIONS AND ORGANIZATIONS:
Most HACHETTE BOOK GROUP books are available at quantity discounts with bulk purchase for educational, business, or sales promotional use. For information, please call or write:

Special Markets Department, Hachette Book Group
237 Park Avenue, New York, NY 10017
Telephone: 1-800-222-6747 Fax: 1-800-477-5925

For Deborah Brooks,
my sister, my friend, my blessing.

Acknowledgments

~

It took a lot of effort and care from a group of talented experts and generous individuals to bring this book to publication. My deepest gratitude goes to all, including:

Literary agent Robin Rue, who has an endless supply of humor, support, and great ideas; and also to her amazing assistant, Beth Miller, who gets 100 percent credit for the title!

Awesome, insightful, and patient editor Amy Pierpont, whose influence can be felt on every page, as well as her equally awesome assistant editor, Lauren Plude, who apparently never sleeps. A special shout-out to the art, production, publicity, marketing, and sales departments at Grand Central/Forever, a professional team that leaves me awestruck every time.

The ladies of Writer's Camp—Kristen Painter, Lara Santiago, and Leigh Duncan—who encourage and inspire me every time we pitch our writing tents. Also, a hug of thanks to honorary camper Louisa Edwards, who is truly a contemporary romance goddess and world-class plotter.

My beta readers rock! In particular, Barbie Furtado should win an award for the number of times she's read this manuscript and left pink-tipped notes during the wee hours that made me laugh and cry the next morning. Thanks to all the lovely readers who suffer through early drafts and make me want to dive into a revision instead of off a bridge.

And to the takers of some frantic research calls: Terry Galloway, brilliant architect and (not so) old college friend; and the lovely ladies at John R. Wood Real Estate in Naples, Florida. You shall all be rewarded with books, I promise!

Finally, the home team: my dearest, most patient, most beloved husband, Rich, who does everything so that I can do this; my wonderful son, Dante, who was kind enough to go to college so I didn't have to hear *Family Guy* in the den while trying to write romance; and my most precious daughter, Mia, who was *not* the inspiration for Ashley…except for the unicorn. You guys are my whole world.

Barefoot in the Sand

Chapter 1

The kitchen windows shot out like cannons, one right after another, followed by the ear-splitting crash of the antique breakfront nose-diving to the tile floor.

Shit. Granny Dot's entire Old Country Rose service for twelve was in there.

Lacey pressed against the closet door, eyes closed, body braced, mind reeling. This was it. Everything she owned—a meager baking business, a fifty-year-old hand-me-down house, and a few antiques she'd collected over the years—was about to be destroyed, demolished, and dumped into Barefoot Bay by the hand of Hurricane Damien.

She stole a glance over her shoulder. Everything she owned, but not everything she *had*. No matter what happened to the house, she had to save her daughter.

"We need to get in the bathtub and under a mattress!"

Lacey screamed over the train-like howl of one-hundred-and-ten-mile-per-hour winds.

Ashley cowered deeper into the corner of the closet, a stuffed unicorn clutched in one hand, her cell phone in the other. "I told you we should have evacuated!"

Only a fourteen-year-old would argue at a moment like this. "I can't get the mattress into the bathroom alone."

The storm was inside now, tearing the chandelier out of the dining room ceiling, clattering crystal everywhere. Pictures ripped off their hooks with vicious thuds and furniture skated across the oak floor. Overhead, half-century-old roof trusses moaned in a last-ditch effort to cling to the eaves.

They had minutes left.

"We have to hurry, Ash. On the count of—"

"I'm not leaving here," Ashley cried. "I'm too scared. I'm not going out there."

Lacey corralled every last shred of control. "We are. Together."

"We'll die out there, Mom!"

"No, but we'll die in here." At Ashley's wail, Lacey kneeled in front of her, sacrificing precious seconds. "Honey, I've lived on this island my whole life and this isn't the first hurricane." Just the worst. "We have to get in the tub and under the mattress. *Now*."

Taking a firm grip, she pulled Ashley to her feet, the cell-phone screen spotlighting a tear-stained face. God, Lacey wanted to tumble into Ashley's nest of hastily grabbed treasures and cry with her daughter.

But then she'd die with her daughter.

Ashley bunched the unicorn under her chin. "How could those weather people be so wrong?"

Good damn question. All day long, and into the night, the storm had been headed north to the Panhandle, not expected to do more than bring heavy rain and wind to the west coast of Florida. Until a few hours ago, when Hurricane Damien had jumped from a cat-three to a cat-four and veered to the east, making a much closer pass to the barrier island of Mimosa Key.

In the space of hours, ten thousand residents, including Lacey and Ashley, had been forced to make a rapid run-or-hide decision. A few tourists managed to haul butt over the causeway to the mainland, but most of the hurricane-experienced islanders were looking for mattress cover and porcelain protection about now. And praying. Hard.

Lacey cupped her hands on Ashley's cheeks. "We have to do this, Ashley. We can't panic, okay?"

Ashley nodded over and over again. "Okay, Mom. Okay."

"On the count of three. One, two—"

Three was drowned out by the gut-wrenching sound of the carport roof tearing away.

Lacey pushed open the closet door. Her bedroom was pitch black, but she moved on instinct, grateful the storm hadn't breached these walls yet.

"Get around to the other side of the bed," she ordered, already throwing back the comforter, searching wildly for a grip. "I'll pull, you push."

Ashley rallied and obeyed, sending a jolt of love and appreciation through Lacey. "Atta girl. A little more."

Right then the freight train of wind roared down the back hall, hurtling an antique mirror and shattering it against the bedroom door.

"It's coming!" Ashley screamed, freezing in fear.

Yes, it was. Like a monster, the storm would tear these old walls right down to the foundation Lacey's grandfather had laid when he'd arrived on Mimosa Key in the 1940s.

"Push the damn mattress, Ashley!"

Ashley gave it all she had and the mattress slid enough for Lacey to get a good grip. Grunting, she got the whole thing off the bed and dragged it toward the bathroom. They struggled to shove it through the door just as the wind knocked out one of the bedroom windows, showering glass and wood behind them.

"Oh my God, Mom. This is it!"

"No, this isn't *it*," Lacey hissed, trying to heave the mattress. "Get in!" She pushed Ashley toward the thousand-pound cast-iron claw-foot tub that had just transformed from last year's lavish expenditure into their sole means of survival.

In the shadows Lacey could see Ashley scramble into the tub, but the mattress was stuck on something in the door. She turned to maneuver the beast when the other window ruptured with a stunning crash.

Ducking from the flying debris, Lacey saw what had the mattress jammed.

Ashley's unicorn.

Window blinds came sailing in behind her. No time. No time for unicorns.

"Hurry, Mom!"

With a Herculean thrust, she freed the mattress, the force propelling her toward the tub, but in her mind all she could see was the goddamn unicorn.

The one Zoe brought to the hospital when Ashley

was born and Ashley slept with every night until she was almost ten. In minutes Aunt Zoe's uni would be a memory, like everything else they owned.

From inside the tub Ashley reached up and pulled at Lacey's arm. "Get in!"

This time Lacey froze, the mattress pressing down with the full weight of what they were losing. Everything. Every picture, every gift, every book, every Christmas ornament, every—

"Mom!"

The bathroom door slammed shut behind her, caught in a crosswind, making the room eerily quiet for a second.

In that instant of suspended time, Lacey dove for the unicorn, scooping it up with one hand while managing to brace the mattress with the other.

"What are you doing?" Ashley hollered.

"Saving something." She leaped into the tub on top of her shrieking daughter, dropping the stuffed animal so she could hoist the mattress over and seal them in a new kind of darkness.

The door shot back open, the little window over the toilet gave way, and tornado-strength winds whipped through the room. Under her, Lacey could hear her daughter sobbing, feel her quivering with fright, her coltish legs squeezing for dear life.

And life *was* dear. Troubled, stressful, messy, not everything she dreamed it would be, but dear. Lacey Armstrong was not about to give it up to Mother Nature's temper tantrum.

"Reach around me and help me hold this thing down," Lacey demanded, her fingernails breaking as she dug into the quilted tufts, desperate for a grip.

Her arms screaming with the effort, she clung to the mattress, closed her eyes, and listened to the sounds of that dear life literally falling apart around her.

It wasn't much, this old house she'd inherited from her grandparents, built with big dreams and little money, but it was all she had.

No, it wasn't, she reminded herself again. All she had was quivering and crying underneath her. Everything else was just stuff. Wet, ruined, storm-tattered *stuff*. They were alive and they had each other and their wits and dreams and hopes.

"This is a nightmare, Mom." Ashley's sob silenced Lacey's inner litany of life-support platitudes.

"Just hold on, Ash. We'll make it. I've been through worse." Hadn't she?

Wasn't it worse to return to Mimosa Key a pregnant college dropout, facing her mother's bitter and brutal disappointment? Wasn't it worse to stare into David Fox's dreamy, distant eyes and say "I'm going to keep this baby," only for him to announce he was on his way to a sheep farm in Patagonia?

Pata-frickin'-gonia. It still ticked her off, fourteen years later.

She was *not* going to die, damn it. And neither was Ashley. She stole a look over her shoulder, meeting her daughter's petrified gaze.

"Listen to me," Lacey demanded through gritted teeth. "I'm not going to let anything happen to you."

Ashley managed a nod.

They just had to hang on and…pray. Because most people would be cutting some sweet deals with God at a time like this. But Lacey wasn't most people, and she didn't make deals with anybody. She made plans. Lots of plans that never—

A strong gust lifted the mattress, pulling a scream from her throat as rain and wind and debris whipped over them, and then part of the ceiling thudded down on the mattress. With the weight of saturated drywall and insulation holding their makeshift roof in place, Lacey could let go of the mattress. Relieved, she worked a space on the edge where the tub curved down to give them some air and finally let her body squeeze in next to Ashley.

Now Lacey could think of something else besides survival.

After survival, comes...what? Facing the stark truth that everything was gone. What was she going to do with no home, no clothes, no struggling cake-baking business, and maybe no customers remaining on Mimosa Key to buy her cookies and cupcakes?

The answer was the thunderous roar of the rest of the second floor being ripped away as if an imaginary giant had plucked a weed from his garden. Instantly rain dumped on them.

Once the roof was gone the vacuum dissipated, and, except for the drumbeat of rain on the mattress, it was almost quiet.

"Is this the eye of the storm?" Ashley asked.

Lacey adjusted her position again to curl around Ashley's slender frame. "I don't know, honey. Hey, look what I brought you."

She fished out the unicorn from behind her and laid it on Ashley's chest. Even in the darkness she could see Ashley smile, her eyes bright with tears.

"Aunt Zoe's uni. Thank you, Mommy."

Mommy just about folded her heart in half.

"Shhh." She stroked Ashley's hair, trying to be grateful for the rare moment when her daughter didn't roll her eyes or whip out her cell phone to text a friend. "We're gonna be fine, angel. I promise."

But could she keep that promise? When the storm passed, the home her grandfather had christened Blue Horizon House would be little more than a memory sitting on a stretch of pristine beach known as Barefoot Bay.

But Mimosa Key would still be here. Nothing could wipe away this barrier island or the people who called this strip of land home. Like Lacey, most of the residents were the children and grandchildren of the first group of twentieth-century pioneers who'd built a rickety wooden causeway to take them to an island haven in the Gulf of Mexico.

And nothing could rid Mimosa Key of its natural resources, like magical Barefoot Bay with its peach-toned sunsets or the fluffy red flowers that exploded like fireworks every spring, giving the island its name. Nothing could stop the reliable blue moon that sparkled like diamonds on the black velvet Gulf every night.

If Mimosa Key survived, so would Lacey.

And there is such a thing as insurance, a pragmatic voice insisted.

Insurance would cover the value of the house, and she owned the land, so Lacey could rebuild. Maybe this was her chance to finally turn the big old beach cottage into a B and B, a dream she'd nurtured for years, one she'd promised both her grandparents she'd pursue when they'd left her the house and all the land around it.

But life had gotten in the way of that promise. And now she had nothing.

Instead of wallowing in that reality, she let the B and B idea settle over her heart once again, the idea of finally, *finally* seeing one of her dreams come true carrying her through the rest of the storm while Ashley drifted off into a fitful sleep.

By the time the howling had softened to a low moan and the rain had slowed to a steady drizzle, the first silver threads of dawn were weaving through the air space she'd made. It was time to face the aftermath of the storm. Using all the strength she had left, Lacey managed to push the soaked mattress to the floor.

"Oh my God." Ashley's voice cracked with whispered disbelief as she emerged. "It's all gone."

Yes, it was. A dilapidated old house that was more trouble than it was ever worth had been washed away by Hurricane Damien's clean-up campaign. Lacey's heart was oddly light in the face of the devastation. Buoyed, in fact, with possibilities.

"Don't worry," she said, gingerly navigating the debris, peering into the early morning light. "It's not the end of the world." It was the beginning.

"How can you say that, Mom? There's nothing left!"

A few drops of warm tropical rain splattered her face, but Lacey wiped the water from her cheek and stepped over broken wall studs wrapped in shredded, sopping-wet attic insulation.

"We have insurance, Ashley."

"Mom! Our house is gone!"

"No, the *building's* gone. The beach is here. The sun will shine. The palm fronds will grow back."

Her imagination stirred again, nudged alive by the reality of what she saw around her. She could do this.

This land—and the insurance money—could be used to make a dream come true.

Beside her Ashley sniffed, wiping a fresh set of tears. "How can you talk about palm fronds? We don't even have a—oh!" She dropped to her knees to retrieve a muddy video-game remote. "My Wii!"

"Ashley." Lacey reached for her, pulling her up to hold her close. "Baby, we have each other. We're alive, which is pretty much a miracle."

Ashley just squeezed her eyes shut and nodded, working so hard to be strong and brave.

"I know it hurts, Ashley, but this"—she took the broken remote and pitched it—"is just *stuff*. We'll get more, better stuff. What matters is that we've made it through and, you know, I'm starting to think this hurricane was the best thing that ever happened to us."

Ashley eyes popped open with an incredulous look. "Are you nuts?"

Maybe she was, but insane optimism was all she had right now.

"Think about it, Ash. We can do anything with this property now. We don't have to pay to remodel a sixty-year-old house; we can start from scratch and make it amazing." Her voice rose as the idea sprouted to life and took hold of her heart. "You know I've always dreamed of opening an inn or B and B, something all mine that would be an oasis, a destination."

Ashley just closed her eyes as if she couldn't even compute an *oasis* right then. "But if you couldn't figure out a way to make it happen when you had an actual house, how can you now?"

The truth stung, but Lacey ignored the pain. This time

she wouldn't make excuses, that was how. She wouldn't be scared of not finishing what she started and she wouldn't let anyone's disapproval make her doubt herself. Not anymore.

"Old Mother Nature just handed us a 'get out of jail free' pass, kiddo," she said, giving Ashley's shoulder a squeeze. "And you know what? We're taking it."

Chapter 2

Six Weeks Later

He's probably at lunch.
He wouldn't take a job this small.
He might refuse to come to Florida in August.

Lacey had plenty of reasons why she shouldn't press the Call button and ask to speak with Clayton Walker, president and CEO of Walker Architecture and Design. A trickle of sweat meandered down her back and trailed into the waistband of the cutoffs Ashley had pronounced too short for a mom to wear.

Too short? Too bad. She could walk around Barefoot Bay naked if she wanted to. Ever since the storm had ravaged the north hook of the island, she and Ashley had been alone out here at the beach. The insurance adjusters had come and gone, promising the rebuilding money, and the bulldozers had already leveled the storm-damaged house. Lacey's two neighbors, one to the north and one to the south and neither very close by, had bailed after settling their claims and promising to sell her their lots for a song.

The next step in her ambitious scheme didn't require age-appropriate attire, anyway. Her sweaty finger streaked the smooth glass of her phone, but before she dialed, she set the phone on the picnic table, one of the few items she'd salvaged from the storm.

What was stopping her from calling the architect?

Fear of rejection? Of course, an architect with Clayton Walker's outstanding credentials, reputation, and portfolio of glorious hotels and resorts might not want to design her beachfront bed-and-breakfast.

But he *had* responded to her e-mail personally. And he *had* said, "Call when you have the insurance money and I'll take a look at the property."

She swiped beads of sweat from her upper lip and scooted the bench closer to the table, trying to slide into the one slice of shade formed by the trunk of a royal poinciana that had survived the storm. Peering through humidity-drenched curls, she studied her daughter at the water's edge a few hundred feet of burning sand away. Madly texting, something she'd been doing more and more of lately, Ashley seemed oblivious to the squawking seagulls fluttering around her.

Ashley had rebounded remarkably after the storm, moving into Lacey's parents' house with a fairly positive attitude, probably since living down on the south end of the island put her closer to more kids she'd be going to Mimosa High with in a few weeks.

Most of the twelve-mile-long barrier island hadn't fared

quite as poorly as the northern end, where Barefoot Bay was located. South of Center Street they'd lost only screens and roof tiles, and a few windows. Businesses were all open in town and life was nearly back to normal down there. Even still, Lacey's parents had decided to stay longer up north with her brother, giving Lacey and Ashley a place to live.

Good thing, because if Marie Armstrong were breathing down Lacey's neck right now, harping on the complete impossibility of these plans, Lacey would never have the nerve to make this call.

She angled the phone and eyed the architect's name, imagining the conversation with a man she considered a legend. She'd seen his picture on the company Web site and on the Internet. The guy looked like Colonel Sanders with all that white hair and a Southern-gentleman bow tie. How scary could he be?

Okay. It was time. She turned so the sight of Ashley wouldn't distract her, and put her finger on the phone.

Wait.

Should she call him Mr. Walker? His e-mail seemed so casual, at least for an architectural genius. So maybe he wouldn't want—

A voice floated up from the beach. A male voice.

Lacey glanced over her shoulder, inhaling a quick breath at the sight of a man five feet away from Ashley. A half-naked man, wearing nothing but low-hanging board shorts and sockless sneakers. Shaggy hair, big muscles, and, dear God, was that a tattoo on his arm?

Was he a tourist? A surfer? More likely one of the many debris scavengers who'd popped up all over the island since they'd reopened the causeway, ready to make a buck off the misfortune of others.

Ashley laughed at something he said, and he turned just enough for Lacey to get an eyeful of sweat-glistening chest and abs and—wow.

Ashley flipped her hair and the man took a step closer.

Okay, stop right there, buddy. Lacey launched forward, driven by primal instinct, forgetting the call and ignoring the fiery sand singeing her bare feet.

"Excuse me."

They both turned at her words, Ashley's body language screaming disgust as she rolled her eyes. But Lacey barely saw her. Her gaze was locked on the predator, preparing her counterattack in full mother-lioness mode, quickly assessing his danger level.

His danger level was...hot.

Ridiculously so.

He stunned her with a blinding smile. He disarmed her with a shake of his honey-colored locks, revealing a handsome, tanned face and a tiny gold hoop in one ear. Then he stopped her in her tracks by stretching out his hand.

"I'm Clay Walker."

What?

"Are you Lacey Armstrong?"

"No. I mean, yes. But..." She froze, completely thrown, her brain short-circuiting at his words.

Colonel Sanders he was not.

He looked nothing like his picture. No white hair, no bow tie—no shirt! He absolutely couldn't be Clayton Walker because, well, he was gorgeous.

"What are you doing here?" she demanded, not caring that she was a sweaty mess of venom-spewing, short-short-wearing, almost-thirty-seven-year-old mom staring at his washboard abs. Or that she still held the phone that she was just about to use to call him. Well, not him. Colonel Sanders.

"I told you I'd check out the property."

"Oh, I expected someone..." *Older. Dressed. Not gorgeous.* "...after I called."

"I didn't want to wait," he said. He kept his hand out and she had no choice but to take it, her hand instantly lost in big, calloused, masculine fingers. "I was too intrigued by the idea of building here."

"So am I." Intrigued, that was. Intrigued and wary.

"I hope you don't mind." He gave a cursory glance to his naked torso. "It's hot as hell here."

"It's no problem," she lied, extracting her hand and forcing her eyes off his body and onto his face. Like that was any less stupefying. "But there's been a mistake."

Dark brows shot up, revealing eyes just about the color of the water behind him. "A mistake?" he asked.

"You're not Clayton Walker."

"I go by Clay." He smiled, kind of a half-grin that crinkled his eyes and revealed straight white teeth. "Got ID in my truck if you want me to get it."

The hint of a drawl fit him as well as the shorts that hung off narrow hips. "That's not necessary because I've been to the Web site and I've seen Clayton Walker, and he's not..." *Sexy.* "You."

"Don't tell me." The smile turned wry. "You were expecting Clayton Walker *Senior*?"

Senior? Like his *father*? "I was expecting the owner of the firm." The man who designed some of the most stunning hotels in the world, who probably didn't have hair to his shoulders or an earring or a tattoo of a flame-encircled star on a sizable bicep. "*The* Clayton Walker. That's who I e-mailed."

"Actually, you e-mailed me," he said simply.

"I got the contact off the Web site."

He shrugged a brawny shoulder. "I guess my name's still there. It wouldn't be the first time someone's made the mistake."

"Do you work for him?"

"No, I don't have anything to do with my father's business anymore."

"Oh. That's a shame." Disappointment dribbled in her stomach and mixed with some other unfamiliar tightness down there.

"But I am a contractor," he said, an edge taking some of the smoothness out of his voice. "And a builder."

"But you aren't *the* Clayton Walker."

He laughed softly, a rumbly, gritty, sensual sound that reverberated through Lacey's chest down to her toes. "Look, I've been checking out this property for a couple of days and, based on that e-mail you sent, I'm totally capable of doing this job for you."

Except he wasn't capable because he was too young and too inexperienced and too...shirtless. "Are you an architect?"

"Technically, it depends on how you define architect. I am, but not completely licensed, so not officially." He fried her with another smile, taking a step closer, giving her a better look at his really remarkable blue eyes. Not that she was looking for remarkable eyes on her architect. Which, by the way, he wasn't. Not *officially*.

"Why don't we take a look at the site and go over some ideas I have?" he suggested.

"How could you have ideas when I haven't even told you exactly what I want?" She didn't mean to sound snippy, but she couldn't possibly trust this young man with her dream. She'd have to get rid of him and find out how to get to the real Clayton Walker.

"Maybe we want the same thing." His gaze dropped ever so quickly over her, a stark reminder that she wore far too little today. And it was hot out here.

Oh, no. No no *no*. Don't you dare go there, brainless hormones. This guy was twenty-nine on a good day, at least six or seven years younger than she was. The *son* of the man she wanted, not *a man* she wanted.

"When were you here?" she asked. Since the storm she'd been up here almost every day. "I haven't seen you." Because she sure as hell wouldn't have missed him.

"A few days ago." He finally tore his mesmerizing gaze from her and focused on the property behind her. "This is a truly legit location for a resort."

Legit? He sounded like Ashley's friends. Maybe he was even younger than she'd thought. "No resort," she corrected. "Just a little B and B is all I have in mind."

"Really? I'd dream bigger than that, Miss..." He inched imperceptibly closer, a smile lifting the corner of his mouth. "It is 'Miss,' isn't it?"

Was he hitting on her? "Miz," she said, a little edge in her voice. "And this isn't a dream, it's a plan for my— our—future. My *daughter's* and mine." Did he get the emphasis? "I have very specific plans." *But they don't include you.* "And I was hoping to meet—"

"My dad, I got that. He's not who you want for this, trust me."

Trust him? Not likely. "Your father's a legend in his field."

"But he's in North Carolina, and I'm here," he drawled with one more brain-numbing smile. "And I already have a couple of ideas for the kind of place you could put here."

"Well, I have ideas, too. A...vision, actually." And a bedroom-eyed, not-yet-thirty not-officially-an-architect wasn't part of it.

"God, Mom, just give him a chance."

Ashley's voice startled her. She'd forgotten her daughter was there, taking in the whole exchange, and, of course, having an opinion. "Honey, this isn't your concern. And, Mr. Walker—"

"Clay. The younger one."

"I have to be honest with you," she said with a sigh of resignation. "This is obviously a huge commitment for me, and I had my heart set on the man who designed Crystal Springs and French Hills, which, as you probably know, were built by Clayton Walker. *The* Clayton Walker. I'm sure you're very good at what you do, but I want someone with more experience."

His expression grew tight and cool. "Sometimes experience can work against you and what you need is"—he ran a hand through sixteen different shades of caramel hair, leaving it just a little more tousled, a lock falling to one eye—"a fresh perspective."

Behind him, Ashley was staring at his *backside* perspective.

No. Yeah. Wow. This guy had to go. "I'm really sorry, but I don't think there's any reason to pursue this. Good-bye."

He half laughed in disbelief. "Good-bye?"

"And thank you."

He took one step backward. "I'd say you're welcome, but I have a feeling you don't really mean that."

"Well, I do mean good-bye."

With his head at a cocky angle that somehow managed to say "You will regret this," without saying a word, he tipped a nod to Ashley and turned to jog off in the opposite direction.

"Mom!" Ashley choked with exasperation. "You were such a b-word to him."

"I didn't mean to be rude, it's just that he's not the person I want to hire. He's not Clayton; he's not the man I wanted."

"But he's obviously the man you e-mailed."

She fired a look at Ashley. "In error." Or was it? "Or maybe he hijacks his father's e-mail or something, looking for lonely women." Not that she was lonely.

"Well, I bet he finds them."

"Dear God, he's twice your age."

"Is that why you sent him away?"

"No. He's too young."

"You just said he was too old."

Frustration zinged through her. "Too old for you to ogle, too young to build my dream." *And for me to ogle.*

Ashley pulled out her phone and thumbed the screen. "Great excuse, Mom."

Chapter 3

I had my heart set on the man who designed Crystal Springs and French Hills.

Well, you had him, darlin', right in your silky little paw. Of course if she called Clayton Walker Architecture and Design, she'd get a different answer.

He ran hard, each jolt of packed sand fueling his determination. He wanted this job. He needed this job. And he had to close the deal before she hooked up with the legend who would squeeze out any competition, including his very own son.

Especially his very own son.

Damn it. He wasn't about to let C-dub near this one. It was a matter of pride. Hell, it was a matter of survival.

And all that stood between him and what he wanted was a closed-minded, uptight, opinionated, voluptuous strawberry blonde. How could he change her mind?

From the minute he'd heard of the hurricane grazing Mimosa Key, he'd known it was the perfect solution. Remote, untouched, and off the competitive radar, he could get the soup-to-nuts job he needed to reinstate himself professionally. Post-disaster rebuilding wasn't his favorite thing, but people in this situation tended to move fast and not take months to bid out work to competitive firms.

There had to be a way to win her over.

Well, there was the obvious. She *had* been pretty busy eyeing his personal landscape. While the idea of spending a long, hot summer night convincing her he was the man for the job had definite appeal, using sex to get the job was flat-out cheesy. It was bad enough that she thought he'd stolen the lead from his father—an understandable mistake since his sister refused to take his name off the Walker Architecture and Design Web site contacts. He wasn't going to try to screw the work out of her, too.

Of course, she'd have the old man on the phone before Clay got back to his truck. The thought made him run faster, hurdling a fallen tree to get to the clearing in the road where he'd parked.

So call him, Strawberry. There's nothin' I love more than a challenge.

He opened the door to climb into the truck, glancing in the back cab at the sketches he'd brought. Bet she'd change her mind if she saw his ideas.

But maybe not. She might not have that much imagination if all she wanted to build on that gem of a property was "just a little B and B." She'd go traditional. Cookie-cutter. Dull as dirt. Come to think of it, Dad would be perfect for her job. Reaching back, he grabbed the sketches.

After his first drive to this beach, he'd raced back to the rental unit to draw page after page of thumbnails. Nothing too detailed, just his gut-level reaction to the pristine, tropical hideaway of Barefoot Bay. It had all come together, too, looking like the success he needed so he could give the finger to his father and take the first step to rebuilding a reputation.

But Lacey Armstrong wanted the legend. The legend who would slap down a four-story stucco box, adorn it with Palladian windows, and pronounce it La Bella Vista at the Sea.

Damn stupid woman with her sexy thighs and preconceived notions.

He slid the rubber band off one sketch and studied what he'd drawn. How the hell could he convince her to look at these? And if he did, would it be enough to stop her from calling his father?

Just as he was about to toss them back, an engine rumbled from around the bend, and a muscular, roofless, high-end Jeep Rubicon accelerated toward him, a woman at the wheel, another next to her, and one in the back. Bass-fueled rock music blared from the speakers.

He was checking out the wild blonde hair, sunglasses, and tanned skin of the driver when one of the others yelled, "Stop, Zoe! Ask that guy!"

Tourists, no doubt. The Jeep came to a screeching stop fifteen feet away from him. The driver threw it into Reverse, fishtailing as she backed up to him.

"Excuse me!" she called, turning down the music. She glanced over her shoulder to say something to the other two as he came around the truck to get closer.

The one in the back didn't look like a tourist, more

lady exec with black hair secured in a ponytail and a crisp white shirt. She didn't reply to what the driver said, but the woman in the passenger seat laughed softly, leaning forward to look at him, dishwater-brown locks falling over an angular face.

Blondie slid her sunglasses into her mane. "We're trying to find Barefoot Bay, but the roads aren't marked at all up here. Do you know if we can get through this way?"

Some time to come for vacation, ladies. "The beach is right there." He pointed behind him. "Your best bet is to park here and walk down, or drive a little farther that way. You can get through, but there's a lot of storm damage and the road gets pretty dicey."

"Let's go straight through," the business-like one in the back said. Probably the Realtor helping them snag a cheap lot, he mused. Good luck with the bitchy property owner. "Once we get closer," she added, "I'll recognize Lacey's place."

Oh? Friends of Strawberry's?

"Thank you," the blonde said to him, adding a dazzling smile. "I really appreciate it. Looks like you've been to the beach."

"Zoe," the passenger said, giving the driver a nudge. "Do you have to flirt with every man?"

"Only the good ones," she teased with a laugh.

"'S okay," Clay assured her. "Yeah, I've been up there."

"Is it a complete wreck?"

He gave in to a wry smile. "Complete."

"Oh, man, what a shame." She swiped her hand through her hair, sharing a look with her friends, then beamed another thousand-watter with dimples at him.

"Well, thanks again. Is that your truck? Do you need a ride or anything?"

Oh, yes, he needed something. He couldn't help smiling, because sometimes it seemed that whenever he faced a wall, the universe handed him a ladder.

"As a matter of fact, did I hear you say you're headed up to see Ms. Armstrong?"

"Yes, we are," Crispy said from the back. "Why?"

"Well, if it's not too much trouble, could you give her these?"

"Of course." The driver reached out and he met her halfway, handing off his ideas, which were immediately flipped into the backseat. "Are your name *and* number on there?"

"Tell her they're from Clay Walker. *The* Clay Walker."

Lacey had wasted way too much energy worrying about how to talk to Clayton Walker—Senior. He was unavailable at the moment. That was all Lacey could get from his arctic assistant, even after Lacey told her exactly why she was calling and how much she needed an architect for her inn at Barefoot Bay. She got to leave sketchy details of the land and job, which she doubted Miss Ice Cube was writing down, and only got a promise that Mr. Walker would call when he had a moment.

Which might be never, the bitch managed to imply.

Don't let this be the excuse that stops you, Lacey chided herself as she and Ashley climbed into her mud-covered VW Passat. She'd call again to—

"Someone's coming up the road," Ashley said, holding up a finger to indicate the not-so-distant sound of a car engine.

Oh, God. Maybe he was coming back.

The thought gave Lacey's heart a jump so unnatural and infuriating she twisted the key with a jerk just as a huge white 4x4 rolled over some debris and hit the horn loud and long enough to block out everything else.

"What the—"

"It's Aunt Zoe!" Ashley shouted, throwing off her seat belt.

"Not just Zoe!" Lacey slapped her hand over her mouth, sucking in a shocked gasp. "They're all here!" Tessa and Jocelyn waved and hollered from the roofless vehicle.

Zoe squealed the Jeep to a stop and all three of them scrambled out, running and dancing toward Ashley and Lacey, arms outstretched.

In an instant it was a huddle of hugs. Even Ashley joined in, jumping up and down as they squeezed and shrieked and an avalanche of explanations came pouring out.

"We wanted to surprise you!"

"We're here to cheer you up!"

"We've been planning this since the hurricane but knew you'd tell us not to come!"

Lacey reeled, holding each dear friend in her arms, choking on laughter and disbelief and joy. Finally the eruption ended and she managed to get her head around the fact that her best friends had come to help her pick up the pieces of her storm-shattered life.

They'd come from across the country and, in Tessa's case, the world.

"Tessa Fontaine!" She put her hands on clean, fresh cheeks, as always unadorned by makeup but so naturally pretty. "I didn't know you were back in the States."

"I just got back while you were dealing with this," Tessa

said, her voice as soft and earthy as her hair, shadows of sadness making her deep brown eyes so serious. "And, by the way, it's Galloway again. I've officially dropped Fontaine."

"Oh, Tess." The divorce, of course, must be final. "Sucks."

"Tessa lives with me now," Zoe announced.

"You do?"

"Not forever." Tessa shrugged a shoulder, which was toned from hours of farmwork in dozens of distant countries. "I went to Flagstaff to hang out with Zoe for the past month, but we didn't bother you with any of that, since you've had your hands full."

"We decided we just had to get out here and lift your spirits." Zoe squeezed Lacey's hand, her other arm already hooked over Ashley's shoulder with casual affection. "And see our group goddaughter, who is getting way too grown-up and gorgeous."

Ashley beamed a mouthful of hot-pink-banded braces at her. "Thanks, Aunt Zoe."

Lacey turned her attention to Jocelyn, the only person on earth who could ride in a 4x4 down a beach road and not have a hair out of place.

"And it only took an act of God to get Jocelyn Bloom back to Mimosa Key," Lacey exclaimed. "There must be a dozen L.A. movie stars who are paralyzed right now without their life coach."

Jocelyn flicked off the comment with dismissive fingertips. "All I need is a phone and Internet and I can work from here for a while. You've always been there for each of us, so it was our time to come to you."

"I'm sorry it took so long," Zoe said, her green eyes

sparkling with the joy that always seemed to light her from inside. "My job took off, so to speak."

They all laughed at that, and Lacey could feel the pressure that had crushed her for all these weeks lift as easily as one of the hot air balloons Zoe piloted for a living.

"I already feel better just looking at you three," Lacey said. "I can't even remember the last time we were all together."

"Tessa's wedding," Jocelyn said, probably able to tell them the date and what each of them wore.

"Uh-oh," Tessa moaned. "This adventure better turn out more successful than that one."

"Tess, c'mere." Lacey reached to give her a hug. "You've been through hell this year."

She took the squeeze, but not for long. "Hell is living through a hurricane. Zoe told me you stayed alive in a bathtub! Is that true?" she asked Ashley.

"Totally true," Ashley confirmed. "Mom was incredible. If it weren't for her, we'd have died in her bedroom closet."

"Ohhh!" The outcry was in unison and came with more hugs, but the tears in Lacey's eyes burned from the sweetness of Ashley's unexpected compliment.

"Hey, Ashley propped me up a few times, trust me."

"Lacey's always been our fearless leader," Zoe said. "The RA who kept us out of trouble for our entire freshman year of college."

"Like anyone can keep you out of trouble, Zoe," Tessa said.

They laughed again, but Jocelyn broke away to look around in disbelief at the bare trees, the piles of debris, and what once was a lovely beachfront property.

"God, Lace," she said, turning slowly. "It's like Barefoot Bay was demolished."

"We got creamed up here," Lacey agreed.

"Almost everything is gone," Ashley said, an understandable whine rising in her voice. "Mom managed to save like five things of mine but everything else is bulldozed or blown away."

Tessa gave her a sympathetic look. "That has to be tough on you, honey."

"I'm telling you, sugar"—Zoe leaned into Ashley's ear—"shopping op!"

"And you guys are living with your parents, Lace?" Tessa asked.

"In their house on the other end of the island, but they're staying up in New York with Adam."

"They don't want to come back and help?" Jocelyn gave Lacey a look. "I know your mom likes to, you know, have opinions."

Lacey bit back a laugh. "My dad offered, but honestly, the last thing I want..." *Is to deal with Mother at a time like this.* But she wouldn't admit that in front of Ashley. "Is for them to have to put up with all the construction. But there's plenty of room for you guys," she added. "We'll squeeze in."

"Actually, I'll stay over the causeway in a hotel," Jocelyn said quickly.

"Like hell you will," Zoe shot back.

"There's plenty of space and we'd love the company. Right, Ash?"

"Oh my God, totally," Ashley agreed, still holding on to her beloved Aunt Zoe. "You have to stay with us."

Jocelyn shook her head. "Nope, sorry. I'm still on the

clock with at least six clients and I've got to be available to them. I booked a room over at the Ritz in Naples, so I'll stay there and come and go with you guys when I can."

"La-dee-dah at the Ritz," Zoe teased, lifting her nose into the air. "We'll be having slumber parties and drinking wine all night." She eyed Ashley. "Not you, of course. Show me the beach, doll face."

Zoe dragged Ashley away and they ran arm in arm toward the sand.

Lacey let out a slow breath, watching them, then turned to Tessa and Jocelyn. "I can't believe you guys are here."

Tessa wrapped an arm around Lacey and tugged her toward the gutted foundation. "I can't believe you lost everything."

"Everything," Lacey confirmed. "Baby pictures and memories, keepsakes and—oh, every day we think of something else."

They tsked and sighed in sympathy.

"But, really, getting wiped out like this teaches you those material things aren't important. What matters is that we survived, and are moving on."

"To think I could charge a client three hundred an hour for doling out that advice," Jocelyn said wryly. "And you figured it all out by yourself."

"I figured a lot out while I was holed up in a bathtub and the world was falling apart around me."

They walked as a threesome, arm in arm. "Like what?" Tessa asked.

"Like it's time to use that three-quarters of a degree in hospitality I have. And I don't mean a shoestring cake-baking business I run from my kitchen."

"That inn full of antiques you've talked about since

college?" Tessa stooped to pluck a stray orange flower that somehow had survived, rolling it in her fingers and giving it a sniff.

"Exactly."

"And how's that working out for you?"

"It's not yet," Lacey admitted sadly. "I thought I had an architect, but I don't think I can get the one I want."

"So you're giving up?" Tessa's voice had a familiar edge of frustration in it. "The world is full of architects, Lacey."

"I need one with the right vision and credentials."

The other two women leaned forward to share a look. "I smell a full-blown Lacey Armstrong rationalization coming on," Jocelyn teased.

"No, no. I want to do this and I have the insurance money, which is enough for a really nice B and B, even a little more if I could swing it, which"—she gave a soft, self-deprecating laugh—"is always the question with me."

"Now you know why we're here," Tessa said softly.

"Why?"

"To stop you from coming up with reasons why you can't build this place and build it right."

"You guys have always been good to me that way." Lacey looked from one to the other. "What do you mean by 'right'?"

"Finished," Jocelyn said. "Up and running and making money."

"I don't know if I can…" Her voice trailed off at their stern expressions, and she laughed. "Okay, okay. And I'm going to need that money because my business is completely shut down now, and I'm living off savings."

Jocelyn settled on the edge of the picnic table. "You want money, you gotta pamper the clients."

"Clients? I can't even get the architect I want to agree to come down."

"You need a spa," Jocelyn said, ignoring her comment. "I can send half of L.A. here if you offer a lava shell massage."

"How about gardens?" Tessa rounded the table. "You have to grow your own food."

"That would be awesome, Tess, but as you can see, we're a long way from a crop of gourmet greens."

Tessa waved a little flower she still held. "But you've got a live *Ixora* 'Nora Grant,' which, I guarantee you, is edible when properly cooked, and quite healthy." She grinned when the other women rolled their eyes. "You'll be back in bloom before long. I was in Borneo after a rough storm and we had an organic farm up and running by the next growing season."

"Oh, definitely go homegrown organic," Jocelyn agreed. "You can totally overcharge for that."

"I love that you guys are planning the spa treatments and menu items and I don't even have building plans yet."

"Lacey." Tessa squeezed her, pulling her to a stand. "Quit finding a reason to say no to everything."

Just then Zoe and Ashley came tearing up from the beach, sand flying in the wake of their happy feet. "Ashley hasn't laughed like that since before the storm."

"Why do you think we put up with Zoe? She's comic relief."

"And she's managed to stay planted in Flagstaff for, what, three years?" Lacey asked. "That's some kind of record for our tumbleweed."

"Her great-aunt Pasha keeps here there, I've discovered," Tessa said. "Or she'd be gone with the next phase of the moon."

"Are you talking about me?" Zoe accused, breathless from the run. "Because I know when that little coven of yours gathers the topic is, What are we going to do with Zoe?"

"Not this time," Tessa said smoothly. "The topic is, What are we going to do with Lacey?"

Zoe fanned herself and cupped her hand over her eyes. "Can we discuss it somewhere shady? Preferably with cocktails? It's hotter here than Arizona and you've got a flippin' beach."

"It's Florida in August, Zoe," Jocelyn said. "That's why they invented air-conditioning."

"Which we didn't have at Nana's house for almost three weeks," Ashley told them. "But we do now."

"Thank God," Zoe said. "Or I would be at the Ritz with Jocelyn, because I don't sweat." She nudged Ashley. "I glisten and glow."

The banter continued as they walked to the cars, but Lacey held back, her arm still around Tessa. "I didn't know how much I needed you," she whispered, her throat suddenly thick with emotion. "Thank you so much for coming, Tess. I know this has been a positively horrific year for you, waiting for the divorce to be final."

"Not horrific for Billy. He's got a girlfriend."

"The bastard."

"She's pregnant."

Lacey froze like ice water had been poured on them. "You have *got* to be kidding me."

"Would I kid about something like that? Five years

I've traipsed around foreign countries to build that organic-farms business with him, growing every seed but the one I wanted."

"Oh, honey." Lacey took both of Tessa's hands.

"He's all smug, too, like he's a real man now that he's finally made a baby." Her voice cracked a little, like it always did on this subject. "He just texted the other day, and she's only like three weeks pregnant."

"I'm so glad you're here now," Lacey said.

"It really was Zoe's idea. But I was on it in a heartbeat."

"And, miracle of miracles, you got Jocelyn to set foot on Mimosa Key again."

"Yeah, sort of." Tessa eyed Jocelyn and shook her head. "Of course you can't get anything out of her she doesn't want to give, but one thing is clear: She won't go south of that road that cuts across the middle of the island."

Where her dad still lived, Lacey thought. "Hey, she's here, Tessa. We'll work around her issues."

"Like that control freak would give us a chance to do otherwise. And, speaking of issues, have you heard from David lately?"

"Oh, Lord, please. Last I heard he was on an icing expedition in Antarctica or maybe he was trekking in Tibet. I lose track."

Tessa rolled her eyes as they reached the Jeep. "So he's still Peter Pan."

"He sends money and Christmas cards," Lacey said, the odd urge to defend Ashley's father and her former boyfriend rising up.

"Hardly enough."

"Enough for me."

"Anybody at all in the romance picture?" Tessa asked.

Lacey just snorted. "What picture? I've dated the few single men on Mimosa Key and I don't feel like bar hopping in Fort Myers with a teenage daughter at home."

"Maybe we can join an online dating service together."

"Get real, Tess." Although Lacey had certainly considered it when she'd looked at the calendar and faced facts. She was going to be thirty-seven, and if she were ever to have another baby...No way she'd bring that up with Tessa now.

Thankfully, Jocelyn ended the conversation by waving her phone. "I need to check into the hotel," she announced. "Client emergency. Why don't you guys put your bags in Lacey's car and ride with her? I'll take the rental."

Next to her, Lacey could feel Tessa tense for an argument, so Lacey jumped in, unwilling to ruin this perfect reunion. "Do what you need to, Joss. I'm just glad you'll be close by."

"Oh my God, Lacey, I was supposed to give you these." Hanging over the driver's seat of the Jeep, Zoe held up a few long cylinders. "They better have Hot Surfer Dude's phone number on them."

Lacey's heart hitched as she took the tubes of paper. "What hot surfer dude?"

"Somebody named Clay Walker."

She almost dropped the rolls. "You saw him?"

"Zoe practically ate him," Tessa said.

"Like you wouldn't have taken a bite," Zoe shot back.

"He was the guy Mom totally dissed on the beach," Ashley said.

"I didn't dis him." Lacey swallowed, the paper sticking to her damp palms. "What did he say?"

"Nothing," Zoe said. "He just gave us those to deliver to you and told us to tell you they were from Clay Walker."

"No," Jocelyn corrected her. "He said *the* Clay Walker, the sign of a massive ego."

"He should have an ego, 'cause that dude was smokin' hot." Zoe elbowed Ashley. "And kinda nekkid, too. I'd like to take a ride on those shoulders."

Tessa covered Ashley's ears. "Nice in front of the kid."

"I'm fourteen, Aunt Tessa."

"I don't give a damn about his shoulders." Lacey snapped the band holding the papers together so hard it broke. "He came here under false pretenses, probably some kind of impostor who hacks e-mail to get work."

Zoe choked. "Yeah, there's a lot of that on the Internet. Like he couldn't get work as a male pros—model."

Lacey spread open one of the rolls on the hood of her car. "We're going to get a lot of con men down here after the storm...so..." *Good God in heaven.* "We should be..."

"We should be what, Mom?"

A slow, prickly chill climbed up her arms, raising the hair on her neck.

"We should be careful," she whispered, staring at the simple ink sketch that took everything she couldn't imagine but felt in her heart and brought it to black-and-white life.

"Careful of what, Mom?"

"Jumping to the wrong conclusion." She stepped back, her hand to her mouth, her breath captured in her lungs, her legs a little wobbly. "Like I just did."

"Wow." Jocelyn leaned over her shoulder. "What do you need to do to get him to build that? 'Cause I'm pretty sure Zoe will do it for you."

"I need..." *An architect with vision.* "A second chance."

Chapter 4

ᗰ

"Hey." Lacey tapped and pushed open the door to her childhood bedroom to find Ashley curled on the bed over her brand-new laptop. The one that had been deemed a "necessity replacement" days after the storm.

Ashley instantly lowered the screen, looking up with surprisingly bright eyes.

"You okay?" Lacey had to fight the urge to launch forward, arms out, maternal instinct at the ready.

"Fine." With one finger she gingerly snapped the computer closed, shutting down whatever she'd been doing.

Lacey ran through a list of possibilities. Nine times out of ten, it was teen-girl drama that brought color to Ashley's cheeks and fire to her eyes.

"You still want to go over to Meagan's tonight?" Lacey asked, walking that fine line between privacy and parenting. Most of the time privacy won, because if anyone knew firsthand what a meddlesome mother could do to a teenage girl, it was Lacey.

"Oh, yeah."

"What's going on, then?" And sometimes parenting won.

"Nothing, Mom. I'm just Facebooking." Evidently, that was a verb now.

"Anyone special?"

"No." She scooted off the bed. "They're waiting for me at Meagan's. Can we go now?"

"Absolutely." Lacey jangled her keys. "Zoe and Tessa and I are going to drop you off and go out to dinner."

"Not Jocelyn?"

"She wanted to stay at the hotel."

As Ashley scooped up a turquoise Hollister tote bag—another post-storm necessity—and grabbed a pillow from the bed, she threw a dubious look at Lacey. "Why does she come all the way across the country to see you and hole up at some hotel?"

Good question. "You've seen the Ritz in Naples. Hardly 'some' hotel."

"But, Mom, I don't get it."

Neither do we, Lacey thought. "You know she grew up here and her mom died a while ago, so she has sad memories of this island." Before a more elaborate explanation was required, Ashley's cell phone vibrated and took her attention.

She read, and shrieked. "Oh my freaking Gawd!" Her fingers flew over the screen.

"Ashley, don't talk like that."

"Tiffany says Matt's breaking up with Cami Stanford! It's totally over!" She clicked more, the text winning over an explanation.

"Tiffany? Tiffany Osborne?" The one who was caught with pot in her locker in eighth grade? "Is she going to be at Meagan's tonight? I didn't think they were friends."

"Maybe I have a chance with Matt now."

Lacey tensed. "Have I met Matt?

Ashley put away her phone and gave Lacey a look that said it all. *Back off, Mom*. And because her own mother never had, Lacey let the conversation go as they piled into Lacey's car and headed toward Meagan's house.

"Would you look at that?" Zoe mused as they cruised through town.

"Look at what?" Lacey asked.

"Interesting," Zoe said, sliding a look to Tessa that Lacey didn't quite get.

"What's interesting?" Lacey pressed.

"Just that little place with the drunk-looking bird on the front. It's cute. Let's have dinner there."

"The Toasted Pelican?" Lacey shook her head. "No way we're going there. They have sucky bar food. I think we should either go to South of the Border for Mexican or see—"

"I want to go to the Toasted Pelican," Zoe said. "It looks like fun."

"It is, if you want to get drunk and meet locals who live, breathe, and sleep fishing."

"Maybe you'll meet a nice guy, so I want to go there."

"Mom doesn't date, Aunt Zoe," Ashley told her. "But if you go to South of the Border will you please get me a doggie bag of enchiladas? They rock."

"Why doesn't Mom date?" Zoe asked pointedly, turning around in the passenger seat to look at Ashley.

"Because she—"

"Because she isn't interested in any of the men on this island," Lacey interjected, watching the yellow light at Center Street, ready to roll through it. "And my nonexistent dating life is not of any interest to my daughter."

"Mom doesn't date because she'll never find a man like my dad."

Lacey's foot jammed on the brake in shock, jerking them all forward into their seat belts. "Sorry, the light was..." Her gaze shifted to Ashley in the rearview mirror. "Honey, where on earth did that come from?"

"Truth hurts, Mom."

Lacey searched her daughter's pale green eyes, exactly the color of David's.

"That's not why I don't date," Lacey said after a long, awkward pause. "I just haven't met anyone interesting."

"Which is why we're going to the Toasted Pelican for dinner."

"Zoe!" Lacey switched her attention to the other wayward child in the car. "I'm telling you, the food, the atmosphere—it's not our kind of place."

Zoe just lifted one eyebrow. "You might change your mind."

Lacey was still too shaken by Ashley's comment about David—which had happened a few other times recently—to argue over where they were eating. Silent, she took the next left and made her way to Meagan's house, where three teenage girls were hanging out in the front, waiting for Ashley.

"Who are those other girls, Ashley?"

"Meagan's friends."

Lacey took a breath. "I mean, what are their names?"

"Oh my God, Mom. You've known Meagan since I

was, like, in preschool. Bye, you guys. Have fun!" She was out before another question could be asked.

Lacey eyed the group but Tessa gave her shoulder a tap. "She's fine, Mom. Anyway, they remind me of us at Tolbert Hall."

"That's the problem," Lacey said. "I know what we did in college."

"She's in ninth grade. Don't worry." The girls were headed toward the house, heads close, giggling. "Nothing like a foursome," Tessa added wistfully.

Lacey glanced over her shoulder. "Hey, you want to drive to the mainland and surprise Jocelyn? I hate that she's alone tonight."

"She doesn't," Tessa said. "You know solitude is like air to Jocelyn. She needs it to survive."

"Anyway, we're going to the Toasted Pelican now," Zoe said again, this time with little humor and plenty of determination.

"What is with you?" Lacey demanded. "That place is a dive, the food is greasy, and the wine is watered down."

"And an extremely sexy architect who may or may not be officially licensed but definitely appears to have some kind of magic drafting tool just walked in the front door. So move your ass, Armstrong. You got work to do."

Lacey's jaw dropped. She'd told her friends about meeting Clay on the beach and the story he'd given about his experience in the field, but clearly they weren't dismayed by his lack of qualifications.

Tessa gave Lacey's shoulder a nudge from the backseat. "C'mon, Lace. You know you want to."

"That's not how I want to talk to him, in some bar. I'll…call him. After I hear back from his father. And check out his credentials. I don't know anything about him and..."

Her voice faded, met by dead silence and "get real" stares.

"C'mon, you guys. Tonight's for us. This is our reunion, a chance to catch up and talk, not worry about him and—"

"Lacey." The warning came in unison and hit a bull's-eye. They were right, damn it.

"You know, girls, sometimes nothing beats a watered-down wine."

Zoe held up her fist for celebratory knuckles. "That's what I'm talkin' about."

Clay looked from one woman to the other, still having a hard time remembering who was Gloria and who was Grace.

The two had flanked him fairly quickly at the bar. They were not-unattractive MILF-y types, late thirties or early forties. Both looked vaguely familiar, but Mimosa Key was small enough that even in his few days here he'd gotten to know some local faces.

Gloria was the dark-haired one, with thick bangs and big brown eyes, a little younger and more reserved than the other. Grace had frosted hair, a spray-on tan—which struck him as odd in Florida—and, despite the thick gold band on her left ring finger, seemed far more physically aggressive.

Grace's first question was where was he staying.

"Hibiscus Court near the harbor," he replied, sipping a lukewarm draft and fighting the urge to check out the bar for anyone else he might recognize. Not that he expected Lacey Armstrong to show up in a place like this. He'd come to grill the locals and find out what he could about her, so he forced himself to focus on the women who'd zeroed in on him as soon as he'd arrived.

"You planning to stay awhile?" Grace asked. "That's a furnished rental, but I know Chuck Mueller wouldn't let you sign less than a three-month lease."

"I'm still deciding, but I wanted to keep my options open." He'd signed that three-month lease, but he was optimistic like that. "And there aren't a lot of other places to stay around here unless I go to the mainland."

Grace's smile widened as she exchanged a look with Gloria. "You just aren't talking to the right people, hon. I'm the owner of the Fourway Motel."

"There was no vacancy."

She lifted an eyebrow and gave him a deliberate once-over. "Then my husband must have been working the front desk, and he's easily intimidated by big, handsome men."

He laughed off the compliment. "The Fourway, huh? Interesting name."

"If you're in Mimosa Key long enough, you'll know what a Fourway is." She gave him a teasing wink. "My cousin, Gloria, and I will teach you."

"You're going to scare the life out of him, Grace," the other woman said, giving a dismissive wave. "The Fourway is the intersection of Center Street and Harbor Drive, the historic site of the first traffic light on the island." She added a shy smile. "There's a long history on Mimosa Key, you know. Our mothers are the daughters of the first pastor when the island was founded back in the 1940s."

"Which explains your names."

"And theirs," Gloria said. "My mother is Charity and Grace's mom is Patience, and they own the Shell Gas Station and Super Mini Mart Convenience Store, also known as the Super Min, located at—"

"The Fourway," he finished for her.

"You're catching on," Grace said as she leaned in close. "There might be a town council, a mayor, and few influential big mouths on this island, but the fact is, we practically run the place." She trailed a long, white-tipped nail over his knuckles and held his gaze. "So you'd be smart to keep us on your good side if you're looking for business." Her finger continued to his bicep. "I assume you're in construction."

"Are you?" Gloria asked. "Because Beachside Beauty, where I work, lost a few windows and the guy who was supposed to install them never showed."

"I don't do windows. I do full buildings." At their questioning look he added, "I'm an architect."

"Whoa." Grace backed up an inch. "Who's hiring an architect?"

No one yet. "Some of the places in Barefoot Bay were demolished and need a full rebuild."

"Like what places?" Grace asked. "It's mostly wilderness, scrub, and mangroves up there and only a couple of old houses."

Here was the perfect opening to get some information on Lacey Armstrong. "Maybe not for long," he told her. "Could be a bed-and-breakfast going up."

Grace's jaw dropped and all the friendliness went out of her eyes "I don't fucking think so."

Clay blinked at the unexpected profanity. "Why's that?"

"Zoning ordinances," she said, shifting her gaze to her cousin to share silent communication. "Nobody can build a hotel, motel, inn, resort, B and B, nothing. Won't happen. Better look for work elsewhere, Frank Lloyd Wright."

Everything in her body language changed; her back stiffened, her nostrils flared, and she downed half a glass of wine in a single gulp. Then she stared at him, all the friendliness gone.

"Who's building it?" she asked.

As much as he wanted to know more about Lacey, instinct told him to keep her name out of it. "One of the residents up there."

"Everham? Tomlinson? Who?" Grace asked, her brows knitting as she thought about it. "Surely Lacey Armstrong isn't going to try to put me—try and build some kind of motel."

"But why wouldn't she?"

"I just told you." Grace moved in to make her point, a whiff of bitter Chardonnay on her breath. "Ordinances. Changing them would require approval from the town council, which is controlled by the mayor." She angled her head and gave him a smug smile. "Who is controlled by my mother."

"Really?" Ah, the intricacies of small-town politics.

"Really." Grace signaled the bartender. "Need my bill, Ronny."

"I'll take care of it," Clay said.

But the woman's look was cold. "Trying to bribe me?"

"Trying to buy a lady a drink."

"We're done here, Glo," she said, standing up. "Let's book."

"I'm not ready to leave, Grace." Gloria gave her some not-so-subtle wide eyes.

"Yes, you are."

Gloria smiled apologetically at Clay. "Listen, if you do stick around and you ever need a haircut, stop by Beach-side Beauty. We do men." She laughed self-consciously at the double entendre. "You know what I mean. Anyway,

I'll cut your hair, but"—she reached up to flutter a lock on his neck—"it'd be kind of a shame to cut this off."

Just as she tugged some of the hair he hadn't cut since the day he'd quit working for his dad, the front door opened.

Gloria leaned over and whispered in his ear. "Don't get on Grace's bad side."

At the door, three women walked in, one with copper curls cascading to bare shoulders and a yellow dress cut low enough to steal a man's breath.

Well, holy hell. Look what the wind blew in.

Then all the sounds and smells and sights of the neighborhood bar faded into gray silence as Lacey and Clay's eyes connected for the space of four, five, six rapid heartbeats.

It took a nudge from the blonde he recognized as the Jeep driver, but Lacey slowly made her way toward him. God-*damn*, she looked good. Shiny, curvy, bright, and beautiful.

When she reached him she bit her lower lip hard enough to wear away the gloss and leave a little white spot and took a breath deep enough to strain some soft flesh against the scooped neck of her sundress.

He let his gaze drop there for just a moment before standing and reaching out a hand. "Of all the gin joints in all Mimosa Key..."

Her glossy lips lifted in a smile that rivaled the blistering sun he'd spent the day under. "You walk into mine," she finished.

Oh, man. He'd just met his match.

Chapter 5

Lacey couldn't let go of his hand. Not just because his fingers were strong and calloused, or because just the sight of him made her knees a little wobbly, but because...

Of all the gin joints.

He'd quoted her number-one all-time favorite movie. *Her* movie. "You've seen *Casablanca*?"

"A dozen times." He guided her to the stool next to him, empty now that Gloria Vail had scooted away.

"Really?" She glanced over her shoulder, but Zoe and Tessa had found a table on the other side of the bar, as planned. Lacey was only supposed to get the drinks and casually "bump into" Clay Walker.

Not sit on a bar stool next to him exchanging movie quotes.

"Why are you surprised? It's a great movie." His leg brushed hers as he sat down and settled too close, sending an electric jolt through her. "At least it would be if they'd changed the ending."

"Change the ending? Of *Casablanca*? Why ruin perfection?"

"Perfection?" Bone-meltingly blue eyes lingered one more time on the sweetheart neckline of her dress, which seemed summery and safe for a night out with the girls but suddenly felt really sexy.

"The wrong guy gets the girl," he said softly. "So that's not perfection."

"The wrong guy?"

"Rick gave up too easily, if you ask me." Almost imperceptibly, he moved closer. "I would never give up that easily."

For a world-tilting second she forgot what they were talking about. Forgot why she'd come to the bar or what she wanted to say to him. Might have forgotten her own name.

"So, this is a really nice surprise," he said. "You a regular here?"

"I just popped in with some friends." *To tell you I love your sketches.*

"Can you forgive me?" he asked.

Forgive him? She was the one who'd kicked him off the beach. "For what?"

"For not liking the ending of *Casablanca*." He gave her a slow, easy smile, all deadly and dreamy at the same time. "And for not being my father."

She had to do this. Had to. No excuse in the world could stop her from jumping through the opening he'd just made. *I like your ideas.* Very simple, very honest. A little crow as an appetizer.

But they just looked at each other, waiting for the other to move first, until the bartender arrived and broke the moment. "What can I get you, miss?"

"Wine . . . three white wines."

Clay leaned into the bar. "Ronny, put those on my tab."

"That's not necessary."

He held up a hand to stave off her argument. "And take two of them to those lovely young ladies by the window. Miz Armstrong will have hers here." Somehow, he combined that southern drawl with easy authority.

Ronny splashed some yellow liquid into a cheap wine-glass and slid it toward her.

"One drink," she agreed, settling on the bar stool.

"That's all I need," he replied.

"To do what?"

He held up a half-empty glass of beer. "Here's lookin' at you, kid."

"Oh, now you're not playing fair." She touched his glass anyway and sipped hers, making a face. "Now that's a fine-tasting nail-polish remover."

He laughed. "So why'd you come in here if you don't like the booze?"

Carefully placing the stemmed glass on a cocktail napkin, she flipped through a bunch of possible, plausible answers. None was the truth.

"I came in here because we spotted you walking in."

His brows raised.

"I'm not a stalker," she assured him. "I just wanted to say . . ." She took a steadying breath. "I really loved your sketches and—wow, where did you get the idea for that overhang in the front, because it was . . . *spectacular.*"

"You know what?" He leaned closer and took one

ringlet of her hair, pulled it, and let it bounce back to a natural curl, making blue-white sparks snap at her nerve endings. "So are you, Strawberry."

Oh, he was good. Young, gorgeous, sinfully good. And even nail-polish-remover-tasting wine could take away a woman's inhibitions. She took another drink and gathered more courage.

"Actually, Clay, I think I'm the one who should ask if I'm forgiven for being a total bitch on the beach today."

"I might forgive you," he teased. "What else did you like about the sketches?"

She closed her eyes, picturing the way he'd tucked the building under foliage that wasn't even there anymore, and the way he'd captured the essence of what was meant to be built in Barefoot Bay. "I didn't like the sketches," she said, getting a surprised look. "I *loved* them."

He grinned. "Then you're forgiven."

She tried to back away but couldn't. The guy was a damn human magnet. "Although what you drew looks like a much, much bigger place than anything I want to build."

"Why not go big?"

"Why? Because I can't afford a *resort*, just a little inn."

"Get investors."

"I've never even run a B and B, so I'd be totally in over my head."

"Hire people."

"Hey, don't bulldoze my excuses," she said on a laugh. "I'm trying to tell you all I have is a foundation and..." *A dream*. "An insurance check."

"You have an architect. That is, if I get the job."

Oh, Lord, it would be easy to say yes to this man, yes

to a lot of things, some of which had nothing to do with buildings or dreams. Well, maybe some dreams.

"Do I have it?"

She laughed. "I thought southern gentlemen were supposed to be slow. You move like a bullet train."

"Why waste time?" He leaned a little closer, a whiff of something woodsy and pure shooting right into her brain and directly to her sex hormones. "When something's right, it's right."

"This is right?" She tried to make it a question, but that smell, that hair, those eyes; her voice cracked in the face of it all.

"You know it is."

"But we have a lot to talk about first." Like fees and plans and ideas and when they would—kiss. No, *start.* "I'll grant you a job interview. How's that?"

"I thought that's what this was."

Laughing, she took a sip of lousy wine, which, somehow when shared with the company of this man, didn't taste so bad. "You don't have a resume with you."

"You saw the sketches. What else do I need?"

"Credentials. Education. Experience."

"I've got 'em all, ma'am."

She cringed. "Ouch, I've been ma'amed."

"Southern habit, I swear. And aren't my drawings creds enough?"

Oh, he was good. And evasive. "You said you weren't 'officially' an architect," she said. "What does that mean?"

"That I don't have a piece of paper that doesn't amount to"—he winked—"a hill of beans."

"Don't do that." She pointed a warning finger at him. "Don't toss *Casablanca* quotes. That won't get you the job.

And, honestly, that stuff makes a damn big hill of beans' difference to me. I wouldn't go to a lawyer who wasn't licensed to practice law or a doctor who wasn't board certified. Why would I hire an architect who isn't officially approved by . . . whoever officially approves architects."

"The AIA and the NCARB," he said.

"No alphabet soup, either. Spell it out in English that a thirty . . . something-year-old mother of one can understand."

"You're sensitive about your age, aren't you?"

"I just think you might be too young for—"

He put a hand over her mouth, silencing her. "I'm twenty-nine, not too young for anything." Slowly he removed his hand, turned it, and waved his fingers in front of his face. "I knew I smelled strawberry," he said with a smile. "It's your lip gloss, not your hair."

"I don't know what kind of architect you are, but you sure are proficient at changing the subject."

"I'm proficient at a lot of things, Lacey."

He said her name like . . . sex. Hell, every time he breathed it was like sex. "I'm only interested in your architectural credentials, Mr. Clayton Walker. *Junior.*"

"Ouch. Okay, we're even for the 'ma'am' now." He inched away, sipped his beer, gave her just enough space to make her want him to come back. "I finished a five-year architecture program at the University of North Carolina."

"I thought you said you weren't an architect."

"I *am* an architect and I'm completely capable of designing any kind of structure or facility you want, and contracting the right people to build it."

"Are you licensed and board certified?"

"Pretty much."

"Pretty much?" She choked softly.

He shrugged one shoulder. "It's just that there's some more, you know, *stuff* to getting licensed in North Carolina."

"Stuff such as..."

"A two-year internship, which I completed at Clayton Walker Architecture and Design, Inc."

"I thought you said you have nothing to do with him or his business."

"I'm on my own now," he said simply. "I learned a lot from working with my father's company, paid my dues, and sat for one of the licensing exams. Then..." Another way-too-casual shrug. "Anyway, the exam was in planning and design, which, you have to admit, is a great place for us to start. Listen, Strawberry—"

"Did you just call me Strawberry?"

He smiled and plucked another curl. "My favorite fruit. I'm telling you, tests don't make you an architect."

She tried to take a breath but got a lungful of man again, the smell of someone who did not take no for an answer. And called her *Strawberry*.

"Life gives you enough tests," he said.

Like how long could she sit here, inches from the sexiest man she could remember meeting in her life, and not kiss him? That right there was a real test.

"True success comes from meeting and beating every one of the challenges you're thrown." He inched a little bit closer with every word.

Words that, she realized as she stopped inhaling and admiring and started listening, were as hot as he was. *If* he meant what he said and wasn't just handing her a load of BS.

"Let me ask you something, Clay."

"Anything."

"Do you always get everything you want?"

Something flickered over his features. A memory, maybe. But it was gone in an instant. "Everything," he assured her. "Even if I have to change what it is that I want."

She smiled, totally understanding that.

"Here's all you have to know about me, Lacey." He brushed her knuckles with his fingertips, ostensibly to underscore the point he was about to make, but the touch sent chills over her skin and made her curl her toes around the bar stool just for something to hang on to. "I don't believe in obstacles, brick walls, barriers, roadblocks, or anything else that says I can't. There's a way around everything and everyone, and I find it. I get what I want and I don't quit until I have it. I give you my word on that. Now, can I have the job to design and build your resort?"

Oh, boy. *Casablanca* was a turn-on, but someone who didn't quit? Didn't give up? Didn't find excuses? Wasn't that exactly what she needed?

"I suppose we could meet at the property."

He put one finger under her chin and tilted her face toward his. "Just say yes."

Like a living, breathing human female could say anything else. "After you've come up with some ideas. Right now I can't—"

"Let's agree not to use the word *can't*. Ever. Let's just call it a four-letter word we don't use."

She smiled. "I can't." Then laughed. "You don't know me. I'm . . . cautious."

He ran his thumb across her bottom lip, a move that, seriously, just ought to be outlawed. "If you were cautious, you wouldn't have followed me in here."

"My friends talked me into it," she admitted.

"Then send them the finest bottle of nail-polish remover. When do we start?"

When do they start what? That was the question. *Come on, Lacey.*

"We'll finish this interview tomorrow morning at ten o'clock at Barefoot Bay," she said, searching for the strength to escape his lethal touch and coming up with nothing. "Bring your drawings and your imagination, samples of your work, and references." *And, for the love of God, don't bring that thumb that's turning me into a puddle of hormones.*

For one more suspended second, they stayed two inches from each other, sparks and heat arcing between their mouths. If he had kissed her, she'd have kissed him right back.

But somehow, she found the strength to walk away.

Chapter 6

Lacey pulled into the Super Min wishing she could fill her tank without having to go inside. The Sisters of the Holy Super Min, as Charity Grambling and Patience Vail were known around town, would surely both be working this morning. But Charity refused to install credit-card-accepting pumps in the only gas station in this part of the island, so Lacey had no choice.

Now that their daughters, cousins Grace and Gloria, had met Clay, it was only a matter of time until Lacey's plans were public. Would there be pushback against leveling her grandparents' ancient house to build a bed and breakfast? Probably. Definitely.

With Clay's definition of "true success" still ringing in her ears—and his sexy scent still torturing her memory—Lacey squared her shoulders and entered the Super Min.

A bell tinkled with an old-fashioned preciousness as

the door opened, just as Charity shoved the cash-register drawer closed and dismissed a customer with a tight smile. The bell was the only thing "precious" about the Super Min or its owners.

"Well, it's about time somebody got dressed up around here," Charity remarked.

"Not exactly up, but dressed." Lacey paused in the heavenly rush of cool air. "I have a meeting."

A construction worker passed Lacey on his way out, giving her a once-over and zeroing in on her chest.

"I'll meet with you," he said with a wink.

So much for the "too professional" blouse Zoe had mocked and Lacey thought underplayed her boobs. Those suckers did not underplay easily.

Clay Walker was already a professional risk; she didn't want to encourage a personal one as well. So she kept telling herself that if he got the job, if he proved himself to her, and if they had to work side by side for a year or more, she would just ignore the fact that he turned her into a quivering bowl of Jell-O.

"Bet I know who you're meeting with." Charity situated her bony backside on her stool, smug and cocky.

"I wouldn't be surprised if you did, Char." There were two forms of news delivery on this island: the *Mimosa Gazette* and Charity Grambling. "Forty dollars of regular unleaded," she said, holding out her money.

Charity took the cash and lifted partway off the stool to peer over the counter and get the full view of the white slacks Lacey had switched to when Zoe had called her other choice mom jeans.

"You're going up to that mess in white pants?"

News *and* editorial.

"Yep." Lacey met Charity's judgmental gaze.

The door to the back office flipped open and Patience Vail, who only answered to the nickname Patti, ambled into the room.

"Lacey's got a meeting," Charity said, pressing way too much emphasis on the word. "With *someone*."

Patti lifted her dark brows. "That same someone you were practically licking down at the Pelican last night?"

Oh, boy. This actually could be fun if it weren't true. "There was no licking, Patti." Lacey gave an obviously impatient look at the cash register. "You know, until you press that button, I can't pump the gas."

"I know." Charity situated herself on the stool. "I gotta tell your mama, Lacey. You know that, don't you?"

Lacey rolled her eyes and almost laughed at the warning, like she was a teenager caught shoplifting in the Super Min or something. "My mother's up in New York at my brother's place, Charity."

"I know where she is. We're Facebook friends."

"Well, no need to report anything, Charity, because last time I checked, I was thirty-six years old." About to be thirty-seven, but no need to give them that ammo.

Patti and Charity shared a look. "He isn't," they said simultaneously. "Bet he isn't thirty yet."

Now she couldn't help laughing. "Did you girls get a picture? 'Cause then you can post that on Facebook, too." She started to back away, but Charity's inch-long crimson nails lingered over the computer key, holding Lacey captive. "Any minute now, Charity. I'm kind of in a hurry."

But Patti put a hand on Charity's arm, further stalling things. "Maybe she *is* the one."

What one?

Charity considered the question, eyed Lacey suspiciously, then shook her head. "Nah, she'd never do something that stupid."

"You're right, she wouldn't," Patti said, like they weren't talking about her in the third person.

Lacey refused to take the bait, though.

"'Course not, Pat," Charity continued. "Lacey wouldn't do anything *stupid* with that old house from her grandfather, who was one of our daddy's *dearest friends* and, of course, one of *the founders of Mimosa Key.*" She practically breathed fire on the last words. "Or did you forget that your grandparents were pioneers who had a vision for this place? A vision, Lacey. And it included some ironclad rules of the road. Do you know what they are?"

Lacey shifted from one foot to the other, the pressure of being late for a ten o'clock meeting in Barefoot Bay almost as weighty as her curiosity, and a growing concern. What was the issue here? "Not sure where you're going with this, Charity, but I would really appreciate if you'd free the gas pump so I'm not late for my meeting."

"With an architect?" Charity prompted.

She looked from one to the other, knowing that a lie would be discovered and the truth would be broadcast to the next thirty customers. "Yes."

"Uh-huh." Charity nodded, slowly, her lips curled in an "I knew it" smirk. "My Gracie said she met an architect in the Pelican last night, and when she and Glo left, you all but fell into his lap."

"Not exactly." She pointed to the register. "Please?"

Patti, a much bigger woman than her sister, worked her girth around the counter to give Lacey a hard look. "He said he might be building an inn of some kind."

Lacey just stared at her, saying nothing, reality dawn-
ing. Grace and Ron Hartgrave owned the Fourway Motel,
and no one in the extended family run by these two matri-
archs would like the competition. But they couldn't stop it.

Could they?

She cleared her throat and met Patti's beady gaze. "Nothing is set in concrete," she said. "I'm looking at all the possibilities." Damn, she wanted to have more conviction than
that, but these two, they were not to be messed with.

"Well, look at this possibility." Charity whipped out a
binder and slapped it on the counter. *The Building Code and
Bylaws of Mimosa Key* was typed across the top. Literally
typed. By a typewriter. Probably before Lacey was born.

Charity flipped open the cover and pointed to a page
already marked with a bright pink Post-it note. "Says right
here that no structure that contains more than five bedrooms
can be built on Mimosa Key."

Lacey almost choked. "That code was written in the
1950s, Charity. It—"

"Still holds true," Patti interjected. "You don't see any
six-bedroom houses on this island."

"Which is the problem," Lacey shot back.

"What do you mean?"

"Well, if we would let some people build big houses, we
could be the next Jupiter Island or take some of the money
that gets poured into Naples' real estate. Mimosa Key is ripe
for big money, and I can't imagine who on the town council would be opposed to having more tourist dollars on this
island."

They both stared at her, but it was Charity whose eyes
narrowed. "So it's true. You're trying to ruin this island."

She fought an exasperated sigh. "No, Charity. I'm

looking for ways to expand it, make it better, bring in jobs, and—"

"We don't need any more jobs," Patti insisted. "We want it just like it is, young lady."

"Oh, now I'm young. A minute ago I was too old for the man I was talking to last night."

"Don't you get snippy," Charity warned.

"That's right," Patti chimed in. "Because your Granny Dot and her dear Theodore would roll over in their graves if they knew what you were planning to do with that beautiful old home they built for you when they founded this island."

She didn't even know what she was planning to do, how could Granny?

"And that home is gone," Lacey said softly, hating that the loss she felt could be heard in her voice. "And so are my grandparents."

"Then you should respect their memory," Charity said.

But Granny Dot always wanted a B and B. She'd been the one who'd planted the idea in Lacey's head years ago. But Lacey wasn't about to share that with these two old witches.

"You don't have your facts straight, Patti," Lacey said. "And you're jumping the gun. I'm not sure at all what I'm going to build on my property. For the most part, I'm just happy Ashley and I survived."

Charity sniffed. Patti crossed her arms. So much for the sense of community and helpfulness that had arisen after the storm. But for one minute, in the face of expressions that looked a lot like her mother's most disapproving scowl, Lacey considered changing her mind.

Was this dream worth getting the doyens of Mimosa

Key riled up and ready to wreck her life? Was it worth fighting for?

Behind her, the bell dinged with a new customer and all Lacey could do was exhale with relief. At least now she could pump her gas.

"Mornin', Strawberry."

The words went into her ear, down her spine, spun through her belly, and gave her knees a little push.

"Strawberry?" Charity choked.

"It is you, isn't it?" He put two strong and solid hands on her shoulders and slowly turned her around. "Yeah, I'd recognize that hair anywhere." He closed his eyes and sniffed. "And the scent."

Oh, Charity ought to have a field day with that. "What are you doing here?"

"I'm addicted to gas-station coffee, so I thought I'd get us some."

Us.

"Introduce your friend, Lacey." Charity tapped impatiently on the counter. "As if we don't already know who he is."

Lacey gave him a secret eye roll and silent warning. "Clay, this is Charity Grambling and Patti Vail, sisters and owners of the Shell Gas Station and Super Mini Mart Convenince Store, also known as the Super Min. Ladies, this is Clay Walker."

"The architect," Patti said. "We've heard *all* about you." She threw a smile at Lacey that gave the distinct impression that *all* they'd heard came right from Lacey herself.

"Mornin', ladies."

Charity's gaze wandered up and down Clay's T-shirt and jeans. "You don't look like an architect."

"Looks are deceiving," he said, stepping toward the coffee station. "Man, that smells good."

"So are you rebuilding Blue Horizon?"

He gave Lacey a questioning look.

"That's what my grandfather called the house," she said, even though she suspected his unspoken question was more along the lines of *Am* I rebuilding it?

"If you are, you better familiarize yourself with this very important piece of historical documentation." Charity lifted the binder. "We have rules against certain-sized buildings and nothing can be, you know, gaudy." Charity dragged out the word and wiggled her fingers. Like those talons weren't the gaudiest things that ever came out of Beachside Beauty.

"I'm not building anything gaudy," Clay said as he filled two large cups.

Patti stepped forward. "'Course you couldn't build that big a place. Your land isn't that sizable, after all. Unless you're planning to buy Everham's and that plot on the other side of yours."

The Tomlinsons'. Yep, that was exactly what Lacey was planning to do. But she just gave a noncommittal shrug.

"That'd be quite a piece of land if you pulled that off," Patti said, proving that speculation was all she needed to turn something into fact.

At the coffee machine, Clay glanced at Lacey. "How do you take your coffee?" he asked, their eyes connecting in silent communication.

"Cream and sugar." She could kiss him for not responding to Patti. Oh, she could kiss him just for standing there like a golden, gorgeous, glorious god, too, but mostly she loved that he didn't take the bait these two were throwing out.

"We're just counting on our Lacey to do the right thing," Charity said. "Seeing as she's part of the very special family of people who built this island for the distinct reason that they wanted to avoid the hellhole of highrises over in Naples. We want things to stay just the way they've always been."

"Change is good," Clay said, giving Lacey one of the coffees and placing a twenty-dollar bill on the counter. "Can I have some?"

Charity didn't move. "Change isn't good for Mimosa Key and we don't need some big-time architects building eyesores on Barefoot Bay."

"I'm not big-time, and I'm not building an eyesore," he said, putting a hand on the book. "But if you'd like, I'd be happy to give you some ideas about how you could make the elevation of this little convenience store even more attractive, and then when the nice people come to stay at Lacey's new place, they'll all stop here on their way in and out to buy your"—he sipped the coffee and nodded approvingly—"fantastic coffee."

Charity yanked the book away and pushed his twenty back. "The coffee's on the house."

"Much obliged." He toasted her with the cup. "For the coffee and the history lesson."

He shouldered open the door, holding it for Lacey, who walked into the sunshine and let out a long, slow breath.

Clay dipped his head and whispered in her ear as the door closed behind them, "You gonna let two little old batshit crazy ladies be a roadblock?"

"No." Maybe. He didn't know how much power they wielded on this island.

"Good." He put his arm around her, pulling her into rock-solid muscle in a dizzyingly casual and intimate move. "Now, let's go look at your property and see how many more people we can piss off."

Chapter 7

The first thing Jocelyn heard when the elevator doors opened to the Ritz lobby was the ring of Zoe's laughter echoing through the cavern of marble and glass. The sound made her realize how much fun she'd missed the night before. Still, no amount of fun was worth the risk of seeing...someone she did *not* want to see. She'd stay here for Lacey as long as she could, but nothing could make her venture south on Mimosa Key.

Which is why she loved that Zoe, Tessa, and Ashley had sweetly agreed to come to the Ritz for lunch today while Lacey met with her architect. Of course, without Lacey to run interference, they might press her a little about coming over to the island, but she could always manufacture a client crisis. Considering she'd just spent the last half hour on the phone with a weeping Coco Kirkman, there wouldn't be too much manufacturing involved.

The three of them stood outside a high-end boutique, Zoe's arm draped over Ashley's shoulder, their heads close as they discussed the bathing-suited mannequin in the window. As she approached, Tessa turned and brightened at the sight of Jocelyn.

"I never thought I'd utter these words to you, Jocelyn Bloom: You're late."

"Client crisis."

"We were forced to window-shop at the overpriced hotel stores." Zoe tugged Ashley closer. "And decided you might have to buy us all one of those adorable bikinis in different colors."

Jocelyn hugged them all, an extra squeeze for Ashley. "I just might do that after lunch. Ashley, you're a doll to give up your day and hang out with us."

"It's cool," Ashley said, her eyes dancing with youthful happiness. Had Jocelyn's eyes ever danced at that age, she wondered idly. No. Not once. Not ever. Which was why she had to stand her ground and stay off the south end of Mimosa Key.

"I'm really having fun," Ashley added.

"Mom's ignoring our texts while she makes out with the smokin'-hot architect boy," Zoe added. "So we can do whatever we want, including buy skimpy bikinis. Right, Ash?"

The light in Ashley's eyes dimmed. "She's not making out with him."

"A figure of speech," Zoe assured her, leaning behind Ashley to share a secret look with Jocelyn. "She almost did last night," she mouthed.

As they crossed the lobby to the terrace restaurant, Ashley fell a few steps behind, reading her phone.

"C'mon, Ash," Jocelyn prodded, waiting for her.

Ashley quickly covered her phone.

"I'm not going to read your texts," Jocelyn teased.

"I know, but it's private."

"A boy?" Jocelyn asked in a whisper.

Color burst on her cheeks. "No."

Her tone was indignant enough for Jocelyn to let it ride. They followed a maitre d' to a window table with a perfect view of the pool and beach. As soon as they were settled in with iced tea and sodas, Tessa gestured toward the vista.

"I could get used to this," she said. "It beats planting organic gardens in Sri Lanka."

"You love planting," Jocelyn said.

"Not in Sri Lanka."

Out of the corner of her eye Jocelyn noticed Ashley pulling out her phone, but she kept her focus on Tessa. "I thought you loved globe-trotting."

Tessa lifted a shoulder. "My ex-husband loved it more than I did."

Next to Zoe, Ashley flicked her finger across the screen and Tessa reached over and put her hand on the phone. "Hey, no texting at the table," she chided.

"I'm not texting," Ashley shot back.

"Then no e-mail at the table."

Ashley rolled her eyes. "E-mail is so last century, Aunt Tessa."

"Then no doing whatever the heck you're doing. It's rude."

"Facebooking. Sorry."

Just the thought of what would have happened to her if she'd used that tone at the table put an ache in Jocelyn's stomach. "Let her go, Tess. It's no big deal."

"But she's right, Ash," Zoe chimed in. "Cell phones

are not cool at the table. Especially in zee Ritz-Carlton, dahling."

Instead of joining the joke Ashley narrowed her eyes at Zoe. "I'm not your daughter."

Whoa. Something inside Jocelyn twisted. Instantly, she put a gentle hand on Ashley's arm. "But you're our god-daughter, honey, and we don't see you that often. So what do you think of your mom's idea for a B and B?"

Ashley shrugged, obviously unhappy about putting down the phone. "'It's cool if she really does it. She's been talking about it forever."

"This time is different," Tessa said. "I think she can really make it happen."

Ashley's phone vibrated and she sneaked a peek, then let out a soft cry. "Oh, he wrote back."

He. Tessa started to say something, but Jocelyn shook her head quickly, sensing that they had to let go of this one.

"So, have you ever stayed at this hotel, Ashley?" she asked. "Maybe you could spend a night here at the hotel with me sometime. Maybe you all could."

That earned her a big, bright smile. "That'd be cool."

"Perfect timing, too," Zoe said. "We could give Lacey a night alone to play with Clay." She grinned. "He'll be putty in her hands. Hah! I'm so punny."

Ashley's tell-all expression shifted right back to the other side of the pendulum. "That's just gross, Aunt Zoe. The guy's not much older than me."

"Oh, yes he is," Tessa corrected. "I'm guessing thirty, which makes him perfectly acceptable as a builder, archi-tect, contractor, and anything else your mother wants."

Ashley squished up her face. "She doesn't date."

"So you've said." Zoe pulled her straw out of her iced

tea and tapped it, then used it to point at Ashley. "And that might be half her problem."

"She doesn't have a problem." Ashley sneaked a peek at the phone.

"You have an issue with her dating, Ash?" Tessa asked.

"No, no, of course not."

"You don't sound too convincing," Zoe prodded. "She's gone out with a few guys. Did you not like any of them?"

She shrugged. "Nobody was right for her."

"Maybe she ought to be the one to decide that," Jocelyn suggested.

"Well, what if my dad wanted to get back with her?"

The question silenced all of them. Jocelyn knew that Lacey did her best not to paint a negative picture of the absentee father, and it sure wasn't her place, or any of their places, to hit Ashley with the truth. Her dad was a thrill-seeking, adrenaline-junkie, trust-funded, part-time cook. He wasn't ever getting "back" with Lacey.

But Jocelyn took a deep breath and went for a technique that worked with some of the more stubborn clients who hired her as a life coach. "Ashley, do you really think that's possible?"

"Of course I do. They don't … hate each other. They're not divorced; they never even got married." Her voice rose, along with a little color on her cheeks. "Things happen like that, you know."

"In books and movies," Tessa said. "Not so much in real life."

"I don't think that's going to happen," Jocelyn agreed, sensing that Ashley was harboring some serious delusions. "There's a lot of water under that bridge."

"And then he burned that bridge," Tessa added.

"After he bungee jumped off it." Zoe grinned at their surprised faces. "You know I'm right."

But every ray of light disappeared from Ashley's face as teenage frustration pulled at her brows. "None of you know what you're talking about."

"Actually," Jocelyn replied, keeping her voice calm. "We do know what we're talking about, Ashley. But you know what? That's not what's important. What matters is that your mom is happy, right?"

"Well, some creepy guy with a tattoo isn't going to make her happy."

"You told me you thought he was cute," Zoe said.

"And your mom thinks he might be the right architect for her project," Tessa added. "You do know how important this dream is to her, Ashley, don't you?"

"She ought to be building a house," Ashley muttered.

"Excuse me?" Tessa leaned closer.

"I said she ought to be building a place for us to live, not for people to come and have us wait on them."

Is that how she viewed her mother's plans? "Honey, you're not going to wait on them, and I'm sure you'll have a place to live."

"Really? In a bedroom in some inn where strangers are walking around in their bathrobes?" Her voice hitched a little. "Isn't it bad enough I've lived in a dump up in Barefoot Bay for all these years while my friends are, like, normal? And now..." She shook her head, fighting to control her emotions.

"I hate to break the news to you," Jocelyn said. "But some of those so-called normal people aren't nearly as happy as you are. They don't all have moms who dote on them."

"But they have dads."

"Oh, honey, sometimes no father is better than—" The words trapped in her throat and she felt all eyes boring through her. Jesus. Now what? "Than a father who—"

Ashley's phone rang with a rap tune. "I have a text."

Thank God.

"It's Mom." She tapped the phone, letting her hair fall over her face to cover her expression.

They all looked at each other, this time with well-deserved guilt. They'd ganged up on her. While Ashley read, the salads were served, giving the three women a chance to exchange a silent agreement to lay off and give Ashley space.

"So, what did she say?" Zoe asked when the waiter left.

"She said we can meet her at the beach later, in a few hours when she's done with her meeting," Ashley said.

Jocelyn stabbed a cherry tomato. "Can't. Sorry."

"She just wants us to bring a cooler and suits and stuff to Barefoot Bay," Ashley said. "She thought you'd be okay with that, Aunt Jocelyn."

Was she? If she didn't have to go too far south, she'd love a day at the beach. "I guess I could do that."

"We just have to go back to Lacey's and get suits and stuff," Tessa said.

"Hey, I have a better idea." The words were out before Jocelyn could stop herself, and even before she really did have a better idea. But she needed one, fast, because there was no way she was driving to Lacey's parents' house. It was too close for comfort.

"Yeah?"

"We…" She snapped her fingers and pointed to Zoe, who'd be all over this idea. "We shop for everything we need, including new bathing suits, even one for Lacey, right here at the hotel. My treat."

Ashley and Zoe gave each other high fives and whoops, the tension of the last few minutes forgotten. Money might not be able to buy happiness, but sometimes it bought distance.

An hour and a half later they left the Ritz dressed in new suits and cover-ups. The girls had driven up in Lacey's father's van, which they'd parked in the lot, but while they waited for the valet to bring the rented Rubicon for Jocelyn to drive, the discussion was all about the logistics of who was going in which car.

"I want to go in that car," Zoe joked to Jocelyn, pointing to a gorgeous red Porsche that pulled up to the hotel. As a man climbed out of the driver's seat, though, Zoe's expression froze.

"Oh my God," she whispered.

"What is it?" Jocelyn asked.

Zoe didn't speak. In fact, she didn't breathe.

"Someone you know?"

"It can't be him."

Jocelyn squinted at the man as he gave his hand to a beautiful brunette gliding out of the car with preternatural grace and poise. "It can't be who?"

"He's a doctor. In Chicago."

"There's an oncology conference here this week," Jocelyn said, eyeing the man, who was as good looking as his woman and his car. He looked to be six-two or -three, with clipped dark hair, great features, and an even better build. "Is whoever he is an oncologist?"

"Maybe." Zoe suddenly looked left and right. "But I don't want to see him. I don't want to talk to him."

"Why?" Tessa asked, stepping closer to Zoe when she sensed something was up. "How do you know him?"

Jocelyn stepped right in front of Zoe to block her from his view, the instinct to help her friend overriding any questions. Just at that moment the valet drove the giant white Jeep Rubicon up to where they waited.

"Get in," Jocelyn ordered Zoe, ending the discussion.

Muttering thanks, Zoe climbed up to the passenger seat the second the valet opened her door. The man and woman walked right in front of the Jeep as another man approached them.

"Oliver!" the second man exclaimed, reaching out a hand to the man Zoe was avoiding. "So happy you could make it."

Jocelyn slowed her step to hear his response.

"Happy to be here, Michael. You remember my wife, Adele."

"Of course."

Jocelyn missed the rest of the conversation when the valet ushered her into the Jeep.

In the passenger seat, Zoe bent over as though she were getting something off the floor, hiding completely. In all their years of friendship Jocelyn had never seen Zoe shy away from anyone.

Jocelyn pulled away, waving to Tessa as she and Ashley got into the van behind them. "Coast is clear, hon."

Zoe rose and took one more look as the man walked toward the hotel.

Jocelyn waited, but Zoe was uncharacteristically quiet. No jokes, no snide remarks.

"You okay, Zoe?" Jocelyn asked, putting a gentle hand on her friend's leg. "Who was he?"

"Don't ask."

"But I never—"

Zoe turned to her, her green eyes narrowed to slits, all

humor and joy and Zoe-ness gone. "We're not asking you about certain things, so... please. Don't ask, don't tell."

She couldn't argue with that philosophy, Jocelyn thought as she drove toward Mimosa Key. But she had to wonder: How many secrets should there be between best friends?

Chapter 8

The noon sun pressed like a blow torch, burning Lacey's skin and leaving a fine sheen of perspiration that probably smeared her makeup and surely curled her hair. But Lacey wasn't thinking about her hair or her makeup as she and Clay slowly circled the perimeter of her property and the land adjacent to it.

She wasn't even thinking about the attractive man who walked a few steps in front of her, giving her a perfect view of a T-shirt molded to ripped muscles and jeans that curved over his backside and down the length of long, strong thighs.

The truth was, he was as skilled verbally as he was physically, and his words were painting a picture so vivid and alluring that Lacey felt as though she'd stepped into his imagination.

And his imagination, it seemed, included villas. The

idea was so out there, so creative, and so perfect that she almost didn't want to let it get too comfortable in her head. But she couldn't stop thinking about it.

"You really think we could do villas?" she asked.

"Why not? Lots of resorts have cabins and separate structures."

"This isn't a resort."

"It ought to be."

She knew that. Deep in her heart, she knew that was what Barefoot Bay needed. But did she dare think that big?

"I don't know," she said quietly.

"Look." He pointed to the slight rise in the Everham property, where a small house had once stood but now only the foundation and some studs remained. "Right there. Picture individual, private villas with cozy patios and intimate rooms. Sleek African mahogany floors and sheer netting over every bed."

Cozy. Intimate. Sleek. Sheer.

Bed.

His words were as hot as the sun, and the images he conjured had her dreaming of a lot more than profit potential.

"Sure, you can have a few rooms or suites in the main building," he continued. "That's where the lobby and restaurant and offices will be, maybe a spa. But the thing that you can do with this virgin area is give people an oasis. High-end, expensive, one-of-a-kind villas that offer a vacation experience unlike—"

"Unlike a bed-and-breakfast, which is all I was prepared to undertake."

He smiled down at her. "You're not letting those two bags of wind at the Super Min scare you off, are you? I'm sure we can find a way around some ancient zoning ord.

Especially with villas, if there's a limit to the number of bedrooms you could have."

He was right about that. But still. "Clay, I don't have the money for what you're talking about. Insurance will barely cover a four- or five-bedroom inn."

"Building a place like this requires investors. We'll get money, Lacey."

"Will *we*?" she asked. "This is still a job interview, you know. I haven't agreed to become a 'we' yet."

"You will." He took her hand, the touch as thrilling as his confidence. "C'mon, let's go look at the view of the beach from that spot. Let's see this place the way your guests will."

So positive. So confident. So attractive. Of course she followed him. Yeah, this was some tough job interview. Who was she kidding? He had the job. Because with every imaginative suggestion, with every "just out of the box enough to be brilliant" idea, with every demonstration of a keen working knowledge of design and building, Lacey was more certain she'd found her man.

His fingers tightened around hers and a thousand butterflies took flight in her stomach. *Easy, Lacey.*

"You certain you can buy this lot?" he asked.

"This one and the one on the other side. I've been in touch with both neighbors and they jumped on my verbal offer. They're just waiting for final paperwork from their insurance company so they can have access to the house deeds at the bank." She'd only planned to buy the lots to make sure no one built too close to her B and B, but the idea of villas had just changed everything.

"How many villas do you think?" she asked. "How big? How...much?"

"You're not asking the right questions, Lacey." At the

top of the slight rise he paused, turned her toward the Gulf. He put his hands on her shoulders, pulling her a little too close to him. She could feel the warmth of his body against her back, the power of his muscles, the length of his legs.

For a few minutes they stood very still, nothing but heat and sun and humidity pressing down.

"Ask yourself this question," he finally whispered into her ear. "What would someone pay to wake up to this view, in a private villa, with coffee brewing and a tray of home-grown fruits waiting on their patio? Someone—two some-ones, probably—who would roll out of bed and bask in the sunshine just like we're doing now?"

Roll out of bed . . . oh. Did he *have* to say that?

"They'd stare at that gorgeous blue horizon all day, romp in the waves, roll in the sand, and appreciate this magical place until the sun kissed the water and turned the sky pink gold. Then they'd uncork a bottle of wine and cozy up on a chaise to watch the moon rise and dapple the water."

She closed her eyes, awash in peace, serenity, even hope. Could she create a place like that? It was so much more than she'd ever imagined. It was terrifying and thrilling and daunting and *fabulous*.

And way out of her price range and capabilities. "I can't—"

He squeezed her shoulders. "Hey."

Laughing softly, she dug for a better way to use the banned word. "I *can't* imagine how amazing that would be."

Another squeeze, this one more affectionate and tender, his thumbs on the nape of her neck, buried in her hair. The move was intimate but completely natural and nothing in heaven or earth could get her to step away from this man or this moment.

"Do you know how rare and valuable this land is, Lacey?" he asked. "You can get loans and investors just based on the value of the property."

"True, if I want to go deep into debt and make promises I might not be able to keep."

"You'd keep them. And you wouldn't be in debt long, not if the resort was like no other around here."

There was that word again. "Resort."

"Doesn't that sound better than bed-and-breakfast?"

"It sounds . . . big." *And better than a bed-and-breakfast.*

"Big and bold and beautiful." He threaded his fingers deeper into her hair and pulled her body closer. "Go big or go home, I say. And, come on, it would be a crime not to build something unforgettable here. There aren't many beaches like this left in America."

"All the more reason to keep it pristine."

"You sound like Charity."

"I just want to build something that belongs here. It has to be true to the land."

"I promise I will," he said softly, the words pouring over her like the sunshine. "But in the process you can make Mimosa Key the next St. Simons or Tybee or Cumberland."

She snorted softly. "Patience and Charity would love that."

"They just need to see you as a source of income and not competition. You could single-handedly turn this island around."

The thought made her dizzy. Or maybe that was his hands, his chest, his hard body behind hers. His seductive voice and even more seductive ideas.

David.

David? What the hell made her think of David at time like this?

Maybe the seductive voice and ideas. David had had both, and it had cost her.

"I don't know," she said on a sigh. "I just wanted a little inn."

"And a little in-come," he said wryly. "Why settle for that?"

"Because...because..." There was no reason. She was just scared. She'd never tried anything so big. What if she failed? "I just can't—sorry, but I can*not*—figure out a way to afford that."

He didn't say anything for a moment, but stayed very still. Had she disappointed him? For some reason she didn't want to let him down. She wanted to impress him, to appeal to him, to think as big and wild as he did. But—

"What if your architect was free?"

This time she stilled, and he eased her even closer, taking away all space between them, nestling her head under his chin like it was the most natural place in the world for her to be.

"You would do this job for nothing?" she asked.

"I'd get something out of it."

Could he mean... "What, if not payment?"

"Credentials." He whispered the word, making it sound like pure gold to him. Maybe it was. Maybe becoming "official" mattered more than cash.

"So, you want to work for free." She reached up to close her hands around his so she could uncloak herself from his arms, but he just gripped her tighter.

"I want to work for you," he said, honey over gravel in

his voice. "I won't take a dime until your resort is profitable. How does that sound?"

Very, very slowly she managed to turn in his arms, brushing his body as she did, painfully aware of every masculine inch, every hard bump, every relentless angle, but forcing herself not to let the amazing sensation cloud her brain. He wasn't asking for sex; he was asking to work on spec, for the experience.

"It sounds tempting." Like everything else about him. "But I need you to be perfectly straight with me. Why would you do that?"

"I need this project in order to prove to the Arch Board that I can sit for the exams," he explained. "So it's a win-win for everyone."

"Why couldn't you just take the exams? How can they stop you?"

He stabbed his fingers in his hair, hesitating as he considered his reply. "I need one significant project under my belt," he said slowly. "I left my dad's firm before I got it. After seeing this place and what could be done here, I know that this is the project I not only want to do, but I'd love to do. Enough that I'd do it for free. And that solves some of your money problems."

Some, not all. "It also makes me wonder if I'm getting a good enough architect."

"Fair enough. You can fire me at any time and keep all the work I've done to date. I need the project and you need a partner who can give life to your vision."

She gave him a slow smile. "Except sometime in the last ten minutes, it became your vision."

"It could be our vision, Lacey."

"It could be," she agreed. She did want a partner. She

did want a vision. She did want something as big and bold as he described, especially if she didn't have to attack that challenge alone.

"I guess it's possible."

"Anything is possible, Strawberry."

Right then, with this man holding her in the sunshine, giving her strength and ideas and throwing reason and excuses out to sea, she actually believed that.

"C'mon, I want to show you something." He took her hand again and pulled her back down the hill, toward her property, while she dug for a reason why she shouldn't follow him.

For once in her life, she couldn't think of a single excuse.

Clay almost ran down the sandy slope, light from the weight that had just left his shoulders. When the idea to work pro bono hit him, he didn't even have to think about it. This was the perfect solution to his problem. He needed a significant project to take to the board, exactly like the one he visualized. No one could claim nepotism, no one could suggest that anything untoward had happened, and no one could deny him the chance to get the licenses he needed to move forward.

Lacey Armstrong offered a way out of the Catch-22 he'd been caught up in, and he wanted it. Okay, he hadn't told her everything, but he'd told her enough. And he would give her the whole ugly story, but only after they'd established a level of trust and a deeper connection. Which felt inevitable.

But now he had to close this deal. And he knew exactly how to do that.

He'd left his tools on the picnic table at the edge of her property, situated in the small bit of shade from a tree too stubborn to give in to the storm. Sitting on top of the table, he took out his pencils and pad and gestured for her to sit across from him on the tabletop while he worked.

"I'm going to draw, Lacey," he said. "And you can ask me anything you want. This'll be that job interview you wanted so much."

"Can I watch you work?" She leaned up to look over his sketch pad.

"No." He moved the pad away, out of sight. "I'll show you when we're done. And then you tell me if I can be your architect or not."

Leaning back on her hands, she just watched him for a few moments, quiet.

"No questions?" he asked. "I expected an ambush."

"All right. Why don't you work for your father anymore?"

He feathered a few pencil strokes, starting where he always did, with the first of the two vanishing points, where the horizontal lines would come together if the structure were long enough.

"My father," *speaking of vanishing points,* "is very competitive, and remarkably insecure. We just couldn't work together anymore, so I left."

"On good terms?"

"We talk." *When absolutely necessary, which would be almost never.* He looked up to see her surprised expression. "You were expecting something else?"

"I guess," she admitted. "Something like your ideas are too avant-garde and his old-school approach makes you crazy. Something more...cliché."

What had happened with Dad was a cliché, all right. Right out of a soap-opera script. "He loves my ideas," he said in response. "Steals them all the time, as a matter of fact. Like your favorites, French Hills and Crystal Springs."

"Those are your designs?"

"While I was an intern, so no real credit." But they were his ideas.

He sketched some basic triangles, rounding them off like the buildings he'd been looking at online last night. Almost immediately the bones of the structure started to appear.

"Any siblings?"

"A sister, Darcie, who's a year younger than I am and still works at the firm."

"She's an architect, too?"

"No, a numbers person. Accountant, Web site maintenance, marketing, handles a lot of real estate and contract issues."

"Are you close to her?"

"Yep." He paused at the first window. Arched or square? He went for a soft arch and decided she should know he had more family than just Darcie. "I also have a brother, Elliott."

"Oh, older or younger?"

He smiled. "He just turned one."

"You have a one-year-old brother?"

"Half-. My dad remarried, and they have a child." He congratulated himself on keeping the darkness and anger out of his voice. Maybe he was over it after all.

"And your mother?"

"She's . . ." *Coping.* "Funny line of questioning for a job interview, Strawberry."

Lacey laughed, lifting up her hair to get some air on her neck, looking so sexy and sweet he wanted to put down the sketch pad and kiss her. No, he wanted to sketch her. Just like that, hair up, guard down, eyes bright, smile even brighter.

"I'm just trying to get to know you. You give everyone a nickname?"

"Only if I really like them."

Color darkened her cheeks. "You don't even know me."

"I like what I know of you so far. I know you're a good mother, and I like that."

"How would you know what kind of mother I am?"

He turned the pad to deepen the perspective of one wall. "You'da killed me if I'd gotten any closer to your daughter yesterday. How long have you been a single mom?"

She didn't answer right away, just turned her profile to him. He stopped drawing to study the shape of her nose. Not perfect in a classical sense, but really perfect for her face.

"I've never not been a single mom," she answered, still not turning to him as if the confession embarrassed her. "I didn't marry Ashley's father. I've raised her alone from day one."

It did embarrass her; he could tell by the note of defiance in her voice. "You've done a great job," he said simply. "I'm sure it's been tough."

"My parents are local, and they've helped, but, yeah, it's a challenge. Especially now because she has an opinion on *everything*."

"Did she have an opinion on me?"

She just laughed. "All of us had an opinion on you."

"You mean your friends that were in the bar last night? What did they tell you to do? Run as fast as you can, Lacey; he's got an earring and a tattoo?"

"No, that'll be my mother when she gets back from New

York. Of course, that's not saying much because I've pretty much made a second career out of disappointing my mother. But my friends? They totally encouraged me to give you a chance." She grinned. "Especially Zoe."

"The blonde?"

"The pretty blonde," she added.

He started to outline the balustrade, the vision so clear in his head he wasn't even thinking as his pencil worked. "She's not my type," he said.

"What is?"

He glanced up. "Job interview question?"

"Curious woman question."

"You're my type, Lacey."

"Oh, please. You've already said you'd work for nothing. You don't have to throw in gratuitous praise to get the job."

He stopped drawing and looked directly at her. "You are my type," he repeated.

"I'm older than you are."

He shrugged. "Wouldn't have noticed if you weren't obsessing over it. Ma'am."

Laughing, she shook her head. "So you like well-endowed redheads who use the word *can't* and have teenage daughters with too many opinions? Why do I find this hard to believe?"

"I like curvy, sexy, gorgeous strawberry blondes who are willing to take risks when something is important enough." The fact that she was a single mother spoke volumes about what kind of woman she was, whether she realized it or not. "I also happen to think we're more alike than you realize."

He finished the balustrade, and considered showing her the drawing, but something was missing.

"Why are you frowning?" she asked.

"I'm not done yet and I can't decide what I've left out."

She leaned forward. "Can I look yet?"

"No. But..." He wanted to ask her to hold perfectly still, just like she was, with dappled sun turning her hair to spun gold and highlighting each little freckle on her nose.

"All right. I got it. Just keep talking. Tell me more about your mother who you constantly disappoint."

She laughed. "You picked that up, huh? No. I'll tell you about my dad, though. He's the only person in my immediate family I've told about the B and B. I wanted to clear the idea of leveling the house with him because his parents built it, as you know, and my dad was born on the kitchen table."

"Really?" He looked up, surprised. "That's a cool piece of history."

"I know, but the kitchen table"—she turned toward the water and closed her eyes—"is gone."

"Must be awful to lose everything."

She nodded. "I go through some bad nights, remembering things, and then I say, Hey, we survived. That's all that matters."

"But you lost your home."

"I'm building a new one," she said with false brightness. "We'll live in the, uh, *resort* someone wants me to build."

He smiled. "I like that."

"And, honestly, I don't want you to think we lost some amazing architectural wonder. My grandparents never did anything to improve the house, then they willed it to me, and it was, honestly, on its last..."

"Support beams?"

"Precisely. Or it might have survived that storm. But

for the years I lived there, all I could really do was piece-meal repairs. I wanted to do more, promised my Granny Dot I'd do more, but I always had…"

"A reason not to," he finished for her as he took out a package of colored pencils and began the job of adding blues to the water and browns to the building and just the right colors to capture his vision.

"Bingo." She pointed at him. "I have a daughter and a small business. Life in general was plenty of reason not to take a huge risk like this. Then the hurricane came and I… faced death."

"Whoa." He stopped shading and studied her. "Seri-ously?"

"Yep. I climbed into a bathtub that is now in a stor-age facility in Fort Myers, and used a mattress to keep my daughter alive." Her voice wobbled a little. "After you go through something like that, it seems stupid to worry about antique tables and even stupider not to take some chances."

The look in her eyes said that chance was on him. And right there, at that angle with the blue-on-blue horizon cutting a perfect plumb line behind her and determination setting her jaw at a defiant angle, Lacey Armstrong was completely lovely, strong, and sexy.

He slid his pencil across the page, a power moving his fingers like he had no control. But he had plenty of con-trol, and he used it.

"You're drawing so fast."

"I'm inspired by you." Low in his belly, a slow burn started. Natural, being this close to a woman he found attractive, but surprising, too. Intimate. Hungry. Hot. "In fact, when I'm finished, we should go skinny-dipping."

Her jaw dropped in pure shock, then she let out a pretty laugh. "You do? Well, I don't think that's part of the job interview. Unless..." Her voice trailed off, but he didn't take his eyes off the page. The drawing was going too perfectly.

"Unless what, Lacey?"

"Unless you think you're applying for a completely different job."

"One for the day, one for the night." He smiled but kept his head down, his pencil flying. Couldn't stop now, not even to flirt with her.

"That would be..."

He waited for her to finish. *Crazy. Impossible. Unthinkable.* What would it be? When she didn't say anything else, he tore his gaze from the work and met hers.

"That would be what, Lacey?"

"Something new for me."

"How's that? No men in your life, ever?"

"Not many, not recently. I just don't have the time or interest." She didn't sound convincing.

"Ashley's father?"

"I haven't seen him since she was a baby, and he's not in the picture."

"Good, then maybe I could talk you into, you know, my special Architect with Benefits program."

She laughed. "Pro bono and benefits? I'm starting to wonder if I won the lottery."

"You like the idea?" Because he did. A lot.

"Maybe." She brushed a hair off her face; the golden red curl caught in her fingers like her voice caught in her throat. "I'm not going to lie and act like..."

"Like you haven't thought about it."

For a long, heavy moment, neither spoke. Then she whispered, "I've thought about it."

"Me, too," he said, setting down the pencil and slowly turning the pad toward her. "See? I'm thinking about it right now."

The look on her face was priceless and every bit as beautiful as he'd drawn her.

Chapter 9

~

Oh." It was the best Lacey could do. Just *oh*.

There was so much to take in. So much to absorb. A tiny structure with a sloping roof and cozy patio faced the Gulf, the beach scene beautifully rendered. But the villa and the water were not the focal point of his drawing, just an exotic backdrop for her. "That's me."

Drawn completely and utterly naked, she was stepping from the villa to the sand. He'd captured her copper curls, the shape of her face, the slope of her neck, and, of course, her voluptuous breasts. But it wasn't just the nude body that mesmerized Lacey. This woman exuded power. With squared shoulders and outstretched hands, a confident stride and a fearless look in her eyes, she was the woman Lacey wanted to be.

"That's how you see me?"

"That's how..." His words faded as he touched the

picture, his long, lean finger following the lines of her body, the effect as thrilling as if he were touching her skin.

"Yes?" she prompted.

"You know how some people draw from memory? Or maybe they use an object to copy? I draw from my imagination or, rather, my fantasy." His finger lingered on the two-dimensional drawing of her breast.

"That's quite a talent." Which might be the understatement of the century. "How did you do that?"

"I draw moments that I'd like to see. That's how I design buildings, something I'd like to walk out on the street and see. This villa"—he gestured toward the structure in the sketch—"is something I'd like to walk onto the beach and see."

"Is there a villa in this picture?" she joked. "I can't get past the naked lady."

He laughed. "Look at the building, Lacey. Really. What does it remind you of?"

She studied the villa for a few seconds, then it hit her. "*Casablanca*."

"I was inspired when I watched the movie last night."

"You watched it last night?" That gave her a little jolt as sexual as his drawing of her.

"When I came home from the bar, I found it on the Internet and watched the whole thing. I still think the wrong guy gets the girl," he said quickly, "But it totally inspired me for your property. What do you think?"

"I love the shape and design of that villa." She'd never seen anything like it, certainly not on Mimosa Key and maybe not in Florida. Instead of the standard Palladian windows and faux Spanish style, this was earthier, cozier.

"I kind of see an all-Morocco-themed architecture,"

he said, excitement making him talk a little faster and get a little closer. "White stucco walls and dark wood floors, the curved windows and low-slung archways. I know it's different, but the buildings are made for intense heat, so it would really fit in around here."

He was right. God, he was a genius.

"Kind of a waterfront paradise without the tacky, typical, tropical feel," she said, tearing her attention from the page to look at its creator. "I love it, Clay."

He beamed a smile at her. "I even have a name for it."

"I was going to keep Blue Horizon House as, you know, an homage to my grandparents."

"And I'm sure they'd love that, but we're not building an assisted-living facility, Strawberry." He was so close their faces almost touched, but neither made a move to back away.

She laughed softly. "So what are *we* building, Clay?"

"You already said it. Casablanca. But I suggest two words. Casa Blanca."

"Spanish for 'white house.'" She sighed, closing her eyes, leaning her head back just to let the beauty of the idea wash over her. "That's perfect."

And so was the kiss he placed on her mouth.

The pressure of his lips was so soft at first that she wasn't sure if the kiss was really happening. Her eyes fluttered open as a breath flickered between their mouths. He slid a hand around her neck, his fingers delving into her hair again. His other hand cupped her jaw and held her face just to make the angles of their lips fit perfectly.

A soft moan escaped her throat as she opened her mouth to him, letting their tongues dance at first, then coil more comfortably, then slide against each other. Lifting her hands to his shoulders, she pulled him closer and made absolutely no effort to stop. It felt too good.

She kept her eyes closed and he kissed her cheek, like a little finishing touch on something that was already flawless.

"You like my ideas, don't you?" he whispered into her mouth.

Oh, she liked more than his ideas. "I like your hands."

That made him chuckle and tunnel deeper into her hair. "How they draw?"

"How they . . ." She closed her eyes and let her forehead fall against his, their noses lined up, their mouths close enough for him to feel the warmth of her breath. "Feel."

He kissed her again, getting their bodies closer on the picnic table, building heat that could rival the tropical air around them. Cicadas buzzed and waves lapped, but all Lacey could hear was the thrum of sex and desire shooting off to every nerve in her body—and the intrusive vibration of her cell phone. The interruption jerked them apart.

"I bet it's Ashley," she said. "She's with my friends and was supposed to call when they're five minutes away."

"Oh, there go all my skinny-dipping plans." He kissed her again, longer, open mouthed, pulling her closer to him on the tabletop. "I was really starting to like this job interview."

"I was really starting to forget this *was* a job interview."

He backed away, holding her face tenderly. "Ms. Armstrong, can we please make this official?"

A crazy thrill electrified her, the question so like a proposal. His eyes were sincere, his mouth still parted from the last kiss, a lock of his hair falling over a brow and making her brush it away.

"I have to think about it," she said. *A lot. For hours.*

Like all she wanted to think about was him and this and Casa Blanca. "How about I tell you tonight?

He just kissed her again, another clash of tongues, until the phone vibrated one more time. She broke away and pulled it out to read the text.

"They're on their way."

He dragged his hands down her bare arms, letting his fingers brush the sides of her breasts. Like he'd touched a magic switch, her nipples budded through the cotton. "Then I'll see you tonight. I think we should watch *Casablanca*."

She laughed softly. "You watched it last night."

"It inspired me." He kissed her mouth. Her nose. Her forehead. "Who knows what could happen if we watched it together?"

Uh, she knew exactly what would happen.

"I'll call you tonight, okay?" he whispered. "We can watch at my place."

Yep. They both knew where this was headed.

"Oh, I forgot." He tore off the picture and handed it to her. "Here's my resume."

She laughed softly, the drawing stealing her attention again. Good heavens, could she do this? Could she let him have the job, talk her into a resort much bigger than anything she'd imagined, and also—

He started to laugh.

"What's funny?" she asked.

"I can see you rooting around for some reason to say no and you can't find one."

It was true. He was right. "Call me around seven and we'll see if I found a reason to say no."

"Don't look too hard. This is right, and you know it."

She just sat there holding his "resume" until she heard his truck rumble away, taking all her excuses with it.

"Mom!"

Lacey jumped off the picnic table, completely unaware how long she'd been sitting there mooning over Clay Walker.

Long enough for the girls to arrive in two cars, which meant they'd brought Jocelyn, who could practically read minds and body language. Would they notice that the "job interview" had shifted into a little make-out session?

Ashley didn't need to know the details, but she'd tell the girls everything about Clay, from his fabulous ideas to his even more fabulous kisses. This new development was too much fun not to share.

"We got you a bathing suit!" Climbing out of the van, Ashley held a colorful shopping bag in the air. With the other hand she lifted her T-shirt. "I got one, too! It's a push-up!"

Oh. *Thanks, Zoe.*

Behind her, Tessa and Jocelyn hoisted a Styrofoam cooler and Zoe jumped out with arms full of towels and two beach umbrellas.

"You bought me a bikini?"

"You're going to hate it," Tessa predicted.

"She's going to love it." Zoe dropped the umbrellas on the sand.

Lacey looked to Jocelyn for the tie-breaker. She just shrugged. "It was two against two. Zoe's exuberance won, as usual."

Ashley shoved the bag at Lacey. "Don't worry, Mom, yours isn't a push-up."

"A minor miracle." She didn't know whether to laugh

or throw the bag at Zoe, who pushed her sunglasses into her hair so Lacey could get a good look at her why-the-hell-not expression.

"For God's sake, Lacey, you're in your mid-thirties and you are not a nun."

No kidding. *You should have seen me ten minutes ago.* "Yeah, but you know how I feel about my boobs. They're too big."

"Your boobs are gorgeous. Own them." Zoe trotted off toward the beach without waiting for a response.

Her boobs *were* gorgeous...the way Clay Walker drew them.

"Oh, Mom, you'll love it," Ashley insisted. "Aunt Jocelyn bought us all new suits and, oh my God, they all cost—"

Jocelyn slammed her hand over Ashley's mouth. "Not important."

"Jocelyn," Lacey said, shaking her head. "That wasn't necessary."

"Expediency is very valuable."

"Expediency?" She must have wanted to avoid south Mimosa Key.

"I couldn't wait to get to the beach. Where should we put this?"

"Let's go down by the water." Lacey took in their haul. "God, look at all this stuff. What, no blow-up tubes and rafts?"

"They're in the car," Zoe said on her way back up from testing the water. "Don't worry; we didn't forget sunscreen. Walgreens had everything the Ritz didn't."

Ashley ripped off her T-shirt to expose a minuscule lime green halter bikini with plenty of padding, and tore off for the gentle swells of the Gulf.

"My suit better be bigger than that," Lacey said to Zoe.

"Not much," Zoe replied. Then she leaned in to whisper, "How'd it go with the big stud? That's an architectural term, you know."

"Really good. We made so much progress."

"Really?"

"He has all these amazing ideas, I mean you can't believe his vision for this place. So, so much bigger than anything I've ever dreamed of."

Tessa and Jocelyn came closer, carrying a cooler between them. "Really? Like what?"

"Like villas! Individual, adorable villas. And the style! So beautiful, all Moroccan and *Casablanca*-inspired."

"Ooooh," Jocelyn cooed. "Your favorite movie."

"I know, right? We're going to watch it tonight for more inspiration."

Zoe choked softly. "Is that what you kids are calling it these days? Hah." She turned to the water and reached out her arms. "Here I come, ocean!"

"It's the Gulf!" Lacey called to her, getting a "whatever" wave in response.

Jocelyn looked skyward. "Ignore her. If you want to meet with him tonight..." She frowned at Lacey. "She's right, isn't she?"

Lacey couldn't hide the smile. "I gotta say, there is some smokin'-hot chemistry between us."

"That could complicate things," Tessa said.

"It already has," Lacey agreed. "But you know what else? He wants to do the work for free. So he can...What?"

"For free?" Jocelyn almost choked. "Why would he do that?"

"He needs the creds. And with his ideas, I need to save

money. I can't afford what he wants, but, oh, God, I want to. I'll tell you all about it later. How's Ashley been?"

"She's fine," Tessa said. "Just a little cell-phone-aholic."

"She is that," Lacey agreed. "Sorry. I'll talk to her about it."

"You might have to talk to her about more than that," Jocelyn said as they walked across the sand.

"What do you mean?"

"She thinks you're going to get back together with David."

Jocelyn's words brought Lacey to a dead stop. "*What?*"

"It's true," Tessa said. "I drove over here with her and she dropped enough hints that I am certain she thinks this storm is bringing him home."

"Home?" Lacey had to laugh. "He's been here one time, when she was a year old. Twice if you count meeting my parents when we were dating. Mimosa Key has never been his home. And you know that man couldn't be less interested in being a father." She heard her voice rise and didn't care. "And just for the record, I couldn't be less interested in ever seeing him again."

"Shhh. Don't let her hear you," Jocelyn said, giving up the cooler to put her hands on Lacey's shoulders.

"But doesn't she know that he's had every opportunity to visit and has done nothing but send money?" Little bits of anger and resentment, sharp as nails, pressed against the inside of her chest. How long had Ashley been harboring these ideas? "What started this, the hurricane? Having her home blown away? Facing death at a young age?"

"Maybe all of those things, but..." Jocelyn shook her head. "My guess is it's a pretty natural thing for a fourteen-year-old to have Daddy fantasies."

Daddy fantasies? "Whoa, those are worse than the fantasies I've been having all day."

"She's not happy about you lusting after the architect, either," Tessa added.

"I'm not." She closed her eyes, not about to lie to her best friends. "Okay, I'm lusting. I mean, like whoa and damn, yes, he's so freaking hot I could jump his holy bones. But—"

"Oh my God, don't let Zoe hear you," Tessa warned. "She'll be buying condoms on our next stop at Walgreens."

"Maybe she should."

"I like the sound of this," Jocelyn said. "Go change into your suit in your dad's van. We'll wait for you. I want to hear about these big ideas of his."

Lacey dug into the bag and pulled out something fuchsia, about the size of a Band-Aid. "There better be a cover-up in here, too."

"Ashley said you have a ton of them."

"At home."

"No one's here, Lace," Jocelyn assured her. "Go. We'll set up camp."

Jogging up to the van they'd borrowed from her dad, Lacey squeezed into the back, stripping down and tsking over the price of the suit that barely covered her breasts and bottom. It was cute, but still.

She glanced down at her cleavage, and the rest of her. And all she could think of was the way Clay had drawn her. Did she really look that beautiful to him? That strong and capable? There were no words for how much she wanted to be the woman in that drawing.

The drawing! She had to go snag it before Ashley did. She'd tuck it away somewhere safe so she could pull out it out whenever she felt weak and insecure. Those times when she'd want to be reminded that a gorgeous, smart, funny, kiss-you-crazy man saw her exactly as the woman she wanted to be.

She rolled up her clothes and let her mind drift back to Ashley. Why this sudden preoccupation with David? Was it because she thought Lacey might be truly attracted to another man? Did she sense that Clay Walker was somehow different from the men she'd dated in the past.

Because he was.

She'd talk to Ashley tonight, before she spent another minute with Clay. They needed to be open and honest about this. And about Ashley's father, who was never, ever coming to Mimosa Key.

Opening the back door slowly, she squinted into the bright sunshine as she climbed out.

"Wow. Pink is definitely your color."

At the sound of a male voice, she gasped, spinning around to see a man silhouetted in the sunlight. She was vaguely aware that he held a paper. The sketch, her sketch, but that was not what short-circuited her brain. Oh, no. It was the complete impossibility of what she was seeing.

All she could do was croak his name. "David?"

Chapter 10

⌒

It's Fox."

Lacey just stared, and tried to breathe despite the six-hundred-pound boulder that had just landed on her chest.

"I go by Fox now." He took a step closer, the world behind and around him fading into black and white as David Fox, a man she had once loved with every fiber of her being and more, stood bathed in sunlight, a dark-haired, green-eyed devil.

"You look fantastic, Lacey." He held out the drawing. "Self-portrait?"

She snatched away the paper, her heart wrenching as a corner tore in her hand. "What are you doing here?"

"I came to see Ashley. And you, of course. And... wow." He angled his head and openly admired her. "As good in three dimensions as"—he nodded to the drawing—"two."

She covered her chest with the paper, painfully aware

that she was in nothing but bright pink strips of silk that barely covered breasts that David had once suggested she have reduced.

"So how are you?" he asked with a wide smile that showed masculine dimples in hollowed cheeks with a hint of whiskers. A linen shirt hung over his lean body, and despite the trousers he wore, he didn't show a bead of perspiration anywhere. In ninety-two degrees.

"I'm..." *Dizzy. Stunned. Hoping to wake up any second.* "You might have warned me you were coming."

He gave her a look of disbelief. "Didn't Ashley tell you?"

Ashley?

She thinks you're going to get back together with David.

"Have you talked to her?"

"Not exactly," he said, turning to look at Ashley in the water, offering his classic, handsome profile to her. "We've been communicating online. Today, in fact. She told me you'd be here."

He was chatting online with her daughter?

"Is it safe for her to be out that far?" he asked.

Lacey took a few steps to see over the rise to the water. "She's just past the sandbar. The water's still shallow there, but it drops off after that."

"I don't know. It looks far."

Irritation fired through her. "She's with my friends. She'll be fine, David."

"Fox," he said. "I really don't answer to David anymore. Are your friends CPR trained?"

She choked a little. "Seriously? After thirteen years of doing a complete disappearing act, you're going to show up here and question my parenting skills?"

"I'm not questioning them." He squinted at Ashley. "She seems well adjusted enough."

Seems? He'd determined that from "communicating online" with her and seeing her from three hundred feet?

"She is," Lacey said. "But this is going to throw her for a loop."

"Are those the same women from the dorm you RA'd in college?"

"Yes." She wasn't surprised he remembered them. The year David and Lacey had been together, she'd spent every other minute with her three best friends.

"David, why don't we go somewhere and talk?"

"I want to see Ashley."

Her heart sank. "Just let me…" *Get my head around this.* "Talk to you. Privately. So you can tell me why you're here and how long you're staying."

"I told you why I'm here. And I'm staying for a while."

A while? What was a while? Five minutes was too long a while. "You'll find it pretty boring here, believe me. No cliffs to scale, no rapids to navigate, no icebergs to climb."

"But one very beautiful woman to thaw." He did the head-tilt thing again, letting his gaze roll over her as slowly and sensually as the waves on the sand. "If she'd just relax and say hello." He held out his arms.

Instantly she backed away, toward the van. Feeling silly, she turned and lifted the hatch door, tucking the drawing away safely and grabbing the shirt she'd just taken off.

"I can't believe she was e-mailing you," she said.

"Not e-mail, exactly. We message on Facebook."

"You're her Facebook friend?" Why, oh why, had she stopped looking at Ashley's Facebook page? Because it was a bunch of "you've been tagged" photos and silly middle-school jokes and Farmville announcements. There'd been no *David Steven Fox* when she'd last checked Ashley's page.

"She friended me."

"Of course. You'd never seek her out."

He made her jump by putting a hand on her shoulder. "I'm here, aren't I? Can't I get some credit?"

Actually, no. "Look," she said, letting out a breath as she stabbed her arms into her shirtsleeves and buttoned up with maddeningly unsteady hands. "This has really thrown me, David."

"Please call me Fox. I have a new career now and, as part of that, I legally dropped David from my name."

"A new career? I didn't know you had an old one."

"I've been studying with some of the greatest chefs in the world. What started out as a new adventure became my passion. You know I love to cook, and now I'm formally trained."

"That's great. Congratulations." She still didn't see why he'd change his name, but it didn't matter. What mattered was that he was here and Ashley—

Surely Ashley wouldn't go running into his arms after being ignored her whole life? She glanced again at the beach. Ashley was still swimming, just past the sandbar but visible.

"Let's go over by the table and talk."

He started to follow her through the reeds of sea oats. "You can't keep me from her forever," he said softly.

"David—er, Fox. You can't just spring yourself on a fourteen-year-old who's been through a trauma."

"Ashley told me you spent the storm in the bathtub."

Resentment coiled through her and knotted deep in

her gut. It was bad enough that Ashley had told him about their ordeal and forgotten to mention that she was on Facebook with her father who hadn't seen her since she was a baby. But the slight reprimand in his tone really irked.

"There really wasn't time to evacuate safely," she said. "And I kept her alive."

"She shouldn't have been here." Nothing slight about that accusation.

"Oh, right, David, like you would have been a better parent. Like you wouldn't have her hiking into African villages for an evening of body piercing."

"She should see Africa. Once you've slept in the mud houses of the Bamako, you see life differently."

"She sees life fine." Lacey leaned against the trunk of the poinciana for support. "I don't know how your appearance is going to affect her."

"I'm her father. And it's a reunion, not a return from the dead."

"Reunion?" She had to laugh softly. "You haven't seen her since the week of her first birthday." When he'd stayed exactly forty-eight hours. She could only hope history repeated itself.

"I've sent her cards and presents."

"And she saved every one," she assured him. "But Hurricane Damien stole them, along with a lot of stability. So I'm just really worried about ... *this*."

"And the money?"

Was he accusing her of taking it? "Ashley has an account with every dime you've ever sent her. You are free to audit that. I'm saving it to pay for college and whatever else she needs. She knows you've sent it and appreciates it."

But the truth was that every check seemed to make

Ashley sad, and Lacey's heart had broken for her daughter, who deserved to be loved, not bought.

"You owned this house outright, didn't you?" He gestured toward the exposed foundation.

Just how much had Ashley shared with him? "Granny Dot left it to me when she died, about a year after my grandfather died. Ashley and I'd been living in an apartment, so it was a blessing. Without any rent or mortgage, I was able to start a small baking business, mostly cakes for weddings and functions."

His eyes lit. "So we're both in the food industry."

"No. I'm... doing something different."

"What's that?"

She took a deep breath and jumped. "I'm building a resort." Ooh, that sounded nice. "As a matter of fact I just hired the architect."

He nodded, gave a slight smile. "I saw his, um, blueprint."

Heat burned her cheeks. "You have no idea what you saw, David. But none of that concerns you."

"Everything about Ashley's life concerns me."

She reared back as if he'd hit her. "Really? Is that a fact? Is that why you've been completely missing from her life even though I told you you could see her anytime?"

"I understand you might be bitter, but I really hope that we're all mature enough to co-exist, and maybe even forgive."

Could she forgive him? His choice to leave her had hurt Lacey, but his decision to stay away had hurt Ashley. And that was unforgivable to a mother.

"I forgave you long ago," she said brusquely, not wanting to get into it with him now or ever.

He was looking around at the post-hurricane mess,

his brows knit. "How on earth are you going to afford to build a resort, Lacey? Don't you think you should start with something a little more modest?"

Exactly the opposite of what Clay thought she should do. That gave her a boost of confidence. "Insurance. Investors. Loans." She tilted her head up, smiling. Clay had done that for her, she thought fleetingly. In one morning, he'd given her confidence. "I have a plan."

"A plan, huh? Not always your strong suit." He tempered the tease with a smile and leveled her with that magnificent green gaze that had melted the clothes right off her about forty-eight hours after he'd guest-lectured in one of her college classes.

"I've changed," she announced.

"You have." When his eyes crinkled she could see his lashes were still thick, and the tiny crow's-feet just made him great looking instead of merely good looking. "And you look terrific, Lacey, considering what you've been through."

"Fourteen years of single parenthood?"

"I meant the hurricane," he said. "But I don't imagine either one was easy." There was an apology in there, she could sense it, and the tone brought her resentment down a notch.

"Thanks, David. Fox. You look good, too." He was thirty-nine now, a full ten years older than the man she'd been with all morning. Ten years and ten million miles apart, she mused. Clay Walker was light, bright, sexy, easy, sunny brilliance. David Fox was dark, threatening, difficult, a sliver of cloud-covered moon impossible to follow and even more impossible to hold.

Reminding her that regardless of his latest career

move, David's next trip to Timbuktu couldn't be much farther than his next breath. That's how he rolled. Away.

"Can I stay with you at your parents' place?" he asked.

What *hadn't* Ashley told him? She tried to think of a good, reasonable explanation for saying no, but none came. Except that she was kind of planning to have sex with her architect.

"Yes, of course you can. For a few..." *Minutes.* "Days. I'm very busy with my building proj—"

The scream from the beach made them both whip around, startled.

"Ashley! There's a shark!"

"Oh my God!" Lacey leaped forward.

"*Helllllllllp!*"

All three women stood on the beach screaming at Ashley, who was frozen on the sandbar, the Gulf waters splashing at her thighs. She looked to her left, the horror on her face visible even this far away.

The fin popped up not twenty feet from her, between her and the beach.

Lacey ran, shells stabbing her feet, a scream caught in her throat. Before she'd even reached the girls David tore past her, his long legs eating up the sand, kicking it in his wake, his arms outstretched. Fully clothed, he bounded into the shallow waters, headed directly for Ashley, who kept screaming.

The four women followed, running toward the water, gasping and calling in horror.

The fin popped up again, directly between David and Ashley, making her wail.

"Don't move, Ash!" David called to her, and she froze, staring at him now.

Once again the shark emerged and David lunged in the opposite direction, forcing the creature's attention to focus on him, making it leap and turn toward him, the white teeth of a tiger bared for a horrifying split second.

"Run, Ashley!" David yelled before throwing himself in the water, drawing the shark farther away.

Ashley screamed again and followed the order, her skinny arms flailing as she stumbled through the waist-high water. Lacey ran toward her just as David made a loud noise and—dear God, had he punched the shark? Kicked it?

The fin disappeared, then popped up again, fifteen feet away and headed out into the Gulf.

Instantly David dove into the shallow water toward Ashley, popping up in front of her just as Lacey reached them both.

She threw her arms out to grab Ashley, but her daughter turned and fell into David's embrace.

"Daddy!"

"Baby girl." He kissed her head and hugged her like . . . like he actually cared about the child he'd demanded Lacey abort.

"Daddy, you saved my life."

"No, sweetheart, you saved mine."

Crumbling into the water, an adrenaline dump and cold reality bit Lacey harder than the rare tiger shark in the Gulf of Mexico ever could. Silhouetted in the sunshine, Ashley and David hugged like there was no tomorrow.

But there was, only now it included a man with the totally apt name of Fox.

Chapter 11

After dinner, Lacey could hear David and Ashley laughing in the living room, a bittersweet sound to a mother's ears. She loved to hear Ashley happy, with a giggle that was quick, easy, and joyous. Despite the history, the absence, and a lot of unanswered questions, Ashley had just seamlessly accepted David into her life.

It was shocking, really, that she didn't harbor more of a grudge. Was the loss of her home and all her stuff enough to make her realize what was important in life? At fourteen? If so, Lacey could learn a lot about maturity from her teenage daughter.

Then again, David had a gift. He wielded that irrepressible charm like a razor-sharp blade, slicing away anything that got in the way of people liking him. Somehow, when he teased Ashley he made the empty years disappear, and when he enthralled her with a colorful story about diving with crocodiles in Botswana, Lacey could see her daughter's eyes fill with awe and forgiveness.

Ashley could forgive David, so why couldn't Lacey?

Because she didn't have to. They had made an arrangement many years ago. David held no paternal rights to Ashley, and any gifts and money he gave her were out of concern and care. No strings attached. In return, Lacey had told him he could see Ashley whenever he wanted.

She just hadn't thought he'd ever want to.

She pushed the faucet handle, making the water run louder into the sink, scrubbing the pan with vicious swipes, drowning out the sound of all that happiness in the living room.

Her hands itched to do something other than clean. She eyed her mother's pantry, knowing it was stocked well enough now that she could knock out something simple for dessert. A cobbler, maybe. Or tropical napoleon, which she'd been testing before the storm. He'd be impressed with that.

She grunted softly and whipped the wet sponge. Why should she impress him?

Although he'd certainly impressed them with his cooking skills, making a remarkably good country-style chicken and not letting any of the girls lift a finger.

How could she not invite him to stay here, sending Tessa and Zoe to the Ritz to bunk with Jocelyn for a few days? Lord, she hoped it was a few days. Or less.

Yes, the invitation made sense; the house was too crowded and the decision to move everyone around to accommodate David had seemed smart when adrenaline was soaring and arms were hugging and rational thinking took a backseat to dramatic life-saving dives.

A few minutes ago, when she had a moment to say good-bye to the girls, Zoe had whispered, "Bet he planted the shark."

Zoe meant it as a joke, but part of Lacey—the dark, nasty, resentful, unforgiving part—wondered exactly what David Fox was capable of doing just so he could redeem himself in his daughter's eyes.

"We're going over the causeway!" Ashley burst into the kitchen, practically vibrating with excitement. She hadn't brushed her hair after swimming, so it was a wild mess, and she still wore the bikini Jocelyn had bought her, with a tiny pair of gym shorts rolled down nearly to her pelvic bone. She looked like a delicate flower, lithe, tan, reedy, and blown by the exciting winds of life. No, David Fox wasn't a wind. He was a cat-five hurricane and, damn it, she'd already weathered one of those.

"Now?" Lacey asked.

"We have to get some games! Grandma doesn't have any."

Of course not; they never played games in this house. Unless you call "count Lacey's faults" a game.

"Okay, you can take my car." Because the alternative, the motorcycle David had arrived on, was not up for negotiation.

"Mom, we're riding bikes."

"You're not going on his—"

"Bicycles." David popped in behind Ashley, a glint in eyes that were so identical to his daughter's that the sight took Lacey's breath away. "Relax, Mama. Ashley says you have a couple of beach cruisers, and I saw a Wal-Mart right in Fort Myers. It'll be no problem."

"Over the causeway?" Yes, she sounded lame, but Lacey had never let Ashley ride that far, even if there was a bike lane. "It'll be dark before nine and the tires need air and—"

"It's only six-thirty, Lace," he said, putting a possessive hand on Ashley's shoulder. "We'll pump the tires at a gas station and I'll take good care of her. I can't believe she's never ridden bikes over the causeway. That's the first thing I'd do if I lived here."

"No, you'd dive off it."

He grinned, clearly delighted with the comment. "We'll work up to that."

Lacey glared at him. "Not funny."

"Chill, Mama."

She gritted her teeth to keep from demanding he stop calling her that.

"I already saved her once today," he said.

Ashley turned to look up at him, adoration in her gaze. "He's my hero."

Oh, puh*lease*. "Can't you just stay on the island tonight? Maybe take a drive over the causeway tomorrow? We have a deck of cards, that I'm sure of."

"See, this is why we never made it, Lace."

"Excuse me?" He was going there now? In front of Ashley?

"You're so risk averse. You can't live like that."

"Actually, you can live longer like that." She resisted the urge to snap the dish towel at him. Instead she dried the pot, maybe a little more furiously than necessary.

"And, sorry, but I'm a parent, David. With that title comes certain responsibilities. Like keeping your child safe."

"Mom! He freaking tore into a shark with his bare hands to save me today."

"Not exactly."

"Exactly!" Ashley stood next to David, metaphorically and literally aligning herself with him. "And I totally trust him and, seriously, like everyone I know rides bikes over the causeway, so we're going. Let's go, Fox."

"You can call me Dad."

Cripes, pick a name already. And not *Dad*.

"Dad." Ashley couldn't keep the smile out of her voice. "We'll be back before it gets dark, Mom."

"Wait a sec, Ash." David stepped closer, taking the towel from Lacey's hands. "I'd be happy to forgo a bike ride if you'd come with us."

She swallowed hard. "I'm going to bake you guys something. A surprise."

He nodded knowingly. "So you still head to the flour and sugar when you're strung out, huh?"

"I'm not—"

"Mom, he so knows you!" Ashley exclaimed, delighted. "Mom always stress bakes. It's awesome." She stopped, realizing what she said. "I mean, not that you're stressed, just that we get to eat your amazing cakes and stuff."

"It relaxes her," David said knowingly, that insider info just irritating Lacey more. "Then I'm ordering something light and delicious. Oh, Lace, remember that French apple tart you made once at my apartment?" He slapped his hand to his chest. "Mother of God, I think that's when I knew I loved you."

She just stared at him, numbed by the comment. "I lost my tart pan in the storm," she said softly. "How about meringue cookies?"

"Perfect." For a minute she thought he was going to kiss her good-bye. And it seemed so natural. But he didn't, instead backing away and gesturing to Ashley. "Let's go, kiddo."

They were out the door before Lacey could think of any reason to make them stay, any reason that wouldn't make her sound like a petulant child or a big old jealous meanie.

Anything like *Ashley, he's going to leave and break your heart again. That's what he does, baby.*

She walked to the door, watching them round the yard toward the garage.

"Ashley!" Lacey called, and even as she did she couldn't think of a thing to say. She had no parting shot, no special warning. She just had to see her daughter's face.

"What?" But Ashley didn't turn.

I love you. "Do you have your phone?"

"Don't need it."

Since when could she not be tethered to that damn phone? Since David-Fox-Dad showed up.

And they disappeared, with more happy laughter in their wake.

Back in the kitchen, she headed to the oven to flip the dial and preheat just as her cell phone rang. And she remembered Clay.

She stood stone still, long enough to debate what to say to him. And long enough to let the call go to voice mail, the technology most adored by chickens.

Of course David's appearance shouldn't and wouldn't change a thing as far as Clay, but it was a wrinkle she didn't know how to smooth out yet.

Clay would think she'd made up an excuse. But she certainly couldn't slip out on a "date" tonight to watch *Casablanca* at his apartment. Instead, she listened to his message, enjoying the tenor of his voice as he promised to call later if he didn't hear from her. Maybe she'd answer that call, but she wasn't seeing him tonight.

With a sigh she opened the pantry, stared at the pathetic baking shelf. Mother hated to bake, but there was probably enough to—

I think that's when I knew I loved you.

She slammed the door closed, biting her lip as if that could stop the sting behind her eyes that had started when Ashley first called him Dad.

Had he forgotten? Had he blocked out that conversation in Gainesville, the day he'd told her a child "doesn't fit my lifestyle"? Well, at that age it hadn't fit her lifestyle, either. And she'd had to deal with her parents. Her mother. The face of disapproval.

Not that she'd been mad that Lacey had gotten pregnant. Oh, no. What upset Marie Armstrong was that Lacey didn't have what it took to get David to marry her.

She abandoned the pantry and the kitchen altogether to change the sheets on the guest bed. Passing the den, she glanced at the bookcase, her gaze drawn to photo albums that filled one shelf. There, in the middle, stood an album neatly labeled 1996–1997.

Kind of a wonder Mother didn't call that the Year of David.

She pulled out the album and tucked it under her arm, heading to the backyard to curl up in what had become her favorite getaway lately, the hammock her dad had hung between two queen palms.

Cocooning into the canvas, she opened the photo album and started turning the thick, plastic-covered pages, stepping back in time to the red brick buildings and moss-covered oak trees of the University of Florida. Those were happy days in Gainesville, especially the year she RA'd at Tolbert—and had met David.

She'd finally settled on a hospitality major after trying and quitting at least three others. So even though that decision was going to cost her an extra year, she was certain she'd found something to see through to completion. And, of course, she'd made great friends on the fourth floor.

She paused on a picture of the dorm on Halloween night, smiling at Zoe channeling her inner Posh Spice. And Tessa dressed to climb Mount Everest. Jocelyn hadn't gotten into costume that night, but even if she had it wouldn't have hidden the sadness around her eyes that remained there almost the whole year.

And there was Lacey, beaming behind her girls, and bone skinny, damn it. She went as Little Red Riding Hood in a scarlet leotard and boots. The Big Bad Wolf showed up just a few weeks later when she'd gone to hear a guest lecturer speak for her Asian Cultures class, a world traveler doing a slide show on his near-death experience hiking Mount Huashan.

To this day, she couldn't remember a thing David Fox had said about his brush with Huashan Death, but she could describe the shades of green in his eyes, the music of his easy laugh, the strength of his hands, the shape of his lips. By the end of the lecture, she was fantasizing about marrying him.

And he, she learned later, was fantasizing about something else with her.

He got his way, and they were lovers by their second date.

She flipped to the back of the book to spring of that year, the weekend she'd brought David Fox home to meet her parents. It was Easter, and she was two weeks pregnant but had no idea. She was also as in love as a woman could be, and would have given anything to spend her life with David.

Anything but the child she carried inside of her, and that was what David wanted her to sacrifice in order to travel the world with him. Not only did she not want to travel the world; she wanted that baby.

That baby, and more, to be honest. But that was not the life David envisioned.

She rocked the hammock, leaving the book resting on her knees, open to the picture. David's hair had been black and long, curling over his collar, reminding her a little of someone else.

Clay.

The realization hit her hard, making her heart squeeze. Sexy, seductive, so good at talking her into things. Charming, smart, and completely compelling. Look what he'd done already.

In the space of two hours she'd agree to let him work for her without proper credentials, to build an over-the-top five-star resort that would tax her professionally, financially, and emotionally, and she'd all but made a date to sleep with him.

He'd done that with one scintillating conversation, a sexy drawing, and a few hot kisses.

She pushed the hammock from side to side with all the resentment and second-guessing that was building inside her. What was *wrong* with her? Hadn't she learned anything from her experience with David? Sure, she'd been careful with men for the last fourteen years, maybe too careful. But Clay Walker was David Fox all over again and she wasn't going to make the same mistake twice.

Tears stung and she blinked against them. Damn it, why did David have to show up now and make her realize exactly how wrong Clay was? Just when she was about to have some fun? She *never* had fun, not the kind this young, hot, carefree guy was offering.

All she did was scrape together a living baking cakes and trying to drum up business, then she gave every ounce of remaining energy to drive Ashley around and make sure her daughter had everything she wanted and needed. In her spare time she'd held that old house together with duct tape and hope. She'd had exactly six dates in the last five years and not one of those men had made a single cell in her body tingle.

And then she'd met Clay and, well, forget tingling. He made her feel like she'd sucked her finger and stuck it into a light socket.

But that's how you get electrocuted, Lacey.

A lump of confusion mixed with bitter self-pity filled her throat, sending a teardrop down her cheek. She swiped it. She had no time for this kind of wallowing. She had to be focused and serious about building a new life, not dreaming about sex with the architect she'd hired to do it.

Screw that up and what would happen? She'd quit, like always.

No, she couldn't have the complication of sex with Clay. That was the one thing that had to go. If she didn't sleep with Clay, then she wouldn't be making the same mistake twice and she wouldn't be risking her heart along with her building project.

The minute she saw him again she'd tell him she couldn't—

"So, I'm guessing you dug deep enough to find an excuse to blow me off."

She turned suddenly, the album tumbling off her stomach. She lurched to grab it and rolled right out of the hammock onto the grass, staring up at the most gorgeous man she'd seen since, well, since that morning.

And, damn it, all she wanted to do was reach up and kiss him. Just for *fun*.

Chapter 12

Clay kneeled next to Lacey, setting down the six-pack of beer he held in one hand and the DVD from the other. She didn't move right away, looking up at him, her hair spilling everywhere, a tear streaking her cheek.

"Are you crying?"

"I'm fine." She let him help her sit up, and just the contact with her bare shoulders made his hands itch for more.

"Really? 'Cause you don't look fine." He couldn't fight the urge to brush a wayward curl from her forehead, getting a flash of gold in her eyes in response. "Is this why you didn't answer my call?"

She tried to swallow, and it looked like it took a monumental effort. "Something came up."

He gave her a wary smile and lifted the six-pack of Mich he'd grabbed on the way to her house. "Better watch it. I brought Excuse Juice. Every time you make one, you gotta drink. I should have you good and loaded if you're starting off with 'something came up.'"

She laughed softly, pushing herself up and making another quick swipe at her eyes. "I'll take one of those. How'd you find my—never mind. You went to the Super Min, didn't you?"

He smiled. "Gloria was covering the register, and she told me where your parents' house is."

He eased her back into the hammock, which swung under their combined weight and pushed their hips right next to each other. "You all alone out here, Lacey?"

Pulling a bottle out of the carton, he kept his gaze on her while he twisted it open. "Where are your girlfriends? Where's Ashley?"

"My friends are staying on the mainland. Ashley is..." She hesitated, then finished with, "She's out."

"What's going on?" He handed her the bottle and she took it, puffing out a long breath and nodding thanks.

"I'm just thinking."

"About what? Never mind, I know. You're having second thoughts about what we discussed today."

She lifted one corner of her lips in a wry smile. "I'm past second and rounding fifteenth."

"Let me guess." He took his own beer out of the carton and uncapped it but didn't drink. "You think I'm some kind of lunatic stalker serial killer who draws naked women and works for free."

A smile threatened. "Possibly."

"And all you wanted to do was build a little five-room inn—in keeping with zoning code, I might add—with frilly bedspreads and antique water pitchers, but I planted visions of Moroccan villas with imported hardwood floors in your head."

This time she nodded slowly and started to talk, but he silenced her with a finger to her lips.

"Wait, wait. I'm not done. Just to make things worse, the first thing we did when we were alone together was make out like a couple of teenagers and practically agree that we'd end the night in the sack. And you're freaked out about that."

"And you're a mind reader."

"No, but I can read your expression and what I see is a woman who is not only trying to decide how far to run but how fast and how soon. So you decided to blow me off tonight." He held out his bottle for a toast. "You're easy to read, Strawberry."

She dinged the glass. "All of that may be true, but there's more to it." His gaze shifted to the book or whatever it was—a photo album?—that had fallen to the ground. It was closed, but he could see someone had handwritten 1996–1997 on the spine.

Simple math told him that would be close to the year her daughter was born. So maybe she'd had an argument with Ashley. Maybe the teenager had stomped out and left Mom crying. Maybe this had nothing to do with him and what she needed was a friend to talk to.

"Then tell me," he said, finally taking a sip. "What else is bothering you tonight?"

"What isn't bothering me tonight is a better question," she said on a quick laugh. "It's kind of complicated and personal."

"I can do complicated and personal." He situated himself on the hammock, carefully sliding one leg around so she had no choice but to lean back next to him. The canvas was wide and comfortable, and easily accommodated two.

She didn't lean back, though. Instead, she gave him a wary look. "I think this is a bad idea."

"I just want to talk."

"And he gives me the oldest line in the book."

"Okay, I don't just want to talk, but since you stood me up and I found you weeping alone in the backyard, I figure talking's all that's on the agenda tonight." He eased her closer. "C'mon."

"I'm not weeping. I'm just emotional."

"Whatever you want to call it." He searched her face, looking past the dusting of freckles and the soft lashes around big eyes. "I can see fear in your eyes."

"You are right that I'm a little scared of…what you proposed today. It's more than I bargained for."

He wasn't sure if she meant the resort or the invitation for sex, but they were probably both more than she bargained for.

"Well, I have good news," he said, turning so that she had to lean into him or fall out of the hammock again. She chose him. "I've been working on blueprints of Casa Blanca, making some calls about resort zoning, and I even started the ED—that's the environmental determination paperwork—and ordered an auto-CAD system to—"

"Stop, Clay."

"Why?"

"I'm not…I can't—"

"Hey, we had a deal. No *can't*-ing."

"No, please." She curled her legs up into the hammock, tucking them under her, making herself into a ball like she wanted to protect herself and not fall into him or his ideas. "This is happening too fast."

"There's no other way for it to happen. You don't want to sit around for months and think about building something, do you?"

The look on her face said she wanted to do just that. "A project this size takes a lot of time and money and—" She closed her eyes. "When you add the complication of our attraction..."

He laughed softly. "The 'complication of our attraction'? Well, gee, when you put it that way, it's *really* sexy."

"You know what I mean." She elbowed him. "You scare me."

"Why?"

"Because...you're...scary."

He took her beer bottle and carefully set it back in the cardboard six-pack along with his. Then he eased back and she had nowhere to go but next to him. Once they were side by side, pressed together in the hammock, he curled a hand into her hair and forced her to look at him. "You're not scared of me. You're scared of sex."

"No, I'm not. I'm scared of...involvement."

"Then we're good. Because with me there's no involvement, other than our business arrangement. All you need to do is relax and have fun."

She smiled, tilting her head so her soft curls brushed his hand. "I was just thinking that I don't have enough fun in my life."

"Then I'm your man." He leaned toward her a little more, the curve of the hammock forcing her a little closer. He tangled his hand in her hair and brought her face closer to his.

"I bet you're a lot of women's man."

"Not really."

"No one in your life? No one up in North Carolina thinking you're just down here on business, not fun?"

"No one at all."

"Why not?"

He dropped back, looking into the purple twilight sky, thinking of the twenty different ways he could answer that question. Hadn't met the right girl. Too busy with work. Standards so high they're rarely met. All true, but none the real reason there was no girlfriend or wife up in North Carolina.

"I had a bad experience," he finally said.

"How bad?"

"Disgustingly bad. Scarred-for-life bad. Keep-all-my-relationships-superficial bad." He didn't turn to look at her. In fact, he closed his eyes and braced for the nasty job of telling his ugly story.

"Are you going to tell me what happened?"

"Only if you're prepared to lose respect for someone you have on a pedestal."

"Someone *I* have on a pedestal?" She sat up a little. "Who?"

"*The* Clayton Walker."

"Your father? You said he was remarried and had a..." Her voice trailed off. "How does that affect your love life?"

It had ended his love life. "Well..." He let a few seconds drag out. "The woman he married was my girlfriend."

He didn't have to look. He knew her jaw must be open, her eyes wide, her breath sucked in with shock. He'd seen the expression on every face, every time he told the story. Which wasn't often.

"Oh. Wow."

"Yeah." That would be the typical response. "So, I'm

pretty much sworn off anything beyond fun, therefore you have nothing to fear from scary me."

"How did it happen? I mean, if you don't mind telling me."

He minded. A lot. But he'd told the story before and survived, so he could do it again. "Jayna was my dad's admin at the firm. When I interned there, we...were together. She's a few years older than I am." He caught her little wince and instantly took her hand. "Trust me, that's where the similarities end."

She nodded, waiting for more.

"We were pretty tight." *Like she was picking rings.* "It was pretty serious." *Like every weekend and most nights were spent in the same bed.* "I was pretty..." Gone.

"Doesn't sound pretty to me."

He smiled. "I admit, I kind of broke it off first. I got gun shy 'cause things were going fast. I'd just finished school and was really serious about training and learning this business. You have to understand that I've been in and around architecture my whole life. I've been working in some capacity at my dad's firm since I was fifteen and I finally had my degree and was interning, really doing some amazing work."

She searched his face. "Like the French Hills."

He barely nodded, turning to face the sky again to corral his emotions. Damn, when would this wound stop festering?

"Anyway, I got some majorly cold feet. I wasn't sure if she was right for me. I wasn't sure if I was ready. I took off for a summer in Europe to just look at the architecture and get my head together. She—Jayna—read that as a permanent breakup. And..."

"And she moved on to *your dad*?" She asked the question like anyone would: with complete disbelief and disgust.

"I think it was the other way around." His throat desert dry, he reached for his beer, slugging the bitter brew quickly, making the hammock sway. "Hey, if you think I'm persuasive with the opposite sex, you ain't seen nothin' till you meet C-dub." Which she never would. Ever.

"C-dub. For Clayton Walker. And they got married?"

"She got pregnant while I was in Europe, so, yeah. He divorced my mom and hopped on a charter to Vegas to make Jayna the next Mrs. Clayton Walker."

She dropped back onto the hammock as it all sank in. "And that's why you left the company?"

Actually, no. But now he was getting into some dangerous territory. Telling her any more tonight, when she was feeling this emotional? Bad idea.

"More or less," he said vaguely.

"What kind of relationship do you have with them?" she asked after a minute.

"My dad and Jayna? I'm not gonna lie. I can't stand the sight of either one of them and I don't feel like taking the high road." Plus, Dad wasn't even done ruining his life, trying to make himself look good and Clay look like a criminal. "I see my half-brother when my sister, Darcie, babysits him. I don't do holidays or birthdays or happy family reunions. Jayna got what she wanted: a husband. And Dad got what he wanted."

"A trophy wife?"

Dad got what belonged to Clay. "My dad's a small-minded, jealous, insecure son of a bitch who resented everything I had because he didn't have it."

"That's not very . . . fatherly."

He snorted softly. "That fucker doesn't know the first thing about being a father. Pardon my French, but he . . ." *Brings out the worst.*

"Sounds like he earned that."

"He did."

She didn't say anything for a long time, the only sound the crickets in the trees and some traffic in the distance. Then, "So that's why you want a no-strings-attached sexual relationship?"

"Honestly, Lacey?" He turned to her. "I don't ever plan on putting myself in the line of fire again, no. I want to do my job really well and use my gifts. I want to fix my—build my own reputation in this business, make top dollar, and . . . avoid anything that tears you to shreds when it ends." He looked hard at her. "But that doesn't mean I can't enjoy myself. It doesn't mean we can't enjoy each other, if you're comfortable with that."

"You know, five minutes before you arrived, I was swearing off sex and now you're basically offering just that."

Just that. "Dumb thing to swear off." He kissed her nose, her eyes, and her mouth again, letting the hammock rock itself so he could use his free hand to trail a finger path down her neck and into the V of her top. "Damn, I thought about you all day."

Color and goose bumps rose on her creamy skin. "What did you think?" she sounded as if she were afraid to ask.

"Well, I didn't think you'd stand me up," he said, faking a frown. "I thought I could get you to my apartment and we could watch your favorite movie from under the covers."

Her eyes widened.

"And we could argue about how the wrong guy gets the girl," he continued. "In between, we could..." His finger reached the rise of her abundant breast, and his mouth nearly followed. "Would you like that?"

She let out a shuddering sigh, rolling her body even closer to his. "Of course I'd like that, but we can't."

"That's funny, Lacey. I could have sworn I heard you use the C-word." He underscored the tease by dragging his finger lower, into the lace of her bra, and leaning forward to kiss the flesh of her cleavage.

"I might have." The confession was buried in a sweet moan of helpless pleasure.

"You like that, too?" he asked, his body reacting as it had been all afternoon: on the brink of an erection.

"I do, but..."

"Sounds like someone needs some Excuse Juice."

"No, I don't. I need"—she stabbed her fingers into his hair, guiding his mouth lower—"this."

"Told you." He rolled so that he could press himself against her hip, hard enough now that she could feel exactly what her body was doing to his.

"Clay," she said, easing away. "We really can't. Not here, not now."

"Okay." He eased off the next kiss. "Your daughter's coming home?"

"Well, yeah, but there's someone—something—else. This afternoon—"

"Mom, where are you?" Ashley's voice cut her off and they both bolted upright, making the hammock sway so hard they almost fell out.

Clay was still processing Lacey's last words. Had she said there was some*one* else?

Lacey face was more panicked than he'd have expected, considering they weren't doing anything.

"I'm out here," she called as they got to their feet. "I didn't get a chance to tell you."

"Tell me what?"

The sliding door to the house opened and instead of the sandy-haired teenager he expected, a man walked out. Tall, dark, commanding, and instantly focused on Clay.

Yep. She'd said some*one* else. Damn it.

"Mom, did you start the cookies yet?" Now the teenager charged out, a smile that could light the universe on her youthful face. It disappeared the instant she saw Clay. "What are you doing here?"

"Ashley," Lacey reprimanded. "That's rude. Mr. Walker is here to discuss the building project."

The man crossed the grass with an easy grace, lanky, tall, and confident, reminding Clay of someone but he couldn't quite grasp who.

"I'm Fox," he said to Clay, extending his hand. "Ashley's father."

Ashley's *father*? Clay shook his hand, meeting green eyes the precise color of Lacey's daughter's eyes. "Clay Walker," he said, returning the shake.

"I understand you have some outrageous ideas for our—for Lacey's property."

"Don't know if I'd call anything outrageous," Clay replied, his brain spinning through what he knew about Ashley's father. Hadn't Lacey said he was out of the picture? Like, seriously, gone for the past fourteen years?

Ashley muscled into the middle of the group holding up two bags. "Dad found you a tart pan and Masterson's was open, so we got apples. He got the clear glass kind, like you want. He knew you can't stand to bake with metal or dark glass, so now you can bake the tart that made Dad fall in love with you."

Fox chuckled, putting a warm, fatherly hand on Ashley's shoulder, eyeing the six-pack on the ground. "It looks like your mama's a little busy now, Ash."

Ashley lowered the bags, disappointment making her expression fall.

"No, we were just...meeting," Lacey said quickly.

"And we're just about done," Clay added. "So y'all can bake your, uh, tart."

"Southern boy, are you?" Fox stooped over and picked up the DVD Clay had brought over. "And look at this. Lacey's all-time favorite way to lose two hours. Can we watch it after we bake the tart?"

"It's all yours," Clay said. "I brought it over for Lacey."

"Oh, I'm sure she has a copy, but this is a digital remaster. Ever seen this, Ashley?"

"Mom's tried to make me watch it but, whoa, boring." She rolled her eyes and sang the last word.

"I'll make you love it," Fox said, putting an arm around Ashley and nodding to Clay. "Nice to meet you, Clay. Lace, just come on in when you're done with your meeting. Ashley and I'll start the dough and we can watch the movie while it chills."

They disappeared into the house and Lacey stayed perfectly still, watching them, silent until they'd closed the door. "I wanted to tell you he showed up quite unexpectedly this afternoon and that's why I didn't take your call. I'm sorry."

"No apologies necessary." But he didn't want to hang around and hear the gory details about their reunion. And go through pictures of their life together. "I'll keep work-ing on the blueprints and sketches. And I'll call you in a few days."

Some storm clouds passed her eyes. "Clay, I—"

"Mommy, hurry up! We can't do this without you!"

Lacey closed her eyes. "I don't want to watch that movie with them."

"Of course you do," Clay said. "You love that movie. Even the end."

She looked up at him and smiled. "When the wrong guy gets the girl?"

He laughed softly and backed away toward the gate. "Yep." And wasn't that the story of his life?

Chapter 13

ᴥ

Lacey had backed out of the baking and the movie, claiming exhaustion and the need for a long bath. True enough, as excuses went, so she spent most of the evening in her room—well, her parents' room because she didn't even have a room anymore—in the tub and then on her laptop, digging up resort-management sites and thinking about Clay.

Around ten, David tapped on her door. "Lacey, Ashley's gone to bed. Any chance you want to take an evening stroll down to the beach?"

She closed her computer and rolled off the bed to open the door. He was in sleep pants, his bare torso lean and fit. She refused even to look at a single hair on his chest, meeting his eyes instead, with one hand on her half-opened door. "Ashley went to bed? It's so early." And she hadn't said good night.

He gave a slow, sly smile. "I think she wants us to have some alone time."

Oh, God. "Well, I have no desire to go to the beach," she said.

"That's too bad, because I need to get out."

After a few hours? Really, how long could this man last on Mimosa Key? She nodded toward his bare chest. "Better put a shirt on or the Mimosa Key sheriff'll haul you in for indecent exposure. They're tough like that here. Excuse me." She brushed by him, walking down the hall to Ashley's room.

The door was closed, so she tapped and pushed it open, expecting to find Ashley crouched over her computer or on her phone.

But the room was dark, except for a beam of moonlight that highlighted some clothes on the floor. That mess would normally be the source of a conversation, but, whoa, Lacey had bigger problems than keeping the house clean.

"You really asleep, Ash?"

"Almost," she said groggily, sliding around in the bed. "You and Dad going for a walk?"

"Ashley, do you have to call him that?"

She sat up with a loud tsk. "He's my father, Mom. Why are you so determined to keep us apart?"

Lacey squeezed her fists and let the wave of fury pass. "I am not determined to keep you apart. I've let him stay here."

"Well, where else would he stay?"

A hotel. On another continent. Where he's been for fourteen years. "Did you like the movie?"

"We watched *Rio* instead."

For some reason she was relieved. *Casablanca* was her movie.

"Are you two going to take a walk?" Ashley asked again, hope in her voice.

"I think he is, but I don't feel like it."

"You should go, Mom. I'll be fine here alone."

"I know you will. I just…" She sighed into the darkness. "I don't want you to get too attached to him."

Ashley reached over and snapped on the light, her eyes blazing. "Why not?"

"Because you don't know him. He'll just—"

"Why can't you just accept that people change, Mom?" Her hands clutched the comforter in frustration. "People grow. He has. He'll tell you. I think he's amazing."

"I'm sure he is, but—"

"But what? What is with you?" She gave her big put-upon huff of breath. "I mean, most moms in this situation would be thrilled that their daughter wanted to have a relationship with her dad. I could hate him, you know?"

"Yes, I know."

"I could push him away and say 'no way, you've been missing for my whole damn life, so screw you.'"

"Ashley, don't talk like—"

"I could! But I'm not and I think that's very mature of me."

"Yes, honey, it is mature." And instead of sounding like her own mother and finding fault with Ashley, Lacey knew she should be congratulating her daughter on her behavior. But she couldn't. "It's also dangerous."

"Dangerous?" She practically sputtered. "He wouldn't hurt a fly."

"Not intentionally." How could she warn her daughter

that loving this man could mean deep and profound hurt? "But he hurt me."

"Mom, that was fourteen years ago."

"But it shows you that he's the kind of man who can, and does, leave when something more exciting comes along."

"Oh, that's just a lame excuse so I don't get close to him." She sank back on her pillow. "I think you're jealous."

"I think you're..." *Absolutely right.* "A little out of line talking to me that way."

Ashley made a pouty face but withheld an apology.

"Don't you see, honey?" Lacey sat on the edge of the bed to get closer and make her point. "I'm terrified that he'll get you all wrapped up in a father-daughter relationship and then, you'll see. He'll get a call from a friend in Madagascar to go zebra hunting or rock climbing or jungle hopping and, wham, you're all alone."

"He said he's done with all that travel, Mom. He's a chef now. He wants to open a restaurant." She leaned forward, grabbing Lacey's hand. "Ohmigod, Mom, what if he opened one here on Mimosa Key?" Her voice jumped an octave in excitement.

"Honey, please don't start harboring those fantasies."

"It's not a fantasy. He likes it here. And, Mom, he still cares about you. I could tell when he picked your tart pan."

"It takes a lot more than a tart pan to demonstrate love," Lacey said. It took trust and sticking it out through tough times and it took a commitment. Nothing Lacey'd ever gotten from any man, least of all David Fox.

Ashley grinned, looking suddenly much younger than fourteen. "Mom, haven't you seen the way he looks at you?"

"At me?" She waited for the expected impact of those words, but there was none. No feeling, no happiness, no excitement. "You're always imagining things, Ash."

"Aunt Zoe noticed, too."

"She's *always* imagining things, too."

"Maybe you're just too busy making out with that architect on the hammock to notice the guy who really matters."

Was she? "We weren't making out. Okay, a little."

"Ewww, Mom. He's too young for you!"

"No, he's not."

"Won't you even give Dad a chance? It would be so awesome if you two got back together."

Lacey just shook her head, very slowly. "I gave him a chance, a long time ago."

Ashley leaned forward, taking both of Lacey's hands. "Don't you feel anything for him? Just a little gooey inside when you look at him?" The sheer desperation in her voice almost broke Lacey's heart.

"No," she said honestly.

"Well, can't you try? For me? So we could have a family? He could buy us a house and, and, we could get all the stuff we lost and—"

"Oh, Ashley, please don't put that on me. I don't want your happiness to be contingent on this...this fantasy you have about David and me getting back together." Because it was almost impossible for Lacey to say no to her daughter.

"Just give him a chance, Mom."

"He's staying with us for a few days. That's enough of a chance."

"A step in the right direction." She gave a secret smile.

"And I promise I won't check to see if the guest room's been used."

"Ashley!" Lacey flicked her fingers on the blanket, tapping Ashley's leg. "Don't even *think* about that."

"Why not? You were thinking about it with that Clay guy."

Lacey reached over and switched off the light, her only defense against a rising blush. "End of conversation."

Ashley just tunneled into the covers and turned over. "It's okay, Mom. Clay's cute and he obviously wants to get into your pants."

"Ashley Marie Armstrong, you cannot talk like that. Go to sleep and stop having opinions."

Ashley laughed softly at the admonition. "Only if you stop flirting with boys and give my father a chance."

"Good night, Ash." Lacey closed the door on her way out, ready to warn David to quit planting these stupid fantasies in Ashley's head.

The rest of the house was quiet, so David must have gone for his walk alone. Relieved, Lacey went into the kitchen to make some tea, stopping to examine the tart pan on the counter. The bag of apples sat untouched next to it.

The gesture had been sweet, she admitted to herself. Fingering the pan, she pictured the blossoming rosette of apple slices covering a sweet compote and buttery crust.

Without giving it much thought, she preheated the oven, loaded up the counter with flour, salt, butter, and some ice water, and mentally calculated some recipe amounts that would kick up the flakiness, which made this tart so divine.

She'd like to use her mixer with the paddle, but...

Don't think about what you've lost, Lacey. But the

homey scents of flour and salt alternately soothed and tortured her, reminding her of all that was gone.

Would she bake at Casa Blanca? she wondered. The resort name still felt unfamiliar and awkward in her mind, so new that she couldn't imagine that it might ever exist, let alone become a place for her to live and bake. Was that possible? Or would she and Ashley find an apartment when Mother and Dad came back?

The thought made her dig deeper into the coarse and crumbly dough, the simple action sending a soothing, sweet numbness up her arms. Of course she'd bake wherever she lived. She'd need to, because—

The back door opened as David walked in, looking with surprise at the counter.

"A walk would have de-stressed you, too, Lace. It's a gorgeous night out there."

She wiped a hair away with the back of a floury hand. "Thanks for the tart pan," she said. "It's a nice one."

"You're welcome. Here, I brought you this." He held up a bright pink bougainvillea blossom, then sniffed it. "Smells like Indonesia."

"I wouldn't know what Indonesia smells like, David."

He chuckled. "Okay, you can call me David. But only you. Is Ashley asleep?" He came closer, laying the flower on the counter while her gaze flitted over his loose-fitting T-shirt and cargo shorts.

"No. But she's having dreams."

He looked at her, a frown making him no less attractive in the soft kitchen light. "How's that?"

She shook her head, not quite ready to start that conversation and kill the mellow happiness of making dough. "When were you in Indonesia?" she asked instead.

"When I got serious about cooking, as part of my internship with the Aman Resorts, a corporation that owns some of the most amazing luxury hotels in the world."

She stilled her fingers. "You worked for a resort company?"

"Don't be so surprised. I am capable of holding down a job," he said, grabbing the bag of apples and dumping them in the sink. "I know you think I'm a trust-fund slacker."

"You *are* a trust-fund slacker."

"I'm not a slacker and the trust fund is well invested. I can't just hop from one adventure to the next, Lacey. A man's got to settle down at some point. Where's the peeler?"

She nodded toward a drawer. "Should be in there. What did you do for this company?"

"I started as a busboy and worked my way up to chef. There's not a kitchen in the Aman organization where I haven't worked, and that includes Cambodia, Laos, Thailand, French Polynesia, Montenegro, Turkey, Morocco—"

"Morocco?"

"Yes, and, trust me, it's nothing like your movie."

Her movie. "I understand you went with *Rio* instead," she said, lifting the dough ball out of the bowl to turn it on the counter. "Good choice."

"And, believe me, that cartoon was no more realistic a depiction of Rio de Janeiro than *Casablanca* is of Morocco."

Morocco. Even the word reminded her of Clay and how much she would have liked to have watched their movie together.

Oh, now *her* movie was *their* movie. "Did you like Morocco?"

He shrugged, starting to expertly peel a Granny Smith. "What I saw of it. Mostly I worked."

"That's not like you. Usually you trek."

"I still do now and then," he admitted. "Once I finished my time with Aman, I took a year to hit a few of my favorite haunts, like Kuala Lumpur and, of course, Chile and Argentina."

"Of course." She knew what was down there in Chile and Argentina. "You've always had a soft spot for Patagonia."

He had the apple peeled and cored in a matter of seconds, his hands smooth as silk and lightning fast. "That didn't take too long."

"The apple?"

"The Patagonia dig."

She smiled, shaking her head and giving the dough another fold. "This has to chill for a while," she said. "I can finish the apples."

"Let's do them together," he said. "Do you prefer to peel or slice?"

She wrapped the dough in plastic, then opened the fridge. "You look like you're pretty handy with the peeler. I'll slice."

They worked in silence for a few minutes, the only sounds the sweep of his peeler and the slide of her knife as she made the paper-thin slices. When she started on the second apple, she took a breath and decided to attempt the more serious conversation.

"So, David. What exactly are you doing here?"

The peeler slowed infinitesimally. "Does my being here upset you that much, Lacey?"

"What upsets me is the ideas that are being planted in Ashley's brain. Ideas that will never happen."

"You never know what's going to happen."

"But I know what *isn't* going to happen: You and I are

not getting back together to live happily ever after as Ashley Armstrong's married parents."

"Married?" he choked softly. "You know I don't believe in marriage."

Oh, yes. That she knew for sure and certain. "I know you don't believe in marriage," she replied. "I think that's why we're in this situation to begin with. I *do* believe in marriage."

"Then why aren't you married?"

She should have seen that coming. "Because I haven't met a man I think would be an ideal partner, a perfect father to Ashley, and a great husband."

He finished an apple and put it on her cutting board, the sweet smell making her want a bite of one of her slices. "Maybe you've already found that man."

She looked up at him. "Clay?"

He let out a sharp laugh. "I meant me."

"You?" A thousand responses warred for air time, but she glommed on to the easiest one. "You just said you don't believe in marriage."

"And you think that twenty-something longhair with a tattoo does?"

"Now you sound like a parent."

"Well, I am a parent, and my daughter's well-being is at stake."

What was he saying? "You think Clay could hurt her?"

"I think Clay could hurt you. It's obvious what he wants, drawing naked pictures, bringing beer over to your house, rolling around on the hammock."

It was so obvious she couldn't argue the point. "He's going to work for me. He's doing the work pro bono."

"Oh, he'll get paid all right."

She turned to him, lifting the knife from the apple just

enough to make her point. "Watch it," she said. "You're over the line."

He held up both hands and took a step back. "You're right. I'm sorry. I'm just jealous."

Jealous? "All right, then, color me confused. I mean, how can you be jealous? Why? You've been gone for a lifetime. Suddenly you care who I'm involved with? About Ashley's well-being?"

"I've always cared about Ashley's well-being."

She focused on the blade, sliding it through the apple and letting it thunk to the board. "Then you had a lousy way of showing it," she said. "Or are we supposed to just erase the years, like your absence didn't hurt her?"

There was no answer from him as he worked his magic on one more apple, flipping the fruit like a seasoned pro baseball player handling the game ball.

"I screwed up," he finally said.

The apology didn't feel good, but it didn't hurt, either. In fact, when Lacey looked up at him, met the eyes that had once melted her, she felt...nothing at all.

Well, maybe a little relief *because* she felt nothing. But she wasn't inclined to let him off the hook that easily.

"Yes, you screwed up, David. There were too many Christmases and birthdays with not even a phone call."

"But I could make it up to you," he said. "If you'd let me."

"No, thanks."

"Lacey, I screwed up the past. Let me change our future."

"*We* don't have a future," she said. "There is no 'our' in our future, David. There is a daughter, yes, and I have never, ever tried to deny you the opportunity to know her. Not doing so has been your choice."

"I know—"

"From the beginning," she interjected, dark emotions building inside of her, words she'd wanted to say for years finally getting a voice. "You made that choice from the day I told you I was pregnant, as I recall."

Again, silence.

"And we both know what you wanted me to do." *Take care of it, Lace. It's legal.* She could still hear his voice.

"That would have been a grievous error," he said.

"No shit, Sherlock." She spat the cliché, not caring if it made her sound more like Ashley than a rational adult.

"And you've done a marvelous job with her."

"Don't patronize me," she said. "I've done all I could and it hasn't been easy."

"She's a lovely young lady."

Lacey snorted softly. "Most of the time, yes. But she's also a teenage hormone factory at the moment, given to drama and self-absorption. More than anything, she's a girl searching to fill a great big hole in her life that happens when you are raised by a single parent."

"Which brings us right back to why I'm here."

Suddenly she suspected she knew exactly why he was there. "Is it possible, David, that you're here to fill a hole in your life, not hers?"

"Anything's possible, Lace," he said as gave her the last apple, then nudged her out of the way. "Let me." He took the knife, gave his shoulders a little flex and started slicing like a human food processor.

"Holy shit," Lacey murmured, rearing back in surprise. "Where'd you learn to do that?"

He grinned at her. "All over the world."

She leaned over, propped her chin on her elbows, and

watched him work, unable to hide her admiration. David Fox was once the man of her dreams and she'd loved him with everything she had.

And he'd crushed that love with a hiking boot.

But the act of baking late at night, talking and sharing and not being alone, the comfort of it, pulled at her heart. Not that she wanted David Fox to fill that role, but, Lord, she wanted someone.

And her most recent find had just hours ago admitted that he'd been so burned by love he only wanted sex. *Lacey, girl, you sure can pick 'em*.

"I'll start the compote," she said, pushing off to grab a bowl and the sugar.

"You know, Lacey," he said, letting her take over and start sugaring the apples. "One of the reasons I'm here is because I had an epiphany a while ago."

She looked up from the bowl, some sugary apples slipping through her fingers. "An epiphany?"

He leaned back against the edge of the counter, crossing his arms, his expression distant. "I was in Bolivia hiking the salt flats. We left late in the day and ended up having to spend the night in this little village, if you can even call it that, across the border in Chile. There was no hotel, no nothing. We stayed with locals, in a hut. They cooked the most amazing food, and the stars that night? You've never seen anything like it."

No, she hadn't, and probably never would. Bolivia held no interest for her. Which was why they were so wrong for each other.

"The next morning," he continued, "just before sunrise, I saw the woman who lived in our hut—a girl, really, barely twenty—outside nursing her baby." He gave her an expectant stare, like she should react to the monumental power of his story.

She didn't. "And?"

"The moment was suspended in time, like God's tableau. A young mother, her black hair falling over her face, her breast giving sustenance to an infant who clung to her with two tiny hands." He held up his own hands as though clutching a breast, which struck her as melodramatic and bizarre, but Lacey just listened.

"And it hit me, Lacey. This girl was just about your age when you had Ashley. That thought just speared me in the gut like nothing I've ever felt before."

She layered the apple mixture over the baking pan, furious that her hands shook a little. But how could they not? It had taken him fourteen years to figure all this out?

"What exactly got you, David? The fact that you ditched me for sheep in Argentina or the fact that the last time you saw your own daughter she was a year old?"

Putting his hands on her shoulders, he turned her from the apples to face him. "The raw power of procreation."

She wiggled out of his touch, an old fury bubbling up. *Little late to figure that out, Daddio.* "It is powerful."

"No, no, Lacey, it's *everything*. It's all that matters. It's the reason we are alive, not to see the seven or seven*ty* wonders of the world. Every single person on this earth is a wonder, and what we need to do—what *I* need to do—is…is…" He balled up his fists like he was grabbing something. "Seize the life we made. That's why I came here."

"To seize Ashley?" Her heart skipped. "You can't take her."

"I don't want to take her, Lace," he assured her, putting his hands on her shoulders again, too tight for her to escape. "I want to be with her, near her, to have a father-daughter relationship with her. You never said I couldn't."

No, she hadn't. But she never thought there was a remote possibility of it happening, either.

"When I looked at that young mother, so connected and alive because of the life she created, I knew that what I'm doing with my life is meaningless. Even the chef's work, which I love, doesn't fill a hole in me. Everything is meaningless without that connection to another human that is part of you."

"I was just thinking that," she admitted. "Although not quite so eloquently."

"Of course you were, because family *is all there is*, Lacey." He pounded his fist on the counter with each word, making the pronouncement like he'd invented the concept. "Nothing else matters. Nothing."

So now he wanted her family? No, not happening. "Family is important," she said, choosing each word carefully. "So why don't you go see yours in New York? They matter, too." *Plus, added benefit, they're a thousand miles away.*

He gripped her shoulders again, doing his damnedest to inch her closer. "Anyway, I'm not talking about that family. I'm talking about our family."

Our. That word again. "We don't have a family, David. We have a child and two separate lives."

"But why?"

"Why?" Was he serious? "Because you had to go to Patagonia. And Namibia. And Botswana. And—"

"Shhh." He put his fingers over her lips, another intimate breach of personal space.

"Don't shush me," she ordered. *And don't touch lips that hours ago were kissing another man.*

"Then don't say things that don't matter anymore. I went. I'm done. I'm back. Why can't it be that simple?"

"Because it isn't simple at all. For one thing, you can't come 'back' to a place where you've never lived or spent more than a week. This is my home, not yours. And she's…" *My daughter.*

But she couldn't say that. She was his daughter, too. Biologically, anyway.

"I had another epiphany in that little village, watching that girl."

Watching that girl's breast, more likely. "Which was?"

"I'm still in love with you." His voice was husky. "In fact I never stopped—"

"Well, stop now." She put up both hands in the international sign for shut-the-hell-up. "You aren't in love with me. You don't even know me anymore."

He gave her a patient smile. "And I'm here to rectify that. And I know this: I loved you once." The words, a direct hit at her heart, left her speechless. "And I think—I *think*—I could love you again."

She stared at him. He reached for her, but she grabbed the baking sheet and whipped around to the oven.

He was next to her in a second, opening the oven door for her. "I believe that deep down, in your heart of hearts, you feel the same."

She stuffed the sheet onto the rack. "Then you'd be wrong."

"Now I am, maybe. But if I'm here long enough, you might change your mind."

How he could he not get this? She felt nothing for him. But there was no way to convince him of that right now. Instead, she closed the oven door and stepped away from him.

"However long you're here, David, I don't want you to make promises to Ashley. Do you understand? I will not have her getting hurt."

"And what about promises to you?"

"You can't hurt me anymore, David," she said simply. "But I admit you can annoy the hell out of me."

"That's a start."

How could he be so dense? No, he wasn't dense. He was David. And he'd never had any trouble with her in the past; she'd gone along with his every idea except that she terminate her pregnancy. That one, thank God, she'd stood her ground on.

And she would with this, too.

"Look, this is my life and my family and my dreams, and, I'm sorry, but you are fourteen years too late and not invited to be part of it. Can I make myself any clearer, *Fox*?"

"You're clear," he said with a soft chuckle. "Perhaps you're forgetting how I love a challenge. I live for a challenge. I can climb Kilimanjaro and I can change your mind."

No, he couldn't. She started to wipe the counter with long, sure swipes. "I'm going to read while the dough chills and these apples cook."

"We could watch the movie," he suggested.

No, they couldn't. "I'll pass. You should go to bed. Surely you have jet lag or something."

He just laughed. "All right. But I have to tell you one more thing because I believe in total honesty and having all my cards showing."

She gathered a palmful of crumbs. "Yes?"

"Lacey, I want to have another baby."

A baby? He didn't want the child he had. "Well, good luck with that."

"I want to have another baby with you."

Tiny little flour crumblets slipped through her fingers and fluttered to the floor. She stared at the dusting on the tile, unable even to look at him. "Why would you even say something like that?"

"Because you're a wonderful mother, a lifelong friend, and we make beautiful children together."

She brushed off her hands, let more crumbs hit the floor, and finally lifted her head to check the clock. Because never in her life had she needed to beat out her misery with a rolling pin more.

Of course she'd always wanted another child. Just not with him.

Chapter 14

ﮐ

"Another baby?" Zoe actually spewed her coffee, splattering a few drops on the glass table at the Ritz-Carlton poolside restaurant.

Tessa and Jocelyn's response was slightly more in keeping with the posh surroundings: silent, gaping mouths of utter disbelief.

"What did you tell him?" Tessa finally asked.

"I told him he's crazy." Lacey picked up her napkin and dabbed at the coffee droplets.

"You don't want another baby?" Tessa asked, a little accusation in her voice. Tessa and Lacey had talked about this, and Lacey had long ago admitted she'd like another baby someday.

Lacey looked up and met her friend's eyes, seeing the battle scars of Tessa's long fight with infertility. "Not bad enough to hook up with David Fox," she said. "I do, but I haven't met the right guy." A thought of Clay flit through her mind. "Definitely haven't met the right guy."

Jocelyn leaned forward. "David's an alpha dog, Lacey. Always has been, always wanted control over you. When he couldn't control you, and force you to have an abortion, he ran. He sees you as a mountain he couldn't climb, a thrill he couldn't conquer."

"Easy, Sigmund," Tessa said. "I suppose there is a possibility the guy's legit."

"And maybe pigs can get airborne," Zoe shot back.

Lacey was definitely on Zoe's side. "Still," she told them. "He did say he worked in the kitchen of this huge five-star resort corporation. He knows how to run the kitchen of a resort. If I go with this idea of Clay's, I'm going to need to talk to someone who's done that."

"Talking to someone is not bearing their child," Zoe said.

"A lot of people have worked in resort kitchens," Jocelyn added quickly. "And they aren't the father of your child or the man who broke your heart."

All three of them looked at her to underscore the warning.

"You guys, I am not interested in him, honestly." In her purse her phone vibrated and she pulled it out, unable to avoid having Tessa read the name on the caller ID.

"Clay Walker texting," Tessa said. "Aren't you going to read it?"

"Later." But she was itching to read what he'd written.

"C'mon," Zoe said with a nudge. "Let's hear what the hottie has to say."

"I heard plenty last night." Lacey folded her napkin

and placed it on the table, over the phone, aware of their curious looks. "He showed up and laid his cards out on the table. Well, the hammock."

"You were on the hammock with him?" Zoe sat up. "Did he lay anything else out?"

"A very ugly story," Lacey said, and they all automatically leaned in closer.

She told them everything about the girlfriend who married the father, and got the expected responses. Tessa was disgusted. Jocelyn quoted Jungian psychology. Zoe said the old man must be hung like a horse.

They spent a good ten minutes imagining how something like that could have happened, how it felt, and what it did to a family.

"I don't know about his family, but Clay's scarred pretty badly," Lacey said. "He's not even going to pretend a relationship could be for any other reason but sex."

"At least he's honest," Zoe said dryly. "'Cause some guys would take you for a major ride, believe me."

"So what are you going to do?" Jocelyn asked.

Lacey shrugged. "I don't know. I have one guy I don't feel a thing for asking to share his life and have his baby, and one I've got the hots so bad for that I can't think straight around him and all he wants is to get laid. What's a girl to do?"

All three of them looked at her like she'd grown another head.

"What?" she asked. "You think I should? Get laid?"

"Why not?" Jocelyn asked.

Lacey frowned at her. "You're not usually the one pushing casual sex, Joss."

"Yeah, that's my job," Zoe said, dinging her spoon

against her glass. "But thanks for the support. So let me repeat: Why the hell not, Lace?"

Lacey looked at Tessa, hoping for the voice of reason but getting a shrug. "I saw the guy. Put me in the why-the-hell-not camp."

"Are you guys serious?" Lacey could barely keep her jaw from hitting the table. "You guys think I should..."

"*Yes.*" They answered in unison.

Lacey didn't know whether to laugh or talk them out of this lunacy.

"Without any kind of relationship? Or, worse, *with* a working one? What if we have some messy breakup and have to—"

"You can't technically break up if there are no strings attached," Jocelyn said. "So I don't see that as a problem."

"What about the example I set for my daughter? Do you see that as a problem?"

Tessa took that one. "She's not a baby, Lace. She wants you to be happy. You can be cool and not all in her face about it. You'll be working with the guy. Working *nights.*"

"She wants me to be with David," Lacey replied, each excuse sounding weaker even to her ears.

"You can't let her control you like your mother did."

"Whoa," Zoe held up her hand for a high five to Jocelyn. "Sigmund's on fire today."

Jocelyn tapped palms, but her attention was directed to Lacey. "I'm serious, Lace. Maybe Ashley doesn't spend every breath telling you what you're doing wrong like your mom, but she does use her behavior to get you do what she wants you to do. It's time to not give her that power."

Lacey just blinked at her. "Well, then, I guess I..." *Am running out of reasons why this affair was a bad idea.*

"Are you out of excuses?" Tessa asked.

"Seriously, Lace," Jocelyn said. "When was the last time you did something just for fun? For you? For the pure pleasure of feeling…"

"His magic drafting tool," Zoe said, getting a loud burst of laughter that drew a few harsh looks from the other Ritz patrons.

Jocelyn slid the leather bill folder to the side of the table. "Let's take this inside or down to the beach, ladies," she said. "I don't think the Ritz can handle the Fearsome Foursome of Tolbert Hall."

"Ah, the good ol' days," Zoe said as they pushed back their chairs and gathered their bags. "When we had nothing but a few finals and frat boys to worry about."

"You had frat boys," Tessa said. "I had agriculture-major nerds."

"And I had the good luck to meet David Fox."

Zoe put an arm around Lacey. "I believe I tried to talk you out of Asian Cultures that semester."

"No, you tried to talk me into a linguistic class on Elvish."

"I was in my *Lord of the Rings* phase." She squeezed Lacey's shoulder and indicated the phone. "I'm dying here. Read the text, Lacey."

"All right."

"Out loud," Zoe insisted.

Lacey clicked on Clay's name, really wishing that simple act didn't make her heart ratchet up. But it did. "Heard there's a secret Mexican restaurant on this island. Need a local to get a table. Dinner tonight? I have something I want to tell you."

"Mexican?" Zoe did a little dance, shouldering Lacey

across the lobby into the apothecary shop. "Someone's getting the whole enchilada."

"Stop it, Zoe," Lacey said, but nothing could stop the smile that had started just by reading his name on her phone.

"We'll get you all ready," Zoe said, ignoring the order. "Clothes, hair, makeup." She snapped her fingers as if a light bulb had gone on in her head. "And I do believe I saw a condom display in that cute little apothecary in the lobby." She grinned, delighted. "We'll pop right in there and pick something perfect."

She pulled Lacey toward the shop. "Lacey needs to grab something in here," she said to the others. "We'll meet you up in the room, okay? And, Joss, can you throw your weight around and get my friend here an appointment for a wax? I'm thinking the whole shebang, huh?"

"Absolutely," Jocelyn said. "How about a pedicure, too?"

"You guys." But Lacey knew her protests were falling on deaf ears.

"What are you wearing?" Tessa asked.

"Whatever Zoe picks for me," she said, any chance of a fight gone. Besides, she didn't want to go home and dress for a date with Clay while David and Ashley looked on.

"Tell him yes," Zoe prodded, pointing to the phone. "C'mon, before you find some reason not to."

Lacy looked at the phone, typed "Sure," and hit Send before she could do exactly that. "Done."

"Safety first." Zoe guided Lacey into the store, past displays of gifts and toiletries, all the way to the back. "Really, you should see the selection."

"When I was younger, there was only one brand," Lacey said. "Trojan."

"In three sizes. There was Color Me Happy Large, This Will Have to Do Medium, and Oh Isn't That Thing Cute Small. Here we go." They arrived at the condom rack.

Lacey grabbed the first one she saw. "What's this? A warming condom?"

"Oh, they're nice," Zoe said. "Thinner and they get kind of hot. I like these, too, the Pleasure Shaped."

"Do you know all of this from firsthand experience?"

"I read a lot." Zoe flipped the box over. "Stimulates nerve endings and heightens sensitivity. Oooh. Lovely."

"Put that back," Lacey said, giving a nervous glance as a couple entered the little store. "My nerve endings are stimulated enough just by being in the same room with Clay. Are you sure I need these? I think we're jumping the—"

"Here's Durex Tingling Pleasure with a spearmint lubricant." She slipped the box off the wire hook. "Tasty *and* safe."

"Shhh," Lacey warned. "Just pick one. Large. No, extra large."

Zoe gave a soft whoop of approval, flipping through some more boxes. "Oh, my God, French ticklers!" She struggled to get the box off the hook as the man separated from the woman, looking at them, then taking a few steps closer.

"Zoe, quiet."

"These have the most amazing little nodules." She yanked the box and suddenly the whole top row of the display popped off, hooks and all, sending a shower of condom boxes everywhere.

"Oh, shit!" Zoe shrieked a laugh, hands out, missing more than she caught.

The man kept coming toward them, so Lacey gave

Zoe a nudge to start picking up the mess. As she crouched down, Zoe was laughing so hard she lost her balance and tipped onto her backside, letting out a howl as she landed in a sea of condom boxes.

She whipped one out from under her butt holding it up like a prize just as the man walked up behind her. "And the winner is . . . Kiss of Mint non lubricated, safe for oral—"

"Zoe."

"—sex with a reservoir tip for heightened—"

"Zoe Tamarin?"

"—male . . ." The arm waving the box overhead froze, but Zoe didn't look up. ". . . sensation."

"Is that you, Zoe?"

She didn't move. Not a single muscle so much as twitched on a woman who couldn't do "still" with a gun to her head.

"I recognized your laugh," he said.

Dead silent, she put her hand on the floor and started to push up. Instantly, he reached down to help her, and she wrenched her hand out of his, standing on her own.

Lacey was vaguely aware that he was tall and dark-haired, a striking figure with bold features and broad shoulders. But she didn't do a close inspection because she was more concerned with Zoe, who seemed almost unable to face him.

Zoe, who didn't know the meaning of shy with strangers and especially not with great-looking men who already knew her name. When she turned, her fair complexion had gone bone pale, her green eyes as flat and dimmed as if someone had reached inside and turned off her switch.

"Hello, Oliver." And she didn't seem the least bit surprised to see this man, whoever he was.

"Zoe." He said her name on a long, soft sigh, breaking into a huge smile, searching her face like a starving man being dragged past a banquet. "What are you doing here?"

She held up the condom box and attempted a funny face. "Stocking up."

He barely smiled, giving her with a look so intense even Lacey could feel its power. "I mean, in this hotel?"

"Visiting a friend." She gave him a tight smile and tapped the green Kiss of Mint box on her cheek. "Obviously, a good one."

"Obviously."

"Oliver!" The woman he'd come in with called from the front. "I'm ready."

He held up a single finger to the woman without taking his eyes from Zoe. He looked like he wanted to say something but no matter how deep he dug, the right words eluded him.

"Your wife is waiting," Zoe said in a voice that was no louder than a whisper.

"Zoe…"

"As I recall, she doesn't like to wait."

He closed his eyes like she'd kicked him in the stomach. "It was…I can't believe—"

"Oliver, I told the limo driver we'd be right there. Hurry, sweetheart."

"Bye!" Zoe said with completely false brightness, using the condom box to give a stupid little wave.

"I'm sorry," he whispered, the words so soft Lacey wasn't sure she heard right. "I'm so sorry."

Zoe's brightness flickered for a second, but that wasn't joy. It was hate. "Go. I have nothing to say to you."

Without so much as a glance at Lacey he pivoted and returned to the front, where the woman grabbed his arm and nudged him toward the door. "What were you doing back there where they keep the sex toys, you animal?"

Zoe stood transfixed, watching them leave.

"Who was that?" Lacey asked.

Zoe just closed her eyes and collapsed into a heap of fallen condoms, no doubt preparing a punch line she'd deliver with impeccable timing and sarcasm.

Instead, she quietly started to cry.

Chapter 15

Clay only half listened to his sister's account of her latest dating debacle as he strolled through the waters of Barefoot Bay. His other ear was trained on the road that led to the beach, hoping the sound of Lacey's little VW would be the next he heard.

"Do I have a loser magnet hanging around my neck, Clay?" Darcie asked. "I mean, is it me or is it just that all men are assholes who only want sex and games, with no strings attached?"

A little guilt tweaked him, but he shoved it away. "It's all men."

"Not you."

Yes, him. Now, anyway. "Just be careful, use protection, and don't get your hopes up. It's hell out there."

"Great advice, oh cynical brother. Aren't you ever going to get over your heartbreak?"

He snorted. "First of all, I'm honest, not cynical. Second of all, nothing broke except my career. And third, I'm over her, Darcie. I was over it long before the day they got married."

Darcie was quiet for a minute. "He's actually been really good with little Elliott."

"Nice to hear. Change the subject or I'm hanging up."

He heard her sigh softly. "How's it going down there? Getting what you want?"

"Working on it," he said with another glance at the road. "I was right about the job; it could be big. It looks like I'm going to get it from planning to finish, which would be exactly what I need to take to the AIA for certification." He waited a beat, debating how much to tell her. "The owner's nice, too."

"Nice? What do you mean, nice? Like he won't go looking for references or digging up dirt?"

"I mean nice, like *she's* pretty hot and we have good chemistry."

"Ohhhh." She dragged the single syllable out to a full chorus of multiple notes. "Well, use protection and don't get your hopes up."

"Touché."

"And be careful, Clay."

"Don't worry. I'm not going to get hurt again." He wasn't that stupid.

"I mean professionally," Darcie said. "If Dad finds out—"

"He won't," he assured her. "This place is completely remote. I'm not going to file anything official with my name on it that could get on the Internet. Once I finish the job, I'll claim it with the board and fight for a chance to sit for those exams. No one can stop me if I've finished designing and building and have all the personnel here, and the property owner, to support me."

"Are you going to tell her everything?"

"I actually asked her to dinner tonight for that very reason. I'm going to tell her the whole miserable story."

Darcie was quiet too long.

"Darcie, can you think of a better way out of this? Dad has tied my hands and threatened to cut them off."

"No, I think you're being very smart and strategic, but maybe you should try talking to Dad first."

"And throw myself at his feet? No, thanks." He was the prick who moved in on his own son's girlfriend. And she was the one who—

Let it go, Clay.

"I came up with a way to save my own ass, and Lacey Armstrong is the ticket."

"Pretty name. What's she like?" Darcie asked.

"Pretty lady, too. Smart, funny." There was so much more to Lacey he didn't even know what to focus on. "Good mother." Why had he picked *that* out of the hat?

"She has a kid?" Darcie sounded shocked.

"A daughter, fourteen." And an ex, but before he could tell that to his sister, he heard the sound of a motor, too loud to be the Passat but definitely coming this way. "Hey, I gotta go, Darcie. I'll call you in a few days."

"Okay, Clay, but please . . ."

The motor had his attention, but so did the little note of sadness in his sister's voice. "Hey, Darce, you'll find the right guy. Don't worry."

"That's not it. I want you to . . . maybe think about . . ."

He knew where this was going. With Darcie, the family

peacemaker, it was always the same. "I'm not going to forgive him, so drop it."

"Life's short, Clay."

"He should have thought about that when he banged my girlfriend. Bye." He hung up without waiting to hear Darcie's reply, standing still to identify the engine he heard.

A motorcycle. He made his way up the beach to Lacey's property, lingering far enough off the road so he could see who it was without being spotted. The rider was helmetless and Clay instantly recognized Lacey's ex, Fox, perched on an expensive BMW bike.

Fox rolled up to the foundation and cinder-block base of the old house, a good fifty feet away from Clay, shut off the bike, and pulled out a phone. Clay had run here and his truck was parked two miles away, so Fox probably thought he was completely alone. But just as Clay was about to call out to him, Fox spoke into the phone.

"Mr. Tomlinson?" His deep voice carried across the open space, loud, like a man who liked to be heard. "I'm here. Are you on your way?" He was silent for a beat, then, "Well, please hurry. I'd like to get this done as soon as possible."

He shoved the phone into his pants pocket, taking a minute to survey the property.

Clay cleared his throat, instantly getting Fox's attention.

"I didn't see you there," Fox said, accusation in his voice. "What are you doing out here?"

"Working," Clay said. "And you?"

"Same." He walked toward Clay with purpose, his gaze direct, a hand extended when he got close enough. "Good to see you."

Was it? Clay shook his hand. "Working on what?" Clay asked.

"A surprise for Lacey." He smiled and slid his hands into the pockets of crisp khaki pants, then took an expansive look around. "Kind of a magical place, don't you think?"

Once again, something about the guy seemed familiar, or at least he reminded Clay of someone. "Absolutely magical," Clay agreed.

"I saw some of your sketches and it sure looks like you captured the possibilities of the place."

She'd shown him the sketches? For some reason that bugged him. "There are plenty of possibilities," he said vaguely. "I'm sure it'll be beautiful when we're done."

The other man snorted softly.

"You don't agree?" Clay had to ask.

"You obviously don't know Lacey." He shook his head, amused. "She's big on plans. Not so big on finishing things."

"Maybe she's changed. I get the impression you've been more or less gone most of the last fourteen years."

"I've been gone, but she hasn't changed." Fox walked toward the water, gazing out. "But I'll give her the benefit of the doubt on this idea. And I want to help her."

Clay said nothing, the sensation that he knew this guy still nagging. "How do you plan to do that?"

A big fat investment? Lacey could use that when it came time to break ground.

Fox just shrugged. "Oh, I'm working on some plans." He kicked a shell and put his hands on his hips, looking around like he owned the place. And the woman who came with it. "Fact is, Lacey and I have a connection."

Yep, definitely the woman who came with it. "You have a daughter," Clay corrected.

"Indeed we do, and that's a connection in and of itself. But..." He lifted his brows. "We also have a *history*," he said. "A long, emotional, passionate history."

What was his point? Throwing down a gauntlet? Warning Clay off?

"History means it's over," Clay said. "Is it?"

"At the moment," Fox acknowledged. "Is anything going on with you and Lacey?"

Clay refused to react to the bluntness of the question. "We're working on a building project."

"Looked to me like you were working on more than that."

"I don't think that's any of your business."

"I'm making it my business." He turned to face Clay, his expression sheer determination. "I'm putting my broken family back together again."

Clay just looked at him, a lot of different responses in his head, but all he heard was the echo of his sister's words. *Life's short.*

He wanted Lacey, no question. And he wanted this business. But he sure as hell didn't want to be in the middle of another broken family.

"Lacey's a grown woman," Clay said. "Old enough to decide what she wants."

"Absolutely," Fox agreed. "And what she says she wants is this pipe dream."

Clay laughed softly. "I think it's a little more than a pipe dream." *It sure as hell better be.*

"You do? Well, here's where my long-term knowledge of Lacey Armstrong and your short-term attraction to her comes into play. As I told you, she's big on starting, big on planning, big on hoping and dreaming and talking. That's a large part of what took us apart. She just couldn't—" He shook his head, a little condescending, a little bemused. "Just wait until the first or second obstacle. She'll stop cold, give up, and start on her next dream. Believe me, I know her."

"Yeah, but you don't know me."

That earned him a look of surprise. "Maybe I don't, Clayton."

"Clay." God, he hated to be called Clayton.

That's who he reminded Clay of…his father. The thought made him a little sick.

"And I know what she needs," Fox said. "And, even more important, I know what Ashley needs."

"How could you?"

He gave Clay a wry smile. "I take it you don't have any children."

"None."

"And probably don't want them."

He didn't take the bait, but shrugged silently.

"So you cannot even imagine what I feel for that girl, and, by virtue of the way nature works, what I feel for her mother."

That stopped him cold. He was right, damn it. He couldn't imagine how this guy felt about a daughter, even one he hadn't bothered to see for more than a decade.

"More critical," Fox continued, "you cannot imagine how much Ashley needs to be part of a strong, loving, solid family again."

Actually, he could. "I'm sure that's a universal desire," he said.

"Indeed it is. And you're getting in the way of it."

"By helping Lacey build a resort and giving her a way to show Ashley how to go from disaster to a success?" How was that getting in the way?

"So you've really bought into Lacey's fairy tale."

"Hell yeah, I have. And I'm going to help her realize it." Wasn't he? Or was he going to use her to get out of his own professional jam?

"Very noble of you, Clay."

Okay, maybe not so noble.

"On the other hand," Fox said, "I'm going to help her make another dream come true and teach Ashley another important lesson. I'm going to be a father to our daughter, a partner to my former lover, and a presence in her life. I can provide her with stability, family, and"—he tilted his head in acknowledgment—"quite a bit of money."

Holy shit, no wonder the guy reminded him of his old man. He was more like Dad than Dad was. And Clay'd had this conversation once before, and lost.

"And I agree with you." Fox took a few steps closer, leveling Clay with a cold look. "It *will* be up to Lacey to decide if she wants stability, family, security, and love or"—he gestured toward Clay—"the thrill of the younger man. Which, I don't deny, is probably making her feel very girlish and giddy. She certainly sounded giddy with you."

A car engine on the road denied Clay the chance to reply.

"Ah, there's the person I'm meeting. Do you mind? I need some privacy."

Yeah, he minded, a lot. Right now he minded everything. Mostly he minded that he hadn't been completely straight with Lacey, and before they went one step farther toward the bedroom, he needed to tell her exactly why he was there.

If he lost the job, or a chance with her, or if that sent her into the arms of this guy, then she wasn't the right partner for Clay. Partner...of any kind.

Chapter 16

Lacey had assured Clay that he'd never find the place the locals called the SOB, since South of the Border had no sign, no written menu, no bar, no reservations, and very few tables. So they'd agreed to meet in the parking lot of the Super Min and walk to the restaurant.

Problem was, he couldn't find a damn parking spot. He finally pulled into the lot of the Fourway Motel across the street and, just as he climbed out of his truck, two familiar faces cruised by in a Mustang convertible that slowed down when the driver recognized him.

The G-girls. From behind the wheel, the frosted blonde, Grace, if he remembered correctly, gave him a long, slow once-over. Gloria was in the passenger seat.

"Gotta admit I didn't think I'd see you here tonight," Grace called out, turning down her car radio. "Hate to break the news to you, but this is a private party."

So what? He couldn't park in the motel lot? "I'm meeting someone," he said.

Next to her, the other woman leaned forward, her dark eyes much less predatory than her cousin's. "Don't tell me Lacey's going to be here?"

Okay, he wouldn't.

"She better not be," Grace said, all playfulness gone from her voice as she answered before Clay could. "Like I said, private party."

"I'll move the truck," he said, not sure what to make of the woman or what she was implying. "No worries."

Grace narrowed her eyes at him. "I'm not worried about your truck, honey. Believe me." With that, she hit the accelerator and drove off, disappearing around the corner.

"What the hell was that all about?" he asked out loud.

"That, my friend, is the Wicked Witch of Mimosa Key riding her red broomstick."

He turned at the sound of Lacey's voice, and any comeback caught in his throat as he checked her out. And checked her *out*. Whoa.

She crossed the street, high heels clicking to a rhythm that suddenly matched his heart as he drank in the tight black tank top, short jeans skirt, and some very sexy, strappy sandals with red toes peeking out.

"And you must be the Blistering Hot Witch." He reached out both hands, drinking in the sight of her. "Dressed to turn heads and break hearts."

Her reddish blonde curls had been straightened to a sleek and sexy sheen. She wore more makeup than he'd seen her wear before, including something really shiny on her lips that he just wanted to lick.

"This isn't a business meeting?" There was just enough tease in her voice to make him give in to the urge to put his arms around her and pull her close. When he did, woman's curves pressed against him top to bottom, and he closed his eyes and inhaled.

"Strawberry."

"I'm starting to get used to that nickname."

"I smell it."

"Not my idea, I have to admit."

"I like it." He nuzzled her in and took another whiff, letting his lips brush the ultrasmooth hair. "And this no-curl look is pretty, too." He inched back, grinning. "Did you get all dolled up for me?"

"I spent the day with my girlfriends at the Ritz and they were all about doing a shopping and beauty day, so I had a little pampering." She gave him a flirtatious wink. "The strawberry body splash was on the house."

"Then I love that house." He took her hand, her fingers silky from all that pampering, and started walking. "It's a good thing one of us spent the day working since the other was at the spa."

"I was working," she insisted, matching his steps. "Resort research. You mentioned that Casa Blanca really could use a good spa. The girls and I were dreaming up ideas. Jocelyn assures me we could make a mint, especially if we go organic. What did you do all day?"

"I did not get a strawberry pampering or"—he leaned down to look at her feet—"a bright red toe job."

She laughed, a feminine, sexy sound that did stupid things low in his belly. "Then what did you do?"

"Set up a CAD system in my apartment and did the first blueprint for a villa."

"Oh, really? That's..." Her voice trailed as her gaze slipped past him to a group of people across the street, and she frowned. "What's going on tonight?"

"I don't know, but G and G said it was a private party."

Her frown deepened as she surveyed the cars in the lot. "Why are all those are town council members going into the back of the Super Min?"

"Big run on milk?"

She shook her head. "I didn't read about any emergency sessions and, even if there were, they'd be in town hall. What did Grace and Gloria say?"

"Just that whatever it was, it was private. And they seemed surprised you'd be here."

"Grace Hartgrave is all talk," she said. "If you came anywhere near her, her husband, Ron, would sit on you and, trust me, you'd be crushed. She's a lot like her mother, Charity, a major busybody with too many opinions, but Glo, Gloria Vail, her cousin, is pretty cool."

"She seemed a little more laid-back," he agreed.

"I always liked Gloria." Her attention focused in on the group outside the convenience store. "What the heck are they doing?"

"I don't know, but I'm starving. Let's—"

"Lacey!" A woman called in a hushed whisper. "Lacey, come here."

Lacey turned, and they both spied a petite woman ducking behind a van in the Fourway parking lot. "Speaking of Gloria," she said. "What the..."

The woman looked terrified, gesturing wildly for Lacey to come closer while she looked left and right as if she would be caught any second. Lacey headed toward her and Clay followed, curious and on alert.

"What are you doing, Glo?" Lacey asked.

The other woman reached out and pulled Lacey closer, her big brown eyes wide. "Probably getting myself disowned, that's what. Listen, Lacey, I have to tell you something."

"What's up?"

"You are about to get screwed, that's what's up. And my family—my cousin and my aunt, especially—are holding the screwdriver. I hate that they're doing this to you, and behind your back, like cowards."

"What are they doing?" Lacey asked.

The woman looked pained, like she'd already said enough. "You just need to..." Gloria blew out a breath, then took another look around. "They're in the back of the Super Min having a totally off-the-books secret town council meeting. Well, not really a meeting, because then it wouldn't be off the books."

"To do what?" Lacey asked.

"To make sure you don't build a B and B, for one thing. A couple other people are getting stopped from building, too, but your plans are front and center."

"Why?" Clay asked. "What's the basis for the opposition?"

"Competition," she said. "My cousin and her husband, Ron, don't want any competition for the Fourway, and Aunt Charity wants Mimosa Key to stay firmly in the 1950s where, as you know, it is."

"Which is just stupid," Lacey said.

"Well, not to her. My Aunt Charity gets all kinds of tax revenue through all these loopholes. She's doctored up that bylaw book so bad it's like a novel she's written." The woman practically spat in disgust. "I'm the only one in the family who doesn't own a business, since I just work at Beachside Beauty, but I talk to a lot of people and they're sick of my aunt's hold on this place. She knows it, she's scared, and she's trying to make the town council work for her."

"What can she make them do?" Lacey asked.

"Tonight, she's making them read the bylaws and understand how it applies to zoning, then convincing them they need to have an emergency zoning meeting tomorrow that will uphold the five-bedroom maximum. The Fourway Motel, of course, is grandfathered in, and therefore remains the only hotel or motel on the island. There's a few long-term rentals, but not enough to make a dent in Charity or her kids' business."

Lacey looked at Clay, concern in her eyes. "What can we do?"

"Crash the meeting," he said.

"You have to," Glo agreed. "You have to get in there and fight my Aunt Charity or she is going to make all kinds of promises to the council that you can't possibly counter."

Clay snorted, understanding immediately. "Graft and corruption are the lifeblood of the building industry, I'm sorry to say. She wouldn't be the first business owner to throw money, booze, or votes at the people who make zoning decisions."

"So we just walk in and say she can't?" Lacey shook her head. "You don't know Charity Grambling."

"I know this business," he said. "If we go in there and point out the discrepancies in the bylaw book—"

"How can we do that tonight? We don't have that book."

Clay gave her arm a squeeze. "I have a copy in my

truck. I got it out of the Mimosa Key Library right after our first meeting. If the one she has doesn't match what was on record, that'll take some of the teeth out of her bite."

Glo beamed at him. "That's exactly what you need to do. But Lacey has to do the talking because this is Mimosa Key and strangers count for nothing."

"I will." Lacey reached over and gave Glo a quick hug. "Thanks for this." Then she turned to Clay. "Guess we better get those bylaws and kick some town council ass."

As they walked away, he put his arm around her shoulder and nestled her closer. "I like your new attitude, Strawberry. Is it the shoes?"

"And the company."

Lacey didn't let go of Clay's hand all the way back to the truck. She had no idea how to kick town council ass, but when he looked at her like that, she was ready to use these heels for more than making him notice her legs.

So what if the good ol' boys and girls of Mimosa Key were not her favorite people? Not all of the current town council members were in that clique. She and Clay would have to focus on the newer members and hope for the best. Surely she'd baked for some of them over the past few years. Didn't that count for something?

"All you need to remember, Lacey," Clay said as they crossed the Fourway Motel parking lot after retrieving his copy of the bylaws, "is that we have one single objective."

"To build?"

He laughed softly. "We are so far from building it isn't funny. There are about six thousand pieces of paper we need first, and the most important one from this group is a zoning permit. But we aren't ready to get that yet."

"Will we be by tomorrow?"

"No," he said, making her heart slip a little.

"But if they call an emergency meeting—"

"Page fourteen, section three." He held up the binder. "Nothing can be decided in an emergency session of the council that impacts the bylaws without a written notice that is posted a full two weeks in advance."

"You memorized the bylaws?" She couldn't believe it. "I've never even looked at them."

"You should. They're fascinating and totally old school. Of course I read the bylaws regarding building. Oh, and there is no such thing as a secret council meeting. In fact, according to page four, section five-A, if all five members of the town council are in a room together, any citizen of Mimosa Key has the right to call order and take notes, then publish those notes in the *Mimosa Gazette* the next day."

"Seriously?" She slowed her step, looking up at him, knowing there was awe on her face and not caring.

"What?" He laughed. "Did you think I wasn't a legit architect just because I didn't take some stinkin' exams? I'm doing my job. Although I like when you look at me like that. It's hot."

"Yeah? So are you."

He took the time to share a sexy smile with her. "Hold that thought for later. Now we have to concentrate on our goal."

"And you still haven't told me what it is."

"Buy two more weeks. If they want to call an emergency meeting tomorrow, they can. But our little book here says that they can't do anything in that meeting except set an agenda for another meeting two weeks later. We need those two weeks to find a loophole in the law that lets us build whatever we want. Which"—he squeezed her arm and reached for the door—"I think I've found."

"Really?"

He didn't answer because about ten sets of eyes greeted them on the other side of the door. The small group sat in an informal circle of chairs, as innocent as a church meeting but with a lot more guilt on their faces.

"Lacey!" Charity stood up, her arms planted on her narrow hips, her long nails crimson like blood drops against ill-fitting white pants. "This is a private meeting."

"No such thing," Lacey said, her voice cracking as she felt the weight of so many gazes on her. For a moment she had a flash of walking into the kitchen to greet her mother and getting a different version of the same comment every day.

You're wearing that *to school?*

And then she'd start to back down. Change her clothes. Question her decision. Doubt herself.

She cleared her throat. "I came to take notes that will be published in the next issue of the *Gazette*."

"What?" Three people asked the question at the same time.

She glanced around to do a quick count of council members in the gathering. Sam Lennox, the mayor; George Masterson, one of his cronies; a woman named Paula, who was a former neighbor of Lacey's; and that new guy with the heavy New York accent. That was four. Only four?

"Would you care to explain that, Lacey?" asked Sam

Lennox, a fairly reasonable mayor despite Charity's claim to have him in her back pocket.

But Lacey was still doing the math. If there were only four present, the plan wouldn't work. They couldn't threaten to take notes and publish them. They couldn't—

Her gaze fell on the face of Nora Alvarez, who headed up the Fourway Motel cleaning crew. Yes! She had been voted onto the council last month, no doubt through strings Charity and Grace pulled.

"It's in the bylaws," she said authoritatively. "It's on page..."

"Four," Clay supplied.

"Section..."

"Five-A," he finished.

Lacey threw him a grateful look. "I'm a citizen and resident of Mimosa Key and I have the right and privilege to attend any function where all five members of the town council are present and take notes." She beamed a smile right at Charity. "Our forefathers and -mothers were so smart and careful like that."

"I don't remember seeing that rule," Nora said, sliding a look to Charity.

Mayor Lennox stood. "Actually, Lacey's right. Come on in, Lacey. And bring your friend."

"This is Clay Walker. He's the architect I've hired to rebuild my property in Barefoot Bay." Just saying the words made it real and right. They'd never signed a contract, but Lacey didn't care.

They took two empty chairs slightly outside of the main circle of people and, after an awkward moment and some very dirty looks from Charity, talk continued.

Lacey tried to focus, but found herself returning the

glances of her neighbors. Glo avoided eye contact altogether, but Gracie stared her down, and so did several
others.

Charity remained standing as she spoke, her back to
Lacey and Clay. "As I was saying before we were so rudely
interrupted, in light of recent events we should have a brief
meeting—"

"Excuse me, Charity." Lacey interrupted and Charity
turned very slowly, her dark eyes tapering.

"Yes, Miss Armstrong?" she asked with the exaggerated patience of a kindergarten teacher who doesn't want
questions. "Would you like the full spelling of my name
for your report in the paper?"

"What recent events are you referring to?"

"The hurricane. Do you remember it?"

Several people laughed, but not the dark-haired young
man whose name Lacey didn't remember. "Aren't you the
one who rode it out in your bathtub with your little girl?"
he asked, that nasal Bronx sounding so out of place here.

"I am," Lacey said.

A few more mumbles and Charity's back grew stiffer.
"May I continue? As I was saying, we need to have an
emergency town council meeting tomorrow to review the
existing zoning restrictions as they will apply to multiple
new buildings that are proposed to—"

"Excuse me, Charity."

This interruption got a sigh of disgust that Ashley
would envy. "What is it, Lacey?"

Next to her, Clay gave a little nudge with the binder he
held. Taking his cue, Lacey stood. "You can't have an emergency town council meeting that affects zoning without two
weeks' written notice."

Charity stared at her, then tilted her head. "You're wrong."

"I'm right," Lacey replied. "I have the bylaws right here."

Charity reached under her seat and pulled out her heavily tagged binder. "Trust me, I know them. My father wrote them."

"With my grandfather," Lacey reminded them. She took the book from Clay, letting their fingers brush, which gave her a surprising kick of confidence. "I'd ask you to please look at..."

"Page fourteen, section three," Clay prompted.

A few people chuckled, but not Charity. She flipped open her book and ruffled pages with slightly shaky hands.

"There is no section three on page fourteen, Lacey. Perhaps you have an outdated version."

Was that possible? Did the library have an old version and she was about to look like a total fool? "I-I..."

"This book was notarized last year as the latest version of bylaws," Clay said, standing next to Lacey. "I was shown the paperwork by a lady by the name of Marian."

"Marian the Librarian," someone said. "She's never wrong."

Under thick powder blush, pink circles of frustration darkened Charity's cheeks. "Well, my version, which isn't notarized but is quite accurate, contains no such pronouncements, Lacey, and I—"

"Let me see it," Sam said, reaching for her book.

She held it. "No, Sam, this has been in my family for years. Only Vails and Gramblings handle this. It's like a Bible to us."

"Then open it and let me see it, Charity," Sam said. "And Lacey, bring that book here."

Lacey went forward, holding the binder open on page fourteen, her finger on section three, her heart hammering with every step. God, if Clay was wrong...

"Nice shoes, Lacey," Grace said as she passed. "You know what they're called, don't you?"

Lacey ignored her.

"Fuck-me pumps," Grace whispered under her breath, getting a laugh from the two people around her.

Sam took her book and placed it next to Charity's, frowning. For a long, quiet minute, no one said a word. Then Sam looked up and handed the book back to Lacey.

"This is for official record," he said to Nora. "So, as the secretary, I want you to note that for some reason these bylaws don't match. However, we will err on the side of caution and post a two-week notice before holding a zoning meeting."

A small murmur of voices filled the room as Lacey turned to give Clay a victorious smile.

"But in the interest of fairness and expediency," he added, "we'll meet tomorrow to set the agenda for that meeting. The town council can approve an agenda and if a citizen fails to get on that agenda, they can wait up to a year for the next zoning meeting."

A year? "How do I get on?" Lacey asked.

George Masterson stepped forward. "Any property owner who wants to have a structure approved that requires rezoning will have to appear at that meeting with preliminary plans detailed enough for the council to agree to put them on the agenda two weeks later."

Preliminary plans by tomorrow? Lacey swallowed. "How detailed?"

"Very detailed," Charity said.

"Define 'very.'" Everyone turned when Clay spoke, including Lacey. He stood now, and, like a lion ambling across the plains, he walked to the center of the circle, in complete control.

And poor Charity was his prey.

"Because, ma'am, if you'll turn to page twenty-five, section eight, and read real carefully and slow..." Clay drawled out the last word enough to send a little flutter through Lacey and maybe a slight sigh among a few other females in the crowd. "You'll see that getting on a zoning meeting agenda requires the property owner only to give a verbal description of the proposed structure, a timeline for building, a general budget estimate, and a declaration of intent to improve quality of life on Mimosa Key."

That was all? Lacey could have kissed him.

Charity, on the other hand, looked like she wanted to sucker-punch him. "That's correct, young man. And anyone"—she lifted a brow in Lacey's direction—"anyone who thinks they can cavalierly change the status quo of this island will find that last little item very hard to get by my, er, this council."

"What the heck do you mean?" Sam asked Charity.

"I mean, Sam, that quality of life is subjective and I expect this town council to recognize that fact no matter what smoke and mirrors and ridiculous promises Lacey or this tattooed man think they can throw at us tomorrow."

Clay bit back a smile. "We're up for that challenge, ma'am." He took the book from Sam's hand and nodded to Lacey for them to leave. "We have some work to do, Lacey."

He reached for her hand to walk her out. As they passed by Grace, Clay leaned down and whispered, "Actually, they're called fuck-me-*senseless* shoes. They're my favorite."

Chapter 17

Lacey practically fell against the door when they closed it behind them. "I can't believe we did that."

"We did that," Clay said, pulling her into him for a hug. "You were awesome."

The compliment warmed like a straight shot of whiskey, and the embrace was like a full-body all-muscle chaser that made her dizzy with joy.

"*You* were awesome." She held on to his biceps as he lifted her. "With the pages and the sections and the big save at the end! It was like a movie!"

He laughed, spinning her around, and, when her feet hit the ground, he kissed her. A celebratory kiss that didn't last long enough. She wanted more. She wanted so much more.

But he quickly turned them toward the car, wrapping an arm around her. "You still hungry?" he asked.

Not for dinner. "Maybe we should do takeout." *At your apartment.* "We have a lot of work to do tonight."

"Oookay." He drew out the word.

"What does that mean?"

"It means we might not get enough work done. We might get senseless."

She leaned close and lowered her voice to a whisper. "I can do senseless."

"Really." Very slowly, he turned so they were facing each other. "You're full of surprises, Lacey Armstrong, you know that? You rose to the occasion, headed into the lion's den, beat the crap out of your opponent, and now you want to…"

"I want to." Oh, God, she wanted to more than she wanted to breathe, eat, sleep, or live. She wanted him.

"You're sure?"

The question threw her. Wasn't he sure? Hadn't he just told Grace that was exactly what he wanted, or had she misread him?

"Or," she replied cautiously, "we could go to dinner and discuss preliminary building plans." Which wouldn't do a thing to quell the little sparks of need exploding all over her body. "That would be sensible."

"I like your idea better." He dipped his head close to her mouth, then fooled her by sliding his lips to her ear. "Strawberry," he whispered, sending sex-charged chills over every cell in her body.

The girls were right. This would be *fun*.

At the truck, he opened the passenger door for her. "Once we head down that path," he said, "you know there's no going back."

She put her foot up to climb in, the position forcing her

skirt way up her thigh. *Way* up. He stared at the skin the move revealed, then placed one hand right on her thigh, making her muscle tense in his palm.

She looked up at him, ready to hoist herself into the truck, but she stayed perfectly still. "I don't want to go back," she said softly, her gaze dropping to his mouth. "I want to go home with you."

He closed his eyes and stroked her thigh before letting go, the softest sigh in his throat. "Yeah," he said, leaning close to her face. "Yeah."

She closed her fingers around his neck, pulling him in for a kiss. His mouth opened instantly, her tongue delving against his. He returned the kiss as fire licked her lower half and his hand inched higher and higher until his finger grazed a slippery piece of silk between her legs.

"Go, Lacey," he murmured, giving her a gentle shove into the truck. "Hurry. Or this is going to get senseless right here in the street."

During the short drive they hardly spoke, which just made the tension thicker and the anticipation more palpable.

"So what changed your mind?" he finally asked, breaking the silence with a question she wasn't sure she could answer.

"My friends told me I should have more fun."

He laughed a little. "And they dressed you for tonight?"

She nodded.

"They aren't rooting for the ex?"

"I told you on the phone today what's going on there. I don't have feelings for David." Certainly nothing like the fluttery, twisting, rollercoaster things going on inside her right now. "I doubt he'll be here very long."

"I saw him at Barefoot Bay today."

She turned to him, surprised. "You did? What was he doing up there?"

"Walking around. Talking on the phone to arrange a meeting with someone. Warning me to stay away from you."

Who would he be meeting? But Clay's last statement was the one that got her attention. "He really has no right to say that to you. None at all. Other than his being Ashley's father, he and I have no connection."

"That's a pretty powerful connection." He pulled into the rental complex, finally letting go of her leg to shut off the ignition. After a second, he turned to her, all humor gone from his eyes. "Family is the most powerful pull, you know."

There was just enough hurt in his voice to remind her that his family had caused some deep pain. "I know, but he's not my family."

"He wants to be."

She touched his jaw, trailing a finger over the hint of whiskers. "One more word about David and the mood will officially be killed."

He angled his head, got his mouth on her palm, and kissed. "You look pretty with the sunset behind you," he said. "I could draw you like this."

"I'd rather you kiss me like this," she said, closing the space to take what she wanted. This kiss was softer, easier, slower than any other. When they parted, neither spoke, but opened their doors and climbed out of the truck. She waited by her side, unsure of where to go until he came around and led her toward the one-story stucco building.

"You want to walk on the beach first?" he asked.

"No."

He put his key in the door. "You want to order pizza?"

She almost laughed. "No."

"You want to start working on the presentation?"

"Absolutely not." She stepped inside the darkened apartment and he followed, closing the door. "Do you?"

He paused, something unreadable in his eyes.

"Didn't you say you wanted to tell me something?" she asked. "When you texted about dinner?"

"Later." He locked the door behind him. "Right now I just want to be one hundred and fifty percent certain you know exactly what you're doing."

"I know what I'm doing."

He put his hands on her waist, very carefully, like she was made of glass. "What I want to avoid is any miscommunication. You know where I stand, right?"

No commitments, no relationships, no women who might break his heart. "I do." She slid her hands around his back, pulled him into her body, and stood on the tips of her sexy shoes to whisper in his ear. "You know what's wrong with you, Clay Walker?"

"What?"

"You have too much sense for me and my senseless shoes."

He didn't need to hear another word, devouring her mouth and dragging her into the golden shadows of sunset that warmed the apartment.

He crushed her lips with a kiss she couldn't have stopped if she'd wanted to, tongues clashing with purpose instead of play. Heat licked up her belly like an electrical current, sending fire everywhere he touched.

Everywhere. Down her back, over her rear, up the sides, and—oh, then he cupped her breasts with strong, capable, determined hands.

She cried softly at the touch, arching her back to force her stomach against his hard-on until he backed her against the wall.

"Bedroom?" she murmured.

"Too far." He pushed against her and she rocked right back, driving her hips into a hard-on that strained his zipper, already moving the way they were meant to move, already gripping his backside and holding him right where she wanted him to be.

He dragged her T-shirt up, revealing a lacy black bra that brought a soft moan of appreciation from his throat. Not bothering to take off her shirt, he palmed the flimsy lingerie, her nipple straining against the satin cup.

He tweaked and stroked, whispered her name, and trailed kisses into her cleavage. Hot, wet, hungry kisses that made her worship his mouth and what it could do to her. She bowed her back so he could undo her bra with one hand. Together, they pulled the shirt and bra over her head, sending all of it down to the floor and leaving her breasts naked and exposed, raw and achy.

"Let me look at you," he said gruffly, bracing on one hand as she closed her eyes and flattened her arms to the wall, giving him a full view and complete access.

Which he took, greedily, bending his knees to get to her breasts, his mouth seeking a connection, hungry to taste her, pulling more whimpers and sighs and soft, soft cries of delight from her.

She grabbed him by the hair, the shoulders, pushing him down to a kneel. That mouth. That mouth. She wanted him on her, wanted to touch his long, soft hair and guide his lips between her legs.

He caressed her thighs, pushing her skirt up around her waist to reveal her black lace panties.

He looked up with a smile. "Those girls know how to dress you for a date."

"Zoe," she said.

"I like her."

"She tried to get me to buy edible."

He laughed as he kissed her thigh, his tongue already slipping into the edge of the black silk. "I like her even more."

"Clay . . ." She could barely speak, her legs and arms splayed against the wall, her fingers digging in so hard she could peel the paint. "Kiss me there."

"I plan on it." He used one finger to tug the silk away from her, inhaling deeply, appreciatively, making her feel so ridiculously feminine she wanted to sob.

He kissed the swollen spot and she closed her eyes, focused on the incredible sweetness of his mouth. Then he licked, very slowly, dragging the tip of his tongue over her until she thought her legs would buckle and her head would explode and the breath she held would come whooshing out when she cried for mercy.

"Clay," she cried. "Don't stop. Please, *please*."

"Not a chance." He tugged at the panties, pulling them down, helping her step out of them. As soon as they were gone he kissed his way back up her thighs, back to where she wanted him most. There.

Curling his tongue like a ribbon around her skin, he sucked her juices, and she reveled in every sensation and sound, in the blood coursing through her with each powerful slide of his tongue. Lights exploded behind her eyes and her pulse hammered and she felt like she was floating through air, utterly lost. Nothing in the world mattered but the need to roll against his mouth and feel each sensation ripple through her, closer and closer to release.

"Oh my gawd, oh my gawd, oh…my…there." She writhed against the wall, his name on her lips, completely surrendering to his tongue and fingers. A sharp twist of pressure, a sweet twinge of tension, then a peak of delicious pain and pleasure so powerful it was almost unbearable.

She rocked into an orgasm, abandoned and wild, her breath nothing but shallow desperation as she moved against his mouth.

Then there were just tender aftershocks and ragged breaths, and the impossible heavy ache in her legs that made them wobble as she started to slide down the wall.

"Now I know," she whispered.

"Now you know what?"

"Why this is so much fun." She hit the floor with a soft thud, her head hanging to the side like a drunk.

"We just got started having fun, darlin'."

But when she looked at him, something swelled up in her chest, and it wasn't laughter. Something squeezed at her heart and clutched her whole body and made her want to reach out to this beautiful, sexy, amazing man and, dear God, it wasn't *fun*.

It kind of hurt inside. And there was nothing *fun* about that at all.

"Lacey, what's wrong?"

"Oh, shit, Clay. I might have made a mistake."

Big, big mistake. God*damn* it. Clay should have known better.

"There's a reason they call it senseless," he said softly, stroking some hair that had fallen in her face. "Because there's no common sense involved. And now you're sorry, aren't you?"

"Not exactly sorry." She gave him a sheepish smile. "Just a little overwhelmed. That's scary."

Damn it. "You don't have to be scared, Lacey. I won't..." What wouldn't he do? Use her and leave?

Yes he would. He'd use her for a job he wanted more than anything, and sex he wanted just as badly. But, Jesus, he did not want a good woman with a nice kid and a decent life and a heart of gold, because all of that stuff came with too much potential for disaster. He'd had enough family for one lifetime, thank you very much.

"Wow, you look like you're in pain, Clay."

He used the obvious excuse and looked down. "A little."

She reached to the tent of his jeans, her fingers tentative. For a second he did nothing, the need for her to touch him way bigger than anything he felt in his head or heart. But then he closed his hand over her wrist.

"Reciprocation isn't necessary, Lacey."

"I want to."

"You just said you made a mistake."

"I thought sex would be fun."

He gave a rueful laugh. "Sorry to disappoint."

"No, no, that's not what I mean. I thought that's *all* it would be."

He slowly pushed up, still holding her hand and bringing her with him. "I know you did. So what happened?"

"I like you."

"Yep, big mistake."

"Is it?" She sounded hopeful. So damn hopeful. "I just want to work with you. And, you know, *sleep* with you. Only not much sleeping since I have to be home at night."

Of course she did, because she had a family. A daughter who needed her. An ex who wanted her.

She swiped her hand through her hair, frowning as though she wasn't used to the straight locks, and suddenly realizing she was naked from the waist up. "Shit, what a mess."

"You're not a mess, Lacey. You're beautiful. But here, get comfortable." He scooped up her top and handed it to her, helping her slip it over her head, then tugged her skirt back down. Her bra and panties were still on the floor, and neither of them made a move to get them.

But not because they'd be coming right back off. He knew that. "You want something to drink?" he asked. "Water? Soda? Beer?"

"Water." She followed him through the living area, past the drafting table he'd set up, to the galley kitchen. While he got the water, she stood at the sliders that led out to a small deck that faced the indigo water, nearly the same color as the late evening sky.

He handed her a bottle. "I have some fruit and stuff for a sandwich, if you're hungry."

She shook her head and opened the water bottle. "No, thanks."

That look in her eyes fisted his chest again, so he got behind her, sharing the view, letting their bodies touch front to back because, hell, it seemed he couldn't be in the same room without making contact.

"It's going to be one tough resort to build," he said after taking a sip of water.

"Because of the zoning restrictions?"

"Your zone. My restrictions."

"I think I just proved I have no restrictions." She let her

head fall back against his chest, resignation in her sigh. "And you sure know your way around my zone."

There went his damn erection again. "You talk dirty, little lady, and I'm going to start getting senseless again."

She didn't say anything, but the silence and her steady breathing only made him harder against her. One more minute and he would be reaching up to get a handful of soft, gorgeous breast. One more minute and he could turn her around and have that skirt hiked all the way up again. One more minute and he'd lose this fight.

"You're upset with me," she said.

"I'm not upset. I might not be walking normally in the meeting tomorrow, but I'm getting used to the fact that Barefoot Bay sits squarely in the state of arousal."

Half turning, she looked up at him. "Really?"

"You turn me on," he admitted. "You have since the moment I met you on the beach."

"I was a bitch."

"A bitch with a smokin'-hot body and a smart mouth. And, man, that hair."

She shook her head. "I don't have a smokin'-hot body! I need to lose at least ten pounds."

"Not in any of the places I just handled you don't." He took a slide over her hip, just to make the point. Perfect.

"I'm older than you are. By..." She hesitated. "Seven years."

"You worry about numbers too much." He took a drink of his water to wet his throat, which was getting more parched with her ass planted against his poor aching hard-on. "Face it, Lacey, you're just not a roll-in-the-hay-and-walk-away kind of girl."

"I'm not a girl, Clay. I'm a woman."

"I know, I know. Seven years. I heard you. But you—"

She turned. "You're just as afraid," she said, pointing a finger in his face. "You use your bad experience as an excuse, and you're scared to death of failing at a relationship, so you don't try. You know, we're more alike than I realized."

He scratched his chin and thought about all the different ways he could respond, but maybe she was right. "Look, Lacey, I don't want to get so tight with anyone that I get tangled and strangled. Maybe you do, and maybe you ought to give that guy who wants you back another shot."

"I don't want to give him another shot," she said vehemently. "I want—"

Don't say it. Don't say it.

"You."

Shit.

"For sex and fun," she added quickly. "And to stand by my side when I kick more town council ass tomorrow and to help me win the zoning fight and to build this resort. You know, the one *you've* convinced me to build. That's what I want, Clay. You in?"

He smiled slowly. "I like when you get all worked up."

"I'll take that as a yes."

"Yes, but I want to add one stipulation to this verbal contract." He closed his hands over her cheeks and held her face, forcing her to look straight into his eyes, knowing that this was the perfect time to tell her the real reason he'd left his father's firm.

No. Not tonight. It would be way too much for her on top of this, and the unexpected meeting tomorrow. Lacey would lunge at an excuse like that and everything would stop.

In fact, tomorrow he might even be able to go over to

the mainland and get some paperwork that would explain it all to her.

Or was he the one making excuses now?

"You're scaring me, Clay. Why are you thinking so hard about this stipulation?"

"Just trying to get the right words." He took a breath, pulled her closer. "Just listen to me. If at any time this thing, this *us,* doesn't work for you on any level, either professional or personal or physical, just let me know and we stop."

"This us?" she laughed. "When you put it that way..."

"I'm serious, Lacey. Will you agree to that?"

"You know what you're doing, Clay?"

God, no. That was the problem. "What?"

"You're giving an easy way out to a woman who loves to find an easy way out."

He leaned forward and kissed her forehead. "I know what I'm doing." At least, he hoped he did.

Chapter 18

~

"And that is why the proposed structure being built by property owner Lacey Armstrong of Barefoot Bay should be added to the agenda of the next Mimosa Key zoning meeting." Lacey took a deep breath and closed her eyes, so grateful to be done. "Thank you for your time, ladies and—ladies."

Three sets of hands clapped loudly and vigorously from the audience lounging around Jocelyn's suite at the Ritz-Carlton.

"You are going to rock, Lacey," Zoe exclaimed.

"I hope so." Lacey straightened the two presentation boards she'd picked up at Clay's apartment that morning, trying not to think about how dead sexy he'd looked when he answered the door wearing nothing but boxers.

He'd worked all night on some preliminary drawings, focused exclusively on the main building. He'd gone to

Fort Myers to get county permit information he thought they might need, so Lacey had decided to use the time before the meeting to rehearse for her friends.

"Aren't you going to talk about the villa concept?" Tessa asked. "That's what really sets this resort apart."

"We want to hold back as much as we can and drop that bomb in the actual zoning meeting. The only thing that matters today is getting on the agenda. I think this is enough, don't you?"

"Absolutely," Jocelyn agreed. "But it will be bigger, won't it?"

Lacey sighed, curling up on the sofa next to Tessa. "Right now, everything's a pipe dream. First I have to close on the two properties next to mine, and then I have to figure out how much insurance money is left. I know Clay is 'free' at this point, but once we break ground, I am going to need some serious cash." She let her head fall back. "It's so daunting to even think about how to get that money."

"Hey." Tessa tapped her leg. "Don't look at the obstacles. You'll trip."

Lacey smiled. "I'm trying."

When none of them said anything for a second, Lacey opened her eyes just in time to catch some silent communication among the three of them.

"What?" she demanded.

Tessa and Jocelyn shared a long look, but Zoe blew out a breath. "Oh, for crying out loud, tell her now. Don't wait until after the stupid meeting."

"Tell me what?"

"No," Jocelyn said. "I'm still ironing out some details."

"But she should know," Zoe insisted.

"It would help her during today's presentation."

Lacey sat up slowly. "What are you guys talking about?"

Three not-so-innocent faces stared back at her and finally, Jocelyn nodded to Tessa.

"We want to invest."

Lacey blinked at her. "Invest?" For a moment Lacey could only stare. And work to keep her jaw from dropping. "You guys want to invest in Casa Blanca?"

"They do," Zoe said, true sadness in her expression. "I can't afford to give you anything but moral support."

"But we can give you actual cash," Jocelyn said. "And we want to. We really do."

A whole new set of chills danced over her while her eyes filled with grateful tears. "You would do that for me? How can you do that?"

Tessa shrugged. "Billy and I weren't running a nonprofit company to create organic farms, you know. And the divorce settlement was generous." She leaned closer. "I want to do something extraordinary with that money and, Lacey, I believe in you. As long as we can make everything as organic as possible."

Lacey nodded. "I can do organic."

"And," Tessa added, "gardens where you grow your own food. Or..." She dragged out the last word and added a meaningful look. "Where *I* grow your food."

It took a second to sink in. "You grow it?"

"I want to stay and help you, Lacey." Tessa put her hand on Lacey's to underscore the message. "I want to stay here and create a completely natural, all-organic farm that feeds your resort."

"Which means she leaves Arizona," Zoe said glumly.

"And moves here." The idea wrapped around Lacey's

heart so tightly it threatened to stop her pulse. Tessa here, with her. "Oh my God, Tess. That would be heaven."

"You know I'm going to be a pain about pesticides and processed foods, don't you?"

"I will swear off both of them," Lacey promised.

"And if you want to open in a year, preliminary soil preparation should start, like, almost immediately. In a few months at the latest."

The hope squeezed her chest, making her breathless. "Can you come to the meeting tonight? The organic gardens should be part of the plan we present. I think it would go a long way to showing exactly what kind of resort we're building."

"Of course I can."

Lacey turned to Jocelyn. "And you want to invest, too?"

"Silently. I'm not growing anything or making grand appearances anywhere. But, yes." She added her hand to Lacey's and Tessa's. "I'm working on getting you a cash infusion that should help you really get rolling on the building and gardens."

Words just couldn't form. Not adequate ones, anyway. "You are the most amazing friends." Lacey's voice broke.

"I just suck in general," Zoe said. "I don't have a dime and can't leave my aunt Pasha."

"Zoe, just you being here is more than enough," Lacey said. "Will you all come with me this afternoon?"

Jocelyn's smile faded. "Not me."

"Just meet at the town hall," Lacey said quickly. "Please."

Finally, she nodded. "For you. To the town hall."

"Oh my God!" Lacey shrieked softly. "I have partners!"

"Lots of them," Zoe said. "Silent Jocelyn, organic Tessa, and don't forget the man with the magic drafting tool."

"That's just the problem," she confessed on a sigh. "I can't forget him for one minute."

"So when do we get details on last night?" Zoe asked.

"Let's just put it this way: He liked your choice of underwear." And, because they were her best friends *and* partners, she told them everything. Well, *almost* everything.

Word must have gotten out about the meeting. A few dozen people peppered the community meeting room in Mimosa Key's town hall, with Charity and Patience seated in the front, surrounded by supporters. A handful of other familiar faces filled the front row of folding chairs, while others sat in small groups of two and three, and some people stood in the back at a coffee station.

The low buzz of conversation stopped when Lacey entered with Jocelyn, Tessa, and Zoe. Clay had texted that he'd meet them here but hadn't arrived yet, making Lacey taut with nerves and a vague sense of disappointment.

She squashed any doubts. He'd *be* there.

"Where's the one who tipped you off?" Zoe whispered.

Lacey glanced around but couldn't find Gloria Vail. "Not here."

"She's probably swimming in the bottom of the bay."

Lacey bit back a laugh. "They're not that bad." She hoped. Charity was sending some dagger-like looks Lacey's way, and her sister, Patti, offered a cool, but less deadly, nod.

The long council table remained empty as no members were seated yet, so Lacey led her friends to some seats. in the audience. She kept glancing at the door for Clay, but instead saw another man with a familiar face that had graced front pages of the *Mimosa Gazette* for much of Lacey's teenage years.

Will Palmer had been the island's golden boy, blazing through the minor leagues and on his way to the pros, last she'd heard. But in the past few years—

"Oh, shit." Next to Lacey, Jocelyn murmured the curse as color drained from her face.

"What's the matter?"

"My phone's vibrating," she said, stabbing her hand into her bag, lowering her head, hiding her face.

"Jocelyn?" Will approached slowly, but Jocelyn popped up to climb over Lacey to get out of the row.

"I have to take this call."

"Jocelyn," Will called. "Please, wait."

She froze, giving Lacey a pleading look. Then she suddenly composed herself and faced him.

"Hello." She reached out a hand. "How are you, Will?"

His eyes flickered with surprise. "Fine. And you?"

"Great. Oh"—she wiggled the phone—"'scuze me for a second." She walked out, leaving him slightly slack-jawed.

"Hi," Lacey said, trying to cover the awkward moment, looking up at the sizable athlete. "I don't know if you remember me. I'm Lacey Armstrong."

"Hello." He shook her hand, but his attention was still on Jocelyn, giving Lacey a chance to take in how time had changed him. He wasn't as boyishly cute as he had been in his baseball heyday, but he was still seriously tall, dark, and handsome.

"I didn't know you were back in Mimosa Key," she said. "Are you visiting or are you here for good?"

"I'm back," he said. "As a matter of fact, I'm picking

up some work with all the construction going on. That's why I came by today."

Construction? That was a huge step down from major league baseball. "What kind of work? I'll hopefully be looking for some people."

"I've been sort of specializing in carpentry and wood-work, but, really I can do anything. Stucco, drywall, you name it."

"I'll remember that," she said as the council began to take their seats.

Once again Lacey turned to the door, willing Clay to show. Where was he? He'd texted a few hours ago that he was still in Fort Myers but he'd be here on time.

"Where did Jocelyn go?" Tessa asked when she and Zoe came back from a stop in the ladies' room, sliding in right behind Lacey. "She just blew by us in a big fat hurry."

"She's taking a call," Lacey told them.

The slam of Mayor Sam Lennox's gavel silenced the conversation. Lacey once again checked the door for Clay, flinching a little when David entered instead, with Ashley close to his side.

Wouldn't there be enough tension without David look-ing judgmental and Ashley frowning in disapproval at Clay?

If Clay ever got there.

Ashley spotted her and waved, but David guided them to seats across the aisle with a wink to Lacey. "Go get 'em, Tiger," he mouthed.

"Good luck, Mommy," Ashley added. "I love you."

Oh. Her heart turned upside down, tumbled, and landed somewhere in her shoes. Because at the end of the day, Ashley was the one who mattered the most. And, honestly, when was the last time her daughter had said *I love you*?

Was that David's influence?

"Where the hell is Clay?" Tessa asked.

"Good question." Lacey tried to focus, but her mind was whirring. If she had to do this alone, would she?

If Clay didn't show, then she had a good reason—

"Call to order an emergency meeting of the Mimosa Key Town Council!" The gavel slammed a second time, and Lacey scanned the front table for a friendly face.

The mayor was a longtime resident of the island, possibly opposed to changing zoning laws. A political beast who loved the role of heading the town council, he could totally be corrupted by Charity but swayed by re-election votes. Nora Alvarez was on Charity's payroll, but something about her seemed fair and smart. Plus, wouldn't she want to expand her cleaning business to do work for Lacey, too?

"Who's the escapee from *The Sopranos*?" Zoe leaned forward to ask in Lacey's ear.

"New guy from New York," Lacey whispered back. "Rocco something."

"Friend or foe?"

"Don't know."

"And the bald eagle?"

Lacey eyed George Masterson and remembered how he'd jumped to help Charity last night. "I think he's in bed with Charity."

"Ewww. Thanks for that lovely visual that will never leave my brain."

Lacey shushed her as the mayor covered some housekeeping details. When given the floor, George Masterson moved to set the agenda for the September fifteenth meeting, calling to the floor anyone who wanted to present at that time.

Lacey swallowed and gave one last look toward the door, her heart sinking. If no one asked a question that only an architect could answer, she could do this. But she wanted him there. The fact that he wasn't just hurt.

"Hey." Tessa touched her shoulder. "Stop looking for reasons not to get up there."

"I'm not," Lacey whispered. "I just..."

Scanning the room, her gaze fell on Ashley, who gave her a wide, warm smile, her eyes filled with admiration and expectation.

She might have reasons to chicken out, but right there sat the reason to walk up to that council and make her demands. She had to show Ashley how to be strong and independent, had to show her daughter how to get what you want in life, even if your partner lets you down. *Especially* if your partner lets you down.

Slowly rising to her feet, she felt Tessa give her a nudge and heard Zoe whisper, "Knock 'em dead, Lace."

She stepped into the aisle along with a few other people petitioning for something they wanted but might not get. Change was never easy in Mimosa Key, and the knowledge of that was plain to see on her neighbors' faces.

"Let's do this alphabetically," Mayor Lennox suggested. "That'd make you first, Lacey."

"All right," she agreed brightly, carrying the two presentation boards to the podium while the other speakers sat in the second row. Unzipping the case with remarkably steady fingers, she set her typed-up comments in front of her and pulled the first board, Clay's blue-line of the site overview.

They needed only a verbal description according to

the bylaws, but she and Clay both felt that this would be more powerful and sway any council members sitting on the fence.

She and Clay. Except now it was just her.

"Good afternoon," she said, her voice echoing and causing a siren-like feedback on the mike. She backed away and refused to let it throw her. "My name is Lacey Armstrong and I'm here to request a slot on the—"

"I object." Charity stood and stared hard at the mayor. "Save our time, Sam, and let's move to the next person."

A soft murmur rolled through the crowd.

"Excuse me, Charity," Lacey said, "but I haven't even had a chance to show you what I'm building."

"Don't have to. I'm not objecting to your building."

"Then what are you objecting to?" Sam Lennox asked.

"Who's building it."

"What are you talking about?" Lacey asked. "How do you even know who's building it?"

"Because everyone on this island knows you're working, among other things, with that man named Clayton Walker."

"Clay Walker," she corrected, feeling heat rise and wishing to God that Ashley wasn't in this room. "And I fail to see how that has any relevance." His name wasn't even on this presentation. He'd insisted on that.

And he *wasn't even in this room.*

For the first time, a vine of bad, bad feeling slithered up her chest.

"Me too," Paula Reddick chimed in from the front table. "I, for one, would like to see the plans, so zip it, Charity."

The older woman's eyes flew open. "I will not zip it

and I will not allow anything to be built on this island by someone who is not qualified to build."

Oh, *that's* what this was about. His licensing. The tendril of worry loosened as she checked the door again, but no one had entered the room, not even Jocelyn.

She had to do this on her own, straightforward and unafraid.

"Charity, if you're referring to Mr. Walker's licenses, they are not required by any law in any state in order for him to design—"

"I'm talking about his . . . his . . ." She gestured to Patti, who shoved some papers closer. Then Charity adjusted her reading glasses and cleared her throat. "His indictment by the FBI for providing fraudulent documents and attempting to obstruct justice in a case against a North Carolina chancellor of secondary education."

Lacey gripped the podium, because her legs couldn't be trusted to hold her upright.

"What?" She barely whispered the question because there were too many other words swimming in her head. *Indictment. FBI. Fraudulent. Obstruct justice.*

"What exactly are you talking about?" Sam demanded. "What do you have on this Clayton Walker?"

"Clay," Lacey said softly. "His name is Clay." Or at least she thought it was. Come to think of it, she'd never seen a driver's license, let alone an architectural license. She'd never called a reference or seen a resume.

All she'd done was let him melt her brain and body and hand him the job. And now he wasn't even here to face the music. And the tune was pretty ugly.

"I'm talking about *this*." Gripping pages of computer printouts, Charity marched to the front, her sneakers squeaking on the linoleum like Nurse Ratched on her way to stick a needle in someone.

The audience murmured and mumbled, and Lacey stole a look at David, who whispered something to Ashley, then he got up and hustled out of the room. Shame and shock prickled at Lacey's skin, a fine sheen of perspiration tickling the nape of her neck.

Toward the back, Tessa and Zoe held hands, leaning forward like they'd been driven to the edge of their seats. Grace Hartgrave looked smug, and a lot of familiar faces of neighbors, friends, and even some of her baking customers looked confused.

And Clay Walker, or whoever the hell he claimed to be, was suspiciously absent.

Meanwhile, Charity slapped her papers in front of the town council, a copy for each of them, with the officiousness of a teacher handing out failed tests. "I just printed these off today, from the state attorney's office in North Carolina." She turned to Lacey. "Of course, maybe you were too blinded by his good looks to do any of your own homework."

Was that possible? She had Googled him. There was plenty about his father, but no mention of Clay, or the FBI. Her heart slipped down a few notches, like her wet palms on the warm wood of the podium.

Sam rifled through the papers. "Have you seen this, Lacey? Says here Clayton Walker of Clayton Walker Architecture and Design has been indicted—"

"It's his father!" The explanation suddenly seemed so clear she practically barked it into the microphone, shutting up Sam and the audience. "They must be talking about his father, Clayton Walker," she added quickly. "It's a common mistake because of the names and the similar work, but they are two very different men and my architect no longer works for Clayton Walker. Those papers, whatever you have, are not about the same man who's been helping me."

"Actually, they are." Clay's voice came from the back of the room, the door he'd just burst through still open. "Those articles are about me."

Chapter 19

ᨶ

For a second Lacey felt nothing but numb. Blank brain, deadened heart, no sensation. Just shocked and speechless as she watched the man she'd let take her to an orgasm with nothing but his mouth bound up the aisle of the meeting room, his long hair fluttering around his handsome face, his broad shoulders braced as if he were going into battle, his summer-sky blue eyes locked on her.

Charity was right. She'd been taken by his good looks. How could she be such a fool?

"However, every charge was dropped," he continued as he strode toward the front. "That information is out of date and invalid, erased from all records, and I have an affidavit to prove that, notarized just one hour ago by the Lee County clerk of court."

"Just one minute," Charity said.

"Excuse me," Mayor Lennox interjected.

"I will explain everything," Clay insisted.

"No way!" Charity all but stomped her foot. "Page three, section three, subsection B of the Mimosa Key bylaws—and don't you dare try to contradict me, young man—says that unless you're a resident of Mimosa Key, you're not allowed to address this council without prior approval. You don't have it, so sit down."

He kept coming, his eyes on Lacey. Eyes loaded with apology, regret, and no small amount of anger. "Damn stupidest law I ever heard, so I'm going to speak anyway."

"Oh, no you are not." Charity was beet red and nearly choking now. "Everything you say is inadmissible—"

"This isn't a court!" Lacey hollered over the sound of the crowd. "Let him talk, for God's sake."

"It's the way we run our town, Lacey," the mayor said.

"I need to know." She breathed the words, but the microphone picked them up and amplified her heartache all through the room.

Lacey searched his face, looking for the truth, for an explanation, for some sign that he hadn't lied to her all this time.

No need to sign a contract.

No need to put my name on the boards.

No need to contact my father's company. Just let me tell you how ruthless he is.

Had she been played, or what?

"Sorry, son," Mayor Lennox said. "We can't change the rules. I assume Lacey knows all this and she can speak on your behalf."

"I will speak on my behalf." Clay parked himself right in front of the council table. "That account is old and false."

"Were you indicted?" Lacey asked.

"No, but there was an investigation, and every single charge was dropped."

"See?" Charity said, leaping forward and poking a bony finger at Clay as though he'd just confessed murder. "Lacey doesn't even know who she's working with. She doesn't have a clue who this man is and we're going to let him slap down some kind of monstrosity on Barefoot Bay and ruin the unspoiled beauty of the last perfect place on earth? I don't think so."

Charity's dramatic words rang through the meeting room, causing another rumble of response.

"You cannot speak to this council, sir," Mayor Lennox said. "If you don't leave, we will have to get Security to escort you."

Oh, that would be just perfect. Let's bring Officer Garrison in here and cuff Lacey's lover in front of her daughter and the friends who'd just vowed their belief in her. Really, could the day get any better?

"What do you have to say, Lacey?" Charity demanded.

She just swallowed and dug for words of defense, but there were none.

She knew virtually nothing about Clay Walker, and yet she'd opened her business, her project, her heart, and, oh hell, *her legs* to him. Stupid, stupid, *stupid*.

"Let the guy talk, for crying out loud!" Zoe called from the back. "What is this, the Salem Witch Trials?"

That got a small reaction of laughter, but Clay held up his hand. "I'll leave, but, please, the false allegations have nothing to do with Lacey Armstrong's proposed property getting on your September fifteenth agenda. I won't say anything now, but let her speak." He finally looked at Lacey, a world of sorry in his eyes that reached right down her throat and seized her heart. "You don't need me to do this. You can do this. You *can*."

The emphasis on the last word wasn't lost on her as he took a slow step backward, like the move was the hardest thing he'd ever done. How could she know? How could she know anything he'd told her was true, and why hadn't he told her earlier about this part of his past?

Had he even told her the truth about his father and the woman who'd broken Clay's heart? Or was that an elaborate tale to cover the real reason he didn't work for his dad anymore? The real reason he hadn't put his name on any of the presentation boards and no doubt the *truth* about why he didn't have those seven licenses he needed?

He pivoted and walked out, the entire room staring after him. Including Ashley.

Oh, Lord. Ashley had witnessed the whole thing. And now she'd witness her mother crumbling and quitting and buckling under the weight of the oldest excuse of all.

I was duped by a sexy guy.

"You may speak now, Lacey," Mayor Lennox said.

But everything in Lacey screamed not to.

C'mon, Lacey, you can't do this now. Give up, go home, settle for less than you deserve.

Shut the hell up, demons.

Taking a deep breath, she dug for something she knew she had to have, with or without Clay Walker. Resolve. Tenacity. Dogged stubbornness not to let Charity Grambling win and leave Lacey Armstrong with one big *excuse*.

"This information is entirely irrelevant to what I'm asking for today," she said, gesturing to the newspaper that was still being passed among the council members. "First of all, if you look closely at my presentation, there is no specific architectural firm attached to the plans and nothing has yet been filed with the state or county. All I want is to be on the agenda for September fifteenth, which will give me time to address these issues."

"Not enough time," Charity insisted.

Lacey closed her eyes, still mining inner strength. "That's all the time I need," she said.

"Is this man your architect and builder, Lacey?" George Masterson asked, his lip curled as he read the paper.

"I'm not sure who my architect is going to be," she said firmly. "But it's a moot point as far as the upcoming agenda."

"I agree," Paula said quickly. "Let's put her on the agenda and move on."

"I second that," Rocco chimed in. "That account lifted off the Internet is questionable at best. Let her present, let her make her plea, and let her use who she wants and prepare to defend him on the fifteenth." He drummed the table in front of him. "Let's move it. There's a Yankees game on in twenty minutes."

"Sorry, but this newspaper clipping is enough for me to say no," Masterson said.

"Please hear me out," Lacey said, earning instant silence and all their attention. She searched her brain for her opening lines, for what she'd planned to say about her resort and all the jobs it could create and Mimosa Key's need to get into the next century.

But she couldn't think of anything. Except Ashley still sitting in the seat where David had left her.

Ashley.

All the feasibility notes, the town codes, and the target marketing points she'd made for this presentation just evaporated from her brain. None of them mattered, really.

"Six weeks ago, my home and business were wiped away in one storm," she said quietly. "As many of you know, I stayed alive and kept my daughter safe in a bathtub with a mattress over our heads."

A soft mumbling rolled through the room.

Yes, she did.

That's a fact.

She was hit hard up there at Barefoot Bay.

Buoyed by the tiny bit of support, she kept talking. "The only thing that kept me going that night was the chance to realize a dream that I believe could be a long-term and positive change for my family and for this island. All I am asking for is a slot on your next meeting agenda to prove that to you. At that time, I assure you, I will have an architect, builder, contractor, and subcontractors who will all meet with the council's approval. All I'm asking for is a chance."

Every one of the council members stared at her.

"Let's vote," Sam finally said. "Raise your hand if you want to give Lacey Armstrong a slot on the September fifteenth agenda."

All but George Masterson raised their hands. She only needed a majority, and she'd just gotten it.

"Thank you." She gathered her portfolio and resisted the urge to gloat at Charity, nodding when Sam handed her the paper Clay had brought in to clear himself. She didn't even look at it but walked down the aisle.

"Good work, Mom!" Ashley high-fived her when she reached them.

"Way to go, Lace!" Zoe called from the other side of the room. Tessa gave her two thumbs-up.

"Thanks." She closed her fingers over Ashley's hand and gave a squeeze. "I'll be right back."

Because she sure as hell wasn't going to let Clay Walker slink away without a damn fine explanation. Then he could get the hell out of her life, thank you very much.

Chapter 20

❧

God, Clay hated the taste of regret. And he was choking on the stuff right now.

He stuck his hands in his hair, cursing his stupidity. Across the parking lot, he saw David Fox talking to a guy in a business suit in the shade of palm trees. Clay ducked around the side of the building to have his moment of self-loathing in private.

Son of a bitch! He should have just told her and not worried that an inaccurate record of history could cost him the tentative assignment. He should've gone with his original intention of telling her last night, regardless of the town council meeting. She could have handled the facts. Why had he doubted her? And if he'd been straight she wouldn't have been blindsided. So now he had the affidavit to back up his story but she'd been publicly humiliated and no doubt wanted to drop-kick him off the nearest dock.

He'd been scared to lose her. That was why he hadn't told her the truth; he'd been scared she'd walk. And now she surely would.

The door of the town hall slammed against the stucco wall with enough force that he had no doubt who'd flung it open and what she wanted.

"Where are you?" Lacey demanded.

He stepped around the corner to face her but wished he didn't have to see the abject misery in her expression. "I'm right here, Lacey."

"How could you not tell me?" She snapped the affidavit he'd risked life and a speeding ticket to have back here in time for the meeting.

"I made a mistake."

Her eyes blazed. "No shit. Let me put it another way: *When* were you going to tell me?"

"At first, but then you were so unsure of me, so I planned to tell you last night, but when this agenda-setting meeting came up—"

"Along with a few other things, conveniently."

Ouch. "This has nothing to do with . . . that."

"No? Oldest trick in the book, Clay. Screw a woman *senseless*, so she can't—"

"Stop it." He reached out to her shoulders, but she dodged his touch. "That's why I went to Fort Myers today, Lacey. I wanted the affidavit in my hand before I told you. And I thought it might throw you and give you an excuse to—"

"Speaking of excuses!" she hissed. "You're as bad as I am. Worse. I may stop when I hit a brick wall, but I don't *lie* my way through it."

"A lie of omission, and not intentional."

She puffed out a breath of sheer disgust. "Oh, please. Was *this* why your dad kicked you out of the firm?"

"Not exactly."

"Then what was it, *exactly*?" She took a step closer, venom in her eyes. And pain. Pain he'd put there, damn it.

This was why he didn't want a relationship. This: the pain in her eyes.

"I want the truth," she demanded, her voice low and steady. "The whole truth, Clay. No more vague explanations buried in flirting and kissing and drawing. The truth. What happened?"

"I did something to help someone I...cared about. To protect my family and my father, but it cost me a brief investigation, from which I was completely cleared."

She considered that, frowning, thinking, and definitely not buying. "Not specific enough."

He closed his eyes and nodded. "I took the fall when my ex-girlfriend used my father's name on some documents she shouldn't have had. She made a gross error in judgment, and I helped her out of a jam."

Her eyes flickered. "Why?"

"Because..." Not because he cared about Jayna, that was for sure. Probably because he cared about his father, which was the greatest irony of all. "At the time, it seemed like the right thing to do. She was eight months pregnant and extremely sorry for making a really dumb mistake that she thought would never be discovered. It was, and she came to me asking for help, and I gave it and got into a shitload of trouble for the effort. My father assumed the worst about me." *Naturally.*

Because what better way to get rid of his own guilty conscience than to see Clay as a criminal?

"Why didn't you tell him the truth?"

"Because I thought he'd leave Jayna if he found out what she did, and I was worried about that kid. When I was cleared of everything, my father continued to believe I was guilty."

"Why?"

That was one question he could answer without hesitation. "Because it made him feel less guilty about sleeping with my girlfriend."

She searched his face, clearly having trouble with it all.

"This is the truth, Lacey."

"Are you still in love with her?"

The question didn't surprise him, but the little note of hurt or worry in her voice stunned the shit out of him. "No," he said quietly. "I'm not sure I ever really was."

"Then why risk your career and family for her?"

In truth, he'd helped his family by protecting the business. "She forged his name on documents and I let the authorities believe I'd signed my name, to protect my dad's reputation. If his business collapsed, a lot of people I really care about would be out of work. So I took the blame, hired an attorney, and got the charges dismissed."

She shook her head. "Then who took the blame when you were exonerated?"

"The company who'd filed the original complaint went bankrupt and everything was dropped. No one was charged and..." *Jayna came out smelling like a rose.* "I left my dad's firm."

"He didn't believe you even after you were cleared? Your own father? That's preposterous."

"You've never met him," he said quietly, hearing the hate and anger in the undertones of his words and making no effort to hide those emotions. They were too real. "As long as I was the bad guy, everything he did in the past was excused. He even convinced some cronies on the Arch Board to ban me from getting a license and deny me permission to sit for the rest of the exams."

She leaned against one of the white columns of the building. "Is this why you've kept your name off everything? Won't sign a contract? Haven't filed anything formal yet?"

"I will do all that, but I wanted to convince you first of how right I am for the job."

"Why? Why is it so important?"

"If I complete a full project on this scale, I can sit for my exams, get my licenses, and start my own business." He gave her a direct gaze, as truthful as what he was telling her.

"Were you trying to win me over or convince me to hire you by using sex?"

"No," he insisted. "That just happened."

"Not yet it didn't."

"Whether you believe me or not, my plan was to tell you over dinner, but then they made this decision to have this impromptu meeting and I really didn't want to give you an excuse to quit. Plus"—he tapped the affidavit rolled in her hand—"I wanted to get some concrete proof that I'm telling the truth."

She closed her eyes like he'd hit her, saying nothing.

"What happened when I left?" he asked.

"I got on the agenda." The words were barely a whisper, as soft as the sea breeze that lifted a curl of her hair.

"I knew you could do it." He had to fight the urge to touch her. "That's great, Lacey."

She finally opened her eyes, none of the misery gone from their topaz depths. "Why weren't you straight from day one, Clay? Why didn't you tell me that this job could make or break your career? Maybe I would have been sympathetic."

More regret gnawed at him. Why, indeed? "When we met on the beach, you were so certain I was coming at this through the back door," he admitted. "I thought it was smart to prove to you what I could do first."

"Like last night? What you could do up against a wall?"

The words punched a hole in his chest. "No, Lacey."

"How can I possibly believe you didn't just use sex to sweeten the deal and make sure I was too far gone to send you packing?"

He waited a beat, then asked the obvious. "Are you?"

"Am I what?"

"Too far gone to send me packing?"

She didn't answer.

"Excuse me, do either of you know Ms. Lacey Armstrong?" The voice came from the parking lot, making them both turn.

A man came forward. He was heavyset, and thin gray strands of hair lifted as he hustled toward her. Clay immediately recognized him, mostly by his out-of-place suit, as the person David Fox had been talking to earlier.

"I'm Lacey Armstrong."

His face brightened, already pink and sweaty. "Oh, that's fortunate." He reached out his hand. "I'm Ira Howell with Wells Fargo Bank in Fort Myers. Have you presented your plans to rebuild on the Barefoot Bay property?"

Lacey stole a glance at Clay before answering. "I didn't present much," she said. "Why?"

"Do your plans include building on the Everham and Tomlinson properties adjacent to your lot?"

She tensed a little, and nodded. "Yes, they do. Why?"

"You don't own those properties, ma'am."

"I'm in the process of purchasing both lots. I've made offers and am waiting for the paperwork."

"Not anymore you're not. My client closed sales this afternoon on both properties. Your plans will have to be scaled back. Or canceled."

"The Everham and Tomlinson properties sold? That's not possible." Lacey choked softly, stepping back as if the guy had hit her, while a little bell dinged in Clay's head. "Who bought them?"

Clay knew, instantly. David Fox had been talking to this guy and, when Clay saw him at the beach, he'd heard Fox use the name Tomlinson on the phone.

"Can't say, ma'am, but both neighbors closed this afternoon," the banker said.

The bastard had stolen the land right out from under her. Clay was next to Lacey in a flash, his hand on her back.

"That's not possible. I haven't been informed—"

"I'm informing you now." He pulled an envelope from his breast pocket. "The owners have asked me to return your deposit on both lots, along with my client's apologies for the inconvenience."

"Who is your client, Mr. Howell?" Clay demanded. As if he didn't know.

"The buyer prefers to maintain anonymity." He handed Lacey the envelope, added a nod good-bye, and headed back to the parking lot, as efficient as a process server.

"Lacey," Clay said, gripping her arm. "I know who did this to you."

She looked up at him. "Who?"

"David Fox."

She just shook her head. "I can't believe anything you say anymore."

"Well, you better believe this, because I'm right. He had a meeting with Tomlinson at Barefoot Bay. I was there, I heard the conversation, I heard him use the name Tomlinson. And I just saw him talking to this banker guy in the parking lot less than ten minutes ago." He took her hand, pulling her around the corner to see if he could spot Fox again, but he'd disappeared. "Your ex is the client Howell is protecting. He has the money, the motivation, the need to control you."

She held up her hands to stop him, the check in one fist, the affidavit in the other, and an expression of pure distrust on her face. "Please, Clay. Just leave."

"Lacey, I heard him say 'Mr. Tomlinson' on the phone, and I just saw him talking to Ira Howell. I swear I did, Lacey."

"Mommy! Are you out here?"

Lacey's face registered a flash of horror. "I want you to leave," she said in a soft whisper.

"Leave? The island? No, Lacey, I'm not."

"Lace? You out here?" A woman called.

"Leave!" She gave him a little push. "I need to be with my family."

"Meet me at Barefoot Bay tonight, Lacey."

Her jaw dropped. "You have *got* to be kidding."

"I'm not kidding. And I'm not leaving this island. I've

never walked away from any challenge, and I'm not about to start with a woman I care about as much as you."

"A woman or a job?"

Both. "Meet me tonight at the beach at Barefoot Bay. We're not done, Lacey."

But the look in her eyes said they were.

Chapter 21

⌒

"Seriously, Lacey? You're going to believe the accusation of a known criminal over the father of your child? A man who claims to have heard me use a name on the phone twenty feet away?" David lifted his feet onto the ottoman and locked his hands behind his head. "I think you have bigger problems than trying to pin that deal on me."

Lacey glanced at the kitchen, where Tessa and Zoe were making food with Ashley, giving Lacey the quiet moment she'd been waiting for since they'd returned from the town hall. Jocelyn had texted that she was going back to the hotel for a "client emergency," so Tessa and Zoe had returned to the house with Lacey.

"Clay heard you say his name."

"But he didn't actually see me talking to anyone."

"Why would he lie about this?"

David let out a hearty laugh. "Why *wouldn't* he lie is a

better question. Lacey, I really hope you have this cougar fantasy out of your head now."

Irritation stung at the words. "Well, you're not a liar, David, and I notice you haven't directly answered the question. Did you or did you not meet with Mr. Tomlinson at the beach when you ran into Clay?"

He let out a long, slow, put-upon sigh that sounded so much like Ashley when she was trapped and in trouble. "I did meet with him, that's true."

"Why?"

"I thought I could help you."

"How could meeting with Mr. Tomlinson possibly help me?"

Another sigh of resignation. "By buying the property for you—"

"So you did?"

"—as a gift. To save you the added expense and show you how much I care and want to be involved in your life and your project."

Why did every word that came out of his mouth sound like bullshit? Because so often it was. "If that's true, then I can buy the property back directly from you." That might delay things, but at least—

"No, I didn't buy it, Lacey, that's what I'm trying to tell you."

Lacey perched on the edge of the sofa, her hands clasped tightly enough to turn her knuckles white. "Then who did?"

"I don't know. Tomlinson said he had another rock-solid offer that he simply couldn't ignore. Of course, I assumed it was you."

"Did you ask him who the offer was from?"

"I did, because I thought I could go to that buyer. But he said it was anonymous through his bank. So I just let it go as a bad idea and decided to look for other ways to convince you that I care." His face was set in the most sincere expression, his eyes dark with just the right amount of contrition and hope.

God, he was good. Believable. Direct. In some ways, more real than Clay.

Forget Clay, Lacey. But that was the problem. She couldn't forget Clay.

"Why wouldn't you talk to me about it? Why wouldn't you just ask to be an investor? Why go behind my back?"

"I wanted to surprise you. I wanted to show you, and Ashley, that I'm serious about wanting to be a family. Because, Lacey, I *am* serious."

She dropped her head into her hands, grateful that Zoe and Tessa were in the kitchen with Ashley; at least she hoped they weren't listening to this.

"I have never lied to you, Lacey." He stood, the words somehow having far more impact that way.

"I know," she conceded. He was a lot of things—adrenaline junkie, absentee father, even a bit of an actor—but she couldn't remember David lying to her. In fact, when she'd told him she was pregnant he'd been honest in his reaction. She'd hated what he said, but he'd been honest.

Which was more than she could say for Clay Walker.

"I tried to tell you. I wanted to." He took a step forward, looming over her now, making her feel small and helpless. "But you were so preoccupied."

"Don't," she said, pointing a finger at him. "Don't tell me circumstances stopped you from being straight with me. I've had enough of that for one day."

"Then you're over him?"

"I was never under him," she said defiantly. "Whether you want to believe that or not, it's true."

"Of course I believe it." With no warning David was on his knee in front of her, shifting from his power stance to a proposal pose.

"Listen to me," he said, his voice low and pleading, his gaze soft and so damn credible. "I did not purchase that land. Why would I do that and keep it from you? I don't want to stop you from building this inn or resort or whatever you want it to be. I want to be part of it with you."

"And with me." Ashley burst in from the kitchen, Zoe practically running behind her.

"Ashley, I'm trying to have a private conversation with David."

"His name is Fox." Ashley folded herself on the floor right next to David.

"You know the old joke, Ash," David said, giving her hair a ruffle. "She can call me anything she wants, as long as she calls me."

Ashley giggled and, for a moment, for one suspended, stupid, insane moment, Lacey felt like they were a family. Dad trying to tease a smile out of Mom through an inside joke with Child.

An ache she didn't recognize at first welled up inside her. The ache for a real family. A whole family. A happy family. David had stolen that from her with a one-way ticket to Patagonia. But they probably wouldn't have made it anyway.

"Mommy, you're crying!"

Oh, geez. Was she?

"Ash, remember what we talked about." David put a

gentle arm on Ashley's shoulder. "You have to be sensitive to the stress your mom is under."

He was giving their daughter life lectures now? Maybe he was trying to be a real family. But it was too little too late. And not what she wanted. What she wanted was . . .

Clay.

"When did you talk about that?" Lacey asked, sounding as wretched and bitter as she felt.

"When we played chess last night," Ashley said. "When you went out to dinner."

Of course. While Lacey was out on a date with a man who was keeping secrets and trying to talk her into commitment-free sex that they could keep entirely separate from their project, a project he had no right going after.

Guilt strangled her. She should have been home teaching Ashley life lessons, not flirting and kissing and offering sympathy for his sad, sad story about his father and the ex-girlfriend.

"Dad and I talk a lot," Ashley said, pride in her voice as she looked at him. "And I'm really trying to work on my attitude, Daddy."

She was clearly possessed by spirits—or the proper parent. The guilt knife cut a fresh wound.

"The thing is, Mom—and don't get mad at me for listening—but Dad didn't try to screw you out of that property and I think he really does want a second chance at love."

"Don't say 'screw,'" David said.

"Don't say 'love,'" Lacey shot back.

On the sofa, Lacey's phone vibrated softly with a text. "That could be Jocelyn," she said, picking it up.

Clay Walker: I'll wait at Barefoot Bay.

She couldn't do anything but close her eyes against the words, feeling a tornado of emotions swirling right down to her toes. A maelstrom of longing and loss, shockingly strong, and remarkably real. Loss? For a man who'd deceived her? Used her?

But had he? His explanation for not telling her made sense, and he hadn't used her. He'd taken what she offered. And she'd offered it because there was something about him. Something different. Something extraordinary.

"Mom?"

"Lacey?"

Their voices pulled her back, forcing her attention away to the two people who were right here, asking her to be a family. The family she wanted. One of them she loved more than anyone or anything. *Unconditionally.* The other she didn't love, but did he deserve a second chance?

And yet there was Clay. And all this unresolved feeling whirling around like one of the mini-tornadoes that had ripped her home to shreds. Was he going to do the same thing to her heart?

Dear God, she *had to know.*

"What did Jocelyn say, Lacey?" Tessa and Zoe stood in the kitchen door, so close they'd no doubt heard the whole preceding conversation.

"Don't tell me she got on a plane and went back to L.A.," Zoe said. "'Cause she is so dead to me if she did."

"It's not, she's not..." She shook the lie out of her head before she said it. "That wasn't Jocelyn." She slid her finger over the screen and deleted the text, shifting back to Ashley. "Honey, there's a lot more to this than you are old enough to understand. But..." She staved off the argument with a flat palm. "*But* I realize how important it is

that David and I are friends. I hope you see that we are."
And that's all we are.

"Does that mean you guys will stop fighting?"

"We're not fighting," David said quickly, unable to keep the appreciative smile off his face as he reached for Lacey's hand. "It's called discussing. Do you believe me now?"

"I don't know," she said honestly. "Who else would have the money or motivation to step in and buy those parcels out from underneath me?"

"I don't know about money, but motivation? I'd start with that skinny bitch who should be named Uncharitable."

Ashley giggled.

"If I find out, will you believe me then?" he asked.

"I suppose."

That seemed to satisfy him. "All right." He put a fatherly arm around Ashley. "Who's up for a game of Monopoly?"

"I am!" Ashley leaped to her feet, sharing a knuckle tap with David.

"Gonna buy me some Boardwalk, baby!" David exclaimed.

Behind them Zoe stuck her finger in her mouth and fake-gagged.

"Listen, Lace. Jocelyn's not answering her cell," Tessa said, "and she took our rental car. You think you could give us a lift to the hotel?"

Lacey gave her a grateful smile. "Of course."

"They can stay here," David said. "No need for you to go out so late alone."

"Or they can take Grandpa's van," Ashley suggested, suddenly the voice of reason and maturity.

No, Lacey had to get away from this house and talk

privately with her friends, even if just for the forty-five minutes it would take to drive to the mainland and back. "Their stuff is at the hotel and, honestly, David, I want to see Jocelyn. I'm worried about her." None of that was a lie.

Her phone vibrated again and she ignored it, throwing it into her purse without looking at the screen.

"It won't take long," she promised, giving Ashley a kiss. In her purse she felt the vibration of another text. She didn't need to look; she knew it was from Clay Walker, the man who always got what he wanted.

"How long will you be gone?" Ashley asked.

If she went to the beach to talk to Clay one more time? "An hour or two, tops."

Not that she'd even consider something so mind-numbingly dumb.

"David is relentless," Tessa said the minute they were alone.

"I know." Lacey cranked the AC to full blast and whipped out of the driveway. "Do you believe him? Do either of you believe Clay?"

Tessa didn't answer, shifting in the passenger seat to adjust her long, lean frame, and let out a sigh. "I'm the wrong man-hater to ask, I'm afraid."

Zoe picked up Lacey's bag. "Mind if I see if Jocelyn was texting you?"

"You can look, but I think it was Clay. He wants to meet me at Barefoot Bay."

Neither one of them said a word.

"I'm thinking about going."

Still no response.

"Are either of you going to talk me out of it?"

Silence.

"Okay," Lacey said with a soft laugh. "You're not advising me because you know that some decisions a person just has to make on her own."

They shared a look, but not a word.

"Or," Lacey said, "meeting Clay at Barefoot Bay tonight is so flipping stupid the idea has left you two speechless."

Zoe leaned forward and quietly set the cell phone in the console. "Bingo."

"Well, what do you think I should do?" Lacey demanded. "Just let it go? Not talk to him more about why he wasn't honest?"

"They lie once, they'll lie again." Zoe turned to the window, crossing her arms, her expression drawn.

"And you know this from experience?" Tessa said, not the least bit of challenge or sarcasm in her voice.

Zoe was silent. They'd all tried to pry out the story of why the doctor they'd seen at the hotel had made her cry, but she was uncharacteristically quiet on the subject. Just like Jocelyn, who was hiding hurt the size of a small country but refusing to talk about it.

"Damn it, are we friends or not?" Lacey demanded. "Don't friends tell each other everything?"

Zoe finally tore her gaze from the street to meet Lacey's in the rearview mirror. "Friends don't let friends have booty calls with liars."

"I am not talking about Clay. I'm talking about you and that married doctor."

Her eyes flashed. "I'm not considering meeting that 'married doctor' at the beach, Lacey. And, Jesus Christ, can't a person have a single drop of privacy around here?"

Her words echoed into the confined space of the car,

Lacey's heartbeat keeping time with the wheels on the causeway bumps. They never fought, but some things had to be aired out. Didn't they?

"I don't get the secrets," Tessa finally said, a little frustration in her voice. "Maybe we could help you, Zoe. You guys knew every time I got my period and how much it hurt to know I wasn't pregnant. Lacey's told us everything about Clay." She hesitated. "Haven't you?"

"Pretty much. I may have left out a hot kiss or two, but you know everything."

"Well, I for one think you ought to go to the beach," Tessa said. At Lacey's surprised look, she added, "To talk to him. You can't just end this without a conversation. That's why he's waiting there."

"That is *so* not why he's waiting there," Zoe said.

"You're both right," Lacey said. "And I think I should go for a completely different reason. There is something about him that makes me feel wonderful."

Zoe snorted. "Dude, that wonderful feeling is your lady bits getting all fired up. A couple more lies will douse the flames, trust me."

"How can we trust you?" Tessa shot back at Zoe. "You won't tell us anything."

Lacey shook her head, glancing out at the causeway lights dancing on the water as they crossed. "Anyway, it really is more than sex."

"That's what I—" Zoe caught herself and laughed. "That's what all women think, Lace."

"I know," Lacey agreed. "Of course there's a sexual attraction. Shit, it's off the charts. But, I also really connect with him." She took a hand off the wheel to stop the jokes or argument before they started. "I mean I see a fundamental goodness in him. And it makes me hope that…" *He's the one.* "He's really a good guy."

Zoe didn't answer, but Tessa put her hand on Lacey's shoulder. "I happen to agree with you. I think you should meet him."

Lacey looked in the rearview mirror at Zoe. "What's your vote?"

"I think you should make him sweat and dangle a little more."

Lacey smiled. "I hate to break it to you, Zoe, but that magic drafting tool doesn't dangle. But let's let Jocelyn cast the tie-breaking vote. I'll do what she thinks is right."

"Fine," Zoe said, turning back to the window.

"Zoe?" Tessa asked softly. "You sure you don't want to talk about it?"

"There's nothing to talk about. I knew the guy in another life. He screwed me over. It's so not interesting. Let it go."

Because they always gave each other what they wanted, Lacey and Tessa let it go. Zoe didn't say another word until they walked into the suite and found Jocelyn in the bedroom, her clothes piled on the bed like neat little mountains of neutral colors, two half-packed suitcases on the floor.

"What are you doing?" Zoe demanded, grabbing a white cotton shirt and yanking it from the suitcase. "You can't leave!"

"I have a client emergency." She took the blouse out of Zoe's hands and laid it on the bed, smoothing the sleeves.

"What client emergency?" Tessa asked. "That crackpot Coco Kirkman?"

"Or did something happen at the meeting this afternoon that freaked you out?"

At Lacey's question Jocelyn's hands froze. She closed her eyes, then silently folded the crisp pleating on the blouse to a precise right angle, her fingers shaking but her breathing calm and steady.

"The only person freaked out is, as Tessa accurately guessed, my client, Coco. And since she pays me an outrageous sum of money to be her sounding board and voice of reason, I'm going back to work."

"Really?" Tessa asked. "You have to go back?"

They both looked at Lacey, expecting her to chime in with agreement. Or maybe acceptance, because wasn't that what they did? Support each other and whatever decisions they made, dumb or not?

Lacey, about to be queen of the dumb decisions, didn't say a word. After an awkward beat, Jocelyn continued packing.

"I know what you want to hear from me," Lacey finally said. "You expect me to say, 'Oh, what a shame, we'll miss you, but do what you have to do, Joss,' right?" They all looked at her, waiting for the *but* to be added. "But I want to ask you a question instead."

Jocelyn's slim fingers hesitated on the next article of clothing. "Go ahead."

"Why'd you leave the meeting?" Lacey asked.

Three, four, five long seconds ticked by before Jocelyn finally said, "Coco called and that took forever, then I got back here and made my reservations."

She wasn't telling them everything, but how far to push? How much does a friend have to know? Where did they draw the line between friendship and privacy?

"Maybe," Lacey said softly, "you should ignore this plea from a client and face down the things that are making you unhappy."

Jocelyn wet her lips. "And maybe you should solve your own problems before tackling my imaginary ones."

That would be the line Lacey just crossed.

"Oh, shit," Zoe mumbled. "We've had a tough day. Can we just drop all the interrogating of friends and let everyone just do what she wants to do?"

"Because that's not what friends do," Tessa said, sitting next to Lacey in a show of support. "Are you telling us the truth, Jocelyn? Is Coco Kirkman really why you're leaving?"

Jocelyn took a deep breath, pain and angst painted on every delicate feature. "Yes. But I will admit she's a convenience, because I want to go."

Lacey leaned forward. "Is it Will Palmer?"

"Who is Will Palmer?" Zoe asked, sitting up. "That hot guy sitting in Lacey's row? I noticed him. Big dude."

"No, it's not Will Palmer," Jocelyn said with so much conviction Lacey believed her. Jocelyn's pain was never about a guy. Not that guy, anyway.

But her father...

"My issues have nothing to do with him, honestly." Jocelyn dropped onto the bed, letting some clothes tumble. "Listen, you guys. I'm not asking you to just feed me a line of bull and say you understand. I'm not asking any of you to do that. All I'm asking for is some space. I need space."

She always wanted space, and, like good friends, they'd given it to her. Maybe that was the wrong thing to do. Maybe it was the absolute right thing to do. Lacey surely didn't know.

Jocelyn stood and shook her head in dismay. "Now I've wrecked my color-coded packing system."

Zoe grabbed a cream-colored T-shirt. "Someone needs to teach you that black, beige, white, and gray are not colors."

Jocelyn just shook her head and her eyes got watery. "'Scuze me." She dashed into the bathroom, leaving them in shocked silence. Then Zoe put up her hand as if she'd had enough and couldn't bear another word.

Tessa sighed heavily and put an arm around Lacey. "Do you see a pattern here? Our two best friends are not telling us everything."

"Should they?" she asked. "Do we owe each other completely bare souls?"

Tessa shrugged, Zoe shook her head, and Lacey just stared at the door of the bathroom where Jocelyn had gone for her precious space.

"Who's the Will Palmer guy?" Tessa asked.

"It's not about him," Lacey said. "At least I don't think so. Remember how weird she was with her father at her mother's funeral all those years ago? This has to do with him and, honestly, I just don't know how much we should push."

"Thank you," Zoe said, blowing out an exasperated breath. "She'll tell us what she wants us to know when she's ready."

And so, Lacey assumed, would Zoe. "Then maybe that's what friends really do for other friends," she said, leaning her head on Tessa's shoulder.

"What's that?" Tessa asked.

"They wait for each other."

The bathroom door popped open and Jocelyn emerged, her face completely empty of the pain she'd worn when she'd gone in there. Her dark eyes were clear and her color was normal.

"By the way," Zoe said. "We need you to break a tie for us, Joss. We're voting on whether or not Lacey should go to the beach to meet the building stud."

"Do you know what happened?" Lacey asked Jocelyn. She nodded. "They texted me. Why would you go?"

She closed her eyes. Did they have to know everything? Only if they could really help her decide, and, face it, she'd made the decision a while ago. Now she just needed to rationalize it. "I feel like there's a chance for something different with him." Zoe rolled her eyes, but Lacey ignored her. "And I've never wanted anything so much in my whole life. I really care about him."

At their silence, she laughed softly. "I'm making excuses to do something. Is that the same as making excuses not to do something?"

Jocelyn didn't answer at first, but started straightening clothes, methodically folding already crisply ironed khaki shorts. "I think," she finally said, "that you should do whatever you want and not worry about what we think."

"But I need your opinion."

"You need our blessing," Jocelyn continued. "Which you know you'll get for whatever you decide to do. But what's really important is that whatever you decide to do, we'll be there to cheer you on or pick up the pieces." She smiled at the others, a hint of tears in her eyes. "That's what friends do for each other. Even when they don't understand everything."

No one argued with that.

"So," Tessa asked, "what are you going to do?"

"I'm going. And when I get there, I'm going to..." She let her voice trail off.

"Do something that starts with an *f* and has four letters," Zoe said.

"Right," Jocelyn said. "Fire him."

Lacey just laughed. "One way or the other, somebody's going to get burned."

Chapter 22

Clay lay flat on the hard-packed sand, close enough to the water that the occasional wave passed under him, soaking his clothes and digging a sinkhole for his body.

A sinkhole. The perfect metaphor for this mess.

He'd been out here long enough that his eyes had completely adjusted to the darkness, allowing him to see the Milky Way in all its celestial glory. A nearly full moon hung in a cloudless sky, cutting a river of silver over the calm waters of the Gulf. Nothing but the sound of the steady surf and the distant buzz of cicadas interrupted his miserable thoughts.

Thoughts that had turned dark, cynical, and circular as each moment passed and he accepted that Lacey wasn't going to show.

A warm wave punctuated the realization, seeping around

his body again, leaving him wet and chilled, sucking him deeper into the sand.

Who could blame her? He'd lied, even if it was a lie of omission. Sure, he had plenty of reasons—she'd back out, he wanted the affidavit, the allegations were false, the charges dropped—but that didn't change the truth.

And he'd given *her* a hard time for having excuses.

Who could blame her for blowing him off tonight? For staying with her friends and family, or letting her ex-boyfriend work his magic and convince her that he could be a real father to Ashley? Because Clay sure as hell didn't want that job. Did he?

He slapped his hands on the wet sand and pushed up, wanting to wash away the thoughts *and* the sticky muck that had turned his skin and clothes into forty-grit sandpaper.

Popping open his button-down shirt, he shimmied free of the wet sleeves and threw the shirt on the sand. Then he stripped off his sopping wet pants and boxers and tossed them on the pile with the shoes he'd long ago abandoned.

Naked, he strode into the surf, instantly relieved of the sand but not of the agony in his chest. He dove underwater and stayed down; his lungs ached. He popped up and sucked in a mouthful of salty night air, wiping the water from his eyes just as headlights cut a swath across Lacey's property.

Holy shit. She came.

She killed the lights, then the engine, and slammed the car door. He heard footsteps on the cement foundation, imagined Lacey walking around her property looking for him.

Why didn't he move? He couldn't. If she came to him, if she forgave him, if she *joined* him in this water and let him do all the things their bodies wanted and needed to do, he'd say things he'd regret in the morning.

Things like *This isn't casual*.

When, exactly, had that happened? Probably when he'd walked into that town hall and seen the heartbreak on her face—and felt it right in his own gut. She mattered, damn it. She mattered to him *already*.

He caught a glimpse of her hair in the moonlight, and the peach-colored dress she'd worn that afternoon. She stood still by the picnic table, looking around, probably trying to get her own eyes to adjust.

After a few seconds she climbed up on the picnic table, wrapped her arms around her legs, and rested her head on her chin. In a matter of minutes her eyes would adjust and the moonlight would reveal his pile of clothes or his truck parked near the bushes.

But she put her head down and started to sob. Chest-tearing, throat-ripping, nose-sniveling sobs of bone-deep pain.

Oh, man.

Way to go, asshole. Way to crush the spirit of the most spirited woman he'd met in years. Maybe ever.

God*damn* it. He strode forward, unable to stop, scooping up his pants in one move as he walked, barely stopping as he stepped into them, ignoring how wet they were. She didn't hear him over the bawling that already had her shuddering.

He didn't want to scare her, so when he got about fifteen feet away he started to whistle softly. The six notes he often whistled, a favorite song, a simple sentiment, the music from *her* movie.

A kiss is still a kiss.

She stopped crying, but she didn't lift her head.

He whistled the next bar.

Very slowly, she looked up and met his gaze. With each step closer, the moonlight emphasized more clearly her swollen, red eyes, the streaks of makeup and tears, the tremble of her lip.

"Of all the sandy beaches in all the world..."

She shook her head at the lame attempt at humor. "Don't."

He stopped a foot away, aching to reach out and take away all that pain. He went for the obvious instead. "I'm sorry this happened, Lacey."

"Not as sorry as I am." She wiped her face, but that just made her makeup smear worse, and punched his gut a little harder.

For the time it took for two, then three, waves to break on the sand, they just stared at each other.

"Did you talk to David?" he finally asked.

"David didn't buy the properties," she said. "He did meet with Tomlinson, but he said it was to try and buy them as a gift for me, but Tomlinson said an offer was already on the table, which must be the one through the bank. David backed off."

He didn't think that was true, not for one second, but it seemed like a lousy time to try to crucify her ex. "Any theories, then?"

She shook her head. "He's going to try and find out who bought the lots."

"I'll find out."

"How?" she asked.

"How's he going to do it?" he countered.

"The way he does everything: by throwing money around. What's your plan?"

"My sister knows a million mortgage brokers," he said. "She can get information like that."

"Is that legal?" she asked, plenty of disdain in her voice.

"Yes, Lacey, it's legal. I've never done anything illegal in my life. Stupid, short-sighted, chicken-shit cowardly, and badly motivated, yeah. Guilty as charged. I haven't lied to you, except by not telling you everything straight-away, and I haven't broken the law." He blew out a breath but wanted to finish the speech. "I have made some of the biggest mistakes in the name of love and loyalty that a person can make."

She stared at him, still holding tightly to her legs, the skirt slipping down in the awkward position, but he didn't steal a peek at her bare thighs. He was too busy searching for forgiveness in her eyes.

"And I'm still the right man for..." *You*. "The job."

She swallowed, her eyes welling up as she tried to speak. "I know you don't want to hear this, but...I... can't..." Her voice cracked with a sob.

"Forgive me?"

She shook her head. "I can't..."

Again, the word wouldn't come out. "Give me a second chance?"

"I can't..."

"Trust me? I understand all those things, Lacey. I underst—"

"I can't stop *wanting* you."

Oh. "Is that why you're crying?"

"I'm crying because..." She took a deep breath and let out a wry laugh as she exhaled. "Because I thought you left and I felt like a love-sick idiot for coming here."

He came closer, reaching out to her. "We're both idiots, then."

She sniffed and inched back, but only a little. "My friends didn't all agree with this, you know."

"I'm sure they didn't." He sat next to her and she didn't leap away.

"Especially Zoe. And she's been your biggest cheerleader. I didn't want to come here. No, I didn't want to *want* to come here. Does that make sense? Of course it doesn't," she rushed, answering her own questions, barely taking a breath. "Then I got here and I thought you were gone and I can't believe how much that hurt me."

"Shit, I've done a bang-up job with you today."

"I know, right? And still... God, how bad do I have it for you?"

"Bad." He kissed her forehead, then wiped the tears.

"It's like you have some kind of hold, some spell over me, and it's really scary."

"It shouldn't be scary." But were those thoughts that far off from the ones he'd just had? "We're both just cautious," he said softly.

"Cautious means you're scared," she said. "Are you scared?"

To death. "I'm not sure what I'm getting into," he admitted.

She searched his face, practically begging for him to say more. But he was in no position to tell her how he felt for her. He didn't know what he felt for her. Just that he did.

She closed her eyes and leaned her forehead against him. "I'm not a lousy judge of character, usually. I mean, I can spot a bad guy from miles away, and, honestly, I'm not one of those women with a string of loser boyfriends. My heart says you are not a bad guy."

"I'm not."

"And my body . . ."

"I'm pretty sure I know what your body says."

"But my friends say that I should fire you."

"Want to know what I say?" He cupped her face, holding her gently as she nodded.

He didn't answer his question until he'd eased her all the way back on the table and settled so close he was just about on top of her.

"Fire me later," he whispered into a soft, airy, sweet kiss that wasn't anything like the fury and frantic connection he imagined they'd have the first time they made love.

He let her get used to the weight of his body against hers, the sensation of their tongues doing their favorite dance, the pleasure of his erection rising against her stomach.

She gripped his arms like she might fall without their support, squeezing his muscles and sliding her hands over his back and rear end.

"You're covered in sand and you're wet."

"Mmm." He nibbled his way down the V-neck of her dress, which buttoned from her cleavage to the bottom. "I was in the water."

"You were?"

"But first I was lying on the sand." He got the first few buttons of her dress open with little more than a flick, spreading the cotton to reveal a white lace bra. And the swells of her gorgeous breasts beneath it.

"What were you doing in the sand?"

He kissed her creamy skin, thumbed the nipple, earned a whimper of delight. "Thinking about you."

"Thinking about this?"

The next three buttons were just as easy, and then the dress fell all the way open. He kissed her cleavage, down her stomach, then opened another button. "No, I wasn't thinking about sex."

"You are now."

"True, but..." The last three buttons left her bare but for white lace panties. He completely spread the dress open, kissing his way down to his destination. "I was..." He licked her belly button. "Thinking about..." He put his mouth over the silk. "How much I want to..."

She squeezed his shoulders, lifted her hips, let out another groan as he pulled down her panties. The sight of her shot fire and agony and need to his every cell.

"To what?"

He sat up slowly, drawing away from her skin but knowing he'd be back.

"C'mon." He slipped her dress over her shoulders, unhooked her bra, and scooped her naked body into his arms to carry her across the sand to the water.

Halfway there, she let her head drop back, an act of complete surrender.

At the water's edge he put her on her feet and stood back to look at her, bathed in moonlight and glowing from arousal. "God, you're gorgeous, Lacey."

She just smiled. "You know what I think, Clay Walker?"

"What?"

"That nothing you do is casual, even sex."

The water lapped his ankles and, as it ebbed away, the

sand disappeared, leaving him in a sinkhole again. Once again he was digging himself deeper and deeper, but he just couldn't seem to stop.

"You might be right, Strawberry."

When they reached the sandbar, Clay pulled Lacey into his chest, crushing her mouth with a kiss and then leaning her back so that the moonlight poured over her body and her hair skimmed the water.

Every sense was alive and sparking, her hands desperate to feel every amazing inch of him, her mouth greedy for more of his lips and tongue. She felt light-headed from the scent of sex and salt and the sounds of his sexy words and helpless groans.

But another sense sparked, too, an undercurrent of awareness that had nothing to do with sex but everything to do with emotion.

Standing, embracing, entwining, they kissed, the water lapping waist-high, invading her most private parts as his tongue invaded her mouth. His hands were everywhere, on her breasts, down her back, under her thighs so he could hoist her higher. The tide took her right where she wanted to be, up against the shockingly hard length of him, already sheathed with a condom he'd put on before they got in the water.

That strange awareness, that sense of something familiar, teased her again, then disappeared when he turned her around so her backside was tucked into his hips. Nothing was familiar about that.

He positioned himself between her legs, closing his hands over her breasts, stealing her sanity as he caressed her budded nipples and glided his shaft along the super-sensitive skin between her legs.

Waves of déjà vu rolled over her.

How was that possible? Even if she could remember the last time she'd been intimate with a lover, there had been no water, no full-body assault of pleasure from a man who'd positioned himself behind her. Because she wouldn't have forgotten that.

So why did it feel *familiar*?

The question tickled like his lips on her ear. "Do you like that, Lacey? Does that feel good?"

"Yes, I like it. I like this. I like—oh, that. I like *you*." The admission felt good on her lips. Almost as good as his fingertips on her nipples.

"And this? Do you like this?" He dragged his hands down and cupped her backside, holding it firmly as he stroked from underneath with a granite-like erection.

"Oh my God, I like that *so* much." She moaned as the swollen head rolled over her most tender spot, his hips grinding into her backside.

"And that?"

His body was a relentless, unstoppable assault on her senses, making her weak and helpless and lost, still reminding her of something so powerful she couldn't stop it, something scary and huge and life-changing. But what?

She pushed away the thoughts and gave in to the building tension, the twisting, squeezing, aching knot developing low in her belly as his erection slid between her legs, from the back to the front, right over the knot that was about to unravel.

"Clay, if you keep doing that I'm going to..." She lost the last word as he bent his knees so she could sit on his lap, forcing his erection directly and mercilessly over her clitoris. She cried out a little, wild with pleasure when he reached down and used his hand to intensify the sensation, slipping one finger inside her.

"Are you ready, Strawberry?"

So ready. She nodded, unable to speak.

"Do you want me inside you?"

"Yes. Now. Please, now."

"Now." He echoed her thoughts and then turned her around to face him, the buoyancy of the water bringing her to his eye level. "This is it."

For one breath of a suspended moment, they were eye to eye, mouth to mouth, chest to chest, then he lowered her right onto him...and they were body to body. This is it. *This is it.* The words had an eerie echo of the past, a warning and a threat as well as a promise.

Without closing his eyes or kissing or saying a word, he slid all the way inside, as deep as he could go. His breath caught as he plunged deeper, held still, then began to stroke in and out.

Everything faded. Every deliciously intense feeling and thrill faded to nothing but that one place where they were joined. His hands stilled, his kisses halted, even their tattered, frantic breathing suspended into near silence as they both focused completely on the connection of their bodies.

She dropped her head on his shoulder and gave in to the rhythm. Each stroke took her closer to the edge, each thrust shoved her a little past sane, each splash of water between their hips and thighs and mouths and chests nudged her closer to a climax.

Until he froze completely, all the way inside her, looking right into her eyes, and time completely stopped.

Everything was silent. Motionless. Hovering like the calm
before...

"Lacey."

"Clay."

"You can..."

"I know. I'm about to."

Closing the space between their mouths, he kissed her
and started up again, thrusting over and over, deeper and
deeper, faster and faster until everything shattered and
exploded and roared in her head.

And then she remembered when she'd felt this way
before. Exactly this way. Torn and destroyed, then lifted
up with anticipation and optimism. The only other time in
her life when something so powerful crashed through her
world and changed it forever. When a force of nature had
stolen everything she thought she cared about and left her
with nothing but hope.

The hurricane.

Only this time she had no insurance against the damage to her heart.

Chapter 23

⌒

It was barely seven when Lacey's phone buzzed with a text, pulling her out of a watery dream. Clay. It had to be him texting. He'd followed her home from the beach to make sure she arrived safely, which was sweet and had given them another half hour to make out on the porch. When she climbed into bed at almost two, he'd texted one last good night.

She fully expected to see "Good morning, Strawberry" on her phone when she blinked the sleep away to read the message.

Zoe Tamarin: Meet us at airport to say good-bye to J. That is if you are not in use as human canvas for his MDT

Oh, his drafting tool was magic, all right. Smiling, Lacey sat up and texted back. *On my way.*

Fifteen minutes later she tiptoed into Ashley's room

to leave a note, taking one minute to gaze at her sleeping daughter. Why were kids always heartbreakingly beautiful when sound asleep, their needs met, their angelic faces so perfect you'd do absolutely anything for them? God was sneaky that way.

Lacey's fingers itched to touch her child's cheek.

And she *was* still a child, despite the outline of a young woman's body under the sheets and the slow shift in Ashley's features to a heart-shaped face that looked so adult despite a few blemishes every month.

What had happened to her baby? Secure in the knowledge that a freight train could roll through the room and not wake her daughter, Lacey brushed a honey-colored lock from Ashley's face, grazing the cheek she'd kissed a million times.

A mighty ache gripped her heart and closed her throat. Now, this sensation was familiar, a love she'd known since before Ashley was born. A love unlike anything she'd ever felt for anyone or ever would feel. She'd never felt this way about David in their happiest of halcyon days, never looked at either of her parents and felt weak with love, never hugged any girlfriend with the sense of helpless wonder.

This was pure and whole, and so unconditional. When the easy thing to do would have been to give her up or follow David's advice and terminate, Lacey had held on to her princess.

"Princess Pot-Pie," she whispered, the ancient nickname rising up from memories of post-bath cuddles in the rocking chair and early morning walks through town with Ashley still in a stroller. She'd had a million names for her baby, but that was her secret favorite.

The shelf built into the headboard was mostly empty, except for the brand-new iPod Lacey's mother had sent to replace the one lost in the storm. A few hair ties, a *Glamour* magazine Zoe bought her when they'd been at Walgreens the other day. But no well-loved copy of the first Harry Potter book, no pictures from camp last summer, no movie-ticket stubs or eighth-grade yearbook.

The storm had stolen those memories, and Lacey had to remember that the loss couldn't be easy for Ashley. Lacey knew that life went on, and that memories were stored in your heart, but Ashley's world was upside down. They had no home, no stuff, and no way of being sure it would ever come back.

On the corner of the bed Lacey spied Aunt Zoe's uni, awash with gratitude that she'd taken the risk to save it.

But now they were in the middle of another emotional storm and more things were at risk. If a man came into Lacey's life, what would that do to her relationship with Ashley? Would David's reappearance destroy the delicate balance Lacey had cobbled together with her daughter? And what about Clay? Could he ever fit into this tiny family?

An unexpected jolt of desire hit her. She *wanted* Clay to fit into this family.

But by staying close to him, was she distancing herself from her daughter?

Unexpected tears burned and Lacey blinked them away. Had she ever cried this much before?

Ashley turned and let out a quiet sigh and Lacey stroked her head one more time.

"Little Princess Pot-Pie. You know I'll always love you the most." She leaned over and placed the softest kiss on

Ashley's head, loving the smell, the feel, the very being of—

"Did you just call me Princess Pot-Pie?"

Lacey laughed and finished the kiss noisily. "I did."

Expecting mockery, Lacey's tears turned to a smile when two slender arms reached up and wrapped around her neck, pulling her closer. "I love you, Mommy."

She almost folded in half. Instead, she choked a little, mostly because the lump in her throat was strangling her. "I love you, too."

"Oh my God, are you crying again?" Ashley pushed her back to see. "Why are you so weepy all of a sudden?"

"I don't know." But the unexpected tenderness pulled Lacey onto the bed, replacing the need to see Jocelyn off at the airport. These moments with Ashley were too precious and far too rare.

"What's the matter, Mom?" Ashley asked.

"You never say I love you," she replied honestly. "And I've heard it more than once, maybe more than twice, in the last few days."

"I'm sorry. Dad told me I should tell you more often."

Shit. That was not the motivating factor she wanted to hear. "That was…" *A tad manipulative.* "Nice of him."

"Yeah, he's nice. Why are you dressed? Where are you going?"

"The airport, I'm sad to say. Jocelyn has to go back to L.A."

"Oh, no." She sounded truly disappointed. "Will she be back?"

"I don't know, but would you like to come along for the ride? We can spend the day doing something fun on the mainland with Zoe and Tessa, if you like." Which might take care of some of the Mommy Guilt when Lacey stayed out late again with Clay tonight. Because she knew she would.

"Can't. Dad's taking me cave diving."

Cave diving? Lacey almost spat. She couldn't get out the "No!" fast enough. "Not—no! Do you know how *dangerous* cave diving is?"

Ashley squished up her face. "He said you'd say that and we should ease you into the idea."

God, she hated that they were talking about her, about how to *manage* her, while she was gone. *Then maybe you shouldn't be gone so much*, a nasty little voice in her head said.

"But he was going to tell you when you got home last night." Ashley gave Lacey a scrutinizing look. "You did sleep at home last night, didn't you?"

"Ashley!"

"I meant you didn't stay at the Ritz with your friends," she added quickly. Even though both of them knew that was so not what she meant.

"I wasn't out all night," she said. "I got home late, though."

"You were with him, weren't you?"

She swallowed, absolutely determined not to lie. "If by him, you mean Clay..."

"Mom, he's a sleazebag. When are you going to realize that? You called it the day he showed up on the beach trying to get your business by running around half naked."

Lacey dug for the right answer, the way to keep the connection alive but honest. "You've sure changed your tune, Ashley. You thought I was a b-word and he was the cutest thing you'd ever seen."

"Well, he's not. He's a slimebucket."

"Actually, he's not."

"You're going to defend him after what happened at the town meeting yesterday? Mom! What is wrong with you?"

"There are two sides to every story, Ash, and he has one that doesn't paint him as the devil, like Charity Grambling tried to do. He's going to do the job for me—"

"What?" Her eyes bugged out with exaggerated disbelief. "Mom." With disappointment in her voice, she plucked the uni from Lacey's hands, as if she couldn't stand for it to be on the wrong side of this argument. "I can't believe you *like* this guy."

Oh, she liked him, all right. Way too much. "I like his work."

"Yeah, right." She curled her lip. "What were you doing with him at the beach last night?"

"How do you know I was at the beach with him?"

"Because I got up to go to the bathroom in the middle of the night and walked on sand in the hall."

"Oh, boy. Now you're a detective."

"Am I right?"

She closed her eyes, wishing she could lie to her daughter. "We . . . talked. About what happened and how he was wrongfully accused of something, and cleared of it. Actually, he was helping someone out. He had a lot of explaining to do and I listened to him."

"Is that what you call it? Because if I did what you're doing, I'd be grounded for the rest of my life."

"First of all, I'm not doing what you think." Because

Ashley couldn't even imagine anything like what went on in the water last night, so that wasn't a lie. "And, secondly, I'm almost thirty-seven years old, Ashley."

"And he's twenty-nine! Don't you see how gross that is?"

Lacey almost smiled. "Depends on your perspective."

"It's gross."

"Look." Lacey reached for her daughter's hands, but Ashley pushed her away, glaring. "Honey, the point is I'm an adult and I can be with who I want to be with."

"But why can't you be with Dad?"

"I don't have feelings for—can you not call him that?"

"Why not? He's my dad. He's my *father*." She said the word with so much pride it twisted Lacey's heart. "And I know, I *know*. He's been a craptastic father for all my life, but I've decided to forgive that and start over."

"As we've discussed, that's very mature of you, but—"

"Then why can't you?"

"Forgive him?" Lacey shook her head. "I'm not still mad at him. I have forgiven him," she said, picking her words like fragile flower petals. One poor choice, and the whole conversation could fall apart. Farther apart. "I understand why he made the decision he did, and went off to live his life instead of settling down." *Instead of taking responsibility for his child. The one he suggested she abort.*

But she loved Ashley too much to play that card.

"Then why can't you give him a chance? Why can't you be in love with him?" She whined the question. "Then my life would be perfect."

Oh, no it wouldn't be. "I can't make myself love a man I don't have any feelings for. And, I'm sorry, Ashley, I simply can't manufacture those kinds of feelings."

"You've been too wrapped up in Clay Walker, that's why."

Was that true? "I don't think that's it. And, Ashley, it would mean the world to me if you'd give Clay a chance. Talk to him and get to know him."

She folded her arms, narrowed her eyes, got into full adolescent-anger mode. "Only if you give Dad a chance."

"I *gave* him a chance fourteen years ago," she said softly.

Ashley didn't answer, thinking long enough to have another idea. "Why don't you go diving with us? He said we could drive up to this river, the Itcha-something."

"Ichetucknee. And, sorry, you're not going. I knew two UF students who died cave diving there."

"Not with a tether!" She threw back the covers and leaped from the bed toward her laptop. "Let me show you the YouTube videos. Dad's in one of them, Mom. It's so cool. He's done it all over the world, in Indonesia and Africa!"

Her head almost exploded. How dare he talk Ashley into things like this? Fisting her hands, Lacey shook her head. "No, you're not going. No arguments."

Ashley turned from the computer to fire a look of pure contempt, Princess Pot-Pie completely morphing into Nastina. "Why do you always say that? All you want to do is be with that stupid loser guy when Dad is right here trying to win you back!"

Lacey gathered every single bit of calm she could find, taking a breath and refusing to get dragged into this argument.

"That's not true," she said, purposely controlling her voice. "I'm offering to spend the day with you."

She curled her lip. "No thanks. Dad and I are going cave diving."

"No, you're not."

"You can't stop me!"

"Yes, she can." David stood in the door wearing nothing but sleep pants and a morning beard. "Your mom is your legal guardian, Ashley, and she has to sign a permission form for you to dive up there. So, if she says no, the answer is no."

Ashley looked stricken, blinking back tears. "You'd really say no? You'd really stop me from having the most amazing day of my entire life just so you can go off and... and... do it with that guy?"

"That's out of line." This time David's reprimand was welcome, because Lacey could hardly form the words as she stared at her daughter.

"Well, it's true."

Lacey stood, somehow holding it together. "What's true is that your comments are way beyond what's acceptable. You aren't going cave diving and you aren't leaving the house for the next three days."

"Mom!" Tears rolled over those cheeks, not so angelic now.

"Accept your punishment, Ashley," David said, stepping aside to let Lacey by. "You need to know there are consequences for your behavior."

Lacey walked down the hall, bracing for the tirade that would surely follow, but Ashley was uncharacteristically quiet. Had David's presence changed her daughter so much that she would accept punishment without a fight?

She stood in the kitchen pressing her fingertips to

her forehead as an Ashley-argument headache started to throb.

"You made the right call in there," David said.

Irritation and resentment coiled through her, making her want to lash out and remind him that she'd been making calls for years with no help from him.

Instead she just nodded. "Thanks for the backup."

"Hey, that's what parents do."

No, parents stay and raise their kids instead of going to Patagonia. "I'm sorry about wrecking your plans for cave diving."

"No biggie," he said. "We'll go when you're ready. I'd like you to come with us."

She turned to him. "I'm never going to be ready to go on family outings with you, David. I'm not going to change my mind and it has nothing to do with anything going on in my personal life. I'm not interested, okay? You can be her father and forge a relationship with her; I've never tried to deny you that. But let me make this perfectly clear: I am not getting back together with you. You have to stop painting that fantasy in her head because when it doesn't happen, *and it won't*, she is going to be heartbroken and it will be all my fault."

He stood completely still, regarding her. "If she's ever been heartbroken, Lacey, it's because I didn't take responsibility for her."

The admission stunned her, leaving her speechless despite the fact that she had plenty more to say.

"And the real epiphany isn't what happened down in Chile. The real eye-opener for me has been this time with an intelligent, beautiful, inquisitive, delightful—"

"I just told you, I'm not—"

"Daughter." He closed his eyes. "I care deeply for you, Lacey, but the person I love in this house is Ashley, and I only want a chance at being in her life to make up for the pitiful job I've done for the last fourteen years. That's all I want, I swear."

She believed him, she really did. And who was she to deny her daughter that kind of love?

Chapter 24

Lacey whipped open the bottom cabinet and prayed for a small miracle. And got one. She almost clapped her hands with relief.

"There is a God," she whispered. "And He has just provided a silver jelly-roll pan without a dent or a nonstick coating. Now if the chocolate in the fridge isn't ready, I can start a second pan."

From the living room she heard Clay laugh softly, a sound she'd been listening to and enjoying for almost ten days. And a lot of nights, when she could sneak out.

"Nothing is funny about chocolate ruffle cake," she called out, pushing herself up to a stand.

"You're funny when you bake," he replied. "Do you know how much you talk to yourself?"

"This cake is incredibly important, Clay." She set the pan on the counter and took a few steps to the left so she could see him in the living room. "The baby shower is being given by Julia Brewer, who is married to Scott Reddick, son of Paula Reddick, who sits on the town council. She's someone we have to impress."

She bit her lip to see if he'd reacted to the *we,* a word that had popped up between them an awful lot in the last ten days.

He didn't. Instead, he put down a coral-colored pencil and smiled at her, his grin like a bucket of sunshine in the cramped room. "I'm just laughing at how much you talk to yourself when you bake. I probably do the same thing here in my office."

And when had the rental-unit living room become his office? Again, things had just morphed in the last week and a half. Instead of an empty, badly decorated living area in a standard beachfront rental unit, the room had been transformed into Clay Walker's architectural studio.

A giant-screen computer design and drafting system and two other laptops stayed lit with bright green lines and angles and mathematical modelings of floor plans and rooflines and buttresses. Photos of Moroccan buildings were tacked to every available wall space, and a huge drafting table took up almost half the room.

"Well, I'm just happy this apartment came equipped with a decent jelly-roll pan because I don't feel like driving home to get mine and I've got to deliver this cake this afternoon."

He studied her, his head angled, his eyes bright. "C'mere."

And, just like that, she did. He was perched on his stool in front of the drafting table and she reached for him, wrapping her arms around his waist.

He flicked his finger on her cheek, then licked it. "Chocolate on strawberry. My favorite."

She snuggled closer, a familiar warmth folding through her like the satiny cocoa filling she'd just simmered on the stove. "What are you working on?" she asked, looking at the drawing in front of him. Rather than buildings or floor plans, this was a map of sorts.

"The traffic delivery system."

"The what?"

"Roads. To, from, and around Casa Blanca. But I really need to hear from my sister about those properties. She said she'd have information today about who bought them, and she's supposed to call me any minute. Knowing if we can have them really makes a difference in how I design the traffic pattern in and out of the resort."

"What if we don't know that, Clay? What do we present? Ideas with or without the other two properties included?"

"Definitely with," he said. "We'll find out who bought them and we'll figure out a way to get them. That's just an obstacle."

Which never bothered him. If she'd learned nothing else from Clay Walker, it was how to get over brick walls.

"So we are going to present as if we own the land. And we need to address traffic patterns in that meeting."

That meeting. The pressure of knowing that it was less than five days away almost made Lacey hustle back to her ruffle cake for some baking stress relief. But she stayed against Clay's warm body, and the anxiety magically lifted. Another small miracle. Who knew a man could be better than baking?

Not a man. *This* man.

"You look worried," he said, scrutinizing her face. "I can do this segment of the presentation, no fears."

She shook her head. "I'm just worried about everything. Including my ruffles. They can be tricky."

Nuzzling her, he worked his mouth into her neck for a kiss. "I like your ruffles." Sliding one hand over her breastbone, then lower, he caressed her nipple. "And your ridges."

"Very original," she laughed, arching into his touch because she couldn't stop herself. That's what he did to her every time. "And there can be no sex until I finish a second pan of chocolate, then make the ruffles, top the cake and—oh, shit!"

He eased his hand away. "What?"

"I forgot shelf liner to keep the chocolate against the sides. Damn, I shouldn't have agreed to a cake this complicated. No," she corrected herself, "I should have made it at home where I have everything. Except..."

"Except what?" he prodded, pulling her closer.

"Except that isn't home. It's my mother's house and she probably doesn't have shelf liner, either."

"There's a hardware store five minutes away."

Of course, he'd get right over the hurdle. He slid off the stool, wrapping her in both arms just as snugly as she planned to wrap that cake.

"Relax, Strawberry. It's all going to be okay. You'll finish the cake and we'll finish this presentation and we'll even get to sneak into bed later this afternoon and"—he tipped her chin—"we'll finish what we started when you walked in here this morning loaded down with bags of baking equipment."

She tried to swallow but couldn't, choked by desire and disappointment and happiness and hope and fear all at the same time. How was that particular mix of emotions even possible?

"I'm homesick." The admission popped out before she gave it a moment's thought, but the minute it did, all the emotions made sense.

She expected him to scoff, but he didn't, just looked at her with a very understanding expression.

"I miss having my own house. My own stuff. My own mess and special places to keep things. I want to bring you home, not to my parents' house where my ex is hovering like a helicopter and I don't even sleep in a room I can call mine." Her voice cracked again, and this time she couldn't fight the tear that spilled. "You can't imagine how hard it is not having your own place."

"Of course I can," he said. "Look around. You think I want to work like this? But you'll get there."

"Will I? I'm working so hard to build a business and this resort. But that's just a place for other people to have a vacation. Is that any kind of home? How will I raise Ashley there? How can I give her a—"

"Shhh." He put a finger over her lips. "I bet I know how to make you stop crying and start smiling. Come with me." He started walking toward the hallway, but Lacey stayed put.

"You can't take this feeling away with sex, Clay."

"Come on, Lace." He tugged at her hand. "I want to show you something."

"Oh, I know what you want to show me, and I'm telling you, that's not the answer to everything when your heart is breaking. And I need to finish my cake."

He turned, still holding her hand. "Please come in the bedroom with me."

"No."

He closed his eyes, almost fighting a smile. "Okay. Then wait here. This was going to be a surprise after the town council meeting, but I think this is a better time."

He dropped her hand and walked away, leaving her to stare after him. Then, burning with curiosity, she followed, peeking into the bedroom to see him on his knees, reaching under the bed.

He pulled out a few tubes of paper, folded back a corner to read something, then selected one of the rolls, shoving the others back under the bed.

For a moment she thought he was getting her shelf liner, since the paper looked thick enough to use. But then he unrolled the rubber band and spread a large blueprint over the bed. "This is something I've been working on for you."

The sketch of a building was similar in style to what he'd done for Casa Blanca, but this structure looked a little bigger than the villas yet still within the traditional Morocco-blended-with-old-Paris motif he'd captured for the resort.

But this was different, homey somehow. Intimate and inviting. This was like a...

"A house?"

"A home. For you and Ashley."

"Oh. Clay." She brought her hand to her mouth, as if she could contain the feeling welling up inside of her.

"You know that little corner, way at the end of the Tomlinson property line, just off the beach?" he asked. "I think we could build this right there, sort of at an angle facing southwest. You'd see Barefoot Bay and the resort, but be tucked away from the action of the business."

This was perfect. Too much. Too perfect. "How could I afford this?"

"Some creative financing," he said. "I've been talking to my sister about some mortgage options. In fact, that's another thing she's supposed to call me about today."

She looked up at him, a new waterfall of feeling cascading over her. "You talked to your sister about my house?"

"Of course I did. I'm close to her. She's the only family I have now."

"You have—" *Me.* She stopped herself before the word was out. "You have really blown me away with this," she finished, turning to the drawing, kneeling just to get closer to it. "This is just incredible."

"That's just the front elevation," he said, coming right down next to her to turn to the next blueprint. "Here's the back."

"It's even prettier. Is that a balcony?"

"I thought that would be Ashley's room. I gave her the whole upstairs, for, you know, teen privacy. But we could do anything to the floor plan." He flipped another page, and her heart went with it.

We could do anything. Yes, yes they could. Couldn't they? Her eyes filled again, making her vision too blurry to make out the clean lines of a kitchen and family room, a dining room and laundry. It was too much. He was too much.

"I thought we could—"

She cut off the suggestion with a kiss, hard and hot and as forceful as she could make it.

Under her lips, he laughed softly. "I take it that means you like it."

"I like it. I like it. I like *you*."

He chuckled again, the words having become a secret message between them. "I thought you said no sex until you do something to that cake."

"I need to do something to you first." She pressed herself into him, her fingers already grasping for more of him, dragging down his chest, over the delicious muscles, down to the zipper on his shorts.

Heat and desire pooled between her legs as she pushed him back to the floor and he tugged at her top to slide it up and get to her breasts. The instant his hand slipped under her bra her nipple budded in his hand, fireworks crackling through her, a molten ache building for more.

"Wait a second," he murmured, breaking their kiss. "I just heard my phone."

She clutched his hand and pulled him back to her. "Voice mail."

"It's Darcie," he said. "That's my sister's ring. She has a ten-minute window free today and this is going to take longer than that." He kissed her on the nose, pushing himself up. "Hold that thought, Strawberry. I'll be back in a minute, hopefully knowing who bought the land and how you can get a great mortgage on this house. Then we can celebrate all afternoon."

She smiled, watching him hurry to the other room, where he'd left his cell phone.

Sighing, she leaned against the bed and stared at the blueprints again. How did he know? How did he know what mattered so much to her? This wasn't part of the resort he had to build, this wasn't something she'd asked him for. This was just him *getting* her.

That was what caused a whirlwind of emotions every time she was with him. He got her. He understood. Overwhelmed, she let herself tumble back to the floor with a sigh of pure happiness. As she turned her head with a little giggle, she spied the other rolls of drawings tucked beneath the edge of the comforter.

Actually, that paper would make good shelf liner.

Reaching for the closest one, she drew it out, aware of Clay's monosyllabic answers on the phone. Were any of these blank? She uncurled one corner and saw a drawing of—*Ashley*?

Sitting up, she wiped away any guilt, rolling the rubber band low enough so she could see more of the drawing without actually opening it. Yep, it was a sketch of Ashley, looking up, laughing, a hammer in her hand.

Along the outside edge of the paper, in his square architect's printing, Clay had written the word *Family*.

Family? Did he see Ashley as—

No, that could mean anything. Maybe these were more sketches of the house. Should she look?

From the living room she heard Clay's baritone voice, a question, but she couldn't make out what he was saying. She was so, so tempted to open this drawing, but it wasn't her place. She'd ask him when he came back. He needed to explain why he'd referred to Ashley as family.

And then she'd show him just how happy that made her.

Chapter 25

Clay dropped onto the stool in front of the drafting table, picking up a pencil to shade a drawing instead of taking out his frustrations on his sister. "So, basically, all you've got is a Delaware-based corporation."

"And there are a million of those," Darcie agreed, equally frustrated. "This one has no more than a P.O. box, and a bunch of brick walls around that. And they paid cash, so there's no mortgage paper trail, or you know I'd be following it. I'm sorry, Clay. I really thought I got close to a name from a contact in D.C., but the flow of information shut off and now I can't get anything. Do you have a backup plan for the property?" she asked.

"A much smaller version of what we want," he said. And it wouldn't include that home he'd just showed Lacey, damn it. "But if we don't get those two properties, we have to compromise on everything."

"You're starting to sound French, big brother."

"Excuse me?"

"We, we, we. Or haven't you noticed that you never refer to 'the client,' only 'we' and 'us' and 'our'?"

He'd noticed.

"Now, do you want the information on the financing for the residence on the property?" she asked.

"Without knowing if we have those lots, it's moot. E-mail it to me."

"Okay, but…" She dragged out the last word, firing more frustration through him. He wanted to get back to Lacey.

"But what?"

"I have to tell you something." There was the tiniest note of desperation in her voice and it caught him.

"What?"

"Dad had a TIA."

His pencil froze as the words settled on his brain. "What the hell is that?"

"A transient ischemic attack, which, in English, is a mini-stroke. I wasn't going to tell you. Jayna told me not to tell."

A *stroke*? "What happened?" He got up and walked to the balcony, shoving open the sliding glass door and stepping outside into the humidity and sunshine.

"Nothing permanent, we think," she replied. "He just had this weird incident while he was driving."

"He was driving?"

"Yes, but no accident. Jayna helped him pull over and, oh, it was scary, Clay. Elliott was in the car and Dad just kind of blacked out. He couldn't even talk for a few minutes, an ambulance came and—"

"Is he in the hospital? Jesus, Darcie, why the hell didn't you call me?"

"Jayna said—"

He smacked the balcony railing hard enough to make it shake. "Damn it! He's my father I have a right to know if he's sick."

"I didn't think you'd care."

He didn't think he would, either. "Just let me know if anything else happens."

"The doctors are watching him. And Jayna's taking care of him."

"Checking all his bank accounts, no doubt." He regretted the words the minute they were out.

But Darcie just sighed into the phone as if she were so over the old wounds. Of course she was. He had the scars; his sister didn't. "I gotta go, Clay. If I find out anything at all about those properties, I'll call you."

He stood still for a long moment, staring at the Intracoastal Waterway shimmering in front of him, a lone skiff bouncing on the gentle waves. Nothing registered. Just emptiness.

Is this what he'd feel if his father . . .

Holy, holy shit. He couldn't even think the words. If Dad died with all this crap between them, well, that would be on his father's soul and take him right where he belonged, wouldn't it?

But Clay would carry it all around forever, like a bag of wet concrete hanging off his heart.

What the hell was he supposed to do? Forgive him? No way. No, no way.

"Hey, Clay, you coming back?"

"Yeah." Back to the comfort and warmth and escape he needed.

In the bedroom he found Lacey sitting cross-legged on

the bed, leaning over the blueprints, her hair falling into her face.

She didn't look up, mesmerized by the house he'd created. "You know what I love most about this floor plan?" she asked.

Right then, he didn't care. He didn't want to talk about floor plans or buildings or families or fathers he should forgive. Right now he wanted help. And the woman who could give it to him was on his bed.

He stood stone still next to her, his jaw clenched, his hands fisted.

"What's wrong?" she asked, finally looking up, her eyes as bright as sun-dappled whiskey and just as potent for the numbing he needed. "What did Darcie say?"

That my father is sick. "Nothing."

"Nothing? Doesn't look like nothing. Did you find out who bought the property? Oh, God, it's David, isn't it?"

He shook his head, snagging the blueprints and tossing them to the floor. "No, we don't know yet. C'mere." He dropped a knee onto the bed and reached for her.

"Clay, are you going all caveman on me?"

"Yeah." He practically knocked her back, climbing on top of her, kissing her hard on the mouth.

She managed to turn her head. "What the hell is up with you?"

He remained suspended just inches from her, blood already racing south, making him hard and needy.

"Lacey." His voice felt as rough as it sounded. "Don't take this the wrong way, honey, but I don't want to talk." He took her hand and very slowly brought it down to his erection, placing her palm on him.

"Oh. I see that."

Did she? Did she know that needing her physically helped erase the terror of how much he needed her in other ways? In all ways?

"That was a helluva conversation with your sister," she said with a wry smile. "It was your sister, wasn't it?"

"We don't have a buyer's name," he said, swallowing. "And..." *My father might be dying. Tell her. Tell her.* "And she's sending me information on your mortgage."

"And that got you this hot?"

"You got me this hot." He punctuated that with a slow kiss, rolling against her, taking it a little easier this time. "You started it," he said. "I just want to finish."

And then he'd share Darcie's news. When Lacey was naked and in his arms, when he'd given her everything and taken just as much.

"Okay." She kissed his throat, worked her way up his jaw until her lips found his mouth for another long, deep kiss. He slid under her shirt and up to her bra, thumbing her sweet, budded nipple, knowing that always numbed his brain.

She sighed, bowing her back to allow him to touch every inch. He pulsed against her, desperate and anxious, steaming with need. His head buzzed with the sudden loss of blood, his fingers ached to squeeze and touch, his balls tightening, ready for release.

Lifting his head, he bypassed another kiss, hungry to suck her breast and steal some comfort there.

"Clay." She pushed his forehead, forcing him to look at her.

He shook out of her touch, determined to get his mouth on her.

"Clay, what the hell is going on?"

He froze in the act of kissing her breast, realizing what was happening. Holy shit, he was crying.

Very, very slowly he lifted his head. She stared at him, neither saying a word.

He took a few slow, steadying breaths. "My..." He couldn't say the words.

"Your what?" she coaxed.

My dad might be sick. Why couldn't he just tell her? Why couldn't he share this intimate detail with a woman he was so, well, intimate with?

"Is it the resort? Your family? What?"

Your family. There, she'd opened the door wide and still he couldn't step through. Why the hell not? Rolling over, he fell onto his back on the bed, throwing his arm across his face. If he told her, he knew exactly what would happen. She'd tell him to get his ass to North Carolina, mend his broken bridges, forgive the old bastard, and move on. Move on and have a healthy, happy, loving relationship with a fantastic, smart, beautiful woman.

Wait a second. How had he gotten from point A to *love*? His mind, trained in every kind of geometry, couldn't even get around that.

"We could bake," she whispered softly.

"Pardon?"

"I do when something's really bugging me. I could show you how to make chocolate ribbons for the ruffle cake."

He actually laughed. "You want to teach me to bake. Now?"

"Hey, if you can master a Julia Child chocolate ribbon curl, you can master anything. Even whatever it is that's eating away at you right now."

Something warm and wonderful bubbled up in his chest as he looked at her. Something that felt complete. It wasn't what she suggested, it was how. With so much tenderness and caring and genuine concern.

And for some inexplicable reason, that turned him on more than anything.

"We can bake later." He eased his hand under her top again, "And the only thing eating away at me is all these clothes."

But she didn't cooperate with undressing, tracing a line over his face, tapping above his brows. "There's so much going on in here. If you let me in, I could help you."

"Please." He just closed his eyes and pulled her closer.

"Please what?" She leaned over him, her curls brushing his cheeks, her lips close to his. "You want sex?"

"I want you." It was a big admission, and he covered by working her top all the way up, concentrating on her body. "You."

The realization shocked him almost as much as the pressure of her kiss, the truth of it blinding him for a moment. He didn't need this; he needed *her*.

He unclasped her bra with one hand and started on her jeans with the other.

"You can have me," she whispered softly, a vixen with golden red hair and topaz glinting in her brown eyes. She fell on her back so he could suck the peak of one breast and caress the other.

Under him, she rocked her hips and they met in a natural, ancient, unstoppable rhythm, each time he groaned and she gasped, each breath triggering more sparks of arousal and need.

She wrapped her legs around him and he just rode

her, his hard-on so close to where it needed to be, his shorts and her jeans the only thing preventing their bodies from being exactly how they both wanted them to be: connected.

He kneeled up to get rid of those remaining barriers, his gaze locked on her slick nipples, taut and pink, still wet from his mouth. His brain went blissfully blank, his dick mercilessly rigid.

He freed himself while she wriggled out of her jeans, the scent of sex already filling the room and his head, her hands closing over his erection the moment she'd shed her pants.

Rocking into each stroke, he stayed on his knees, head back, eyes closed, pleasure shooting like fireworks up his back, down his legs, and straight through his balls. The world was forgotten, except right here in this room with this woman.

She took it all away.

She sat up, her lips inches from his shaft. He looked down at the very instant she looked up, their gazes locking as she opened her mouth and took one slow lick of his already moist tip. Then she slid him into her mouth. It was too much. A different kind of pleasure, a ripping sensation of closeness that electrified and terrified and stunned him.

"Lacey."

Still looking up, still holding him with her eyes and her mouth—and her heart—she took him even deeper. He wanted to be inside her, he wanted to make—

Pleasure jolted as she sucked, holding him like he was precious to her. Loving him with her mouth and kisses, giving everything just for his satisfaction. The act, as sexual and hot and mind-blowing as anything, suddenly felt like so much more.

Like she was giving him all the comfort he needed, with her mouth and hands and heart.

She licked again, closed her eyes, and slowly, lovingly, sweetly ministered her special brand of comfort. He relaxed into the sensation, letting the thrill of release build and grow and overpower every other thought or feeling.

He lost any shred of control, an orgasm kicking through him, squeezing him until he called out, torturing him while he grew stiffer and more helpless. Sweat tingled and blood pumped and raw, pure, intense pleasure punched through his body until he finally let go of everything. Everything but Lacey. He clung to her shoulders, her feathery silken curls, and spilled into her mouth.

Closing her eyes, she coaxed the very last drop out of him until they both fell back on the bed. He couldn't breathe, couldn't see straight, couldn't talk.

"Clay." She stroked his skin, her delicate touch like a firebrand over the sheen of sweat.

"Mmmm."

"I need to know something."

Of course she did. She needed to know why he had been upset on the phone. She needed to know how he really felt about her. She needed to know when this thing had gone from purely sexual to wildly emotional.

"I just don't know if I can tell you what you need to know, Lace," he said, his voice still raspy from the heavy breathing. But he had to. He had to be straight with her. "But I'll try."

"What are the drawings under your bed?"

He turned to face her. "You looked at them?"

She hesitated, then shook her head. "Not really, but I thought I could use the paper for shelf liner."

He didn't want her to see those sketches. "I have some extra paper like that you can use."

"But what are they?"

"Just ideas I have."

"For what?"

He waited for his heart to slow before he answered, carefully choosing his words. "They are ideas for things I might build in the future."

She studied his face, definitely not sold on that. "Things that include Ashley?"

So she *had* looked at them. "They're personal," he said, a little more gruffly than he meant.

She leaned up on one elbow. "If they include my daughter, they're not personal."

"I told you, I draw what I visualize. It's the curse of an overactive imagination."

"You visualize Ashley with a hammer?"

Was that all she'd seen? It had to be. If she'd seen the rest of those drawings, the one with Ashley hammering a two-by-four would be the least interesting to her. "I expect Ashley to have a role in building the resort and your house, don't you?"

"I hope so," she finally said.

"Well, that's all those pictures are. Memories of moments that haven't happened yet. You know, if I see something well enough to draw it, I can make it happen."

"What else do you see?" The question was tentative, a little scared, and full of hope.

"Right now I'm trying to visualize how you can

make ribbons out of chocolate. Why don't you show me and then we can come back in here and..." *Go ahead, man, say the thing you cannot say.* "Make love." He leaned in to whisper in her ear. "Can you visualize that, Strawberry?"

Because he could. He could visualize it all too clearly.

Chapter 26

ｃ◡

Later that afternoon, when Clay pulled up to Julia Brewer's house, Lacey dipped her head to peer at the minivan in the driveway. "Well, it looks like we're a lot less than six degrees away from Paula Reddick, town council member." She gingerly shifted the chocolate ruffle cake on her lap. "She's inside. Want to come in and charm her?"

He shook his head, opening his door. "I have to call my sister back and ask her about something else while you take the cake in. But hang on. I'll help you get it out."

Lacey's heart slipped a little as he climbed from the truck. The afternoon had been amazing. They'd finished the cake, fallen into bed, and spent the last hour in the shower. And yet he still hadn't told her what had had upset him so much about the phone call with his sister, and she didn't want to whine or beg.

Maybe he didn't trust her, or maybe it wasn't that big

a deal. But, Lord, he'd *cried*. Something had upset him pretty badly.

Jayna?

She crushed the name when it popped into her head. There was no room for ex-girlfriend jealousy in her head or heart. For crying out loud, David was living with her and Clay wasn't acting jealous. But he had gotten off the phone pretty worked up for sex.

No. *Don't think that way.*

He popped open the door and reached in for the cake. "You did an amazing job on this, Lacey."

"I hope they like it. My business has come to a screeching halt since the storm." She stepped down from the running board and took the cake he held. "Be right back."

"Take your time."

So he could call . . .

Don't go there, Lacey. Don't make excuses where none exist. She headed up to the house gripping her ruffle cake with care, grateful when Julia opened the front door and she didn't have to knock.

"Hey, Lacey," Julia said. "How'd the cake come out?"

Lacey looked down at the nest of chocolate ribbons on the cake tucked in a topless box. "Pretty good, I think."

"Wow, would you look at that?"

Smiling at her creation, Lacey lifted it higher. "Yep, it's nice."

"I meant that guy outside."

Lacey followed Julia's gaze, catching a glimpse of Clay leaning against the truck, on the phone. "Oh." She laughed. "That's Clay. My . . ." *Lover. Boyfriend. Main squeeze.* "Architect."

"He can build me a house anytime."

"Lacey's not building a house," a woman around the corner said. Paula Reddick stepped into the entryway, as tiny and trim as she'd been when she'd taught PE at Mimosa High. "She's building a posh resort."

"It's not..." Yes, it was. Posh and a resort. "It's still in the planning stages, as you know. Hi, Paula."

Paula gave a quick smile. "Don't worry, Lace. I like the idea. Charity Grambling may kill me in my sleep, but you have my vote."

"Thanks," she said, handing the cake to Julia. "Keep it chilled until the shower tomorrow."

"Let me go get your check, Lacey."

When she left, Paula moved closer to the front door, peering over Lacey's shoulder. "Did you guys work out his shady past?"

"It's not that shady," Lacey replied. "He's clean."

"Looks dirty." Paula grinned. "In a fun way."

Lacey just laughed softly. Oh, if Paula only knew how Lacey had spent her afternoon.

"What's your plan to counteract Charity's flyer campaign?"

Lacey drew back, surprised. "What flyer campaign?"

"Get thee into town, m'dear. You're up against a street team of people trying to stop you before you start. They're all under her wrinkled old thumb."

Lacey sighed as Julia returned with a check. "Thanks for the business, Julia. And for the warning, Paula. Guess I'll head into town and see how bad the damage is."

As she came out, Clay hung up the phone and opened the door for her. "All set?"

"Maybe not yet. We have to head into town now."

On the way there she explained what Paula had told

her, zeroing in on a bright yellow flyer with bold black letters as soon as they got to Ms. Icey's, an ice cream parlor on the outskirts of Mimosa Key's undersized downtown.

SAVE MIMOSA KEY!

Stop all zoning modifications!

Be heard at the Town Council meeting on September 15 at 10:00 AM!

Don't let progress replace pristine!

"Pull over, Clay. I'll grab it." She climbed out of the car, marching into the store to ask Bernadette Icey to take it down, barely noticing a group of teens at a corner table.

"Mom!" Ashley's voice broke through the laughter.

Lacey glanced at the group, all of their faces unfamiliar to her but one. "Ashley, what are you doing here?"

She popped up and threaded through a few empty tables to get to Lacey. "We just came in for ice cream. What are *you* doing here?" Her eyes were bright, her color high. She definitely hadn't been expecting Lacey to walk in.

Lacey looked at the kids again. "Who are they?"

"Just my new friends. Some of them live down south near us, so I'm getting to know some other people."

"Where's Meagan?"

"Oh, Mom, Meagan is turning into such a—"

"Is that Tiffany Osborne?"

Ashley hushed her, blocking the view. "Mom, you don't have to say her name like that. She's not some kind of pothead."

But Lacey wasn't sure of that. "I have to get that flyer in the window down. Is Bernadette here?"

"Miss Icey?" Ashley turned. "No, but that kid's the manager."

Behind the counter a sixteen-year-old was texting.

"Then he won't care if I do this." Lacey slipped behind the front table and ripped down the yellow flyer. "Go get your stuff, Ashley."

"What? Why can't I stay?"

"Because I don't know these kids." Weak argument, but Lacey had a bad feeling. And Ashley wasn't exactly dragging her over to meet them all.

"Hey, Ash!" A boy with swooping bangs and skinny shoulders called out. "Move your ash back here." The entire table hooted with laughter.

Ashley's cheeks flamed. "Shut up, Matt."

Lacey almost reprimanded her for saying shut up, mostly out of habit, but honestly, that felt like the least of her problems. "Get your stuff and let's go," she whispered. "Now."

"Mom, why?"

"Because…" *I said so* was just lame and this was not the time or place to make her point. She lifted the flyer. "I need your help getting rid of these. They're all over town."

"What are they?" Ashley took the flyer and read. "What the…"

"So get your bag and let's go," Lacey ordered with enough force that Ashley didn't argue.

"Gimme a sec. I'll meet you outside."

Lacey was waiting in the truck considering all the ways this could go when Ashley came out of Ms. Icey's and narrowed her eyes.

"Why is he here?" she asked, yanking open the door to the back cab. "I thought we were going alone."

Lacey ignored the question and whipped around to face her daughter. "I don't want you hanging out with those kids."

"Mom, they're fine. Honest."

"I don't like them."

"You don't know them."

"Then bring them home."

She snorted. "We don't have a home."

Lacey and Clay shared a silent look, and then Lacey let it drop.

They saw about fifteen more flyers on the way through the few streets that made up downtown Mimosa Key, taped to the locally owned storefronts and the old iron light posts that lined the main streets. Every time they spotted another one, either Lacey or Ashley got out to rip it down. With each sighting Ashley grew more indignant.

"This is so wrong!" she said when she climbed in after taking one off the railing by the harbor. "I knew Charity Grambling was a b-word, but this is so unfair!"

"Charity and her friends see our project as competition for their business, and it's a free country. They can fight us," Lacey said.

"Let them lose everything they have and see how they feel."

"You know what?" Clay said, taking an unexpected turn north. "I have an idea."

"Make our own street team and plaster some flyers all over town?" Ashley replied. "'Cause my friends would totally get behind me on this."

"I have the plans," he said quietly to Lacey. "They're under my seat."

The plans to the new house?

"I thought we might go up to Barefoot Bay and check it out," Clay said. "Let's take Ashley."

"Take me where?" Ashley asked.

"You'll see." Clay turned and smiled. "I think you're gonna like it."

At least she didn't argue. When they arrived at the property, Clay brought the rolled-up sketch and they walked north.

"What are we looking for up here?" Ashley asked. "More flyers?"

Clay slowed his step and got on her other side so that he and Lacey were flanking her. "What are *you* looking for?" he asked Ashley.

She scowled at him. "Is that a trick question?"

"Nope, I'm serious. What's missing in your life?"

"A boyfriend, and Mom probably just killed the deal by dragging me away from Ms. Icey's."

"If that Justin Bieber-y thing was your boyfriend—"

"Eww, Mom. Totally gross. Matt's so much cuter than Bieber."

"Answer his question, then. Something more important is missing in your life, isn't it?" Lacey couldn't keep the note of anticipation out of her voice.

She froze, horror on her face. "Oh my freaking God, you two are getting married."

This time Lacey's steps slowed as heat that had nothing to do with the late-day sun blasted her. But Clay laughed easily, seemingly not fazed by the question. Maybe it was so out of the realm of possible that he didn't take it seriously.

"Just answer the question," he said. "What don't you have that you wish you did?"

"Well, besides all my old clothes, my favorite Wii games, my collection of stuffed dogs, my yearbooks

going back to kindergarten, and every Christmas ornament Mom ever got me, I guess my own room."

The list of missing treasures made Lacey's heart hitch.
Clay must have felt the same way, because he put a gentle
arm on Ashley's back and led her toward the far corner of
the Tomlinson property line. "That's right, Ashley. You
need a home."

"No sh—" She stopped again, looking from one to the
other. "I thought you two wanted to build a resort."

"We do, and we will." Clay's confidence gave Lacey
another thrill. "But we want to build something else,
assuming we can get our zoning issues approved and get
these two properties back." He looked at Lacey. "And I
know we will."

"What?" Ashley asked, looking at Lacey for the
answer. "What are you building?"

"This." Clay unrolled the blueprint and spread it on a
patch of grass. "Your home."

"A house? For us?" Ashley's voice rose just enough to
make Clay look up and smile.

"I hope you like it."

She dropped to her knees exactly as Lacey had when
she'd seen the plans. "Ohmigawd, it's beautiful! Mom,
did you see this? It's so awesome." She rocked back. "We
could live there?"

"We're going to try," Lacey said, so completely hopeful about the idea that it scared her. What if it didn't happen? What if she couldn't afford it or the zoning didn't get
approved or the property—

"That's my room?" Ashley shrieked as Clay turned
the page and showed the floor plan, pointing to the space
that said "Ashley's Room" in tiny, squared-off letters.

How did he know? she wondered again. How did he know just what mattered the most? "That whole thing is my room? With my own bathroom?" For a minute Lacey thought Ashley would throw her arms around Clay and kiss him.

Lacey knew exactly how that felt. "Isn't it amazing?" Lacey asked. But what she really wanted to say was *Isn't he amazing? Isn't he brilliant and special and thoughtful and don't you just love him?*

Because sometimes, like at this very moment, Lacey thought she could love Clay. Maybe she already did. Was that possible?

"Look at the kitchen, Mom! All that space for you to bake."

The comment touched Lacey enough to bring her down to her knees.

"She's quite a baker, too, your Mom."

More warmth crawled up her cheeks. Lacey didn't dare look at Clay because she didn't want to see the expression that went with that comment. The chocolate ribbons had gotten pretty sexy.

Wasn't that what he was thinking? While she was standing here dreaming about the L-word? She finally looked at him, self-consciously pushing a hair from her face

His gaze wasn't the least bit sexual. His gaze said he might be thinking the same thing.

"And my dad's a beast cook," Ashley said, crashing the moment with a dose of David. "He'd totally rock that kitchen. In fact, he texted me that he's making steak tonight. You should come over for dinner. Can he, Mom?" The note of hope in Ashley's voice must have surprised Clay as much as Lacey, as he suddenly stood, brushing some sand off his cargo shorts.

"Of course he can," Lacey said.

"Cool. Then we can we show Dad this house. He'll love it." Ashley smoothed down the curling edge of the blueprint. "It might be the kind of thing that would convince him to stay." There was even more hope in that statement. Just enough to break Lacey's heart.

David wasn't staying, but how could she convince Ashley of that? She looked up at Clay, who was gazing out to the Gulf, lost in thought.

And who was going to convince Lacey that Clay wasn't going to stay, either? "Do you want to come over, Clay?" Lacey asked.

"I'm going take a pass," he said. "I need to work through dinner tonight. That September fifteenth deadline looms right around the corner, Lacey."

"Another time, then," she said quietly. "Anyway, Zoe and Tessa are coming over." And maybe they'd talk Lacey off this love ledge before she fell right off and broke something. Like her heart.

Chapter 27

After Clay took a long swim in the warm waters of the Gulf of Mexico, he headed over to the Super Min to buy some snacks to get him through the night of work. Instead of one of the older women he expected to see, Gloria Vail sat behind the counter. He could tell the G-cousins apart now, and Gloria was definitely more friend than foe, and he meant to thank her for tipping Lacey off to the secret meeting.

She sat on a stool, chatting with a man who stepped away from her the minute Clay walked in.

Not a man, though. *The* man. In a sharp sheriff's uniform, a Glock on his hip.

"Oh, hi," Gloria said to Clay, giving her bangs a quick fluff. "Nice to see you again."

Feeling the sheriff's attention on him, Clay gave her a nod, walking to the cooler to get a liter of soda. When he came back, the sheriff had moved to the candy display.

Clay grabbed some chips and his stomach rumbled, reminding him that he had next to nothing to eat in the apartment and he'd turned down a dinner invitation.

"How's it going?" Glo asked.

"Good." The smell of the hot dogs and burritos rolling out of a heated cooking unit drew him closer. "Starved."

"Well don't eat those," Gloria said quickly. "They're awful."

The sheriff chuckled as Clay took the rest of his purchases to the counter. "She's not lyin'," he said. "Charity sells the worst hot dogs on the island. Maybe in the state."

"Thanks for the tip." Clay slid the soda toward Gloria. "That's the second time you've given me good advice."

"Just remember, don't tell my aunt. I'll be disowned."

The sheriff took a step closer, tanned and sharp-eyed, a sizable dude who was no stranger to the gym. "You're too scared of her, Glo."

"I'm not…" She caught the other man's eye and shrugged. "Sometimes. Who wouldn't be, Slade?"

"She can be scary," Clay agreed.

"You two know each other?" the sheriff asked, eyeing Clay a little suspiciously.

"Clay Walker." He held out his hand.

"He's the architect I told you about, doing Lacey Armstrong's property up in Barefoot Bay."

"I'm Slade Garrison." He took Clay's hand and gave a tentative smile but a strong shake. "I heard you landed a few on Charity's chin recently."

"Not literally," he assured the lawman.

"Enough that you've become a little bit of a folk hero around here."

Clay almost choked. "I have?"

"Rumors and stories fly on Mimosa Key," Gloria told him. "By the time the tellin' was done, there were people saying you tore up the bylaw book and threw the paper shreds at Charity just for laughs."

"Wish I'da thought of that."

"I know," she said. "But people like the idea of someone taking her on. And congratulations for Lacey getting on the zoning meeting agenda."

"Any curveballs we should expect?" he asked.

Gloria rang up the soda and chips, shaking her head. "Not that I'm aware of."

The bell behind him dinged, followed by some conversation and laughter, both of which stopped almost instantly.

Clay turned to face the very woman they'd been discussing, Charity Grambling, accompanied by her daughter, Grace, and a heavyset man. Seriously heavyset.

"We get robbed or something, Slade?" the man asked as he headed to the back cooler.

The sheriff crossed his arms and stared the other guy down. "You better plan on walking if you pick up a Bud Light, Ron."

He got a laugh in response. "Like I'd drink piss-water beer. Anyway, Gracie's drivin' and she's sober as a judge."

Meanwhile, Charity leveled Clay with a hard look, moving toward the counter. "Hope you're not planning on hanging any more of these out there." She slammed a fistful of bright pink papers on the counter.

He frowned, looking closer at the words:

SAVE ASHLEY ARMSTRONG'S HOME!!! Vote Yes For Zoning Changes!!!

So Ashley had made her own street team, just like she'd mentioned.

"I had to stop those little hooligans from putting them up outside the Fourway," Grace said, scowling at him. "You should arrest them all, Slade."

"Is it against the law to hang a flyer?" Clay asked.

"Thought you had the local laws memorized," Grace shot back.

"Not against the law to hang flyers, but"—Charity flipped the back countertop and stepped to the register, practically shoving Gloria aside—"last time I checked *the use of marijuana* was illegal." She pointed a finger at the sheriff. "So maybe instead of hanging out in my fine establishment trying to work up the balls to ask Glo on a date, you should be rounding up some criminals down at the Mimosa High football field."

Shit. Was Ashley there?

"You certain about that, Charity?" Slade asked, his voice deeper and more authoritative than when he'd been hitting on Gloria.

Charity put a hand on her hip, snorting softly. "I'm sure. Those kids are hanging around the same place kids have been gettin' high since I was a freshman at that school." She gave him a slow, easy grin, turning her face into a web of creases. "No jokes about what year that was. Get down there now and you'll find 'em. Got all their stupid flyers up and now they're doing what kids do."

Clay grabbed the plastic bag with soda and chips, nodded to the others, and headed toward the door, mentally flipping through his options. Call Lacey and tell her? But could she get up to the football field in time to get Ashley out of there?

He slid behind the wheel of his truck, catching Slade and Gloria walking out in his rearview mirror. They talked for a minute, and Slade put a hand on the woman's shoulder.

Take your sweet time getting the phone number, Sheriff Garrison. Clay needed to get Ashley out of there.

He pulled out of the lot slowly, not wanting to draw Slade's attention, headed down to the first intersection, and then gunned it to the high school. When he reached the side street that ran along the football field, he parked the truck close enough to make a fast getaway and jogged toward the stands.

An impromptu party was well underway, about twenty kids messing around, laughing and standing in small groups. The bittersweet aroma of weed, the sound of teenage trouble, the thrum of a small-town summer night all hung under the bleachers that probably shook on Fridays in the fall.

"Have you seen Ashley Armstrong?" he asked a couple leaning against a post, arms around each other.

The guy shook his head, but the girl pointed to the other side of the field. "She's with Tiffany and Matt."

He had to hand it to Lacey: Her instincts were right on. He rounded the crowd, ignored the looks, and spotted Ashley standing apart from a few kids.

"C'mon, you guys," she said. "I want to hang the rest of these."

A skinny boy with a mop of hair threw a lit cigarette on the ground and stepped closer to Ashley, draping a way-too-familiar arm around her. "Chillax, AshPain. We got your stupid flyers up. Now it's time to party."

Ashley shook him off. "I'm serious. We didn't do half of town."

The boy slipped around behind her, sliding his grimy paws around her waist. "Ashley needs a toke, guys."

She jerked harder. "No, I don't, Matt. I need—get off me."

Instantly Clay launched forward, his fists already balled. "Hey!" he barked. "Let her go."

They all stared at him, and Mop Head let go.

"What are you doing here?" Ashley asked, color draining from her cheeks.

When Clay reached her, he resisted the urge to grab her elbow and muscle her away. The smell of pot was strong, but not on her, and she looked clear eyed and straight. Still, they had minutes until the sheriff showed.

"I'm taking you home. *Now*." She opened her mouth to protest, but instead slid an embarrassed look at the boy.

A girl next to Ashley wobbled a little on too-high platform shoes, long hair in her face, eyes red enough for him to take a guess that this was Tiffany the Troublemaker.

"You're dating Ashley's mom, aren't you?" she asked. "My mom and her friends were talking about you two."

"Want me to call the cops, Ash?" the boy asked. "'Cause this guy looks like trouble."

"No need to call them," Clay said quietly, leaning closer to Ashley. "They're on their way."

"Seriously?" The question came from Mop Head.

"Slade Garrison will be here in one minute."

"Is he really?" Ashley asked, her eyes wide with concern.

"Yes, he is. And you can leave now and I can take you home, or you can call your mom from the police station. Your choice, Ashley."

"He's full of shit, Ash."

But she ignored the boy, looking hard at Clay. "'Kay. I'll go."

She went with Clay, not even saying good-bye to her

friends. At his truck, just as he reached for the passenger-door handle, blue and white flashing lights cut through the darkness, sending the pack of kids scattering.

"Get in," Clay ordered, giving her a shove into the passenger seat before jogging around to climb in the driver's side.

He turned on the ignition and Ashley stared straight ahead until a loud bang on the truck bed made her jump. "Ashley! Help me get out of here."

"It's Matt," she said, turning to the back. "My... friend."

"Didn't act like a friend."

She gave Clay a pleading look. "Can you take him home?"

Clay nodded and Ashley opened her door to yell, "Climb in the back, Matt. Hurry!"

The boy yanked open the back door and slid into the crew cab behind Clay. In the rearview mirror Clay saw fear on the kid's face, and the first hint of whiskers like a dirty mark over his lip.

"Thanks, man," the boy said. "Some prick must have busted us."

"You want to ride in the truck, son? Tell me where you live and shut up until we're there."

Nobody spoke while Clay pulled out of the back of the school lot, easily missed by Slade Garrison. Except for giving directions to Matt's house, Ashley stayed silent until they arrived at a small house in south Mimosa Key, not too far from Lacey's parents'.

When Clay pulled into driveway, Matt threw open the back door. "Thanks for the ride."

"Wait a second." Clay was out as fast as the kid, blocking him. "I need to tell you something."

The boy looked up at him, a whole different kind of scared in his eyes. "What?" He tried for tough, but his voice cracked.

Clay leaned an inch closer, keeping his fists clenched but careful not to touch the boy. "You ever put a hand on Ashley Armstrong again and you'll be sorry."

"Yeah, I—"

"Seriously sorry."

The kid's protruding Adam's apple lifted and fell. "I don't even like her that much."

The little bastard. Clay moved one inch closer. "Then leave her alone."

" 'Kay."

Clay didn't move, but Matt finally stepped to the side, giving a final worried look over his shoulder as he bolted into his house. When Clay heard the side door slam, he got back in the truck, braced for a teenage onslaught of fury.

But Ashley just gnawed on her bottom lip, reminding him very much of Lacey when something troubled her. "What a tool," she finally murmured.

"Yep." He threw the truck into Reverse but kept his foot on the brake, looking at her. "You deserve a whole lot better."

"I thought those kids were cool, but they're not." She turned to him, her eyes moist. "Are you going to tell my mom?"

"I have to."

"Please, please don't. She'll be so disappointed in me." Her voice cracked and she turned to hide her tears.

"Did you smoke pot?"

"No! Honest to God, Clay, I never have. I don't even want to. I was scared of what they were doing, and I was really kind of glad to see you."

The words squeezed his chest, tugging on a heartstring he didn't even know he had. "And you are never going to hang out with that idiot again, right?"

She laughed softly. "Right."

He picked up the flyers she'd left on the console. "Did you make these?"

She nodded.

"How 'bout we hang a few on the way back to your house?"

"Yeah." She smiled at him. "Good idea."

He parked near the Super Min, and Ashley produced a roll of tape she'd tucked into her pocket. They started on the west end of Center Street, slapping up flyers on every light post and storefront, and even the corner mailbox.

"Now that'll get you arrested," he said, ripping it off government property.

She laughed and taped one to the front post on the Fourway Motel sign. "And that'll get Grace Hartgrave's panties in a bunch."

"Damn straight. How about we put them on every car window?"

"Love it!" She grabbed more flyers while he lifted windshield wipers.

"I have to ask you a question, Clay."

"What's that?"

"You want kids?"

His hand stilled in the act of lifting the wiper blade on a Honda Civic. "Not really sure yet," he said slowly, searching her face to determine where she was going with that.

"'Cause, you know, my mom...she should have another baby before she's too old."

Going *there*. "Maybe she should," he said. "She's a darn good mother."

She smiled and pushed a hair out of her face, another gesture so like Lacey it kind of caught his heart. "Yeah, I know."

They tagged a few more cars. "My dad wants another kid," she said.

Of course he did, because he'd been so wonderful with the one he had. Clay just nodded.

"And, now don't take this the wrong way, but if you weren't around making my mom act like, well, all crazy and stuff, then she and my dad would get back together."

He came around the front of the last car in the row. "Do you really believe that?"

"I know it." She rolled her eyes. "I mean, she's all happy and sings and spends hours getting dressed when she's going to see you."

He almost smiled thinking about that. "What's wrong with her being happy, Ashley?"

"Nothing. What's wrong with her being married to my dad?"

Everything. "Hey, we're out of flyers," he said. "I'll take you home now."

"See?" she said as they walked toward his truck. "You don't even have an answer for that. 'Cause you know I'm right. You gave me that lecture about Matt. Well, how about taking one of your own? My mom thinks you're like, in love with her or something."

Or something.

"But all she ever tells me is how my dad is going to leave her, and that's exactly what you're going to do, isn't it?"

Eventually. Wasn't he?

"Isn't it?" she demanded.

He took a slow breath and exhaled it through clenched teeth. "We have to build this resort before—"

"I think she really wants another baby."

Did she? They'd never talked about it, but why would they? They'd known each other a few weeks and right now, it was all about sex. But Lacey was a nurturing woman, and young enough to have more kids. "And my dad wants one, too. I really like the idea of a little brother or sister. A bigger, you know, family."

He knew.

"And my dad, I know he hasn't been the world's best father, but he had an epi...efipan...a moment of knowing exactly what he should be doing."

An epiphany. "I had one of those once."

"Yeah? What did you decide to do?"

To stop trusting in the concept of *family*. "I, um, struck out on my own in business."

"Well, good for you." She put her hand on the truck's door handle. "I'm sorry for being such a, you know, opinionated kid. I just want you to know exactly what you're doing."

The problem was, he didn't have a clue what he was doing. Except feeling things for a woman who probably wanted more than he was equipped to give her.

"Let's get you home, Ash."

"That's not my home," she corrected. "But, thanks to you, I might have one soon. A home and a family."

Yeah. Well, he could help with only one of those.

Lacey, Zoe, and Tessa leaned over the coffee table, oohing and awing over the house plans.

"I just can't believe he did this for you, Lace," Tessa said. "Talk about thoughtful."

"I know." Lacey sighed, stroking her hand over the edge of the blueprint. "I was so touched. I just love..." *Him.* "That he did this."

"Finish the sentence the real way," Zoe said. "You love *him.*"

She looked up, feeling warm blood rush to her cheeks. "Is it possible?"

"Anything's possible," Tessa said, putting a hand over Lacey's. "Only you know in your heart how you feel."

"I feel insanely happy when I'm with him. Completely capable and beautiful and sexy and—"

"Who needs a refill?" David marched in from the kitchen holding a wine bottle but killing the buzz.

The girls shared a look that said the conversation wasn't over but would have to wait.

Misinterpreting the look, David glanced at the bottle. "Unless you want to switch to red because the steak will be ready in a few minutes."

Tessa pushed up. "I'll set the table, then."

"I'll do it," Lacey said quickly.

"No, no. You keep decorating your palace. Fox and I have this covered."

"Thanks, and I'm fine on wine, David. Zoe?"

She shook her head, pointing to the master bathroom. "I'd go for a bigger tub, because I'm starting to think you're going to use it. A lot."

David and Tessa disappeared into the kitchen and Lacey dropped her chin on her folded arms. "Yeah," she said in a dreamy voice. "A tub for two."

"Shhh. Listen." Zoe leaned toward the kitchen, a hand to her ear. "Hear them laughing?"

"Yeah."

"Have you noticed how those two laugh *all* the time?"

Lacey scowled. "Tessa and David? She can't stand him."

Zoe lifted a very meaningful brow. "You know the definition of irony?" she asked in a soft whisper.

"Probably not the way you're about to describe it."

She grinned. "David gets this baby he says he wants from the person who openly longs for one. Tessa."

Lacey's jaw dropped so fast and far she actually knocked her elbows off the edge of the table. "Now that would be . . ."

"Ironic."

"Impossible. She can barely stand to be in the same room with him *and* she's infertile."

The ring of Tessa's laughter floated out from the kitchen.

"Yeah, that definitely sounds like it's killing her to be in there with him." Zoe rocked back on her heels, crossing her arms. "Did you see how she launched into table setting that puts her in the very same tiny kitchen with him and, by the way, for your information, infertility is often a two-way street."

"Billy's girlfriend is pregnant. He's obviously able to make a baby."

Zoe shrugged. "Sometimes it's the chemistry of two people. They can get pregnant with others, but there's something wrong with PH balance or whatever."

"And you know this, how?"

"Because I talked to my Aunt Pasha last night and she was reading her beer bubbles."

Lacey snorted a soft laugh. "Like tea leaves?"

"Exactly, only with hops."

"Okay, and what did the Budweiser say to the old aunt who thinks she's psychic?"

Zoe gave a put upon look. "First of all, she doesn't think she's psychic, she's full-blooded *gypsy*." She dragged out the word as if that explained everything. "And second, she's not that old, somewhere between seventy and eighty; she won't say. And third, she prefers Blue Moon to Budweiser."

Lacey cracked up. "All right, and what did she predict?"

"She doesn't predict, she reads the clues."

"Zoe." Lacey was losing patience. "What?"

Zoe leaned very close to whisper. "She said Tessa's seed will grow in Barefoot Bay."

"And was this before or after you told her Tessa's moving here to run the gardens for the resort?"

Zoe just shook her head. "She wasn't talking about an organic mustard seed, honey."

"Okay, and David? Pasha's never even met David."

"Precisely." Zoe crossed her arms and smirked. "But the Blue Moon bubbles showed the face of a fox."

Lacey's eyes widened. "Are you sure it wasn't a wolf? Bubble art can be deceptive."

"Go ahead, make fun of her."

"Nah, it's too easy. Did you tell her about David?"

"Of course."

"Did you tell Tessa?"

She shook her head. "I'm filing it under one of those things we think is better kept secret."

Lacey took a drink from her almost-empty wineglass. "There's been a lot of those these past few—"

Headlights swept the driveway and a loud car-door slam pulled her attention and got her to her feet. "Oh, thank God, I bet that's Ashley. She went to hang her flyers in town with some friends and told me Meagan's mother would bring her home, but I was starting to—" She stopped cold at the front door, peering through the glass. "That's *Clay's* truck."

Why oh why did that send entire lightning bolts of happiness through her body? Because she was falling in love with him. She threw open the door, her smile faltering when Ashley climbed out of the passenger side.

"Hey, Mom," she called as Lacey stepped out on the patio to greet them.

"Hi. How did you two hook up?"

Clay threw a quick look at Ashley and ambled forward, his hands tucked in his jeans pockets. "I ran into Ashley in town, hanging some flyers, so I gave her a lift."

"Oh, good." She got a better look at Ashley's face, which was pale, and her expression was kind of worried. "Where's Meagan?"

"She, um, didn't go."

Clay reached her and Lacey waited for a quick hug or kiss; she'd gotten used to them over the past few weeks. But he seemed as uptight as Ashley.

"What's going on?" Lacey asked.

"Ashey was..." He gave her daughter another look, obviously opening the conversation for Ashley.

"Mom, I was with those kids you don't like and they got in trouble, but Clay knew about it and he got me home. I'm sorry."

Lacey didn't react, having trained for fourteen years not to be her own accusing mother but longing to know the whole story. "Are you all right?" she asked. "Did you get hurt?"

"Oh, no, not at all. And we did hang the rest of the fly-ers, so it wasn't a complete waste of a night."

Lacey nodded. "Go inside, Ashley. I want to talk to Clay."

"'Kay. G'night, Clay. And thanks a lot." She rushed up the walk and into the house.

"How bad was it?" she asked.

"Your instincts are right about those kids, but I think the night's events scared her enough that she won't hang out with them. You can get the details from her."

"I will." Her arms ached to reach out, but for some rea-son he wasn't coming to her, holding her, kissing her like always. "You okay?" she asked.

"Lacey, I . . ." He drew in a deep breath. "I have a lot of work to do before the presentation."

"I know."

"So, let me get focused on that. The minute I can, I'll call you and we'll start rehearsing."

Which was so not what she wanted him to say.

But how could she expect him to say anything when she was being just as coy and obtuse about her feelings? It was time to tell him the truth. But not here, not tonight.

"When can I . . ." Oh, God, she didn't want to sound desperate. But she was, at least a little. "When will you call?"

"Soon," he promised. He gave her a little smile, one that kicked her heart around in her chest until it felt a little black-and-blue. "You know I can't go too long with-out you."

Did she know that? "Same here." She couldn't help it; she took a step closer and put a hand on his chest, just to feel the strength and warmth of his body. She didn't expect to feel his heart hammering every bit as hard as hers.

"You sure you're okay?" she asked.

"I'm not sure of anything anymore, Strawberry." He gave her a tight smile and took one step back, denying her the chance to feel that beating heart. "But when I figure it out, you'll be the first to know."

Chapter 28

A teenager would do this. A bad, out-of-control, irresponsible, consequences-be-damned teenager like Lacey hoped her daughter never would be. But Lacey was doing it anyway.

Tiptoeing out of the house at one-thirty in the morning, her sandals in hand to be sure she could escape in silence, Lacey turned the knob on the back door slowly to avoid the click. She kept one ear cocked in case Ashley or David sprang from the darkness and caught her sneaking out in the middle of the night to go have sex on the beach.

Outside, the still, silent night air, redolent with the hint of salt that permeated the whole island, sent a chill of anticipation over her skin. She pulled out her phone and texted Clay.

Made it—meet you in 5 min!

Okay, maybe the exclamation point was taking the teenager thing too far. But Lacey couldn't help it. She was *happy*.

He'd finally texted. After almost two days—two long, lonely, empty days—Clay had texted. Okay, it had been after midnight and probably a total booty call, but Lacey didn't care. She needed to see him. She needed to tell him how she felt and, damn it, she was going to do that before the presentation. No excuses.

Holding the straps of her sandals in one hand, she ran fast enough that the air lifted her hair and the breeze tickled right through the thin cotton sundress she wore with absolutely nothing underneath. Every cell in her body tingled in anticipation.

"Strawberry, you have it bad," she whispered to herself, holding the nickname close to her heart. She'd never taste a strawberry again in her life without thinking of him. She could certainly tell him *that* tonight, if not some of her more intense thoughts about him.

The thought sent a shiver through her, this time right down to her bare toes as she scampered over the sandy sidewalk. His truck was already parked in a shadowy section of the lot, the lights off. Even in the waning moonlight, she could see his profile as he leaned against the headrest, eyes closed. She slipped up to the passenger's side and lifted the handle.

"You asleep at the wheel, Clay?"

He looked at her, his eyes clear, his smile a little distant.

"Hey," he said simply, finally dropping his gaze to the open top buttons of her thin cotton dress, the angle, she was certain, making it clear she had no bra on. He lingered there for a minute, then reached to bring her all the way into the truck.

"You look…" He hesitated, and her heart hit triple time as she waited for what he would say. "Just like I imagined you."

"When were you imagining me?"

"Pretty much every minute I'm not with you." Still holding her hand, he pulled her closer and she fell right into him, leaning over the console, anxious to meet his mouth.

"I've missed you," she whispered.

"Yeah, me, too." He kissed her gently at first, but instantly reacted to her heat, opening his mouth, holding her head in just the right place, soft lips torturing and tempting and taking ownership of hers.

Already breathless, she broke the kiss. "How's the work going?"

"Done." He ran his thumb over her lip, studying it as though the shape of it fascinated him. "We can rehearse the presentation tomorrow and present the next day."

"Do you love it?" she asked.

"I love…"

Lacey held her breath, one word pounding in her head like a bass drum. You. You. *You.*

"I love a lot of things about it," he finished, sending a physical jolt of disappointment through her.

"But not everything?" she prodded.

"There are a few things I'd like to change. I'm nervous that we don't have those properties in hand but we're presenting as though we do."

"You thought that was the best way to go."

He nodded. "I still do. I'm just worried about a curveball being thrown at us."

"We'll handle it," she said, leaning in for another kiss. "Are we going to the beach?" she whispered, meaning, of course, the complete privacy of *their* beach on Barefoot Bay. That was where she wanted to tell him how she felt.

He shook his head. "Let's stay here."

More disappointment. But she covered it with a soft laugh. "Could get, um, steamy in this truck."

"Could." He fluttered some of her curls in his fingers, then dragged his hand down to the opening of her dress, his jaw slack as he slipped into the bodice and easily palmed her breast.

They both closed their eyes at the impact.

"I never stop wanting that," she murmured, arching her back so he knew how much she loved his hand on her.

He leaned over and kissed her again, taking his hand out and slipping it under the hem of her dress, up her bare thighs.

"Now I really feel like a teenager instead of the mother of one."

He didn't answer, but inched his hand back down, his eyes flickering with an expression she couldn't read. "Ever think about another one?"

The question threw her so completely she wasn't entirely sure she understood. "Another baby?"

"Yeah, do you ever think about having another one?"

Where had that come from? A low, slow warmth wound through her, completely different from the heat his hands and mouth had been causing. "Why?"

He shrugged, the gesture more casual than the look in his eye let on. "Just wondering. I mean, you're..."

"Getting older," she supplied with a quick laugh. "But not too old."

"That's not what I meant and you know it. I was thinking...."

Hope, unexpected and raw and real, clutched her chest. Did *he* want a baby? Had being with her, and being with Ashley, made him realize how wonderful family could be?

She simply couldn't fight the smile that pulled at her mouth. "If you want to know the truth, yes. I could see myself doing it all again. Maybe better next time."

"You're a great mother, Lacey."

"Better than my own, that much is true, but I could stand for some improvement. And maybe a little help from"—*the right man*—"a good father."

"David wants another, doesn't he?"

"He said so, but we don't really have any reason to discuss it. Who told you that?"

He hesitated, then shrugged. "I'm just observant."

He hadn't been around David that much, had he? "So what brought that question on?" Did she sound needy? Too bad. Maybe this was the opening she needed to tell him exactly how she felt.

I'm falling in love with you, Clay. Maybe he would say it first. Right now.

"I've been thinking about some things," he said, looking away toward the beach.

Her heart did a quick double-beat. "What kind of things?"

"Just things." He still wouldn't look at her, and she fought the urge to reach out for his chin and turn him, just to say *Look at me, damn it.*

But his attention was on the black horizon of the water. And he was silent just a second or two too long, and all that happiness and hope started slowly seeping away like her heart was a balloon and his silence the pin that pricked it.

"I think you'll like the final outcome of the plans," he finally said.

"The building plans." Because she had a feeling they were talking about two very different kinds of plans.

"Of course, the Casa Blanca plans."

She slowly dropped back to her seat as the rest of her air, and hope, slipped away. "I can't wait to see them. To present them."

"And after that . . ." He finally looked at her.

"After that we're building a resort," she said, a little too sharply. "A resort that you designed. With villas and a house." Right? *Right?*

Silence. Oh, God.

"*Aren't* we, Clay?" A bad, bad feeling slivered through her.

"Lacey, I think maybe you should take the project to another builder."

She just stared at him, any chance of taking a breath or firing back a response gone.

"I mean, you'll have what you need to get started and I'll have enough to sit for the exams. And I can consult from North Carolina if you—"

"Consult?" She practically choked the word. "You want to be a consultant?"

While she was sitting here rehearsing the first *I love you*? She grabbed the door, fighting the urge to flip the handle, shove it open, and run.

Instead she squeezed the metal and clenched her teeth. "If that's what you want to do, then fine."

"Lacey."

"What?" She turned on him. "What do you want me to say? Great idea, Clay! Be a consultant from a thousand miles away."

"I want you to have what you want."

"I want *you*." So much for subtle, perfectly timed, romantic admissions.

He took a slow breath. "I can't give you want you want."

"Meaning, what? You can't give me..." *Say it, say it, say it.* "Love."

The word hung like a cloying scent in the car. He swallowed and closed his eyes.

Shit. "I'm taking a walk," she said.

Without waiting for his response she slid onto the running board, then hit the asphalt, congratulating herself on not bolting away like a kid having a temper tantrum.

Instead she took long strides to the boardwalk, then down to the beach, making it about fifty feet before he reached her side and took her arm.

"Lacey, please. This is better for both of us."

"Is it? Well, sorry, I'll be the judge of what's better for me and I can tell you that your going back to North Carolina is not better for me. And David Fox is not better for me. No one is better for me than you."

"Are you sure?" He took her wrist to pull her closer, but she yanked herself out of his grip.

"What do I need to say to convince you? I'm not in love with him. I'm...I'm not interested in having another child with him, no matter what he says or anyone else says."

"I want you to be certain of that, because I can't give you that."

"I never said I wanted a child."

"I can't give you all the things you want. I can't give you the kind of love you deserve. I'm not—I don't have that in me. I have..."

"I know what you have," she said. "Issues. Pain. A hurtful breakup. Problems. It's called life, Clay. And you're using them as..." She laughed softly, the irony of it all hitting her so hard it might be funny if it weren't her heart that was breaking. "Excuses. You're just using your dad and your hurt as excuses not to fall in love, not to have a family, not to have a *life*."

He turned toward the water, away from her. "Maybe I am."

"Well, I'm not," she said, grabbing his arms to make him face her, the power of what she wanted to say and why she wanted to say it nearly rocking her backward. "I'm not afraid anymore. I'm not hiding behind excuses or old hurts." She took a slow, deep breath and squeezed his arms. "I'm falling in love with you."

"Lacey..." But his voice trailed off into silence.

"I'm waiting." She smiled. "And not for you to say the same thing. I'm waiting for some kind of pain to consume me because I know you're *not* going to say it."

Searching her face, he stayed silent. Miserably, woefully silent.

"But that's okay," she said, a weird brightness almost choking her. "That's okay because I feel the pain and the love and the need." She hammered her chest. "I *feel* it right here."

"Then you're really lucky." He took her fist and placed it on his chest. "You know what I feel there, Lacey?"

She shook her head.

"Numb."

Numb. Not the four-letter word she was hoping to hear. "Maybe you're just asleep," she said. "Maybe someone or something needs to shake your heart awake."

Without waiting for him to answer she walked away, the sand cold on her feet, vaguely aware of a buzzing in her head. No, that was his phone.

"Is someone texting you?" she asked. Now? At two in the morning?

He pulled it out, glanced at the screen, his eyes widening so slightly that someone who didn't know his every expression might not notice. But she noticed. He didn't read the text, just stuffed the phone back into his pocket.

When he looked up his entire expression had changed. His eyes were distant, and his brain somewhere else. Who had texted him? That wisp of jealousy she'd felt the other day wrapped around her chest. And squeezed.

Whoever it was had just taken him far, far away from a very important conversation. One she suddenly didn't want to have anymore.

She climbed into the truck, slipped on her shoes, and swallowed hard against the lump in her throat. She would not let him see her cry. When he didn't open the driver's door, she checked the side-view mirror to see what he was doing.

Reading the text. Standing frozen in the moonlight, reading the words someone had sent him, running a hand through his hair, looking up at the sky and closing his eyes like someone had just stabbed him. The way he'd looked when he'd gotten off the phone with Darcie the other day. When he'd teared up and wouldn't tell her why.

He stayed behind the truck for a good two minutes,

long enough for her to start to question everything she knew about him.

Who was texting? Why wouldn't he tell her? Was this text from...

Jayna. The name banged around her brain. Could he be talking to his ex? Still in love with her? Was that why he was numb? Unable to take the next step because maybe he thought there was still a chance with her?

Had he lied about talking to his sister that afternoon? Had he been talking to his ex?

He got in, his expression more frozen than before. They drove the two blocks to her parents' house in a thick silence, the echo of her ugly thoughts all she could hear in her head.

"Look, Clay," she said as he pulled the truck up to the curb. "The zoning presentation is in two days. Let's stay focused on that and when it's over we'll figure out where we go from here, whether it's to North Carolina or..."

"I'm going home." He muttered the words. "I have to."

She had no answer to that, and, honestly, it was obvious he didn't want an argument. He was going home after this presentation.

"I'll walk you to the door." He flipped his phone onto the console and got out.

Her gaze cut to the phone. Her finger itched. Her brain hummed. Her heart rolled around.

With a lightning-quick move she touched the screen, making it light up. Then she touched it again to read the list of texts, the top name the most recent.

Jayna Walker

Oh, *God*.

He opened her door and she turned guiltily from the

phone, inching forward so he wouldn't see the light of the screen in the car. She took a minute to gather her bag, and her wits, and slowly stepped down, certain she hadn't been caught.

Then she saw the moisture in his eyes. Apparently, there was a woman in this world who could make him cry. And it wasn't Lacey Armstrong.

"I want to do the presentation alone," she said.

"What?"

"Just let me make the presentation to the zoning committee on my own."

She waited for the argument, the "Why would you do that?" fight. She wouldn't admit she'd just peeked at who'd texted him, but—

"Okay."

Okay. *Okay*? Had two syllables ever stabbed so deeply? What could she say? *You're supposed to say no!*

"Okay," she repeated, grateful that the word even found its way through her pain-thickened throat.

He didn't respond, his eyes still distant. He was a million miles away—with Jayna.

"I'll get the materials tomorrow morning," she somehow managed to say. "Will you..."

"I'll leave the key behind the mailbox."

In other words, he'd be gone by tomorrow.

"Good-bye, Clay." She opened the kitchen door and stepped inside as fast as she could move, with no regard for waking David or Ashley.

When she closed the door and leaned her head against it, she took a deep breath, but all that came out of her was a low, slow, soul-cracking, heart-wrenching sob.

"Mom?"

She whipped around to see Ashley at the kitchen table drinking a glass of milk, waiting for her like a mother waits for a wayward teenager who's stolen away in the middle of the night. For a moment, Lacey braced herself for the inevitable disapproval, hearing her mother's voice in her head.

I told you he was scum.

I warned you about that boy.

You never pick the right ones.

"What's the matter, Mom?" Ashley stood slowly, her chair scraping over the tile floor, echoing loudly in the silent house.

"It's Clay. He's leaving."

Ashley's hand flew to her mouth. "Oh, no! I'm sorry!"

"It's not your fault, honey."

"But, Mom..." Her face looked stricken as she came around the table, reaching out. "You're crying!"

"I know you hate when I cry, Ash. I'm sorry. I-I just..." The sob caught in her throat, embarrassing her. "I feel so stupid."

"You're not stupid!"

She swiped her eyes, choking a dry laugh. "Honey, when you hand yourself over to a guy and give him everything and he dumps you, you are officially too stupid to deserve happiness."

Ashley hugged her close, squeezing harder than Lacey could remember. "You're not stupid, Mom. And you do deserve happiness."

"Yes, I do, baby. Yes, I do." The problem was she'd just thrown it away. And he hadn't even put up a fight.

Chapter 29

"Why are we waiting?" Tessa asked, leaning against the kitchen counter impatiently. "He said he was blowing out of town, so let's just go get the stuff and start helping you rehearse."

Lacey shook her head. "I don't want to run into him."

"I do," Zoe said. "I want to run *over* him with that big ol' Jeep, actually, then spit on his broken bones and tell him what I think of cheaters and liars."

"He didn't cheat," Lacey said quietly. "We weren't official. I let my imagination run away with me."

"Details," Zoe shot back.

"Excuses," Tessa added. "Where's David, by the way?"

"I let him take Ashley cave diving."

"You what?" Tessa slammed down her coffee cup hard enough to splash the granite. "I thought you were morally, ethically, and parentally opposed to that."

"They got me at a weak moment, and it's really a beginner's cave. I trust him, and I need the day to rehearse and prepare."

And lick my wounds.

"Honestly," she added, "I'm not afraid of him letting her swim tethered in a cave, but I'm scared to death she's going to tell him Clay had me in tears last night, and now David's going to drag the whole story out of her and think he has a chance with me."

"Does he?" Tessa asked.

"Not even a small one."

"Then come on, Lacey, let's go," Tessa insisted. "So what if you see Clay? You know where he stands now."

"He stands with his father's wife." Zoe made a face. "Eww."

Lacey grabbed her purse. "You're right. Let's go."

Zoe drove while Lacey sat in the front and tried not to summon memories from places she'd been with Clay. When they pulled into the parking lot of Hibiscus Court, she couldn't resist looking at his empty parking spot, remembering a few hot kisses in his truck before they stumbled into his apartment, and into his bed.

Memories, all bittersweet memories now.

"See? Coast is clear." Zoe took the space and turned off the ignition, patting Lacey's leg. "You feel better or worse knowing he's not here?"

"I just feel empty."

At his unit, no one answered the knock. She felt even emptier when she opened the door using the key he'd hidden and found exactly what he'd promised: the boards and 3-D model of the resort all neatly lined up on the kitchen table and counter. Everything else—the

CAD system, the laptops, even the drafting table—was gone.

But her stomach turned into a hollow pit when she walked down the hall to the bedroom and saw the open closet door with nothing but hangers inside. The bed was partially made, the comforter sliding off, the sheets pulled up like no one had slept there. In the bathroom a dry towel hung over the shower door, but there was no other evidence that a man had been living here for weeks.

Or that a couple had turned it into a love nest.

"Sucks, doesn't it?" Zoe said, standing in the doorway.

Lacey turned to her, aware that Tessa was already at work taking the first load of stuff to the car.

"What happened?" she asked Zoe.

"You fell in love with the wrong guy, Lace. Oldest story in the book."

"Is that what happened with you and Oliver?"

She paled slightly. "'Fraid so." Instantly Zoe turned back toward the living room. "I'll get the rest of these boards. You say your last good-byes to the fond memory of all those life-changing orgasms you had in that bed."

When she heard Zoe go out the front door, Lacey let out a long, pained breath and sat on the corner of the bed. "They did change my life," she said to herself. "You helped me realize what I was capable of, Clay Walker. So I'm eternally grateful."

She blew a kiss to the pillow and picked up the comforter out of habit. As she pulled it over the sheets, her foot tapped something tucked beneath the bed.

The drawings. Her heart practically launched into her throat.

He'd left the drawings behind.

Slowly she eased out a roll of paper, glancing over her shoulder to see if the others had come back yet. Still alone, she rolled the rubber band off and started to spread one of the drawings out on the bed.

Before it was fully open, her legs felt unnaturally heavy, like she'd had a half of bottle of wine and tried to stand suddenly. She flattened the paper, instantly recognizing his sure hand drawing their favorite beach, and the penciled outline of Lacey, lying back on the sand, a dress falling open, her breasts partially exposed.

Memories of things that haven't happened yet.

She slid the picture to the side and looked at the next one. "Oh my God," she whispered, stunned by the tableau of Lacey and Clay in the water. They were naked, entwined, her backside tucked into his front, her head thrown back as he captured the moment she'd had one of those *life-changing orgasms.*

That particular moment had most certainly happened. It was burned into her personal memory bank.

She was almost afraid to look at the next one.

It was the drawing of Ashley holding a hammer. But Clay was in this picture, too, holding the wood that Ashley nailed. Building the house together?

I expect her to help build the house, don't you?

"What are you looking at?" Zoe asked from the living room.

"I'm not sure."

"More stuff for the presentation?" Tessa walked into the room and stopped. "Hey, is that Ashley? That's good."

Lacey hesitated to slide the picture away, not sure she could take another unfulfilled fantasy of Clay's. "He told me once that he likes to visualize things, then draw them. That's how he gets them to happen."

Zoe came up next to her. "Whoa, who knew? He really *does* have a magic drafting tool."

"So he was hoping for a moment like that with Ashley?" Tessa asked. "That doesn't seem like a man who would jettison at the mention of a commitment."

"What else is there?" Zoe asked. "Let's see the rest."

Lacey moved one picture and smoothed out the next.

Tessa gasped. Zoe let out a soft grunt of disbelief.

And Lacey felt her legs buckle enough to kneel down in front of the bed.

"That's quite the imagination he's got there," Zoe said.

"No kidding," Tessa agreed. "Looks an awful lot like a woman and man getting married at the water's edge to me."

"A woman with curly reddish blonde hair," Zoe noted. "And, oh my God, is that the mayor dude who is marrying you two?"

It was hard to tell because something had dripped right over Sam Lennox's face and smeared the pencil. A tear?

Had Clay *cried* when he'd drawn them getting married?

"And look at the three bridesmaids." Tessa pointed to the row of women Clay had drawn next to the bride and groom.

"Oh, I look so pretty!" Zoe dropped to her knees next to Lacey. "I knew I loved this guy."

"There's one more, Lace." Tessa said gently. "Let's see it."

She looked up. "I'm scared."

"Oh, come on," Zoe said, dragging the sheet away. "First comes love, then comes marriage, then comes—"

Lacey, nude, joyful, laughing—and at least eight months pregnant.

Another tear fell, but this time it was Lacey's. Tessa put her hand on Lacey's shoulder and squeezed. "Maybe we misjudged him."

She rolled the edge of the page, silently closing up the sketch that revealed what really was going on in Clay Walker's fruitful imagination.

But she only heard one word.

Okay.

"What are you going to do, Lace?" Zoe asked.

"I'll save these. I've lost a lot of very real memories in the past few months. It'll be nice to have some new ones, even if they never happened."

"I wonder why he left them," Tessa said.

"They weren't important enough for him to take." Lacey rolled up the wedding picture. "They were just meaningless drawings."

"Maybe he wanted you to find them," Zoe said. "Maybe they're not meaningless at all."

Lacey smiled at her friend, but she knew the truth. And, damn, it hurt.

Fourteen hours after he left Mimosa Key, Clay barreled into the parking lot of Duke Raleigh Hospital and headed straight to the ICU. Darcie was waiting with a quick hug and a soft push through the double doors, not giving him a chance to even brace for whatever waited on the other side. The last time he'd seen C-dub...

A man takes what a man wants. Didn't I teach you anything?

His father's words still echoed, and still stung. A man doesn't *take* his son's woman.

"Go ahead, Clay." Next to him Darcie gave his hand a squeeze, sensing his hesitation. "They won't let us both in there at the same time because there's a limit of two people."

So Jayna was in there. Of course. She'd been by his side since the stroke last night, texting updates to everyone, including Clay.

"He's in the first room on the right," Darcie added.

He nodded, then walked down the wide hall, assaulted by the bitter smell of antiseptic. Turning to the glass doors, he froze at the sight of his father, who looked blanched and—dead. Ice trickled through his veins, so cold it stole his breath.

Jayna looked up as he entered, her eyes red from sleeplessness and tears. She didn't speak or smile, just looked at him.

"He'll be happy you're here."

Clay doubted that, but he slowly approached the other side of the bed, aware of the monitors softly beeping to prove that his father was, indeed, still alive, and breathing through the tubes coming out of his nose. "Will he even know?"

"He knows," she said.

Clay leaned closer, examining the ashen pallor of his father's face and noticing that the left side seemed to droop.

"Is he conscious at all?" Clay asked.

"They're saying he's in a comatose state, but I know he hears us. Take his hand so he knows you're here."

Dad's right hand rested at his side, completely still, but Clay made no move to touch him.

For a moment he imagined Lacey here. Even the thought gave him a surprising comfort, and an ache. If she were here, she'd tell him to...

Take the old man's hand, of course.

Wasn't that why he hadn't told her his father had had a stroke last night? Because she would tell him he had to forgive him, and he refused?

Still, he closed his fingers over older, thicker ones. A hand that had never been raised in anger, he mused. No, this man had other ways to inflict pain.

"Talk to him, Clay," Jayna said. When he didn't immediately answer, she added, "See what happens."

He took a deep breath. "Hey, Dad."

Jayna looked pointedly at the hand Clay held. "I think it's really hard for him to react, but if you talk, I swear you'll feel him squeeze your hand. Right, C-dub?"

His father's hand remained still.

"See?" She brightened. "Did you feel that?"

Clay didn't have the heart to tell her he didn't feel a thing.

She wet her lips, looking down at the hand that held her husband's, then back to Clay. "This might be a good time to tell him something important. Anything."

Like what? *Hey, old man, you're forgiven for being the biggest asshole on the face of the earth. For being insecure and miserable, and jealous of your own son.*

"Like I told him that Elliott drank out of his sippy cup all by himself this morning." Jayna's singsong voice yanked Clay out of his mental musings, giving him a second of emotional whiplash.

"And he squeezed my hand when I mentioned Elliott's name."

Of course he did. He wasn't competing with Elliott—yet.

Clay cleared his throat, repositioned his hand, and leaned closer, no words ready.

"I told him what you did for me." Jayna whispered the confession. "He knows that you did that to help me, and to help him. And, Clay, he only continued to blame you because it made him feel less guilty. You know that, don't you?"

Clay shrugged, ignoring the desperation in her voice. "Kind of moot, now."

Jayna stood slowly, her eyes on her husband. "Why don't you talk to him privately?"

She leaned all the way over and kissed Dad's head, closing her eyes and gently stroking his white hair. Clay stared at the sight, struck by the profound tenderness of the gesture.

She loved the old man. Really, truly loved him.

While Clay, his own flesh and blood, just hated him.

"I'll be back, sweetheart," she whispered. "Listen to Clay. He wants to tell you something important."

What?

Jayna left the room, closing the door with a decisive click, leaving him with the steady beep of life support and his father's limp hand.

Still he didn't speak. The words were there, hovering in his head, on the proverbial tip of his tongue.

I forgive you, Dad.

Why couldn't he say it? Because he didn't forgive him. And if he didn't forgive him, then what did that make Clay? Pathetic, harboring a grudge over a woman who, in the scheme of things, didn't matter. It made him small and guarded and...unable to love, no matter how much he really wanted to.

Unable to love.

Was it possible that this man right here held the key to Clay's deadened heart? No, Clay held it. He just didn't want to turn that key and let Lacey in.

Lacey.

Suddenly he knew what he wanted to say to his father.

"I met a woman, Dad." He cleared his throat again, and powered on. "I met *the* woman." He closed his eyes and pictured Lacey in all the ways he remembered her, and all the ways he'd secretly fantasized about her. Lacey, his lover. Lacey, his partner. Lacey, his...wife.

"She's really something, too." What was it about her he most wanted to tell his father? "She's got a heart like no one I've ever met before. She's determined and kind and smart, and she has a teenage daughter who's a really good kid hidden in a really tough shell." He knew that kid. He'd *been* that kid. "Dad?"

Still no reaction. Dad wasn't hearing this, Clay thought. But that didn't stop him from wanting to say it all.

"I'm in love with her."

Great. He could tell his dad, but not Lacey. What the hell? But he'd fix that. First he had to fix this. No, first he had to fix *himself.*

"I designed something for her. A resort in this place called Mimosa Key. It's down in Flor—"

The slightest pressure squeezed his hand. Clay looked down at the thick fingers around his, stunned. Had his father just reacted, or was that merely an unconscious twitch?

"Dad?"

Nothing. Okay. A mistake. "Anyway, I designed a resort for her and it's going to be—"

This time the squeeze was real and one of the monitors kicked up in speed. Clay looked at the screens, pinpointing the one that had just changed its tune. The heart. His heart rate was up.

"Dad, can you hear me?"

Should he call someone? He inched closer, holding tight to his father's hand.

"So, this project," he said, sticking with the subject because that was what got the reaction. "We're calling it Casa Blanca, and I gave it a really strong Henri Post influence. You'd like it."

Another firm squeeze and the slightest flutter behind his lids. Dad was definitely awake, and reacting to the name of his favorite French architect.

"Do you want me to get the doc?" he asked.

Nothing.

"Do you want me to keep talking?"

Nothing.

"Should I get Jayna? Are you waking up?" Frustration mounted when there was no reaction. "Is there something you want to say, Dad?"

The beep jumped another notch and his hand constricted. Hard.

Clay waited, his breathing as measured and slow as his father's. "Dad?"

Nothing.

"Is it about the building?"

A squeeze. Seriously? At a time like this he wanted to dole out architectural advice? He didn't want to clear the air and put their messy past behind them?

Clay leaned on the bed rail and threaded his fingers through his father's hand.

"The project," he said, getting a squeeze in return. "Is a resort on the beach." Another squeeze. "I'll be perfectly honest: She was looking for you when she accidentally contacted me."

Squeeze. Squeeze. Squeeze. *Beeeeep.*

"Dad, are you familiar with this property?"

Under closed lids, his father's eyes flickered back and forth and Clay took it as a yes.

"Is there something you want to tell me?"

More flickering, squeezing, and beeping.

"Did you—"

The door flew open. "Clay, what's going on?" Behind Jayna a nurse ran in, pushing her aside, flying to the bed.

"Out! Everyone out!"

Clay dropped his father's hand and stepped away from the bed. "Is he okay?"

"He's having another stroke. We need a doctor. Everyone out of here!"

Jayna grabbed his arm and yanked him to the door, everything moving in slow motion. Clay's head felt thick with grief and guilt. Had he brought the stroke on? By talking about architecture and resorts and—

Then he knew. He knew exactly what had brought that on. Goddamn it, C-dub, *why*?

From the other side of the glass he stared at the old man and hoped to God he'd get a chance to ask him that question.

Chapter 30

Lacey finished the last section of the presentation with her voice loud and clear so Zoe could hear it from the kitchen, where she was already opening a celebratory bottle of wine.

"And that's why the Mimosa Key Town Council should vote to amend the zoning restrictions in Barefoot Bay and welcome the potential of Casa Blanca."

Tessa clapped, Zoe hooted, but Lacey just shook her head.

"What?" Tessa said. "You were awesome, confident, unstoppable."

"Thanks, but—"

"It's wine o'clock!" Zoe came in with a bottle and three glasses on a tray. "Well, four. But we can officially drink now."

"In a second," Lacey said. "I need a new name for this place."

"For the resort?" The question was asked in unison, and with matching disbelief.

"It's bothering me here," Lacey said, tapping her chest. "It's our name, mine and Clay's. And if..." It hurt to say it, but she had to be true to herself. "If he's not there, then I don't want to call it Casa Blanca. It's too personal."

"But it's perfect for the design."

"I know, Tessa, but..." She already had the eraser out and walked to the first easel to eliminate the words that were bothering her so much. "I'm just not going to call it anything. The right name will come to me."

Her cell phone jangled and she cursed the way her heart kicked up, forcing herself to act as if she wasn't even thinking it could be Clay.

Zoe snagged the phone from the end table and checked out the screen. "Sorry, it's just Ashley."

Lacey rolled her eyes. "Am I that obvious?"

"Brutally so," Zoe said. "Here. Find out how the cave adventure is going. Maybe David drowned."

"Zoe." Lacey laughed softly and took the phone. "Hey, honey. How's it going?"

"It's David."

Something in his voice. Something bad. "What's the matter?"

"There's been an accident, Lacey." His voice cracked, and so did Lacey's entire being.

"What kind of accident?" She could barely hear him; her pulse beat a deafening thump in her head. "David, what happened?"

Both of the girls were at her side instantly, squeezing her, trying to listen.

"She hit her head."

"What? Is she okay?"

"She's in the hospital, Lacey."

Blood rushed, limbs weakened, and her chest exploded in an agonizing burst of disbelief. Not Ashley. Please, God, not Ashley. Anyone but Ashley. Please. "Please tell me she's okay." *Please.*

"She's unconscious, but alive."

Alive? There was a chance she wouldn't be? "Oh my God, David."

Tessa grabbed the phone. "Where are you, David? Tell me exactly how to get there."

Words wouldn't form. Nothing could come out of Lacey's mouth except shuddering breaths while Zoe calmed her and Tessa got them all into the Jeep to drive wherever David had told Tessa to go.

Zoe swore softly, putting Lacey's seat belt on. "Wait. Your insurance forms. ID. You're going to need that stuff at the hospital."

"My handbag's on the kitchen table and the insurance card is in my wallet."

"Got it. Be right back."

She had started climbing out when Lacey grabbed her arm. "Wait, Zoe. In Ashley's room. Get her unicorn."

"Good thinking, Mom."

"What else did he say?" she asked Tessa when Zoe jogged away.

"Just that she's unconscious. She hit her head on a low ceiling in the cave, and she's breathing on her own, but unconscious."

Everything shook uncontrollably. Her body, her guts, her knees literally knocking as Zoe climbed back in and wrapped her arms around Lacey, cooing soft words to calm her.

"I've got the hospital programmed into the GPS," Tessa said. "Hang on, girls. We'll be there in a couple hours."

"A couple of hours!" Lacey wailed. "What if she—"

"Shhh." Zoe squeezed her. "Just hold on and let's get there."

She couldn't do anything but pray and cry and curse herself for backing down on the cave diving issue. They drove in silence up the interstate.

Tessa had barely reached the ER entrance when Lacey threw herself out of the Jeep and started running toward the doors. Zoe was next to her in a second, taking control, asking the questions Lacey couldn't, calmly following the orders to get them to Ashley.

She saw David first. He sat in a waiting room with his head in his hands, still wearing a bathing suit and a T-shirt and a look of red-eyed anguish, so miserable looking that the worst imaginable thought slammed into her head and she gave voice to it.

"Ashley's dead."

Before he answered a nurse whisked into the room. "Are you Ashley's mother?"

Blood thrummed and a low, guttural grunt of acknowledgment came from her chest.

"Come with me," the nurse said. "Are you related?" she asked Zoe, who shook her head. "Stay here with him, then."

"I'm her father," David said, coming with them.

"Actually"—Lacey held up a hand to stop him—"I want to see her alone."

The nurse pushed her through double doors.

"Please, tell me, is she—"

"Oh, yes, she's awake. Has been for a while. She hasn't sustained brain damage, and that's what we've been watching for. Definitely a concussion, though. She's woozy and on some pain meds. It was quite a serious blow, but we think a monstrous headache will be the worst of it. Here she is."

Lacey took a deep breath as she entered the room, letting it out as a soft cry at the sight of Ashley, pale and thin and tiny in a hospital bed with tubes in her arms, a bandage on her head, her eyes closed.

"Go easy, Mom," the nurse warned.

Lacey nodded, forcing herself to slow her steps as she approached the bed. She touched Ashley's shoulder and her eyes opened.

Thank you, God. Thank you.

"Hey, Princess Pot-Pie." Lacey managed not to sob, but the words were barely a whisper.

"Mommy."

Lacy sucked back tears, willing herself to be strong.

"Please don't be mad."

"I'm not mad, honey. I'm just so grateful you're alive. I won't even say I told you so. How do you feel?" she asked as she tucked the uni into bed beside her beautiful daughter. Ashley smiled and pulled the uni closer.

"I'm okay. My head hurts, but they told me I knew my name and my birthday and my favorite color."

"What is it?"

"Lime green. Mommy, I'm sorry." She started to cry.

"Shhh." Lacey stroked her cheek, her chin, her quivering lips. "You don't have to be sorry."

"I shouldn't have done it."

"I gave you permission to go, angel. It's not like you sneaked away."

"But it's my fault. God's punishing me."

Lacey put her hand on Ashley's head. She *wasn't* making sense. Could there be damage they hadn't diagnosed? "No, not now, baby. Save your strength. We have to get you home and get you all better."

Ashley closed her eyes. "I made Clay leave you."

Lacey leaned in, not at all sure she understood. "What are you talking about?"

"I told Clay. That night he got me at the football field I didn't tell you everything." Tears streamed down her face.

"You told him what, baby?"

"That we'd be a family if he'd just leave."

Lacey stared at her, processing the words, trying to understand. "That's not why he left, Ashley."

Jayna had texted him at two in the morning. He said he wanted to go back to North Carolina. Ashley couldn't take the blame for that, no matter what she'd told him.

"I basically told him to leave, and he was being so nice." She squeezed her eyes. "He's really nice, Mom."

"Whatever you did or said couldn't make him leave or stay," Lacey assured her. "All you need to worry about is getting better. That's all."

"But I think he really loves you."

Lacey stroked her head, determined not to let Ashley's innocent—and mistaken—ideas make her sicker. "Just close your eyes, Ash. We'll talk later."

"I told Dad and he said..."

Lacey waited, curious whether David was behind this confession. Maybe he was all too happy to get rid of the competition.

"Dad said he should leave now and let you have your life." Ashley's voice cracked. "I don't want him to leave, Mom, but I want you to be happy."

"I *will* be happy when the doctors say you are one hundred percent healed. Sleep." Lacey kissed Ashley's forehead, keeping her lips on her daughter's silky hair. "This is no time to deal with the heavy stuff. Rest." She curled her hands around Ashley's much narrower fingers. "I love you so much, Ashley."

"I love you, too, Mom. I'm so sorry I screwed up."

"Honey, you didn't screw up. Please, rest now."

Ashley closed her eyes and breathed the sigh of a child with a clear conscience. In a few minutes she slept, and Lacey returned to the waiting room to update Tessa and Zoe, then headed outside, where David was getting air.

He stood braced against a waist-high brick wall, his face to the sun, his eyes closed.

"Whatever you have to say, you're right," he said without looking at her. "I screwed up royally."

"This is not about you," she said. "She's going to be fine, and that's all that matters. I let her go and you had an accident. I can't hate you for that."

"But you hate me for other things."

She sighed. "David, I don't hate you at all."

"I got in the way of you and Clay."

"No, and neither did Ashley. I appreciate how you and Ashley want to take the blame, but there's none to go around." At least not with these two.

"What did the doctor tell you?" he asked.

"I haven't seen the doctor yet, but the nurse seems to think she'll be fine. We'll monitor her. And she'll have an excuse for every C in math for the whole first semester of high school."

He smiled, hope in his eyes. "Listen, Lacey, I have to tell you something."

"Ashley said you're leaving."

He angled his head in acknowledgment. "I'll be on a flight to Papua, New Guinea, in four hours."

"Really? That's so…" *Far. Soon.* "Not a surprise," she said flatly.

"A few weeks ago I would have taken that response as hope that we could have a future."

"We don't. At least not like you first painted it when you got here."

"I'm trying to tell you I owe you an apology," David said.

She acknowledged his words with a nod. "Accepted, but I'm not going to hold this or the last fourteen years against you. Honestly."

"What I'm sorry for is not just the last fourteen years, because I've told you I regret them every minute I get to know Ashley more. And the way she's accepted me, when any other kid would resent me…" He sighed heavily. "She's amazing."

Lacey smiled, pride welling up in her chest. "Yes, she is, David, and I'm glad you finally know that."

He took a step closer, his eyes moist, struggling to swallow. "What I'm sorry for is how I reacted when you told me you were pregnant."

She didn't respond, leaning against the sun-warmed bricks, the adrenaline and fear dumping out of her, leaving her muscles weak. Including her heart. That might be the weakest muscle of all.

Because she'd never planned to forgive David for that.

For not marrying her, for disappearing, even for showing up now and upsetting an already shaky apple cart, yes. Forgiven. But for pressing to terminate the pregnancy? That seemed unforgivable.

He searched her face as if he could read her thoughts.

"I have no excuse," he finally said. "I mean, I was pretty young, but you were younger. I was restless and unsettled, but you hadn't even graduated. I was scared to be a parent, and you were the one who had to carry and raise her." His voice cracked. "Please, Lace. Forgive me."

She managed to blink without shedding the tears that welled. "It's history."

His expression softened with relief. "Thank you." He reached out for her hand, squeezing it. "Thank you."

All she could do was nod, and wait for the pressure on her chest to ease. Surprisingly, the weight lifted quickly. Forgiveness weighed less than blame.

"You are always welcome in Ashley's life, David," she said.

"Good," he replied. "Because I have an idea how I can help you."

She frowned. "Help how?"

"I'd like to invest in your resort. No ownership, no ties. Just an investment that you can pay back when the resort starts making money."

"I-I don't know what to say, but thank you."

"And, Lacey, I don't know who has this kind of pull, but I can't find out who bought those properties, and God knows I've tried to grease some palms. But eventually the identity of the buyer will be revealed and you need to buy it back. That'll be my investment; I'll pay for those lots no matter what they ask."

"Oh, David, really. Thank you." She accepted the embrace he offered, leaning on his shoulder for a moment. "Thank you."

"And one more thing." He put his hands on her shoulders. "I've been a lousy father, but you are a remarkable mother."

"Thanks." She leaned back to look at him. "Did Ashley tell you she said something to Clay? Something she thinks made him leave?"

"She did, but—"

"But what?"

He gave her shoulders a squeeze. "I think he'll be back."

She cursed the hope that coiled through her. "I don't."

"Well, I saw the way he looked at you, Lace. And that man might not know it, but he's in love."

Maybe he was, but not with her. Still, when David left to say good-bye to Ashley, Lacey checked her phone messages, just in case David was right.

Nothing.

So the right guy didn't get the girl, and neither did the wrong guy.

Chapter 31

~

Mrs. Walker?"

Clay looked up when the neurologist pushed open the waiting-room doors and scanned the small group on the other side, no doubt looking for an older woman. Sorry, doc. Meet the Dysfunctionals.

Jayna stood. "I'm his wife."

To his credit, the doctor didn't show any reaction. "And which one of you is Clay?"

Clay lifted a hand but didn't jump out of his seat. The doctor turned to him and gestured. "Your father would like to speak with you."

"He can talk?" Jayna exclaimed.

"A bit. The second stroke, which wasn't nearly as severe as the first, actually stimulated some activity and brought him out of the coma. I'm going to explain all that to you in a moment, ma'am, but your husband is quite forceful, even after two strokes. He was adamant about talking to Clay, and I see no reason to deny him that."

Clay finally stood. "I'll talk to him." Because the son of a bitch had a lot of explaining to do.

"Clay." Darcie gave him a harsh look, fully aware of what was going on. She'd already used her laptop to confirm what Clay suspected, and they'd been hard at work trying to fix things while the docs tried to fix their father. "Be gentle."

That earned an angry flash from the neurologist. "If you have any other intentions, son, don't you dare go into that room."

"I have no intentions other than to listen to what he has to say." And get his shaky signature. But the doc didn't need to know that.

He headed down the hall with slow, deliberate steps, not in any huge rush now that he'd gotten up here and found out what the old man was really made of. Not that he hadn't already known, but this latest stunt?

Unbelievable.

So C-dub wanted to confess, beg forgiveness, remind Clay that everything he'd ever done was out of fatherly love and driving ambition to build a business. Blah, blah, blah. *Just sign the papers and I'm out.*

The ICU room was quiet again, the beeping machines tapping out a softer, more stable rhythm, and his father's eyes were open. Not focused, but open.

For a moment Clay thought he might be dead. But the easy rise of his chest proved him wrong.

Clay approached the bed slowly, leaning over so C-dub could see him.

"Two strokes," Dad said through clenched teeth, his lips not even moving.

"One more and you're out," Clay said gently. "So take it easy, old guy."

Dark blue eyes shifted toward Clay, but his father's head didn't move. "I'm not going to die."

"I don't think anyone's worried about that. Just how nasty you're going to be when you get home is the real concern."

"Not going to be nasty anymore."

Clay snorted. "Then why'd you buy those two properties in Barefoot Bay?"

"I liked the land."

What the *hell*? "That gave you the right to undermine the whole project?" Clay worked to modulate his voice and keep the nurses at bay.

"I didn't know I was undermining you," his father said through a stiff jaw. "My office got a call about the project and I sent someone down to look at it. Standard procedure."

Lacey had mentioned that she'd called Walker Architecture after he'd left her on the beach the day they met. Of course that phone call would have set some exploratory wheels in process.

"The land looked good," his father said. "And my pre-project guys said there were two lots available for purchase. I bought 'em. You know we'd never put the name of a company on a purchase like that. It's a red flag to others."

The angry fist in his chest loosened its grip. "You didn't know I was involved?"

"I didn't, Clay. But I found out later you were competing

for the project and..." He closed his eyes, a soft grunt of pain drawing Clay closer.

"And what?"

"That's when I had that damn TIA that started all this."

The first mini-stroke? "Never knew you to suffer from guilt pangs."

"I was driving home to call you when it happened. I wanted to tell you, but"—a hint of a smile crossed his lips—"I got scared, Clay."

"Scared of what?"

"I knew you'd never believe me. You'd think I was out to screw you again. You'd hate me more."

Clay couldn't deny that, so he just stayed silent, the sound of his father's steady heartbeat on a monitor the only noise in the room.

"I have to tell you, son, Jayna has taught me about what it means to be a parent."

Clay gave a dry laugh. "The irony in that statement is damn near incalculable."

"Don't I know it. But I'm afraid I'll never have a chance to make it up to you," Dad admitted on a sad sigh.

"Darcie drew up an ad hoc contract to give me the land. Sign it and we're good."

"I will." He blinked back some moisture that on any other man might have been a tear. But this was C-dub, so Clay would bet it was just a bit of garden-variety watery eyes. "But, son, I don't want to die knowing you still hate me."

"You aren't dying." *God, I hope not.* "So don't sweat it."

"Clay, hold my hand."

He took the old man's hand and got a gentle squeeze.

"Only one thing matters, son."

What? Winning the game? Having the most toys? The youngest, prettiest wife, the biggest bank account, the most famous name? He knew what mattered to C-dub, but he came closer anyway. "What's that, Dad?"

"I love you, Clayton Walker." A single tear rolled slowly down his father's cheek, meandering to the side until it fell on the hospital pillow. "I love you."

Dad's heart monitor sped up just a little, eerily matching what was going on in Clay's chest. He couldn't remember the last time his father had said those words.

"Bring me those papers," C-dub ordered. "So I can prove it to you."

Clay stepped away, toward the door, turning before he left. *Say it, say it, say it.*

"I hope you get better, Dad."

Dad managed to look at him. "Three little words, Clay. Can't you say them to me?"

He tried to swallow, but something closed his throat. Those unspoken words, of course, balled up inside of him and keeping him from breathing, talking, or loving.

"Please?" The request was barely a whisper from his father's lips, so soft he may not have wanted Clay to hear him beg.

Clay turned away. "I . . . can't."

Behind him he heard the old man sigh. A sad, resigned, pathetic sound of regret. Clay knew if he released his father, he could release himself.

And about seven hundred miles away, on an island bathed in sunshine and happiness, there was a woman who needed Clay to be free.

"Dad," he said as he slowly turned around. "I forgive you."

"Oh. Thank you."

For the first time in years, they smiled at each other.

Lacey blinked through a haze of sleep, aware that everything hurt as she tried to turn in bed. No, no, she wasn't in bed. She was on a window seat on a piece of foam rubber that doubled as a guest bed in a hospital.

The dawn's earliest light peeked through the blinds, and with it came the harsh memory that the doctors had insisted on keeping Ashley overnight for observation.

She blinked at the sight of someone standing next to Ashley's bed, then gasped when she realized who it was.

"Oh my God, you're here."

Jocelyn smiled and came around the bed to the window, holding out her hands. "Of course I'm here. I got on a red-eye when Tessa called. See? I have the red eyes to prove it."

Of course she didn't have red eyes or bed head or morning breath, unlike Lacey, who no doubt had them all.

"My cavalry comes again."

"The other two-thirds of your cavalry is asleep in the waiting room."

"Oh." Lacey sighed. "Where would I be without you guys?"

"You'll never have to know." She glanced at the bed. "Please tell me it looks worse than it is."

"It does," Lacey confirmed. "She has a concussion, but nothing permanent. We're lucky."

Jocelyn put both hands on Lacey's cheeks. "And how's Mom?"

"A wreck."

"What about the big meeting?"

"It starts in . . ." She looked around the room for a clock. Naturally, Jocelyn wore a watch, which was already set to local time. Lacey took her wrist and did a quick calculation. "Less than three hours. And I'm two hours away. Shit."

"Is that your excuse?"

"No, I have a better one. I'm not leaving Ashley. She's been through enough."

"Poor thing." Jocelyn reached out and touched the blanket but not the sleeping girl. "We'll stay with her. You go and fight the good fight, Lace."

Not a chance. "The meeting's at ten, Joss. I'd have to leave in the next hour to even get down to Mimosa Key in time, let alone shower, dress, and get my act together." She glanced at her sleep-worn T-shirt and jeans, the flip-flops on her feet, and—no, she didn't even want to think about her hair.

"We can go." Zoe stood in the doorway, looking a lot like Lacey felt. "You can stay here with Ashley."

"We can be down there with time to spare," Tessa said, coming up behind her with a sleepy yawn. "We're co-investors. We'll fight the old-school bastards."

Ashley stirred, stopping the conversation as Lacey practically leaped to her side.

"Hey, Princess Pot-Pie. How ya feelin'?"

"'Kay."

"Did she just call her Princess Pot-Pie?" Zoe nearly choked. "Did I hear that right?"

"That's what she calls me." Ashley smiled and brought her stuffed unicorn up to her chin, then her eyes flew open. "Oh! Aunt Jocelyn's back."

Jocelyn reached over and hugged her. "Hey, kiddo."

"Are they going to let me go home, Mom? I really want to go home."

"Not for a few hours, honey."

"Long enough for us to get back to Mimosa Key in the rental car I got at the Tampa airport," Jocelyn said. "We can handle the meeting, or at least start it. When you're done here, you follow. By then we could have the whole zoning issue resolved."

"You can't present," Lacey said, digging for her phone to check for a message she knew wasn't going to be there. "You have to be a resident of Mimosa Key." Nothing on the phone.

How long would she keep checking and hoping for word from Clay?

"Then let's do what Zoe suggested," Jocelyn said. "We'll stay with Ashley and you go."

"Yeah, Mom, that's the best plan."

"No." Lacey shook her head. "I have to sign you out, honey. You're a minor."

"We'll spring her," Zoe said. "Throw her on a gurney and sneak her out the back like they do in the movies."

Ashley giggled. "Fun!"

"C'mon, Lace," Tessa prodded.

"Well, let me talk to the nurse and find out if I can pre-sign or something, then if I leave now . . . but I—"

"Lacey!" They all said her name in perfect unison. "Quit making excuses!"

"Okay, okay." She rounded the bed, kissed Jocelyn on the cheek, gave high fives to Zoe and Tessa, then leaned over and gently hugged her baby. "God, I love the four of you."

She'd made it out the door and down the hall a few steps when Ashley called out, "Mommy! I love you!"

"I love you, too, Pot-Pie!"

The nurse complied with the discharge paperwork, and in less than twenty minutes Lacey was powering the big Rubicon down I-75. By nine-fifteen she was in grid-lock Fort Myers morning traffic, swearing as she watched the digital numbers on the dashboard clock click closer to ten.

Running out of time would *not* be her excuse for missing this presentation, damn it.

By nine-forty she crossed the causeway to Mimosa Key, flew across Center and whipped right on Palm, min-utes from the house. She could do this. Hell, she might even have time to throw on some makeup and brush her hair.

She could *do* this!

She pulled into the driveway, ran up the walk, and stopped dead in her tracks when the front door opened.

No, no. This wasn't *possible*. Anybody, anybody, but—

"Mother, what are you doing here?"

"I live here." Marie Armstrong reached out to yank Lacey closer. Not hug, really, because Lacey's mother didn't actu-ally *embrace* others. She squeezed them into submission.

"We got a call from David that Ashley had an acci-dent. Where is she?"

"You know about Ashley?"

Her mother scowled. "Of course I know. We flew down last evening after David called us. He said not to bother you at the hospital but wanted us to know about Ashley. And David!" She said the name with nothing less than reverence. "It was such a thrill to hear from him, Lacey. He sounded wonderful."

She managed to get inside, brushing by her mother,

hoping for her dad, and scanning the living room for the...

The presentation materials were gone. "What did you do?"

"Lacey, you left an open bottle of wine here. I hope you and your friends weren't drinking and driving, and all those—"

"Where is everything?" Lacey demanded. "The boards? The model? The papers?"

"That mess? I had Dad put it all away in a guest room closet, and that room was not exactly tidy either, I have to say."

White lights practically popped in Lacey's head. "Mother, I'm presenting to the town council in ten minutes!" She started toward the hall, but her mother grabbed her arm.

"Where is Ashley?"

"She's still in the hospital."

"And you *left* her? What kind of mother leaves her child in the hospital for a—a garden club meeting?"

"There's my girl!" Dad came bounding out of the hallway, all bright and white-haired, big and happy. Exactly the opposite of the woman he'd married. But Lacey couldn't even sacrifice one precious minute to throw her arms around him.

"Dad, I need all the materials you just—"

"Paul, Ashley's alone in a hospital somewhere!" Mother cried. "Lacey left her there! We have to go to her right this minute."

"She's not alone," Lacey said through a clenched jaw. "She's with my friends. Tessa and Jocelyn and Zoe are with her."

"Zoe? That wild one? I don't think—"

"Mother!" Lacey snapped the word like a whip in the air, and Marie reared back, penciled eyebrows raised high into her forehead.

"Excuse me, young lady."

"No," Lacey said, her voice low and quiet now. "I won't excuse you. I won't listen to you insult my friends or tell me I'm not a good mother because I left my daughter in their care. In a hospital, I might add."

"But David said—"

"David's gone," Lacey replied, using the shot of adrenaline from her rebellious speech to ease her father out of her way. "Now, you guys could really help me or you can just get out of my way. Right now I'm on a mission to change my life and I'm not going to argue with you about it, Mother."

"We are not going to help you," her mother said. "We are going to the hospital to take care of Ashley."

"She's taken care of. In fact, she might already be on her way here. Dad, please."

"What's going on, Lacey?" he asked. "Are you sure Ashley's okay?"

"I'm positive. And what's going on is too complicated to explain right now. I just need your help."

"Of course. You know what I always say."

As she walked down the hall, she smiled. "There's a reason God gives you two parents?"

He chuckled. "I say that tough things make you tougher. And that granddaughter of mine is one tough cookie."

"Yep, she's going to be fine. I wouldn't have left her if I didn't believe that."

"And what about her mom?" Dad put a hand on her shoulder, a loving, strong, guiding hand that had always been there for her.

"Going to be fine," Lacey said. "If I don't get derailed by disapproval."

Almost instantly Mother was in the room, glowering at them as if her very presence could break the father-daughter bond. But it couldn't; that was one thing Marie Armstrong never could control.

"Her *mom* is very busy instructing *me* to back off," Mother said in response to Dad's question.

"Then maybe you should listen, Marie."

That got him a vile look. "Forgive me for doing my job and giving her advice. I'll never stop, no matter how old I am or how old she is. She doesn't have to listen, do you, Lacey? You never have, anyway."

That was the problem: She'd been listening for far too long. At any other time in her life, this would be the point where she would say something to make her mother feel better and back away from the conversation. Instead, she looked up at her father.

"Dad, I wonder if you would do me a huge favor?"

"Anything, sweetheart."

"Come with me and charm the town council."

"Is that hag Charity going to be there?"

Mother choked. "Charity Grambling is my friend."

"On Facebook," Dad shot back, then winked at Lacey. "I never accepted her friendship. She doesn't floss, you know."

Lacey laughed. Only Dr. Armstrong, Mimosa Key's only dentist for three decades, would know that.

"You are *not* going to confront her in the town hall," Mother said. "Especially looking like that."

"Like what?" She hoisted the 3-D model. "I think I look just fine."

Mother sputtered. "Your hair looks like you combed it with a rake."

"Marie, she looks fine," Dad said.

"And, Lacey, have you put on weight since this hurricane?"

She rolled her eyes and tilted her head toward the front of the house. "Grab the boards, Dad."

He marched right past her mother, who stood with her hands on her hips. "Paul, where are you going?"

"To help our daughter, Marie."

It was going to be okay. Lacey really could do this. She might not have Clay, but she had a little backup and— backbone. Now it was time to use it.

Chapter 32

In the hallway outside the community room Lacey could hear Sam Lennox's gavel slam, his booming voice calling the meeting to order. She shared a quick look with her dad, who, during just the short car ride there, had become so fully invested in Lacey's resort concept that he'd parked illegally right in front of the town hall. Good thing Mother hadn't come.

"Go, Lace," he said, nudging her toward the door.

Inside, the buzz grew louder as a few people called her name, some in support and some not. Sam rapped his gavel again, which did little to quiet the noise.

Of course Charity and Company had taken over the front row on the right side, a group that included her daughter Grace and her sister Patience. Standing next to their row, Lacey spotted Gloria chatting with Sheriff Slade

Garrison, who adroitly divided his attention between Glo and the rowdy crowd.

"I think our team's on the left," Lacey whispered to Dad, noticing him nodding to many friends and familiar faces on both sides of the aisle.

But some folks weren't smiling; not everyone wanted change and progress to come to Mimosa Key.

"Thanks for the support, Dad," Lacey whispered as they walked down the center aisle together. "I know you'll catch hell from Mother, but I really appreciate you doing this for me."

"I'm proud of you, Lacey, and I know my parents would approve of this resort. I'm just glad we could stay gone long enough for you to find your nerve and stand up to your mother. What happened while we were gone?"

She smiled. "A hurricane?"

"Looks to me like that wind swept away all your baggage and left you some confidence." He gave her a squeeze. "Good girl."

"It wasn't the wind." And she hadn't exactly been a *good* girl, but Dad didn't need to know everything.

They found two empty seats but had to climb over a few people, including Will Palmer, who stood to let them go by.

As she passed him he whispered, "Go get 'em, Lacey."

She gave him a quick smile and thought about Jocelyn, but there was no time to pursue that now. Instead she took her seat and scanned the town council table, trying to psych out who'd be on her side.

Paula Reddick, yes. Rocco Cardinale and Nora Alvarez, maybe. George Masterson and Sam Lennox, no way. Well, maybe Sam.

"Call to order!" Sam shouted, smacking his gavel again, to no avail. "Can I please have quiet?"

Finally the murmurs died down.

"We will be hearing four presentations for proposed land use and new structures," Sam said, adjusting his glasses as he read the papers in front of him.

"Alphabetical will put us first," Lacey told him. "As soon as he says the order, let's go get the stuff from the car."

Sam continued reading from notes. "The bylaws state that we hear presentations in geographical order, south to north."

They did? Or was that one of Charity's unofficial edits? Not for the first time Lacey wished she had Clay and his bylaw-memorizing talent with her.

"That'll put us last," Lacey said. "Which is fine."

"More time to gauge the mood of the panel," Dad replied with an encouraging nod.

Sam leaned into the mike to talk. "Up first is John McSweeny seeking to replace signage lost during the hurricane for the bowling alley at 4623 Palm Avenue."

Signage. That wouldn't take long.

"Next will be Barbara Pennick requesting all new windows and a new entry to Beachside Beauty."

From the sidelines Gloria beamed at her boss.

"Third presentation is Lacey Armstrong, Barefoot Bay property owner."

Lacey sat straighter. Wait, how could she be next? She had to have the northernmost property. Unless whoever had bought Tomlinsons' land decided to show.

Her heart jumped at the thought. Was someone proposing to build on that lot? Wiping damp palms on her jeans, she waited for Sam to describe her proposal.

"Ms. Armstrong is proposing a change in"—Sam paused, frowning down at the paper—"town codes, development standards, transportation flow . . ." His voice trailed off as he looked at the crowd. "That one will take a while."

The reaction was a mix of mumbles and nervous laughter, some throat clearing, and a lot of eyes on Lacey, who still didn't know how she could be third out of four presentations.

"What's the matter?" Dad asked.

"There's no one north of me," she said. "Who is presenting fourth?"

Just then she spotted Ira Howell, the banker who represented the anonymous property buyer, leaning against the back wall, a scowl pulling the skin of his bald head.

She gripped her father's hand tighter as Sam started reading again.

"Our final presentation addresses another lot in Barefoot Bay and another change in town codes, development standards, and transportation flow, given by Mr. Ira Howell of Wells Fargo."

No. *No.* Whatever they were building, however they'd gotten on the agenda, she had to stop it. At the very least she had to know *who* she was up against. "This is a nightmare," she mumbled.

Will Palmer leaned over. "You know, Lacey, code changes and development standards could mean they're hard-line environmentalists. It doesn't automatically mean the buyer is building something."

But she needed that land. Tomlinsons' and Everham's properties were north and south of her. They'd close her in. And her house, Clay's house, was supposed to go on the Tomlinson land. She couldn't let go of that dream. And with David's offer of an investment to buy those properties, she'd been certain she could make that dream a reality.

Dad patted her leg. "You can't find a solution until you know the problem, Lace. Let's find out what's going on."

What was going on were fried nerves and bad feelings in her gut.

Charity shot up. "I'm sorry, but Mimosa Key bylaws clearly state that the only speakers at a town council meeting must be current residents of the island. No representative can speak for them. Mr. Howell is not a resident of Mimosa Key."

For once she could have kissed Charity and her damn rules.

Ira Howell pushed off the wall to respond. "I have complete power of attorney for the property owner, Mayor Lennox. I have the paperwork to prove that I can speak on behalf of this individual who owns the land, and is therefore a resident of Mimosa Key."

"That's not good enough," Charity said, getting a loud reaction and a few boos from the crowd.

Ira shook his head. "There's actually a proviso in the bylaws regarding power of attorney if the individual is unable to appear before the council. If it pleases you, Mr. Mayor, I'd like to present that reason exclusively to the town council."

Despite the outcry of the crowd, Sam hit the gavel with authority. "We'll take a short break to discuss this behind closed doors," Sam announced. "Presenters, please get ready."

Lacey exhaled, but then nudged her father. "Let's go get the materials from the car, Dad."

"I'll help you, Lacey," Will offered.

"Oh, that would be great, Will. The car's illegally parked and if I chance it much longer, Slade'll slam me with a parking ticket."

As Ira Howell left with the five members of the council to a private chamber, Lacey, her father, and Will headed out.

"Good luck, Lacey!" A woman who'd had Lacey bake her wedding cake called out.

"You're our hero, Lace!" another said.

She was? She gave a little wave to some friends and a few baking customers, buoyed by their belief in her.

Lacey dashed through the hall and to the main entrance, where Will held the door for her.

She pointed to the big Jeep Rubicon. "That's my car."

Will slowed as the approached the vehicle. "I hoped, er, figured I'd see your friends with you today."

Lacey hesitated. Jocelyn. He meant Jocelyn. "They're out of town now, but they'll be back this afternoon. Joceyln, too," she couldn't help but add.

"Is she going to stay?" Something in his voice said that mattered to him.

"I only talked to her for a few minutes this morning, so I don't know." Lacey opened the back of the Jeep and reached for the 3-D model. The sight of the mini version of villas made her miss Clay with a physical ache.

His work was genius. He deserved to get the credit today, but something, *someone,* was a more powerful draw.

Will took the model, glancing down at structures that stood on a miniature replica of the beaches of Barefoot Bay. "Wow, looks like north Africa."

"Inspired by the architecture of Morocco." *By a very inspiring architect.*

"Very cool. They'd be nuts not to let you build it." He examined it closely, looking from side to side. "Where's Clay?"

"Oh, he's not here."

"Really? Isn't he the architect?"

"Not…" *Anymore.* "Officially. We haven't signed a formal contract, yet. He did this as a favor to me." Good Lord, had she just boiled the past few weeks of life-changing *feelings* into a favor? How sad was that?

"Oh, that's too bad," Will said. "He offered me a job working for him on the resort. And he's obviously great."

Obviously. "Well, if we get approval you can have that job." Except Jocelyn might not like that. "That is, if all the investors agree."

She pulled out the rest of the presentation boards and gave them to her dad. "You guys take that stuff in and I'll move the car and bring the handouts."

With the car legally parked and her arms full of the documents that explained all the financial benefits of her project, Lacey hustled back into the town hall, doubts pressing down like the unforgiving sun overhead, a whole choir of excuses hitting high notes in her head.

Without Clay she should ask for an extension.

Without a chance to talk to Ira Howell about what he was presenting she could be completely blindsided.

And without five minutes to change her clothes, comb her hair, or put on a drop of makeup, she looked a little like a homeless person. Which, come to think of it, she was at the moment.

Still, she felt a smile pull across her face as she mentally squashed every excuse. She wasn't going to let anyone or anything hold her back now.

"Somebody looks happy."

She stopped so suddenly that the papers almost flew out of her hands. The heat and humidity evaporated, leaving nothing but a chill straight to her heart.

Clay.

Chapter 33

Lacey managed a shaky breath when he stepped closer, his hair as disheveled as hers, his eyes a little red-rimmed. Had he been crying or hadn't he slept since the last time she'd seen him?

"Lacey, I have to explain something to you. It's important—"

"Lacey Armstrong!" Grace Hartgrave smacked open both doors in a dramatic, noisy interruption. "Get your tush in here, now. They changed the order of presentations."

Clay nearly lunged to stop Lacey from moving. "No, I have to talk to you."

"Later," Grace answered for her. "The council wants to do the site-development plans first, so that's you and then that guy from the bank who's here because his client has a medical emergency."

"He really is presenting site-development plans?"

Lacey asked. That meant someone was *building* on the land they'd taken out from under her.

"I have to talk to Ira Howell," Clay insisted. "Right now. Right this minute."

Grace physically pushed him away. "Not now." She reached for Lacey. "Hurry up, 'cause right now you just became the lesser of two evils."

"Why?" Lacey asked, her voice as shaky as her legs, her head buzzing with shock and confusion.

Clay turned to her. "It's not what you—"

"Looks like your boyfriend screwed you in more ways than one, Lace." Grace pulled Lacey into the air-conditioning, right past Clay. "My mom got the inside scoop. Clay Walker's building a big-ass resort and spa right smack-dab next to you." She gave Clay a sly smile. "Looks like you've been playing both sides against the middle, Mr. Walker."

Lacey choked as Grace yanked her away and Clay took the other elbow. "No, Lacey, you don't understand."

Dad appeared behind Grace. "Lacey, in here now or you're off the agenda!"

Without even looking at Clay, without taking a minute to figure exactly what he'd done to screw her out of that land and the hopes for her resort, she ran inside.

"Lacey!" Clay called.

"Sorry, pal," Grace said harshly. "Residents only unless you get special dispensation from the mayor or sleep with the right people. You didn't." She slammed the door loud enough to shake the town hall rafters.

Lacey's dad guided her down the wide hallway. "Looks like someone wants to compete with you, kiddo."

Did he? Or was it his dad? *The* Clayton Walker.

God, she didn't know. She didn't know if she could believe him anymore. Her brain flashed to the drawings she'd found in his apartment. Didn't they tell her a lot about him?

Maybe. But he needed to say it. And show her, not just draw her.

Inside the community room, her father kept her marching straight ahead.

She tried to turn. "No backing out or dreaming up reasons to run."

"But Dad—"

"Lacey," he said softly as their steps fell into a matching rhythm and heads on both sides of the aisle turned to look at them. "What does this feel like to you?"

"Hell?"

He smiled and patted her hand. "A walk up the aisle with my little girl."

Her heart dropped so hard it practically rolled out onto the floor. "Dad, please."

"It's okay, Lacey. Unconventional, but okay." He beamed at her, pausing as they reached the front. "Now, you go up there and change your life, young lady. Doesn't take a man to do that for you."

"But Dad, that guy back there—"

"Is not important."

But he *was*. He could have been. He'd changed her and loved her and made her feel strong, smart, sexy, and powerful. How could that not be important?

"What's important is your future." Dad gave her a nudge. "Now go get what you always dreamed of."

What she'd always dreamed of was a guy like Clay. A partner, a friend, a father to her children, a lover for life.

Sam Lennox cleared his throat, making no effort to hide his impatience. "We're waiting, Ms. Armstrong."

So was she—for Clay. For him to run in and explain that this was all a mistake, and, by the way, he loved her and would she mar—

"Are you changing your mind?" Sam asked.

"Thinking about backing out?" George Masterson added.

"Afraid you'll lose?" Charity had to shoot her two cents in.

It would be so easy to quit now.

"No," Lacey said quietly, walking forward. "I'm ready."

At the podium she blew out a breath and looked at the back of the room as the doors opened again. She braced for Clay, but instead a woman she didn't recognize rushed in, hair pulled back under a red baseball cap, sunglasses covering her face.

And then Clay came in and put his arm around the woman's shoulders, speaking softly into her ear.

Jayna?

Instantly Ira Howell lunged out from his chair in the middle, nearly jogging back to Clay to shake his hand. Like they were *business partners*. Could he have secretly planned to buy that land and build on it without telling her?

Why?

Why not? After all, what did she really know about Clay Walker? But those drawings; they were from his heart, weren't they?

He still didn't look at her, didn't even glance in her direction. Instead he put his arms around the woman and squeezed her into his chest, lifting the brim of her baseball cap to give her a smile.

That smile. That heart-stopping smile. Then he leaned

over and kissed her on the cheek. A kiss that, even from here, she could tell was full of love.

"Your microphone is on," Sam said, giving Lacey a start as she imagined that her dark and pained thoughts might somehow be broadcast to the town.

But no one knew what she was thinking. Not even the man she was thinking it about. In fact, he hadn't even glanced her way. Instead Ira had his full attention, and the two men walked right out the back, deep in conversation.

He was gone, but the woman who'd come in with him took a seat in the last row, crossed her arms, and looked at Lacey with profound interest.

Interest in the competition, no doubt.

"Lacey, please." Sam's voice grew irritated. "You have the floor."

She cleared her throat, looked out into the crowd, and found her dad. What had he said to her earlier?

Looks to me like that wind swept away all of your baggage and left some confidence.

And right at that moment she found her voice.

"Ladies and gentlemen, members of the council, honored guests, and my lifelong friends and neighbors. I'm here to present an idea that I believe will change Mimosa Key for the better, will improve our lives, increase our revenue, and ensure that this island remains vital for many generations to come. I present to you Windswept at Barefoot Bay."

It had actually hurt not to look at her. Hurt not to hold Lacey's stunned and devastated gaze and give her some kind of sign that everything would be okay. But Clay couldn't look her in the eye until it *was* okay.

First he had to deal with Ira Howell, who'd promised late last night that he'd honor the change in ownership if Clay made it to Mimosa Key with the official paperwork before the town council meeting.

That had been thirteen hours and seven hundred hard miles ago. And at least six cups of gas-station coffee, all of which burned in his belly right now. Clay had driven to and from North Carolina without sleeping and he felt every mile on his body. But he couldn't rest now. Not yet.

"Do you have everything?" he demanded of Ira as they powered through the lobby and into the lot.

"Do you?" Ira shot back.

Clay guided him to the van with the lettering "Clayton Walker Architecture and Design, Inc." on the side. The van Darcie had snagged the keys to, and warned him that it tended to shimmy when it hit seventy-five so he needed to go easy on the gas. It shimmied at seventy-five all right, and felt like it would implode at ninety.

But he and Darcie had made it from Raleigh to Mimosa Key alive, with the paperwork intact.

"Right here," he said, grabbing the power of attorney forms they'd had notarized at the Raleigh hospital by a person probably more used to signing death certificates than property transactions.

"Because as much as I want to help you," Ira said, "there are some tricky legal issues doing it this way, according to the lawyer at Wells Fargo."

"I have what your lawyer needs. Trust me." Clay handed him the form.

Standing in a strip of shade, Ira opened the letter and read it. "I have to tell you, first of all, I'm very sorry about your father's stroke."

Clay nodded his thanks.

"How is he?"

"He's alive." Why lie? He might not be long for the world, and if he made it, he wasn't ever going to run a business or design a building again. "The second stroke was actually a blessing because it pulled him out of the coma and he could communicate."

Ira used the paper to fan himself, beads of sweat dampening his lip. "He didn't know you were involved when his company bought the land; you know that, don't you?"

"That's what he said." Although part of Clay suspected nefariousness on his father's part, he and Darcie had been able to put the pieces together, and it looked like Dad really had had no idea of Clay's involvement when he'd sent the scout who'd determined that the properties made a great purchase.

"After that last meeting," Ira continued, "I was confused. I couldn't understand why Walker Architecture was staying anonymous when someone with the same name was already involved."

"You told him?" Clay asked.

"I struggled with it; I'll be honest." Ira took out a white handkerchief and dabbed his damp forehead. "I figured it was a family feud and I oughta back out. So I didn't say anything for a while, but then I got wind of some of the stuff going on over here and I contacted the company."

"Why didn't he just terminate the deal?"

"Well, I don't want to make you feel guilty, son, but that day he had a medical, uh, situation."

So C-dub hadn't lied about that at least.

"I guess his health became his focus then." Ira dug into his bag and produced a massive amount of paper that would take at least twenty minutes to sign. Even though it meant he'd miss Lacey's presentation, he took the time because when he walked in there he wanted this deal done. No lies, no promises, no more misunderstandings.

When he put his last signature on the bottom line, Clayton Walker—the *younger* Clayton Walker—owned both parcels of land and he could do whatever he wanted on them. And, God, he knew what he wanted to do.

They shook hands and Clay couldn't resist giving the man a quick pat on the back. "You went above and beyond, Mr. Howell. All that work last night and early this morning to prepare this paperwork was outstanding. Thank you."

"Use my bank for this resort you're planning."

Clay grinned. "We will." The word "we" sounded so right and natural. Now all he had to do was make it so.

He walked inside, where Lacey stood beside the 3-D model of their resort, the main-building front-elevation board propped up next to her.

"Right here you can see how we…" She hesitated when her gaze landed on Clay, color rising to her cheeks. "How *I* propose to handle that."

So she rightly suspected the worst. And judging from the way she looked, she'd had a rough night. Guilt punched, but he knew it was just a matter of a few more minutes. He could wait that long.

He'd waited his whole life for her, so what was a few more minutes?

"How's she doing?" he whispered to Darcie when he sat down.

"Really well. You get 'er done out there?" Darcie asked.

He held up the packet of papers. "I'm the proud owner of ten acres of Barefoot Bay."

"And Dad paid for them."

"In more ways than one," he said. "Has she been through the feasibility and due diligence research yet?"

"Easily. She's just covering the physical buildings now."

Lacey spoke with confidence and pride when she described the villas, the spa, the greenhouse that Tessa wanted so much, even though they weren't sure they could fit it without the other properties.

Now they could. Now they could do so many things, including pick up where they'd left off. Just the thought of Lacey in his arms, in his bed, in his life, made Clay smile.

"Somebody's in love," Darcie sang into his ear.

Clay just grinned more broadly. Somebody *was* in love.

Around him the audience was as riveted on Lacey as he was, even those who looked unfriendly to change. But where was Ashley? And Tessa and Zoe? And David?

Why weren't they here to support her?

"And that," Lacey concluded, turning to the long table of council members, "is why we believe that Mimosa Key can benefit from the world-class, wholly environmentally friendly, revenue-producing, state-of -the-art resort known as Windswept at Barefoot Bay."

Windswept at Barefoot Bay?

Stunned at the name change, he felt his jaw, and his heart, drop with a thud. Only then did she look directly at him, and that expression said everything. An expression that said: *I don't need you, Clay Walker.*

"Hold all questions, please!" George Masterson shouted. "Our next presenter is from Clayton Walker Architecture and Design, and his plans will make all of these null and void."

Lacey closed her eyes as if George's words had kicked

her right in the teeth, but Clay was the one who felt kicked. Now she thought he *represented* his old man. He had to fix this, and fix it fast.

Clay made his way up the aisle with nothing but the packet of property papers in his hands. Lacey stepped away from the podium, turning her back on him to gather her presentation boards.

He stopped behind her, leaning a little too close, feeling her stiffen. But he had no time to set her straight now. Instead he put a hand on her tense shoulder.

"Pay attention, Strawberry. I mean everything I'm about to say."

As long as she didn't leave the room, Lacey Armstrong was about to find out exactly how he felt about her.

Chapter 34

With control she didn't even know she possessed, Lacey turned away from her presentation boards and walked toward the back of the room. She wanted to leave, of course. Wanted to run into the bathroom and howl in pain or possibly throw up.

But she refused to give him that satisfaction.

Her father was in the back row clapping for her. She gave him a smile and was about to sit next to him when the back doors opened.

"Mom!"

Zoe and Tessa each had one of Ashley's hands, and all three wore huge smiles. Ashley's head was still bandaged, but her eyes looked clear and her smile lit up the room.

"Did we miss it?" she asked as Lacey hugged her and led them all to the back wall.

"I'm done. But brace yourself. Things are about to get ugly."

"What's he doing up there?" they asked in unison.

"I'm not entirely sure, but he might be breaking my heart."

They all leaned against the back wall to listen.

"Jeez, he looks worse than you do," Zoe whispered. "And that's saying a lot."

"He does," Tessa agreed. "He looks like he hasn't slept for days."

He looked good to Lacey. Disheveled, unshaven, and was that a coffee stain on his T-shirt? None of it mattered. He was a gorgeous man, who loved...

She glanced at the woman in a baseball cap, who turned and looked right at Lacey. Then she slid off her glasses very slowly to reveal eyes as bloodshot as Clay's and also as blue.

The other woman nodded, and winked. Was that a bitchy move or what? Except it didn't seem as though she was trying to be bitchy.

More confused than ever, Lacey turned back to Clay, her head buzzing like a thousand cicadas invading the beach.

"Ladies and gentlemen of Mimosa Key. My name is Clay Walker and I'm delighted to be addressing you as the newest resident of your fine community." He held up a handful of legal-sized papers and Lacey tried to concentrate on what he was saying, not the baritone of his voice or the music of his North Carolina drawl. "These are the deeds to the properties formerly owned by Mr. and Mrs. Andrew Tomlinson and Mr. Ross Everham. They are now in my name, free and clear."

He owned the lots. *He* did. The betrayal stung like hot needles inside her chest. But she forced herself to listen.

"What do you plan to build?" Charity called out.

Good question, Char, Lacey thought. What *did* he plan to build?

"Something extraordinary."

The whole room went eerily silent, except for maybe Lacey's heartbeat, which surely everyone could hear.

"What kind of something, Mr. Walker?" Mayor Lennox asked, obviously not amused by Clay's obtuse response.

Clay never looked away from Lacey, pinning her to the wall with a dead-serious gaze. "Something everyone wants but not everyone gets."

Lacey's legs weakened and she used the wall to hold her steady. What was he talking about? He was looking at her, but...

Sam Lennox spoke into his microphone because the murmurs and comments and frustrations of the crowd were getting louder. "Mr. Walker, we have given you the floor, and if you can't make a serious and thoughtful presentation, your request for zoning changes will be denied."

"I am making a serious presentation. This land"—he held up the papers again—"will be part of the resort and spa that Lacey Armstrong just presented. With one minor stipulation."

Lacy held her breath.

"The resort is called *Casa Blanca*." He leveled her with a gaze. "Not *Windswept*."

Oh. She dropped an inch against the wall, bracing harder.

"What difference does it make?" Charity barked. "Just tell us what you want."

"What I want..." He inhaled deeply and finally smiled. "Is to spend every day and night with Lacey Armstrong, building..."

She absolutely couldn't breathe, holding his gaze, squeezing Ashley's hand, fighting the burn behind her eyelids.

"A life together."

"Oh my God," Zoe practically cooed in Lacey's ear. "I love him!"

"So do I," Lacey whispered, aware of the tears filling her eyes. "So do I."

"And if she would just come up here and join me"— Clay held out his hand in invitation—"we will answer any questions the good people of Mimosa Key might have so we can assure you that we want to make this island a destination that remains true to its roots but looks forward to the future."

"Amen!"

"Hear! Hear!"

"Go kiss him, Lacey!" The loud suggestion came from the woman in the baseball cap.

Clay leaned very close to the microphone and lowered his voice to dead sexy. "I think my sister just had a very good idea."

His sister? That was Darcie?

Ashley grinned, turning to her. "He likes you, Mom. A lot."

She looked at her daughter, putting a hand under her chin, holding her gaze. "You know that no man, ever, will come between us."

"Mom, don't be weird. Go kiss the guy. Listen to this place. They're going nuts."

The entire room clapped in unison, a chorus of female "Oohs" and "Aahs" adding to the cacophony.

She started up the aisle, and Clay left the podium to meet her halfway.

There, he put his arms around her and pulled her into a deep, dreamy, delicious kiss. The whole audience hooted so loudly she could barely hear when he whispered in her ear.

"Windswept at Barefoot Bay? Are you kidding me?"

She looked up at him. "Only because in *Casablanca*, the wrong guy gets the girl."

"Let's change the ending, Strawberry."

When the last of the council members had cleared out after the vote and a noisy victory celebration, Clay shook hands with many townspeople and promised more than a few job interviews for construction-crew candidates. Even Ashley congratulated him and told him about her own scary trip to the hospital.

Lacey was always nearby with a hand on her daughter's shoulder, giving instructions to her friends as they packed up the car, accepting congratulations as people milled about the meeting hall and eventually left.

He saw her talking to Darcie for a few minutes and then end that conversation with a quick hug.

Finally he made his way over to her, hands outstretched. "Hey, Strawberry. I missed you."

She came right to him, folding into his embrace and offering one of her own. "Oh, Clay, I'm so sorry I thought the worst of you."

"I can't believe you'd really think I'd buy those lots and build on them," he said. "What made you think that?"

"I didn't. I mean, that's not…" She closed her eyes as if just saying the words hurt her. "I looked at your phone the night we went to the beach. I thought you were going back to Jayna."

He let out a sigh, finally understanding. "And I should have told you why she texted. In fact, I should have told you my dad was sick before that, but I really thought you'd preach to me about forgiving him, and I wasn't ready."

"Did you?" she asked.

"Done and done." He held her closer and put his lips on her hair and inhaled, the smell of strawberry mixed with sun and maybe a little antiseptic reminding him that she'd had her own trip to the hospital. "How's Ashley doing?"

"She's fine and very apologetic for whatever it was she said to you that she thinks made you leave. But it was a hellish night, I'll tell you."

He held her again, hoping the hug could express how sorry he was that the last twenty-four hours had happened the way they had.

"I thought I'd lost you," she whispered.

"Not going to happen."

"Even after"—she fought to finish her thought—"even after we're done building the resort?"

"Did you not listen to my big speech?" He slammed a hand to his chest, only partially feigning pain. "I bared it all up there for you, woman."

"That wasn't just to win votes?"

"Maybe a few." He winked, but then his expression grew serious. "I've had a lot of time to think, Lace."

"Thirteen hours, Darcie said."

He sighed, shaking his head, looking into her eyes. "Maybe more than that. But when I talked to my dad in the hospital yesterday, I realized something. I realized that he can be a complete jerk, selfish as hell, and willing to do almost anything for what he wants. A man who hates the word *can't.*"

"You're not like him, if that's where you're going with this, Clay."

But he could be. "I let him go. I let go of all the anger and hate. I forgave him because there's something— someone—I want to focus my attention on. You."

She sank deeper into his arms with a happy sigh. "Oh. I like that."

"I like *you.*" No. This time she deserved more than their inside joke. "In fact..." He lowered his mouth to hers, brushed his lips against hers, and whispered, "I—"

"*Ahem.*"

They separated, turning to face a woman who looked vaguely like Lacey, only older, thinner, colder, and nowhere near as happy.

"Mother."

"I heard you got what you wanted, Lacey. That's good."

Sure didn't sound good. Not in that tone.

"*We* got what we wanted," Lacey corrected her, slowly standing straighter, dividing her attention between her mother and him. "Have you met my...Clay?"

The older woman marched a few steps closer, an amber brown gaze leveled at Clay, the same color as Lacey's but completely flat.

"I've been with Ashley in the parking lot," she said. "I don't think she should be in the sun with that injury. So I let her go off with that Zoe, but—"

"Clay Walker is the architect who is going to build the business I've always wanted to run. Clay, this is my mother, Marie Armstrong."

The woman sniffed, reaching out one hand to shake his, the other smoothing hair he'd never call "strawberry" blonde, although maybe a distant, dull cousin. "Then I guess congratulations are in order," she conceded with a nod.

"For Lacey," he said. "She's the owner, manager, lead investor, brain trust, and inspiration for the whole Casa Blanca concept."

A reddish brown eyebrow launched north. "I'm sure there are a lot of smart people behind her on this. Lacey's a follower. Her brother Adam's the leader in our family."

"Not anymore," he said.

Her mother ignored the comment. "Could I speak with you privately, Lacey?"

"Later," Lacey said. "Clay and I have to get that last model in the car and get—"

"Now."

Lacey froze and a few fireworks of fury sparked inside Clay, but he kept his mouth shut.

"What is it, Mother?"

"Privately."

They faced each other like gunslingers while Clay debated if he should offer to leave. Before he could, Lacey put a hand on his shoulder.

"Anything you have to say to me you can say in front of Clay," she said. "He's my . . . he's my . . ."

"I'm her partner," he supplied, suddenly wishing he could use a term with far more impact and emotion attached.

"I know what he is," Marie said, cutting a cool glance his way. "And, Lacey, I think you're entirely too old for this."

"For what?" Lacey asked with a soft cough of disbelief. "For a man? For a lover? For a business? For a *life*?"

"For a boy." She gestured toward Clay. "And you should be ashamed of yourself, taking advantage of a lonely older woman."

Clay started to laugh. A chuckle at first, then a full, sharp, from-the-gut laugh. "You're funny, Mrs. Armstrong."

But Lacey wasn't even smiling.

"C'mon, Lace." He reached for her hand. "Let's go."

"No." She pulled her hand away from him. "I don't want to go, Clay."

No? Was she going to give in and let this cold, cruel woman do what she'd obviously been doing to Lacey her whole life? "Lacey?"

"Very smart of you, honey." The first bit of softness formed around Marie's eyes, and a spark of satisfaction. "I knew you'd come to your senses."

"I have," Lacey said softly.

Disappointment curled through him, landing low and hard in his gut. Was she this weak? Had he misjudged her that much? A woman he was a breath away from loving?

"You can leave, Clay," Lacey said.

He stood speechless. What power did Marie Armstrong have over her? "Leave?"

"Just go."

Marie wore a smug smile and tipped her head to the door. He opened his mouth to argue but closed it again, taking the few steps to the back door. Pulling it open, he waited for Lacey to change her mind, but she didn't.

Without turning, he stepped outside into the hallway. Behind him the door started to close with the hiss of a pneumatic hinge, slowly enough that he heard Lacey's next words.

"Mother, listen to me."

He slid a hand in the frame to keep the door ajar.

"I don't need to hear your excuses, Lacey. Everyone makes mistakes and he, well, he was a doozy."

"I'm not making excuses, Mother. I want to say something to you. One time and one time only."

Clay inched closer. He had to hear. Had to know.

"Say it fast and then let's go. I can't stand the thought of Ashley with that Zoe woman."

He heard Lacey's intake of breath, as though she were about to start a speech. Then silence.

"What?" her mother demanded.

"I don't know why you have so much anger in you, Mother, or why you are so disappointed in me."

"I'm not—"

"It doesn't matter," Lacey insisted. "Because I forgive you."

Clay closed his eyes at the echo of his own words to his father. He knew exactly how liberating that was.

"I don't need your forgiveness. I don't need—"

"Anything or anyone. I know. But I do." Lacey's voice cracked, making Clay squeeze the door. "I need love and I need that man out there. I need him like I need my next breath."

"You're confusing sex with need."

"I'm not confused about anything." Her voice rose with conviction and clarity. "I love him and I want to spend every possible minute next to him."

Yes. Yes, Strawberry, *yes.*

"Well, you do that," her mother said. "And I'll be there to pick up the pieces when he dumps you for the next girl who gives him what he needs."

"There won't be a next girl." Confidence oozed from every word. "I'm all he needs and all he wants and all he will ever have to have."

He braced for Marie's cutting reply, but there was nothing but silence. And footsteps to the door, fast enough for him to realize she was running. To him.

"Clay!" Lacey called, pushing the door so hard he had to jump back to keep from getting nailed. "Clay! Oh. You're here."

"I'm here."

"You heard."

"Every word."

"And…"

He reached for her, pride and love and something he couldn't even name welling up inside of him.

Completion. That was what it was. Like the final stroke on a drawing that was just waiting for completion. He could see the whole picture ahead and, man, it looked good.

"And I think you are right about everything," he said. "Especially the part about how you are all I need and all I want and all I ever have to have."

Lacey leaned into Clay. "You know what I want to do now, Clay?"

He lifted an eyebrow. "Thank me properly?"

"After that, I'd like to make some of your drawings come to life. And I don't mean the floor plans."

He reached down to kiss her. "Told you, Strawberry. If

I can see it clear enough to draw it, I can make it happen.
Let's make it happen ... together."

"I like that."

He grinned. "I like *you*."

"I—"

He put his hand over her mouth. "Let me say it first. I
love you."

Epilogue

Six Months Later

"Why is everyone whispering?" Lacey approached Zoe and Jocelyn a few minutes after the formal ground-breaking ceremony had ended.

They both shut up instantly.

"Secrets," Lacey said, shaking her head. "Why must we have any secrets? We're best friends."

"No secrets," Jocelyn said. "We're just talking about what a lovely ceremony it was."

"Especially the part where you and Clay did the first big dig." Zoe mimed scooping dirt. "Because nothing says romance like a shovel."

"Who said anything about romance?" Tessa joined them, her fingers wrapped around a small cluster of bright pink mimosa flowers that she'd insisted on planting months ago in honor of the island's name.

"Can't say much else when Lacey and Clay are together," Jocelyn said. "You two are the definition of bliss."

"Speaking of bliss, this afternoon kind of reminds me of a wedding." Zoe slid her arm around Lacey to turn her toward the beach, but Lacey caught Jocelyn and Tessa's sharp look of warning.

"It's okay, guys," Lacey assured them. "When it happens, it happens. We'll know when it's the right time. We have a resort to build, you know."

Again they shared a look that could only be interpreted as—what? Pity? Understanding? Concern?

"You guys, stop," Lacey insisted. "Clay and I don't need a piece of paper. We've never needed that, not even to build Casa Blanca together. It's always been sealed with a kiss."

Which really should be enough when a person is this much in love, right?

"Here, Lace," Tessa said, handing her the flowers. "A gift for you to celebrate this glorious day of new beginnings."

She took the bouquet and smiled, surprised when tears stung her lids. She wasn't disappointed that Clay hadn't proposed yet, was she? No, these were tears of joy and anticipation. They had so much ahead.

"And just look at those two," Jocelyn said, indicating Clay and Lacey's father deep in conversation at the water's edge, silhouetted against the first golden streaks of a magnificent sunset.

"They're like father and son," Lacey mused. They'd formed a strong bond almost instantly and, for the first time since he'd retired from dentistry, her father seemed truly happy. Even her mother...

Well, she was coming around. She'd joined the party today, at least. And Ashley, now halfway through her first year of high school, had managed to forge much better friendships and an improved attitude. Right now she was talking excitedly to Clay's sister, no doubt telling her all about the upcoming spring-break trip to the Caribbean to go snorkeling with her father.

David had been true to his word: He'd invested heavily in Casa Blanca. No word on when he'd be back to visit, but Ashley seemed content with their regular texting and Facebook exchanges, and the promise of at least one adventurous vacation with him a year.

"Hey, Lace." Zoe gestured toward the water. "Your hotter half is waving you down to the beach."

As her father walked up the sand, Clay stayed in the shallow waves giving Lacey a two-fingered come-hither beckoning. "Like I could resist that. See ya," she said, using the flowers to wave over her shoulder.

"Shoes off," he called, already barefoot himself.

She kicked off her sandals and headed into the warm water, letting the froth bubble around her ankles. Clay reached out to her and she slipped into his arms, the warm water of Barefoot Bay tickling her toes just as his first sweet kiss landed on her mouth.

"We did it, Strawberry."

"We sure did." She leaned back, secure in his arms, giving in to the sheer bliss of being held by him. He bent over and kissed her neck, getting some crowd reaction.

"We're drawing attention, Clay."

"Get used to it. We're going to draw a lot more." He smiled at her, a sly, sneaking smile that crinkled his eyes and kind of crushed her chest. "You know, Lacey, your dad reminded me we've forgotten an awfully big step in this project."

"We have?" She frowned. "What is it?"

"Our contract."

"A business contract?" She laughed at the idea, mostly because the notion seemed ridiculous when they'd done this much without one. Or maybe she laughed because, for one crazy second, she thought he might mean another kind of contract.

"I don't think it's smart to go much farther along without one, and your dad agrees."

"Of course. He wants to protect me."

He curled his arm around her shoulder as if protecting her was his job, pulling her into him so she had to put her arm around his waist as they turned to the sunset, their backs to the beach. "You have to admit a contract makes sense."

"If it's important to you…" She let her voice trail off as her eyes drank in the peachy pool of sunlight over the horizon and the violet-tinged sky above it. Beautiful. But she'd rather look up at the man she loved. "I don't think we need one."

"I do. This is a huge commitment, years of work, lots of decisions to make, people who will depend on us to stick together when times get tough, and, of course, there are always complicated legal issues to iron out in case of a dispute."

"I never want to have a dispute." She put her head on his shoulder, trying to just drink up the peacefulness of the moment.

"Just in case, I think it would be smart to have a formal, binding, stamped-by-the-mayor kind of contract that says this partnership is permanent."

She squinted up at him, blinking against the late

afternoon sunshine that washed him in gold. "Let's just seal it with a kiss, Clay, and agree to trust each other."

He stared at her. "A kiss?"

"Is just a kiss." She stood on her tiptoes to peck his cheek. "That's what our song says."

He turned so she hit his mouth and suddenly it wasn't a peck at all, but slower, longer, deeper, and warmer. "Unless it's a kiss like that."

"I'll say," she agreed. "That was pretty binding."

"But not good enough." He angled them both toward the sunset again, the sand squishing in between her toes. "I want legal."

"Okay. On Monday you call the lawyers."

"I don't want to wait until Monday. We have everyone we need here right now."

"Here for..." Deep inside, in the part of her chest that always ached a little when she looked at him, something twisted. "Here for us to sign a contract?"

"If that's what you want to call it." Very slowly, he eased her around, away from the sunset, toward the beach.

Every single person there gathered in a tight group, facing them. Except for Zoe, Tessa, and Jocelyn, who stood off to the side in a row.

"What's going on, Clay?"

"One more ceremony today," he said.

Then the crowd parted down the middle, as if choreographed, and Ashley stepped into the open area, more mimosa flowers in her hands. She looked at Lacey, smiled, and slowly began to walk toward the water, dropping the pink stems as she did.

Tears blurred her vision and a lump formed in her throat. "Clay. Is this..."

"This is it, Lacey."

She let out a little breath of air, suddenly strangled with happiness. "Now?"

"No chance to make a single excuse why we *can't*."

"As if I'd even dream of that."

Laughing, he stroked her windblown hair off her face, then held her cheeks. "That's why I didn't propose."

"Better do it fast."

He got down on one knee, earning a big cheer from the crowd.

"Lacey Armstrong, this beach is where I found you and fell in love with you and built a life with you. So this is where I want to make you my wife, the best friend and forever lover I will cherish, honor, adore, and love for all the days and nights we have together. Will you marry me?"

"Yes, Clay Walker. I will marry you right here and now. I love you, too."

Behind her, Zoe squealed just as Ashley reached them.

"Congratulations, Mom. I love you." She kissed Lacey and hugged Clay. "Welcome to the family, Clay."

She stepped to the side to join the girls, all three with tears that matched Lacey's and smiles that rivaled the beauty of the sunset.

Lacey's parents came next, and, miracle of miracles, her mother was smiling. And Dad was bawling like a baby.

Last was Mayor Lennox, carrying a single piece of paper.

Their contract. Their future.

"Please join hands," the mayor said.

Lacey looked down at her mimosa bouquet, then turned to her friends. Which one of them should get this? Should the bouquet go to Zoe, whose mischievous grin almost hid her long-ago heartache, or Tessa, with her nurturing spirit that couldn't be fulfilled in the garden no matter how hard she tried? Or Jocelyn, who tried to control everything by turning her back on the past?

She wished a lifetime of love for all three of her best friends, but only one could take the bouquet.

"Just a minute," Lacey whispered to Clay. "I need to give these to someone."

Turning, she hesitated, still trying to decide.

"Just throw them," he said. "Let the wind decide."

She tossed the bouquet toward the women. Tessa froze and Zoe reached out with a squeal, but the breeze caught the flowers and took them straight to Jocelyn. She snagged the stems right before they hit the sand, getting a huge cheer from the crowd as she held the flowers with tentative fingers.

"You're next," Lacey mouthed, then sidled closer to Clay.

As the mayor started the second official ceremony of the day, Lacey took a slow, deep inhalation of the salt air of Barefoot Bay. The tangy scent reminded her of the morning of the hurricane, when hope and anticipation and change had beckoned her.

And then love found her.

She joined hands with the man she loved and hung on for dear life. Because life, as it turned out, really was dear.

To her clients, life-coach Jocelyn
Bloom had it all. Only Will Palmer, the
boy who grew up next door, had a
bird's-eye-view of the ugly truth.

When they meet again, can he
help her heal the past?

Barefoot in the Rain

Please turn this page
for a preview.

Something was different at Casa Blanca. Will could practically smell a change in the salty air of Barefoot Bay the minute he climbed out of his truck in front of the resort's construction trailer. To the west, the Gulf of Mexico was dead calm, the cobalt swells barely lit by dawn's fiery rays peeking over the foliage along the east. The construction parking lot was empty, of course, and the structures stood silent in various degrees of completion.

Still, the air pressed, heavy with…change. Funny how he could sense that. Like when the wind would pick up in the outfield, a signal that the game's momentum was about to shift.

Scanning the main building, he noticed a few additions since he'd last been to the job site. Clay and Lacey Walker ran a tight schedule, determined to get the high-end resort up and running within the year, so it was no surprise that the subs had been hard at work on Friday while he'd driven to Tampa to pick up the flooring for one of the villas.

There were definitely more roof tiles on the main structure, the creamy barrels adding to the many textures of Clay's Moroccan-inspired architecture. And the window contractor had been busy, too, leaving at least a dozen giant sheets of plate glass propped along the side and front of the curved entry, ready to be installed when the roof was completed.

But the main building of Casa Blanca was of no real interest to Will. His work centered on the six private villas that the resort's most well-heeled guests would rent. He'd spent most of the last year building those smaller structures, including all of the finishing carpentry in Rockrose, the first completed villa at the north end of the main path.

He peered through the palm fronds and elephant ear leaves that had grown so lush since a hurricane stripped the trees over a year ago, studying the unpaved road that led to the villas. Deep, fresh wheel grooves cut through the dew-dampened dirt. Had someone driven up there on a Sunday?

Even if there had been a sub here on a Sunday—which was really unlikely—the construction crew was primarily focused on Bay Laurel, the villa closest to where he stood now, and the destination of the African wood flooring he'd loaded in his truck.

Why would someone drive up the path? He paused at the passenger door, pulling it open to grab the cup of coffee he'd picked up at the Super Min on his way to the site. As he unwedged the cup from the holder, a drop of hot black coffee splashed through the plastic top, dribbling onto the seat.

Well, not the seat. Onto the newspaper he'd dropped there. And not exactly a newspaper either, unless the *National Enquirer* qualified.

The headline blared and taunted him.

Coco Kirkman Says: My Life Coach Stole My Husband!

Why the hell did he buy that paper anyway? To revel in Jocelyn Bloom's misery? To get the dirt on a woman he once thought was perfect?

Oh, shit, why not face facts? He bought the tabloid on the off chance there'd be a picture of Jocelyn inside. And there was.

Holding the coffee in his right hand, he used the other to lift the front page to see the blurry shot of a woman with long dark hair, big brown eyes, and features so familiar he didn't need some paparazzi's wide-angle lens to capture them.

That face lived in his imagination. And since he'd seen her on TV last Thursday night, dead center in a Hollywood scandal, thoughts of Jocelyn had haunted every waking moment.

Like that was much different from every other day.

Maybe work would distract him. He nudged the door closed with his hip, finishing his coffee, still intrigued by the tire prints in the path. Following them, he strode along what would be the resort's most scenic walkway, canopied by green and lined with exotic flowers.

He passed some of the villas, mentally reviewing each construction schedule, but his thoughts stopped the instant he rounded the foliage that blocked Rockrose, the only fully finished villa.

That's what was different.

He squinted into the sun that backlit the vanilla cream structure, highlighting the fact the French doors along the side were wide open, the sheer curtain Lacey had installed fluttering like a ghost. There was no breeze, so someone had to have the overhead fan on in there.

Shit. Vandals? Squatters? Maybe Lacey's teenage daughter or one of her friends taking advantage of the place?

There was no other explanation. Rockrose had been given a CO two weeks ago. But a certificate of occupancy didn't mean *actual* occupancy, and Lacey kept the secluded villa locked tight so that none of the construction workers traipsed through or decided to use the facilities.

He took a few steps closer, instinctively flexing his muscles, ready to fight for the turf of a building that somehow had become "his."

He took cover behind an oleander bush, slipping around to get a better view into the bedroom. He could see the sheer film of netting Lacey had hung from the bed's canopy, the decor capturing the essence of North African romance.

If anyone defiled one inch of that villa, there'd be hell to pay. Especially Rockrose. He'd laid the marble in the bath, shaved the oak wood in the ceiling, and personally carved the columns on the fireplace mantel. The whole job had given him more satisfaction than picking off a runner trying to steal second.

Irritation pushed him closer to the wood deck. If some stupid kid had—

The filmy gauze around the bed quivered, then suddenly whisked open. Holy Mother Mary, someone was *sleeping* in that bed. He bounded closer, sucking in a breath to yell when one long, bare, shapely leg emerged from the clouds of white.

His voice trapped in his throat and his steps slammed to a stop. The sun beamed on pale skin, spotlighting pink-tipped toes that flexed and stretched like a ballerina preparing to hit the barre.

The other leg slid into view, followed by an audible yawn and sigh that drifted over the tropical air to make the hairs on the back of his neck stand up. He took a few stealthy steps, wanting to keep the advantage of surprise but, hell, he didn't want to miss what came out of that bed next.

The feet touched the floor and a woman emerged from the netting, naked from head to toe, a sleep mask covering most of her face. Not that he'd have looked at her face.

No, his gaze was locked on long limbs, a narrow waist, and curves that begged to be handled. Her breasts were small, budded with rose-colored nipples, her womanhood a simple sliver of ebony that matched the hair tied up in a sloppy, sexy mess on her head.

Finally, she stretched, widening her arms, yawning again, giving him a centerfold-worthy view as her breasts lifted higher. Every functioning blood cell tumbled south, leaving his brain a total blank and his cock well on its way to being as hard as the planks of African wood in his truck.

Son of a bitch. He backed up, ducking behind the oleander and cursing himself for being some kind of pervie peeping Tom. He had to get back down the path, and return—noisily, in his truck—and find out who the hell she was.

A footstep hit the wood deck and Will inched to the side, unable to stop himself from looking. At least she had a thin white top on now, and panties. And she'd taken off the sleep—

His heart stopped for at least four beats, then slammed into quadruple time.

Jocelyn.

Was it possible? Was he imagining things? Was this a mirage spurred by a couple of lousy pictures in the media and three days of fantasies and frustration?

She reached up and pulled a clip from her hair, sending the thick, black mane over her shoulders like an inky waterfall. Shaking her head, she closed her eyes and turned her face to the rising sun.

All doubt disappeared. That was Jocelyn Mary Bloom, the girl next door, the teenager who made his every dream come true, the woman he—

Her eyes popped open and her head whipped around toward him. "Is someone there?"

Make a joke. Say something funny. Walk, smile, talk. C'mon William Palmer, don't just stand here and gawk like you've never seen a female before.

"It's me."

She squinted into the bushes, then reared back in shock as he stepped full out and revealed himself. Her lips moved, mouthing his name, but no real sound came out.

"Will," he said for her. "I thought someone was trespassing."

She just stared, jaw loose, eyes wide, every muscle frozen like she'd been carved out of ice.

He fought the urge to launch forward, take the three stairs up to the deck in one bound and...thaw her. But, holy hell, he knew better with Jocelyn Bloom. One false move and *poof!* Empty hands.

"What are you doing here?" They spoke the words in perfect unison, then laughed softly at the awkward moment.

Not really awkward, though. They'd always been of one mind; she just hadn't realized it. Yet.

"Lacey brought you here?" he guessed.

She nodded, reaching up to run a hand through that mass of midnight hair, then, as if she suddenly realized how little she had on, she stepped back into the shadows of the villa, but he could still see her face. That beautiful face he'd always lo—

"How about you?" she asked.

He cleared his throat and wayward thoughts. "I work here."

She looked completely baffled. "You play baseball."

"Not anymore. I build villas. Like the one you slept in last night."

"Lacey said I'd be the first guest. I'm...staying here."

Hiding here, more like. The pieces fell together like tongue in groove. She'd run away from the mess in L.A., and her best friend had cloistered her in a place that wouldn't even show up on a map, let alone at the other end of a some reporter's camera.

Then another thought hit him like a fastball to the brain. "You alone?" He must have had a little accusation in his voice, because she raised an eyebrow and looked disappointed.

"Yes," she said softly, sadness in her eyes and a softness in her posture.

Shit. He'd hurt her. He regretted the question the instant it had popped out. She was hiding from prying eyes and personal questions and what had he done? Pried and asked.

He held up a hand as though that could deliver his apology and took a few steps closer. "How long are you here? I'd love to..." *Talk to you. Kiss you until you can't breathe. Spend every night in your bed.* "Get caught up."

"I shouldn't be here that long."

In other words, no. "Too bad," he said, hiding the impact of disappointment. "Maybe I'll see you on the south end when you go home."

"I won't go there." The statement was firm, clear, and unequivocal. *Don't argue with me,* dripped the subtext.

She wouldn't see her dad? A spark flared, pushing him closer, up the stairs. She wouldn't even go visit? She wouldn't even do a drive-by to see if her old man was dead or alive? Because he'd bet his next paycheck, she didn't know.

Something hammered at him, and this time it wasn't his heart reacting to the sight of his favorite woman on earth. No, this was the physical jolt of anger and a whole different kind of frustration.

"What do you do at Casa Blanca?" she asked, apparently unaware she'd hit a hot button.

But her casual question barely registered, her astounding near nakedness practically forgotten despite God's professional lighting that gave him a perfect view of her body under those slips of white cotton.

"Carpentry," he said through gritted teeth, a little surprised at how much emotion rocked him. He had to remember what she'd gone through as a child, what her father was in her eyes...but right now, all he could think about was a harmless, helpless old man who had no one to call family.

Even though he had a perfectly good daughter standing right here.

"A carpenter just like your father," she said, nodding. "I remember he was quite talented."

"Speaking of fathers..." He dragged the word out, long enough to see her flinch...like she had whenever her father had taken a step toward her. "I'm back in my parents' house. They moved out to Seattle to be closer to my sister and her kids."

In other words, I live next door to your father. He waited for the reaction, but she just raised her hand, halting him. "I really have to go, Will. Nice to see you again."

Seriously? She wouldn't even hear him out?

She backed into the opening of the French doors, hidden from view now. "I'm sure I'll see you around, though," she called, one hand reaching for the knob to close him out.

God *damn* her. He grabbed the wood frame and held it as tightly as he had when he'd installed the very door she was about to slam in his face. "Jocelyn."

"Please, Will."

"Listen to me."

"I'm sure our paths will cross." But her voice contradicted that cliché. And so did history. One word she didn't want to hear and Jocelyn would find another hiding place in another corner of the world.

Was he willing to risk that? After all his dreams of seeing her again? Of a reunion? Of one more night? One more chance? If he so much as spoke the name Guy Bloom, she'd be on a plane, headed back to California.

He let go of the door and she began to pull it closed. Then something shot through him. Anger. Justice. Vindication. Whatever. He thrust his boot in the jamb to keep the door from closing.

"Will, I have to—"

"I just thought you should know." He had enough strength in his foot to nudge the opening wider and get closer to leave his parting shot. "Your father has Alzheimer's. I take care of him."

He slipped his boot out and the door slammed shut.

Well, he was right about the winds of change. Maybe now, after half a lifetime, maybe now he could finally get over Jocelyn Bloom.

Keep telling yourself that, buddy. Someday you might believe it.

THE DISH

Where authors give you the inside scoop!

♥ ♥ ♥ ♥ ♥ ♥ ♥ ♥ ♥ ♥ ♥ ♥ ♥ ♥ ♥

From the desk of Roxanne St. Claire

Dear Reader,

BAREFOOT IN THE SAND opens during a powerful hurricane that forces the heroine and her daughter to hole up in a bathtub under a mattress and pray for survival. The scene, I'm sorry to say, took very little imagination for me to write. I've been there. On August 24, 1992, one of the worst hurricanes in the history of this country slammed into Dade County, Florida, and changed hundreds of thousands of lives. Mine was one of them.

Exactly one month pregnant with a baby that had taken four years and a quadrillion deals with God to conceive, I decided to spend the night at my sister's house when Hurricane Andrew approached Miami. Despite the fact that the forecasters predicted the storm would turn north before making landfall, my husband and I had worried that our proximity to the coastline made us vulnerable, and that our east-facing double front doors might buckle with the wind. We braced the doors with the living room sofa and evacuated just eight miles north. My sister's house sustained little damage that night, though freight-train winds ripped her patio screen and took down some beloved trees.

We headed home the next morning, and with each

passing mile, it was clear that the southern section of Miami had taken the brunt of the storm. We sure hoped that sofa had held the doors closed.

We still laugh about that because, well, we never did find that sofa.

When we arrived at what we thought was our street— all the trees were uprooted or stripped bare and not a single street sign survived—all we could do was stare. The sofa was long gone (but our neighbor's love seat was in our driveway!), along with our doors, every window, all the roof tiles, the garage doors, and just about everything we'd ever owned. *Everything.*

Inside, all the ceilings had collapsed, leaving snow-drifts of insulation. My beautiful home was covered in mud, drywall, and broken glass. Every remaining wall was green from the chlorophyll in the leaves that had blown around during what had to have been mini-tornadoes in the house.

I stood in the midst of that chaos and started to cry, of course. Shaking uncontrollably, unable to process what might lie ahead, I could barely suck in shuddering breaths and weep at the sight of my rain-soaked wedding album and shattered bits of my precious Waterford crystal.

Everything we had was gone.

Then my husband gripped my shoulders, giving me a stern shake and silencing me with two words: The baby. *The baby.*

Obviously, not everything was gone. When Mother Nature has a temper tantrum and breaks all your stuff, the only things that really matter are the people who are left.

When I needed the catalyst to set Lacey Armstrong's story in motion and start the Barefoot Bay series, the lessons I learned from surviving and rebuilding after Hurricane Andrew were still fresh in my heart, even almost two decades later. It wasn't hard to imagine riding out that storm in a bathtub; I had many friends and neighbors who had done just that. It wasn't impossible to put myself in Lacey's shoes the next day, digging for optimism in a mountain of rubble.

But I also had twenty years of perspective and knew that no matter what she lost in the storm, Lacey's indomitable spirit wouldn't merely survive, but thrive. She not only found optimism in that rubble, she found love.

P.S. "The baby" turns nineteen this year. And, no, we didn't name him Andrew.

Roxanne St. Claire

♥ ♥ ♥ ♥ ♥ ♥ ♥ ♥ ♥ ♥ ♥ ♥ ♥ ♥ ♥ ♥

From the desk of Cara Elliott

Dear Reader,

Psst! I've got a secret to share with you about my hero in TOO TEMPTING TO RESIST. Okay, you already know that Gryffin Owain Dwight, the Marquess of Haddan, is rich, handsome, titled, and an incorrigibly charming flirt. But I'll bet you weren't aware of this intimate little detail—he speaks a *very* special language.

No, no, not French or Italian! (Though as a dashingly

romantic rake, he's fluent in those lovely tongues.) It's the secret language of Flowers, a highly seductive skill. For example, he knows that red roses signify "Love," while orange ones mean "Fascination." He can tell you that yellow irises murmur "Passion" and peach blossoms say "I am your captive."

Now, you might ask how he came to know all this. Well, here's an interesting bit of history (as the author of historical romances, I love discovering interesting little facts from the past): Flowers have long been powerful symbols in Eastern cultures, and in the early eighteenth century, Lady Mary Wortley Montague, wife of the British ambassador to Constantinople (and a fascinating woman in her own right), learned of a little Turkish book called *The Secret Language of Flowers*. Intrigued, she had it translated and brought it back to England with her...and from there the romantic idea that lovers could send hidden messages to each other via bouquets was introduced to Europe.

Today, the symbolic use of flowers is still flourishing. Here's another secret! Kate Middleton's bouquet at the Royal Wedding to Prince William was carefully designed using the language of flowers to express special meaning for the bride and groom and their families: *Lily-of-the-valley*, which means "Return of Happiness" (chosen in memory of Diana); *Sweet William*, which means "Gallantry" (isn't that romantic!); *Hyacinth*, which means "Constancy of Love"; *Ivy*, which means "Fidelity, Friendship and Affection"; *Myrtle*, which is the emblem of marriage and love.

Now, getting back to *my* hero, Gryff has a number of other intriguing secrets. He's a man of hidden talents—and hidden passions. It's no wonder that Eliza, Lady Brentford, finds him irresistibly alluring, despite her distrust of rakes and rascals. She too has an interest in flowers, so when she discovers that he speaks their language...

And how does Gryff use this special skill? Well, that's for you to find out for yourself! I hope you'll take a peek at his story and let him whisper his petal-soft seductions in your ear!

Cara Elliott

♥ ♥ ♥ ♥ ♥ ♥ ♥ ♥ ♥ ♥ ♥ ♥ ♥ ♥ ♥

From the desk of Caridad Piñeiro

Dear Reader,

I've been reading romances for as long as I can remember, going back to when I was twelve and read and re-read *Wuthering Heights* all summer long. At one point the librarian told me I could not take the book out again since other people needed a chance to read it!

Denied my broody Heathcliff and doomed Catherine, I turned my attentions to what some might say were an odd mix: Shakespeare and Ian Fleming.

It's safe to say that those choices as a young reader were later reflected in what I wrote, especially in THE CLAIMED, the second book in the Sin Hunters series.

Action. Adventure. Angst. I've incorporated all those elements that I love into this tale of a determined and broody alpha hero, Christopher Sombrosa, and a woman who is the absolute wrong choice for him, Victoria Johnson.

So why is Victoria *not* the woman for Christopher? Think Romeo and Juliet, Capulet and Montague.

Victoria is destined to be the leader of her Light Hunter clan, while Christopher is not only one of the Dark Ones, he is likewise supposed to assume command of his Shadow Hunter people.

Add to the mix some rather nefarious villains in the form of Christopher's father and ex-fiancée and the betrayal of someone dear to Victoria, and I think you'll find THE CLAIMED will keep you turning pages until the very end.

I am very glad to say, however, that despite the hope-less Catherine, Juliet, and assorted Bond girls who could never win James's heart, there is a path to a new and exciting place for Christopher and Victoria.

I hope you will enjoy their fight for a better tomorrow for not only themselves, but their race of Hunters.